THE PERFECT RETREAT

Kate lives in Melbourne, Australia with her husband and two children and can be found nursing a laptop, surrounded by magazines and talking on the phone, usually all at once. Kate is an avid follower of fashion, fame and all things pop culture and is an excellent dinner party guest who always brings gossip and champagne.

To find out more about Kate visit www.kateforster.com or find her on twitter @kateforster.

D0630341

By the same author:

The Perfect Location

KATE FORSTER

The Perfect Retreat

AVON

AVON
A division of HarperCollins*Publishers*
77–85 Fulham Palace Road,
London W6 8JB

www.harpercollins.co.uk

A Paperback Original 2013

1

Copyright © Kate Forster 2013

Kate Forster asserts the moral right to
be identified as the author of this work

A catalogue record for this book is
available from the British Library

ISBN-13: 978-1-84756-309-5

Set in Minion by Palimpsest Book Production Limited,
Falkirk, Stirlingshire

Printed and bound in Great Britain by
Clays Ltd, St Ives plc

MIX
Paper from
responsible sources
FSC
www.fsc.org   FSC™ C007454

FSC™ is a non-profit international organisation established to promote
the responsible management of the world's forests. Products carrying the
FSC label are independently certified to assure consumers that they come
from forests that are managed to meet the social, economic and
ecological needs of present and future generations,
and other controlled sources.

Find out more about HarperCollins and the environment at
www.harpercollins.co.uk/green

Thank you to my editor Sammia Rafique, for 'getting' my work and then polishing it with no irritation to me whatsoever.

Thank you to Fiona Michel and Emma Assaad for being my first readers and giving me their precious time and their friendship. 'You complete me.'

Thank you to my clever friends Jacquie Byron, Kylie Miller, Jonah Klein and Stef Boscutti who all have helped me professionally and personally. You're the tops, the lot of you.

Thank you to good friend Pippa Lambiase who guided me on speech disorders and treatment for children. You're a good egg Lipsy.

And to lovely David, and gorgeous Tansy and Spike – thank you for everything.

For Tara whose patience, support and guidance
means more to me than she knows.

PART ONE

To Clementina Ferrand, Comtesse de Clermont
Paris,
January 1850

Dearest Clementina,
   This small weight of paper does not do justice to the enormity of my task. It is done. I have fulfilled my promise, and now I hope with all my heart that you will keep yours to me. When I lingered at your side in Paris, unwilling to leave you, you asked me to build you a home.
   It is done.
   My beautiful Clementina, I have included a drawing of our home – if you will let it be such – and I hope it meets with your approval. It is a home for us, and if God is kind, our children.
   I cannot imagine life without you here. Every room calls your name and every tree I have planted asks for you to come and witness its transformation over the seasons.
   The house is named Middlemist, after me. It is a pretty home, resting on a hill, built in a modern style. I have built a ballroom at its heart. I have taken the liberty of including something I have dreamed of: an orangery, filled entirely with clementines. Should you wish to come and be

my wife, you will have all the sweet fruit you desire and I shall have you, the sweetest Clementine in the world.

It may be my misfortune that you have been taken away by another suitor by the time this letter comes to you; and if that is so then I will retire gracefully. I will live with the pain in my heart for evermore.

Although water divides us and some say that time should have lessened our love, you have my heart forever, my darling Clementina. Middlemist is yours and waiting, as am I.

Yours now, for I am no longer my own,
George

Spring

CHAPTER ONE

Willow Carruthers sat in the deep leather chair in her lawyer's office and wrung her thin hands together, oblivious to the scraping sound her rings made.

'No money?' she asked again.

Her lawyer shook her head, the noise of Willow's rings annoying her. 'None, I'm afraid.'

Willow felt the pit of her stomach sink away and she rubbed her eyes, hoping the black spots before them would disappear, smearing her perfectly applied eye makeup.

'How can it be?' she asked. 'I had my own money when Kerr and I married.'

'I know, but you and Kerr never signed a prenuptial agreement. All your money has gone on . . .' the polished woman looked down at the list in front of her, '. . . lifestyle. And some poor investments.'

Willow had the strong feeling she was being judged. Her feeling was confirmed when the lawyer started to speak again.

'Three Aston Martins, two Porches, a house in Vail, a house in London, two castles in Europe, a vineyard in France and an olive grove in Italy, and a luxury yacht which Kerr put the down payment on eighteen months ago. Works of art by Lucian Freud, Damien Hirst, and Tracey Emin. Jewellery . . .'

'I know, I know,' Willow interrupted her.

She knew the castles were too much. She had tried to convince Kerr they didn't need a house in Vail – she hated skiing – but he insisted. He was a rock star cliché and now she had to pay for it. Although she hadn't been too stingy with the credit card either. Harvey Nichols practically closed when she was inside; she often had three people serving her at once. And she had recently spent an enormous amount of money on making the house environmentally friendly.

'Kerr's lawyer has recommended you both sell everything. That will give you the funds you need to pay the taxes. And naturally Kerr will have to lose the deposit on the yacht.'

Willow nodded. The yacht was news to her; she didn't even know Kerr had bought it.

'I . . . I just want to know how this happened,' she asked. Her head was pounding and her mouth felt dry.

The woman looked Willow over, taking in her client's Michael Kors suede skintight trousers and spotless Chloé silk shirt. 'You haven't made a film in six years. Kerr's last album didn't sell as well as he thought, and he took a loss on it. Your lifestyle simply cost more than you were both bringing in. You had no decent money management advice, and the losses your investments made in the US, to put it bluntly, screwed you.'

Willow looked up at her lawyer. 'What am I going to do?'

The lawyer started to shuffle the papers on her desk, and putting them back into a folder, signalling that the meeting was coming to a close. She looked Willow squarely in the eye.

'Get a job.'

Willow left the office in a daze. She looked at her waiting car, her driver ensconced in the front seat. That will have to go, she thought sadly.

8

As she was driven through the streets of London to her home in Shepherd's Bush, she tried to swallow the bile coming up into her mouth. When the pictures of Kerr with some leggy wannabe Russian rock star and her sister were posted on TMZ, she knew she had no other choice but to file for divorce. It was shameful. To see him with one woman was tough, but two? And sisters? Willow had spent the morning she had seen them online throwing up. Thankfully Kitty, the nanny, had left her alone and taken the children out for the day.

The thought of Kitty made her want to weep. She had been with them for three years, since she was eighteen, straight out of school. Not the brightest of girls, but the children loved her. Maybe more than their own mother, thought Willow. Not that she minded. The more time they spent with Kitty, the less time they could spend asking her where their shit of a father was.

Kerr had been missing in action since before their third child was born. Now Willow was the single mother of Lucian, who was five and still not talking; Poppy, who was four and talking for herself and for Lucian; and Jinty, who was one. Jinty was conceived on tour and Willow never regretted her for a moment, although she had had to give up the film she was planning to do once she found out she was pregnant. Kerr was less than enthusiastic. Remembering the fight they had had when she told him after he returned home, she shuddered at Kerr's cruelty.

'Christ Willow! We don't need another fucking kid. Jesus, we can't even get the ones we've got right! Lucian's not right, he's still pissing his pants and he's nearly four!' he shouted across their immaculate bedroom.

Willow hushed him. 'He can hear you, he's not deaf!' she said. 'There's nothing wrong with him, he's just taking his time.'

'You're living in dreamland, Willow. I don't want another fucking baby, you hear me? Get rid of it!'

Willow had been shocked at Kerr's brutality.

Kerr seemed fond of Poppy, but only because she was always in his face daring him to notice her. He ignored Lucian completely. Willow refused to believe Lucian was anything but perfect. *An artist's temperament*, she told people when they asked why he wasn't speaking yet.

So Kerr had moved out when she started to show with Jinty. For the last year, rumours had circled about the state of their marriage, but Willow refused to acknowledge there was trouble, putting on a brave face and keeping her Jade Jagger wedding ring firmly on her left hand. People loved Willow and Kerr; they were rock star royalty in Britain and Europe.

For a year, she refused to see the separation as more than just a hiccup in the marriage. Kerr would come home, she was sure of it . . . until the pictures of him and the sisters emerged. Then the media put an end to its speculation about the health of Kerr and Willow's marriage, declaring him a bastard and a shit. Willow didn't disagree with their assessment privately, but she maintained a stoic silence in public. Even though she hadn't made a movie in years, she was still a popular figure back home in the US, and in the UK.

Kitty was her birth partner when she had Jinty, and Kerr never came to see the baby even though she sent him several messages. Willow wondered how she could have been so wrong about the man. How could you be married for years before you found out that your husband was a complete and utter loser, with no real desire for anything but bags of coke and blowjobs?

Willow realised that she was a liability to Kerr. The rock star lifestyle didn't have much room in it for a wife, three kids and an environmentally friendly home. It didn't help that Willow was still celebrated as one of the world's most beautiful women.

Although she hadn't made a film in six years, Willow's style had kept her in the public eye. She was considered a classic American beauty: blonde, tall, svelte, with an air of entitlement and intellectual superiority. The glossy magazines revered her for being a stay-at-home mother to her children and applauded her for her grace under fire after Kerr's indiscretions were made public.

The green and organic movements loved her for her dedication to their causes, and tabloids loved her and Kerr's constant dramas for helping them to sell millions of copies around the world.

Willow's celebrity still had currency, but even the thought of hustling again to get the next job made her tired. It wasn't as easy as people thought to stay famous. There was always someone else on the horizon: the next Julia Roberts; the next Cameron Diaz; the next Willow Carruthers.

Willow emerged from her reverie as the car pulled up outside her house. She strode up to the front door, ignoring the lurking paparazzi.

As she entered the house, she heard Poppy playing SingStar at the top of her lungs. Putting down her keys carefully so as not to alert the house to her homecoming, she made for the stairs so she could run away to her bedroom and get her

11

head together. But Lucian, who made up for his lack of speech with super-hearing, ran towards her and blocked her path. She smiled. 'Hey Luce. What's new?' she asked.

Her beautiful son stared back at her and then turned and ran away. 'Bye!' she called after him.

She changed her mind about hiding and walked into her living room, decorated with minimalist chic and muted colours but with a rock and roll vibe with the edgy art on the walls. Poppy was wearing the purple Calvin Klein gown Willow had collected her Oscar in, with a red and black striped turtleneck underneath. The dress was hitched up using a ribbon from her box of hair accessories, and underneath Willow could see she was wearing her favourite Nike kicks that Kerr had sent Poppy from Los Angeles.

'Hey pop star!' called Willow. Poppy waved at her and kept singing along to some hideous song that Willow was unfamiliar with.

Willow pressed the intercom to the kitchen. 'You there, Kit?'

'Yep,' came a crackling voice in return.

Willow kicked off her Jimmy Choos and padded downstairs to the kitchen, which was a work of art. Two professional ovens, two fridges, black stone countertops, and French crystal chandeliers over an enormous central bench. The bench was huge and had wonderfully comfortable stools alongside it. The family – Willow, the children and Kitty – sat here to eat their meals.

Kitty was feeding a messy Jinty her lunch and Jinty clapped at the sight of her mother. Willow had felt awful about Kerr and tried to lavish attention on Jinty when she had the time, to try to make up for the lack of her father in her life. Lucian seemed calmer with Kerr gone, Willow had noticed; it was Poppy who suffered. She played her father's music in her room and always ran to answer the phone as soon as it rang. Her therapist said she was mourning her loss and would get over him eventually, but Willow wondered sometimes if Poppy would ever get over Kerr.

Kerr had been Willow's big love – or so she thought. They had met just before she won the Oscar for Best Supporting Actress for her role in an arthouse film, and he had just taken the world by storm with his music. They were untouchable as far as the media was concerned.

When Willow got pregnant, they married quietly in Scotland, in the village that Kerr had grown up in. They were happy for a while and when Lucian was born, Willow was content to let Kerr take over everything else in their life, including their finances.

However the marriage turned sour faster than Willow could ever have imagined. Kerr wasn't interested in Lucian and spent eight months of his first year away on tour. Poppy was conceived during the four months he was home and not holed up in his basement music studio, and Jinty was Willow's last desperate attempt to try and get their marriage back on course.

When she had seen the photos of Kerr and the sisters she had not been shocked or angry, just scared for her and her family's future in the public eye. She had known the relationship was over the minute he suggested she abort Jinty. She had spent the nine months of her pregnancy mourning him and their marriage, and now she was alone. Kerr had not applied for access and his lawyer had made no mention of it. Not that Willow missed him, but 'A child needs its father,'

her psychotherapist mother had insisted over the phone from New York. 'It's a pivotal relationship.'

'Well that depends, Janis,' said Willow, 'on whether the father is a complete fuckwit or not.'

'Yes, Kerr has some problems, but he is still their father after all. They need a significant male in their lives,' her mother's nasal voice had protested over the line. Willow knew not to get into an argument with her.

Willow, Janis, and Willow's father, Alan, also a psychotherapist, were never going to be on the same page. Born and raised in New York, Willow had been homeschooled. Her mother's belief that Willow was the reincarnated spirit of Sarah Bernhardt meant she was enrolled in every drama class New York had to offer, but it was the only formal schooling she had ever had.

Janis and Alan were passionate activists for anything and everything. They lay in front of bulldozers, climbed trees and held sit-ins.

Janis saved everything. She called herself 'Betty Budget' and reused her baking paper. Willow was dressed in vegan shoes long before Stella McCartney had the idea. She was raised on a diet of legumes and literature.

Willow privately thought that growing up with Alan and Janis was almost like being in a cult. Nudity, hand-me-downs and self-proclaimed gurus filled the small apartment. Willow used to escape when she was old enough by saying she had a drama class or a workshop and wander up and down Fifth Avenue window shopping. She loved the clothes and the colours. The leather shoes – how she longed for leather shoes! There were so many shoes she wanted.

Once, she found a Big Brown Bag from Macy's on the

street. She carried her things to drama class in it until it tore from overuse. There was nothing better than shopping, she decided. Once she had enough money, she would spend, and then she would spend some more.

She had been young, rich and fabulous. and her meteoric rise to fame had been helped by her marriage to one of Hollywood's most eligible bachelors. Their subsequent split involved rumours not only of affairs, but also of drug addiction, both on his side.

Now at thirty-one, she was a married woman with three children, her Hollywood career behind her. Willow had very definite ideas about raising her family. She felt homeschooling was the best thing for her children and she was planning to work with Kitty on the curriculum for Lucian over the coming winter. Lucian's development didn't worry her; used to Janis's unusual opinions on child raising, she figured Lucian would find his own way when he was ready. She had disagreed violently when Kerr suggested they send him to a specialist.

With the hindsight so many women have after the failure of a marriage, Willow realised she had been more in love with the lifestyle and the crown that went with being Kerr Bannerman's wife than she had been in love with the man himself. She didn't miss making films and she didn't miss Kerr when he was on tour. She liked being photographed out and about in London, with her perfect flazen-haired children. She was on charity boards and worked in the organic food movement; the most recent publicity she had had was letting their London house be photographed for English *Vogue*, where she spouted the need for people to green their home, no matter the cost.

Looking back, she wished she had perhaps looked at the

budgets a little closer. Perhaps 'Betty Budget' was a role she needed to learn from her mother, who she knew disapproved of her lifestyle. When she had imagined her child as an actor, she had envisaged Broadway. If she had to be in films, she would be the private, dignified type, like Meryl Streep or Woody Allen.

Janis didn't like the magazine covers, the gossip and the drama. She stayed away from London and ultimately her own child and grandchildren, much to Willow's disappointment and relief. She wanted her mother at times, but she knew that with her came the lectures about money and lifestyle and how she raised the children with the nanny.

Watching Kitty as she fed Jinty, she wondered how she would do without her. Kitty had come to her through a nanny agency when she was eighteen years old. She'd had no experience, but Lucian seemed to like her when she came to the house for her interview. That sealed the deal for Willow, as Lucian didn't seem to like anyone. He refused to meet most people's eyes when they spoke to him and ignored most instructions. When Kitty had sat down and asked Lucian to bring her his favourite toy, Willow had been surprised when he quietly left the room and came back with his brightly coloured blocks with raised lettering on the sides. Kitty had received the blocks gracefully and acknowledged the reverence that Lucian bestowed upon them, exclaiming over the colours and the smooth texture of the letters, although she never asked him to read them to her, and she never read them to him herself.

Willow had been in wonder at the girl child in front of her and how Lucian had seemed to take an instant liking to her. Soon Kitty was firmly ensconced upstairs in the nanny's quarters, which she seemed perfectly happy with, refusing Willow's offer to redecorate to her taste.

'I'm fine, really. I come from a crazy old house in the country. I don't need anything else, I swear,' she had said, and Willow had stepped back – although she did get a few new sets of Cath Kidston linen for her. She seemed like a Cath Kidston sort of a girl.

'How's my little Jinty?' cooed Willow at her youngest.

'She's great. Just having lunch and then off for a nap,' said Kitty as she cleaned Jinty's dirty face of the organic pumpkin Willow had cooked for her. This was one area where Willow did not let the children down. Her cooking skills were amazing and there was not a recipe she couldn't master. If she'd had her time again, she often thought, she would have worked in food somewhere. Now she nurtured her children with food, and the two fridges were full to bursting with Willow's meals and treats.

Willow's phone rang and she walked out of the kitchen to answer it. It was her lawyer.

'Willow. Hi,' she barked down the phone.

'Hi,' said Willow bracing herself for more bad news.

'Listen, I've done my best, but the bank are going to court to start proceedings to repossess the house. It's about to become very public, very messy and very expensive.'

Willow sat on the silk-covered armchair in her bedroom. 'Jesus fucking Christ,' she said.

'Exactly,' said her lawyer.

'I'll have to head back to New York,' said Willow, wondering if her parents could put her up for a while and whether Alan would wear clothes around the house, at least for her sake.

'No, you can't,' said the lawyer, as though Willow was an

idiot. Perhaps I am an idiot, thought Willow, feeling sorry for herself.

'Why not?' she asked.

'You can't take the children out of the country until you get Kerr's consent. They are half his after all,' she said. 'And until we find him, you have to stay put.'

'Fuck,' said Willow angrily.

'Call me anytime.' The woman's voice softened. She had seen so many women end up like Willow, having given their power and responsibility to shitty husbands.

'Thanks,' said Willow and hung up the phone.

Thirty-one years old, unemployed, broke, a single mother and homeless. Willow wondered how much her Oscar would bring her on eBay.

CHAPTER TWO

When Willow had left the house that morning, Kitty surveyed the mess that Poppy had left in the living room. 'Poppy, come here please!' she called up the stairs, and Poppy came stumbling down in the purple dress which Willow had tearfully accepted her Oscar in. 'Should you be wearing that?'

Poppy shrugged. 'Mummy put it in my dress-ups,' she said.

Kitty had raised her dark eyebrows. 'Well, if you say so – but I will check with Mummy. OK?'

'Whatever,' said Poppy. It was her new favourite phrase, picked up from the television she watched for hours on end. Willow didn't mind it being on all the time, but Kitty did.

'Can you put these things away please, Poppy?' asked Kitty, gesturing to the clothes, books, dolls and crayons covering almost every surface in the room.

'No,' said Poppy, and picked up a crayon. She held it against the wall, daring Kitty to say something.

'Don't even think about it,' said Kitty.

'Why? I feel like doing art,' she said, and she slowly drew a wobbly line down the Colefax and Fowler wallpaper. Kitty held her breath. Poppy stopped and they faced each other, their eyes meeting.

Kitty won the stare-off, and Poppy walked over to a doll and picked it up. 'What did you say?' she asked the doll, and then held it up to her ear. She laughed and then looked at Kitty. 'Yes, Kitty *is* a fatty,' she said.

'Poppy, you must never call anyone fat,' admonished Kitty. Compared to Poppy's mother, she must seem huge, she thought. She wasn't fat, she was curvy, with a tiny waist and large breasts. She had the kind of body men either wanted to paint or fuck, and she refused either offer, although plenty came her way. Her dark hair and eyes, courtesy of a French gene from way back in her family tree, gave her a sleepy exotic quality and immediately made men fall in love with her. Kitty declined most adult attention, endearing her to children and making her misunderstood by her peers.

Being a nanny for Willow and her children was her perfect job, albeit trying at times like this morning.

Lucian was a dream, although it would be better if he spoke; and Poppy had too much to say. She was wise beyond her four years – she watched television that was too old for her and Willow put no boundaries on her. When Kitty told her off, Poppy either ignored her or laughed at her.

Kitty knew the best thing for Poppy would be kindergarten. She was bright and understimulated at home, and Kitty knew she could be no help in this area. Willow had it in her head that she and Kitty would homeschool the children, but Kitty thought she would have resigned before that happened.

Willow's impending divorce from Kerr was proving difficult for Poppy to understand, and she pined for her father. When she had first started at the house, before Willow became pregnant with Jinty, Kerr was around more. He gave his attention to Poppy and usually ignored Lucian, although once she had caught him calling Lucian a dumb idiot and demanding he spoke, which only made Lucian wet his pants.

Kitty had gently led Lucian from the room, cleaned him up and sat with him on the bed telling him fantastic stories about the boy with magical mind powers until he settled down.

Kitty's relationship with Willow was mostly formal. Willow's aloofness was difficult for Kitty and even the children to penetrate. Lucian didn't bother Willow; his quietness suited her, although it worried Kitty. Poppy was too much for her mother to handle. She was so like her father that Willow often gave in to all her wants and desires, particularly since she and Kerr had split up. Jinty had no idea who her father was. She clung to Kitty as though she was her mother, which Willow encouraged as she had so many other things to think about.

The idea of teaching Lucian and Poppy at home was daunting to Kitty. She hadn't done well at school, leaving as soon as she could, much to her father's disapproval. Her much older brother, Merritt, had gone all the way through to university and was Kitty's father's pride and joy. Merritt was now a garden designer and writer on all manner of gardening subjects, travelling the world and sending her copies of his books whenever a new one was released. Almost twenty years older than Kitty, he was a mysterious brother, whom Kitty shared no similarities with. He was as fair as she was dark, tall and muscular where Kitty was curvy and soft. He could spend hours reading or in the garden, Kitty remembered from her childhood, whereas she didn't know a weed from a petunia and only knew the plots of books if they'd been adapted into a film she'd watched.

In the company of children was where Kitty felt the most comfortable. They had no expectations of her, and she had the ability to calm them down with her stories or comfort them when they needed it most. Kitty's lack of superficiality and her joy in the everyday was what Willow's children loved most about her and she in turn loved their innocence and lack of judgment.

Growing up in Merritt's shadow hadn't been easy, especially after her beloved mother, Iris, died when Kitty was twelve. She had navigated her way clumsily through puberty, school and boys – not that many of them had been interested in her until her breasts began to show. Kitty avoided boys at school and then men as she became older. Moving to London when her father died just as she was turning eighteen, she had moved into a bedsit, leaving behind the house and attempting to leave her memories too.

It was only when Merritt's short-lived first marriage to Eliza failed that she had seen her father angry with her golden brother. She still remembered the shouting coming from downstairs and her father saying how disappointed he was that Merritt didn't have the tenacity to stand up and be a man. Merritt had shouted back and then left the house, not returning for years till their father had died of a heart attack in the garden.

Kitty had not heard from Merritt for those years either. She and Merritt had never been close so she hadn't minded. Kitty had hated Eliza; she thought she was rude and pretentious, always speaking in an affected tone and telling Merritt to get a real job. What did he see in her? she had wondered. When their marriage had lasted for less than a year, Kitty had silently rejoiced.

Eliza had started measuring up Middlemist House as soon as the emerald engagement ring was on her finger. Eliza had pranced around telling everyone it was a Middlemist family heirloom, as old as the house, but Kitty knew her family hadn't even kept hold of any jewellery. If they had, their father would have sold it years before for the upkeep of the house. Eliza's ideas for Middlemist made Kitty feel sick. Working in a modern London gallery, she envisaged Middlemist as a grand modern home. She wanted to get rid of most of the wonderful Gothic features and fill it with giant sculptures of malformed babies and chandeliers made of rubber gloves. Kitty's father had put his foot down and told Eliza and Merritt in no uncertain terms that there would be no rubber gloves as light fittings, and that until he died and was under the ground then the house would remain as it was.

Kitty thought Middlemist was fine as it was, filled with hidden rooms, bay windows and turrets. Her favourite memory of the house was of taking the hidden passage from the library to the dining room on the other side of the building, with only a torch to light the way. Kitty knew every flagstone by heart, she had walked it so many times. Her father said he had walked the same route as a child, and his father before him.

No matter how familiar she became with it, Middlemist House had never bored Kitty. She loved the romance of the balconies and the columns, the dark woods and the sweeping staircases. Her father had told her the house housed many secrets, namely the great treasures his great-grandmother had supposedly spoken of, but the generations that followed had never found them.

Kitty's father, Edward, had been a stern man, more concerned with appearance and the family name than caring for his two children. When Kitty's mother had died, he was

23

caught up in trying to save Middlemist from massive debts and rising running costs. The house was a money pit as far as he was concerned, and eventually he gave up trying to rescue the grand dame. Slowly the house fell into disrepair. Edward managed to sell some land at the back of the property, which paid the debts but that was all. When he finally died he left the house to Merritt and Kitty on the proviso they not sell it for ten years, along with the small amount of cash that he had saved. There were no staff to let go of and Merritt and Kitty had locked the house up after the funeral. Pulling the keys out of the massive iron gates, Merritt had handed them to Kitty.

'Take these,' he had said on the road outside Middlemist. 'I don't want them.'

'What am I going to do with them?' she had asked.

'Keep them safe. I'll call you in ten years when it's time to sell,' he said, looking down the road.

Kitty took the keys and tucked them into her backpack. 'Take care Merritt,' she said to the brother she hardly knew.

'You too, Kitty Kat.' He touched her shoulder briefly with his hand, and then turned and walked down the road without a glance back.

Kitty had got onto the bus at the other end of the road, and when it drove past Merritt walking down towards the village, Kitty had tried to catch his eye. He never looked up, even though he knew she was driving past him.

Kitty had soon moved out of the bedsit when she landed her job with Willow, courtesy of a nanny agency in London. Although she had no experience or references, she had an innocent charm about her that the owner of the agency liked. When the opening came up to be Willow Carruthers's nanny,

Kitty was sent on a whim – partly because when asked if she knew who Willow was, she said she had no idea, and partly because the nanny agency had no one else suitable. Willow's brief was for an English country girl, with cooking skills and a liking for children. The woman at the agency had raised an eyebrow at the last request, but Willow was of the opinion that you couldn't be too careful. Kitty ticked all the boxes, and had been happily ensconced at Willow's London home ever since. She never thought about Middlemist, never told anyone about it, and she hadn't heard from Merritt since that morning outside the house. She still had the keys though, in her jewellery box, next to her mother's locket.

Things at Willow's house had become more and more tense over the last two years. Kerr was a shocking father, worse than her own, and Willow was self-absorbed, although she meant well. Kitty ended up taking on all the duties of a nanny and a parent, but she didn't mind. It was nice to be thought of as smart and clever for once in her life.

Since Willow had come back from that meeting with her lawyer, she had taken a call and then locked herself up in her bedroom for the past hour. Kitty wondered if she should see if she was alright. She was never sure what to do in these situations. She found it best to stay put when faced with the unknown though, so she stayed with the children till Willow made the first move.

After Kitty had put Jinty down for a sleep and Poppy and Lucian were watching some bizarre movie about a hotel for pets or some such rubbish, Willow crept into the doorway of the playroom where Kitty was tidying up the toys and beckoned to her to follow her to the front room. This room was Willow's pride and joy – the children were never allowed in. All lavenders and blue silks, the walls were white and a stunning glass cherry-blossom-shaped light fitting hung over the mantelpiece. Kitty thought that this room utterly reflected Willow: icy, perfect and cool. Willow sat on the blue silk couch and motioned for Kitty to sit down on the adjacent lavender wingback chair.

As Kitty approached she noticed Willow's swollen red eyes. Willow clasped her hands in her lap. 'So, as you know Kerr and I are divorcing,' she said uncertainly.

Kitty nodded, unsure what to say or do.

'Well there is a problem, you see.' Willow nervously cleared her throat. 'It seems that Kerr has spent all of our money.'

As Kitty opened her eyes wide in shock. How could you spend that amount of money? she wondered. Still she said nothing.

'Yes, so it's a big problem. You see I've got two weeks to get out of the house and take what I can and find a new place for the children and me.

'I can't return to America with the children until the divorce is settled, and I've nowhere else really to take them. I've tried to ring my agent to see what work is around, as I will have to get some cash fast.'

Kitty sat still, waiting for the final blow.

'I am afraid, Kitty,' Willow paused, as if swallowing tears, her voice breaking, 'I will have to let you go. I can't afford to pay you until I start to work, and you won't be able to live here as the bank are repossessing. I've tried calling Kerr but he won't answer. It's all a bit of a cock-up I'm afraid. The paparazzi are going to go nuts when they find out. I don't know where the hell we're going to go!'

Kitty stared down at the perfect white carpet, the pile

vacuumed a certain way to make it look as though no one had ever entered the room.

Willow put her head in her hands and the tears started to flow. 'I'm so sorry Kitty. I'm so sorry.'

Kitty got off the chair and knelt on the carpet in front of her boss. 'It's OK – it will be OK,' she soothed, unsure if it was the right thing to say. 'Can I help in any way? Can I do anything?'

Willow looked up at Kitty's kind face and shrugged. 'Do you know anywhere we can hide till I get a job?' she said, sarcasm thick in her voice.

Kitty sat and thought hard. She took Willow's cold, white hands in her warm, soft ones. 'Actually, I do.'

CHAPTER THREE

Willow had jumped at Kitty's idea as soon as she suggested it, and the more Willow thought about it the more she was convinced this was the right idea.

Kitty, however, was regretting mentioning it to Willow; the house hadn't been opened for three years, and god knows what state it would be in. She had hoped to get up to the house as soon as she could to try and make it respectable for Willow and the children, but Willow had kept her busy with plans for their move. Willow had moved everything that she loved from the London house to a storage place, under Kitty's name. Everything of Kerr's, she left in the house, including some of his prized artefacts, such as a letter by J D Salinger that he had paid a huge amount at auction for and a series of artworks that gave Willow the creeps. She hated modern art as much as Kerr loved it, so she left his things on the walls and in the cupboards. She knew from her lawyer that whatever the bank found in the house they would repossess and sell to pay off the debt.

The children's things and some of Willow's personal items were to be shipped to Middlemist in Kitty's name. The plan was that the five of them would sneak out of the house in the night and drive to Middlemist undetected.

On the evening of the planned getaway, Poppy was beside

herself with excitement. 'I saw this on *The Sound of Music*!' she said to Kitty, who was packing the Range Rover in the downstairs garage. 'We are escaping the papanazis,' she whispered.

'Yes,' said Kitty, trying not to laugh. 'The papanazis.'

Willow came downstairs with the last of the food she had packed up from the kitchen, even though Kitty had tried to tell her they had supermarkets in the village. Willow would have none of it. 'Organic, Kitty – we must be organic. Does Middlemist have solar power or is it powered from the grid?'

Willow thought about the flickering lights and the occasional blackouts that occurred for no apparent reason. 'It's a combination,' she said.

'Ah, a dual-fuel house. Very good!' Willow bustled in the car, reorganising Kitty's packing.

'OK, well I'll get Jinty and Lucian and we can head off then,' said Kitty as she went upstairs.

Willow followed her and they stood in the kitchen together. 'Is it terrible?' asked Kitty without thinking. It was a habit she was trying to break.

Willow turned to her. 'What? Leaving the house?'

'Yes.'

'Not as bad as I thought it would be. Not as bad as Kerr leaving. I just want to start again,' she said, looking around the once-perfect kitchen, cupboards open and drawers pulled out.

Willow swept up Jinty, and Kitty went to find Lucian. He was sitting in his now empty room. Kitty went and sat next to him. 'Time to go, Lucian. I'm taking you to my house. OK?'

Lucian said nothing. Kitty continued, used to his lack of

response. 'I have sheep and gardens and exciting things in the house. I think you'll like it. It's fun! There's so much to do,' she said gently.

She stood up and held her hand out to Lucian. 'Come on tiger. Let's go and get dirty in the country!'

Lucian stood up and took her hand. They walked down to the car and found everyone waiting for them inside.

Willow was in the driver's seat. She knew Kitty couldn't drive when she hired her and up till now she hadn't needed to, living within walking distance of everything.

'Hop in Luce. Time to go!' She started the car and opened the garage door. There was no one waiting for them at the front of the house. No papanazis. Willow had chosen tonight as she knew Matt Damon and George Clooney were at dinner together at Nobu. Willow and Kerr were invited but she had begged off, claiming the kids were sick. Every pap in town was over at Nobu waiting for their shot and Willow had a free and clear ride to the country.

Once out of London, the children fell asleep in the back seat and Willow and Kitty sat in comfortable silence.

Willow listened to the sat nav give her directions to the house, which was near Bristol. She turned off the motorway and onto smaller and smaller roads, and eventually they were in front of a pair of enormous gates.

Kitty jumped out of the car quietly so as not to wake the children and pulled the keys from her backpack. Heading over, she found the key to the gates' padlock. She tried to open it but it was stuck, rusted from lack of use over the past three years.

Willow got out, and having watched Kitty's attempts with the lock, went to the back of the car to rustle through the organic cotton bags. She found what she was looking for, walked up and sprayed the lock. Kitty turned the key and the lock opened.

'Organic olive oil,' said Willow as she walked back to the car holding the can.

'I'm impressed,' said Kitty as she swung open the gates. Willow steered the car through them and waited for Kitty to get back in. Lucian stirred and rubbed his eyes to try and focus on the darkness outside.

As they arrived at the house, Kitty suddenly remembered she had forgotten to ring the power company to reconnect the electricity. The house looked black and forbidding in the moonlight and Kitty felt slightly sick at the thought of Willow and the children staying in the dark and cold all night. 'Only for a few weeks,' Willow had promised her, but now Kitty wondered if they would make it through the night. Kitty prayed there wouldn't be any dead birds in the entrance hall. Three years was a long time to leave a house locked up.

Kitty alighted from the car, pulled her keys back out and opened the front door. Willow followed her. The door swung open and the smell of dust and old air filled their nostrils. Kitty made a face as she felt for the light switch, silently praying that perhaps the electricity would still be on, although she distinctly remembered getting it switched off before she and Merritt had left three years before.

The power gods were obviously listening; miraculously the light turned on, and Kitty blinked a few times in amazement as her eyes adjusted to the light. Memories of the house flooded her mind and she stood in the large entrance, spellbound.

Willow was entranced. 'Jesus, it's amazing Kitty! Why didn't

31

you tell me you lived here?' Willow was circling in one spot, looking up at the vaulted ceiling. She stopped and gazed up the magnificent oak staircase that stretched before them.

Kitty was in a trance as she stood by the front door, not hearing Willow. Memories of running up the stairs with Merritt; the sound of her mother in the kitchen. Bach flowing out of the drawing room when her father took to the piano in the evenings. He had stopped playing after Kitty's mother died. It was as though the music in him died with Iris.

'Kitty, Kitty!' Willow's voice shook Kitty from her daze.

'Sorry,' said Kitty. 'I'll go and turn the lights on and unpack the car, if you want to get the children.' Kitty walked towards the kitchen.

'Great, I'll meet you back here,' said Willow, looking happier than Kitty had seen her in months.

Kitty wandered through the house, turning on lights and opening whichever windows would allow her. Some were tightly stuck, but she figured she could get Walker, the local handyman, to get them opened – if he was still working.

As she walked back to the entrance, she could hear Poppy's voice. 'I can be a princess here!' she was yelling. Jinty was crying and Lucian was as silent as ever.

Willow handed Jinty to Kitty, as she usually did when she cried. 'Show me everything,' she said, her cheeks flushed.

'OK, well, this is the entrance. The staircase leads up to the first floor, where there's an ancient bathroom and sixteen bedrooms of different sizes, plus a nanny's quarters and two smaller rooms, including a playroom. There's also another wing, but we never open it as it's just more to look after.'

She walked with a now settled Jinty, who was going back to sleep on her shoulder, towards large oak double doors to the side of the entrance. 'This is the drawing room,' she said as she opened the doors and turned on the light. Willow took a sharp intake of breath. 'My god! Did a *Brideshead Revisited* bomb go off in here and time has since stood still?' she laughed.

Kitty looked at her blankly.

'You know, *Brideshead Revisited*, the book? Evelyn Waugh?' said Willow.

'I've never read any of her work,' said Kitty.

'Evelyn was a man, and *Brideshead Revisited* was the book that made me fall in love with England. I read it when I was fourteen. It's set in the twenties,' said Willow as she walked around touching everything that wasn't covered with a dust-sheet.

Kitty felt embarrassed. Willow was so smart. She was forever offering to lend Kitty books, but Kitty always declined – although she devoured the glossy magazines.

Willow walked around the room looking at its contents. There was no television. The only television they had was in the parlour off the kitchen, where Kitty had hidden herself away after Iris had died. Merritt preferred the library.

'It's a bit out of date, I know. We didn't have a lot of money to do it up with. A house like this eats money, I'm afraid,' she said, rocking Jinty in her arms.

'It's not a criticism. It's wonderful. People go to great lengths to get their houses to look like this nowadays. If it were mine, I wouldn't change a thing,' said Willow, picking up a bronze astrolabe off a side table. 'What's this?' she asked.

'It's some astronomy thing,' said Kitty.

'How do you use it?'

'No idea. My brother knows,' said Kitty as she tried to open a window with one hand, careful not to wake Jinty.

'You have a brother?' asked Willow. 'Where's he? Why doesn't he live here?'

'I don't know,' said Kitty honestly. 'After my father died we went our separate ways and said we would meet again when we could sell the house. There's a caveat on it. We can't sell it for ten years.'

'Don't you and your brother get along?' asked Willow. She had longed for a sibling as a child. The idea of never speaking to one seemed unnatural.

'We get along but we are very different. He's almost twenty years older than me,' said Kitty, feeling the cool night air on her face now the window was open.

'Oh,' said Willow. 'Show me more of the house,' she demanded, and Kitty sighed softly and did what her boss asked.

Kitty pushed open another set of doors and they stood watching Poppy as she climbed the steps and ran around the library mezzanine.

'Careful,' said Willow, as she looked up at the stone vaulted ceiling and the rows and rows of old books. The large reading table in the centre of the room was big enough to seat twelve for dinner and the battered Chesterfield faced a huge and ornate stone fireplace.

'Now this is wonderful. You must have loved this room when you were little,' said Willow, craning her neck to take in the room. The iron spiral staircase had metal serpents winding their way up to the mezzanine. Kitty watched as Poppy flitted about like a hummingbird in her favourite tutu and a purple feather boa.

'No, I didn't like it much,' said Kitty quietly. She had hated the library, with its smell of books and air of seriousness.

'Let's keep going,' said Willow, and Kitty showed her the dining room and the billiard room, where the billiard table was covered in a white dustsheet.

Every room they went into Willow went into raptures over it, exclaiming over the furniture; the carpets; the chandeliers. She even managed to get excited about the small powder room downstairs.

'I'll find it hard to leave,' said Willow.

'Well, you haven't seen the kitchen yet,' muttered Kitty as they walked through to it. It had lain untouched since 1960, when Iris had insisted Edward do it up for her as a wedding present. The old Aga stove had been left, but everything else was avocado laminate and white cane furniture.

Willow laughed as she entered the room. 'This is very Austin Powers.'

Kitty laughed, not because it was particularly funny but because she was relieved to get the joke. She was still ashamed for having thought Evelyn Waugh was a girl in the drawing room.

Kitty walked into the small parlour to the side of the kitchen and set the sleeping Jinty carefully down on the old Laura Ashley sofa. She covered her with the throw that lay along the back of it. 'Alright, well let's unpack then shall we?' she asked Poppy and Lucian cheerfully.

'Why don't I unpack and you go and get the children ready for bed? You can go and choose their bedrooms if you like,' said Willow.

Kitty took her small charges upstairs and put them in a room together in twin beds. The bedrooms were sparsely furnished. Most of the good furniture had been sold over the years to pay for bills or repairs to the house. Kitty found clean linen in the hall cupboard, although it was a little musty. She reminded herself to air it in the morning.

Willow brought the first lot of cases upstairs, which were carefully labelled with each of the children's names in Kitty's childish writing. 'Crazy,' said Willow, looking down the wide hallway with all its paintings and the doors leading off it.

Kitty unpacked the children's clothes and put them into a large cedar dresser, and then she changed the children into their pyjamas. Lucian was silent as she led him through the motions, but Poppy was high on the smell of dust and circumstance.

'I love it here. I don't think we'll ever leave. I am sure I've been here before!' Poppy rattled on, and Kitty nodded and agreed as she wrestled Poppy into her organic cotton pyjamas.

Taking them to the ancient bathroom, she watched as Poppy and Lucian cleaned their teeth and then took them back inside to tuck them up in bed. 'Willow,' she called down the stairs.

Willow came up with more cases and walked into the bedroom. 'Night changelings,' she said as she bent down to kiss them.

'I'll go and make us some tea, OK?' Willow said as she went downstairs again, leaving Kitty humming the children to sleep. Kitty stayed with them until they'd drifted off.

As she walked down the grand staircase Willow touched the worn balustrade. She wondered what it would be like to own this house, to have all the history that Kitty had. Not that Kitty had ever shown it; she had made a huge effort to downplay her ancestral home, although Willow didn't remember ever asking Kitty anything personal since her employment.

As she crossed the landing and continued down towards the entrance she looked down and was shocked to find a man standing in the entrance. 'Who are you?' she asked imperiously, taking on the tone of the lady of the house.

'I might ask you the same thing. What the fuck are you doing in my house?'

CHAPTER FOUR

'It's a plant sample,' explained Merritt to the customs official at Heathrow.

'Right. Got a certificate for it then?' asked the man, shaking the bag. It had a small cutting inside it wrapped in cotton soaked in water and Rescue Remedy.

'Please be careful,' said Merritt.

'Sure, sure,' said the official absently as he glanced at the certificate that Merritt handed over. 'Effilum oxypetalsum,' he read carefully.

'Epiphyllum oxypetalum,' corrected Merritt, trying not to let the disdain creep into his voice.

The man picked up the bag again. 'What's that?' he asked, shaking it vigorously.

'It's a type of cactus,' said Merritt, careful not to upset the officious man, who smelt of Vicks and cigarettes. He was tired and wanted to get out of the loud airport and have a shower and drink.

'I hate cactus plants. When the wife and I bought our house there were so many, and we had them all pulled out,' he said as he stamped Merritt's certificate for approval.

Merritt grabbed the paper from the man, put his plant into his worn leather satchel and walked through to collect his luggage. He had hunted for this sample, a night-blooming

Cereus known as 'Queen of the Night'. It bloomed only one or two nights a year, around the full moon in May. The blooms only lasted for twelve hours or so and then it would take a full year for it to bloom again. He wasn't about to have some tit at Heathrow who was high on the power of his job ruin his dreams of having one back at Middlemist again.

Since he had said goodbye to Kitty three years ago at the elaborate gates outside Middlemist, he had travelled constantly, designing gardens for a sheikh in Jordan, a sneaker entrepreneur in the Hamptons, and a luxury hotel chain in Bali, India and Mexico, which is where he picked up his precious plant sample. In between this he had written three books and filmed a television special for PBS in America.

Then one day, he woke up and wanted to go home. He was exhausted. Whatever he was looking for eluded him, and the thing he was trying to escape from had followed him from place to place. Middlemist had been calling him. The gardens cried for him, and he finally listened.

Returning home, he planned to head straight to Middlemist and then call Kitty. He had thought about her a lot over the past three years. She worried him, but he was not equipped to help her with what she needed. While he was still at home it had been painful to watch her struggle at school, with their father so proud of him but ignoring his daughter.

His marriage and fast divorce from Eliza had rocked his father's world, although he had no idea why it had been so shattering to Edward. In hindsight, he saw that he and Eliza had never been a good match. He was swept away by her vivacity and ability to make small talk, both skills he severely lacked. But Eliza, it emerged, was actually a shameless social climber who wanted to be the lady of the house. She had assumed that Merritt's family had more money than they actually showed off.

The separation from Eliza was swift, partly because he found out she had gone through not only the estate's private accounts but his personal accounts too, but mainly after he had found her astride his best friend from school, Johnny Wimple-Jones, a gadabout and heir to an enormous property and large trust fund.

He had left Eliza and Johnny to each other, facing the disappointment of his father and the gossip of his friends. Such was his pride and shame, Merritt had refused to divulge what had happened in the marriage; not even to his father. It was only Kitty who he had told what had happened after he came back for the funeral. He still remembered her coming into his room in the middle of the night. She had sat on the end of his bed, held his hand and listened as he told her what he had discovered about Eliza. He wasn't sure why he spilled his heart, but she was so unprejudiced about his and Eliza's relationship that he felt himself able to tell her everything.

Kitty had said nothing. She had made soothing noises, which is what she reverted to when she didn't know what to say. Her own memories rendered her silent. She was afraid that should she speak, Merritt might find more out about Johnny than he would care to know, and she would make things worse for him.

The ten-year caveat on Middlemist had always seemed tiresome. Merritt could have done with the money, as he was sure Kitty could have, but now he understood why Edward had created this stipulation in his will. Grief makes people commit impulsive deeds. Deeds like his – heading off around the world in search of something he still hadn't found.

Three years later he could see that Middlemist House was bewitching, but while the Middlemist family name came with great history and once with great wealth, all of that had gone over the years. Now all he and Kitty had were the house and what they earned from their jobs.

Even though the house seemed stuck in time, and the gardens were probably overrun and perhaps even beyond repair, he figured he at least had to try to do what he could. If it proved too much then he would sell at the end of the ten years.

The only preparation he had made for his arrival was to have the power switched on again at Middlemist.

When he arrived at the house he was alarmed to find the gates wide open, and as he drove up the driveway in his rental car he was even more concerned to see a large black Range Rover parked on the gravel.

He got out of his car and peered through the windows of the Range Rover with his penlight torch. He could make out a packet of nappies, a doll and some bags of food. Perhaps Kitty had rented the house out without his knowledge, he thought crossly, striding towards the front doors.

As he stepped through the entrance he saw a very slender, beautiful blonde woman coming down the stairs, looking around in wonder. Maybe she was a squatter, on drugs, he thought. Then he wondered how many squatters drove top-of-the-line Range Rovers.

It was only after she rudely asked who he was that he felt his hackles rise. His retaliation alarmed her enough that she ran back up the stairs, calling out his sister's name.

Kitty came to stand at the top of the stairs. 'Merritt!' she cried, and ran down to him where he caught her in a warm embrace.

Willow stood and watched the family reunion with interest. So, here's the long-lost, astronomy-expert, green-fingered brother, she thought. Hopefully he won't ruin my plans. She needed to stay at Middlemist for as long as she could, or at least until she could work out what she was going to do next.

The older brother was handsome. And so *tall*, she thought, watching him embrace his sister. He had a mop of brown curls with slight greying at the temples, a brown face, and brown arms in his white shirt with its sleeves rolled up. In his worn jeans and work boots, he had an air of the outdoors about him.

Merritt and Kitty pulled away from each other. 'How are you, Miss Kitty?' he asked kindly.

'I'm OK,' she said, grinning.

Willow walked down the stairs, but stopped before she reached the end. Standing on the bottom step, she was nearly as tall as Merritt. He looked at her, and Kitty shook her head. 'Sorry – Willow Carruthers, this is my brother Merritt Middlemist.'

Willow held out her hand for Merritt to take it and plastered a careful smile on her face.

Merritt took her hand and smiled. 'Hello. Sorry about the language. I thought you were a homeless person who had taken over my house.'

'I am,' said Willow simply, and Merritt laughed. He glanced at her, and realised she reminded him of a flower. Which one? he wondered. Her pale face bore a false smile and she was tired; it was as though her bloom had faded. Thin and tall, elegant but brittle. He searched his mind for the plant he was looking for.

Kitty looked at Willow, unsure of what to say next. Willow had told her in no uncertain terms that she was not to let anyone know about her financial situation until she had it worked out. Willow had paid her wages for the next eight weeks, but couldn't promise any more after that until she got back to work.

'Are you a friend of Kitty's then?' he asked.

Kitty laughed nervously. 'No, Willow's my boss. I'm her nanny.'

'Oh great. Good for you,' said Merritt cheerfully. 'Is your husband here?' he inquired politely.

'No,' said Willow. 'I don't have a husband.'

'Right then,' said Merritt, not knowing where to look.

'I don't know why I said that. I'm sorry,' said Willow, her face red.

'Well it's better to talk about it, I've found,' said Merritt kindly, and he looked at Kitty who smiled gently at him in return.

'What are you doing back here?' asked Kitty. 'I haven't heard from you in three years!' she admonished. 'I would have written to you, but you know . . .' her voice trailed off.

'I know. I didn't have an address anyway,' he said. 'Let's have a drink. I'm desperate. I stopped at the off-licence and got some tonic and gin and a lemon. I wasn't sure whether the lemon tree would be kind enough to give me anything after all these years. You up for a G&T?'

'Yes please,' said Kitty.

'Sure,' said Willow, not sure at all of the giant man with worn hands and curly brown hair in desperate need of a cut.

43

Willow and Kitty followed Merritt into the kitchen, where he set about making them all drinks. Willow sat in silence as she listened to Kitty and Merritt talk. Their familiar tone with each other, their joking and laughing, was something she had never experienced. She found it captivating.

He set the drinks down in front of them and sat down at the kitchen table. He looked huge on the delicate cane chair, and Willow tried not to stare.

'So, Willow. What do you do?' he asked genuinely.

Willow looked at him to see if he was joking but she couldn't see any amusement in his eyes. 'I'm an actor,' she said.

'Oh great. I love the theatre,' said Merritt as he sipped his strong G&T.

'More films actually,' she said, with an edge to her voice.

'Right. I don't see many films. Sometimes I see them on the planes but I never pay much attention. Those headphone things are too small for my head,' he said ruefully, rubbing his mop of hair.

Kitty laughed. 'Silly. Willow's won an Oscar,' she declared, proud of her boss.

Willow shrugged. She wasn't proud of her award.

'Wow, an Oscar. Well done you,' said Merritt, looking at her carefully. He knew what flower she was now. A Japanese windflower. Tall, fair, elegant. Liable to snap at any minute, he thought, looking at the dark circles under her eyes.

'You still haven't told me why you're back?' asked Kitty to Merritt.

Merritt turned the glass in his hand. 'I just thought I should check up on the house. And you, of course.'

44

'Well, I'm glad you're back,' Kitty said happily. 'How long will you stay?'

'Not sure yet,' he said vaguely, 'I want to get an idea of how things are here, and if the house can be saved or if we should sell.'

'What do you mean "saved"?' asked Kitty.

'Well, it's in pretty bad shape,' he said, looking around the old kitchen.

'I know,' said Kitty sadly.

The kitchen door opened slightly and the three turned to look. A small face peered through the crack at them. 'What are you doing out of bed?' asked Willow.

Poppy walked through the door shyly and looked at Merritt. 'Who's him?' she asked.

'Who's that?' corrected Willow.

'Who's that?' asked Poppy again, more confidently.

'Hello, I'm Merritt. I'm Kitty's big brother.'

'I'm Poppy,' she said, and stood next to Kitty.

'Poppy – the flower of magic, beauty and imagination,' said Merritt.

'Your name is silly,' said Poppy, and put her thumb in her mouth.

'Poppy!' exclaimed Willow. 'That's rude.'

'No, she speaks the truth,' laughed Merritt. 'It's terrible, I agree, Poppy. It's a family name. Has Kitty told you her full name yet?'

Willow and Poppy turned expectantly to Kitty. She looked down at the table.

'Tell us,' said Willow, not quite believing Kitty had worked for her for three years and she had never known her nanny's full name.

'Katinka Iris Clementina Ceres Middlemist,' she sighed. It was such an awful lot of letters to spell out. It always took her ages to fill in forms, and she had begun to hate it over the years.

Willow looked at her, eyes wide. 'That's quite a name,' she said.

'I know, I hate it.'

'So where's Kitty from?' asked Willow, as Poppy crawled onto her lap.

'My mother called me Kitty-Kat as a baby and the Kitty stuck. I much prefer it.'

'They are all beautiful names though. Katinka Iris Clementina Ceres Middlemist,' she repeated to herself. 'How did your parents come to choose those names?'

'Katinka is a family name – some mad aunt I think. Iris is my mother's name. Clementina is after my great-great-grandmother and Ceres is the goddess of agriculture and the harvest. Merritt's full name is Merritt Edward Oswald Middlemist. It sounds like a name for a duck,' said Kitty.

'Thanks so much. I shall walk about quacking now.' He looked at Poppy and gave an almighty quack.

Poppy laughed hysterically and Willow smiled. 'You have children, Merritt?'

'No.'

'You're so good with them,' said Willow, watching the adoration in Poppy's eyes for her new friend. For a brief moment sadness swept over her and she wished Kerr had been able to have fun with the children, with her.

'Perhaps. Kitty's the one who children love,' he said, and Kitty smiled at him. 'What about your name, Willow?'

'Ah, I was named after Willa Cather.'

Kitty looked at her, puzzled.

'Willa Cather the author – you know, Prairie Trilogy and all that? Perhaps she's not known in the UK.'

Merritt nodded. 'I know of Willa Cather.'

'No middle names?' asked Kitty swiftly, moving the conversation along.

'Nope.'

'Lucky thing,' said Kitty, thinking of all the letters in her long name.

Willow looked down at a tired Poppy in her arms. 'Kitty, would you?'

'Sure.' Kitty stood up and took Poppy from Willow.

'So, just Poppy?' asked Merritt as Kitty left the room with the sleepy little girl in her arms.

'No. Two more. Lucian, who's five, and Jinty, who's eighteen months.'

'Wow, and no husband to help?' Merritt shook his head.

'No, but then who needs a husband when you have Kitty?' said Willow.

Merritt looked to see if she was joking and saw she was serious. 'Fair enough,' he said.

Kitty came back into the kitchen. 'She was asleep by the time I was at the top of the stairs.'

Willow stood up. 'I think I might be also. I might head off to bed. What room should I take, Kitty?'

'The one at the furthest end of the corridor on the left. There are clean sheets in the linen closet as you walk by. Bathroom opposite,' said Kitty.

'Great. Nice to meet you, Merritt. Sorry about the misunderstanding on the stairs,' said Willow.

'Lovely to meet you too, and I apologise for the language,' said Merritt, laughing.

Willow smiled at him. For a moment their eyes met and she felt like she was about to say something, but then it was gone from her mind. Merritt stood waiting for her to speak. She'd looked as though she was going to say something, but then she'd stayed silent. Strange woman, he thought as she walked from the kitchen.

After she had left, Merritt turned to Kitty. 'So what's the story?'

'Well I can't tell you everything – it's all a bit awful – but she needs to escape for a while and so I offered her the house until she works out what she's doing with the divorce and all. If I had known you were coming back . . .' Kitty trailed off.

'No, no, I should have called you. It's fine. I'm just going to do some assessing of the house and the gardens and try and work out a plan as to whether the house will ever be habitable, or whether we'll have to sell to the National Trust.'

'It looks shabbier than ever,' admitted Kitty. 'I hate to think what it looks like during the day.'

'Well, we'll see in the morning,' said Merritt, standing up and stretching. 'What's she like? Your Oscar-winning boss?'

'She's nice. A little bit crazy at times, but she's had a rough time over the years I've been with her. Did you really not know who she was?' asked Kitty, as she stood opposite her brother.

'Of course I knew who she was – I haven't been in a coma – but I wasn't going to let her know that. She has that look of haughty expectation. Way too high maintenance. I wanted her to keep it real.' He laughed.

Upstairs, Willow lay on the flannel sheets she had found in the hall cupboard. They smelt of mildew and violets. Merritt's face crossed her mind. It felt nice that he didn't know who she was. Anyway, she had no idea who she was any more, so why should anyone else claim to know her? Rolling over, she faced the large window with only one curtain drawn. She could see the crescent moon outside.

Now was the time to find out who she was, and there was no better place to do it than here, she thought. She drifted off to sleep, dreaming of staircases and tunnels and violets.

CHAPTER FIVE

The next morning when Willow was still asleep and Kitty was up with the children, Merritt came stomping into the kitchen, his boots caked with mud.

'Fuck a duck, it's a shithole out there!' he exclaimed, and he heard a child laugh.

Looking up he saw three faces staring at him. 'Whoops . . . sorry about the language.'

Kitty frowned at him. 'Be careful what you say. Poppy repeats everything.'

'And what about you? Do you know that swearing is the sign of a low vocabulary?' he said to Lucian as he poured himself a mug of tea from the brown pot on the table.

'Lucian doesn't talk. If you want to tell him anything you have to go through me,' said Poppy with her little arms crossed. This morning she was wearing her pyjamas with a dressing gown that he was sure had once belonged to his father; navy silk with stains and moth holes.

'OK, roger that,' said Merritt, and he raised his eyebrows at Kitty. She met his gaze and shook her head imperceptibly. 'Well, you'd better introduce me then.'

Poppy turned importantly to Lucian. 'This is Merritt Edward Oswald. He's Kitty's brother.'

Kitty laughed. 'She has a mind like a steel trap,' she said to Merritt.

'And who's this seedling?' he asked, looking at Jinty, who was shoving toast into her mouth.

'This is Jinty. She can't talk either. I'm the only one who can talk.'

'Well done you,' said Merritt. 'So, what's on this morning?' he asked.

'Not sure yet,' said Kitty. 'Mummy's still asleep isn't she?'

'Mummy sleeps in every morning,' said Poppy.

'Lucky her,' said Merritt. 'I've been up since five o'clock.'

'Why?' asked Poppy as she peeled the cheese off her toast and ate it first.

'Best time, the morning. Quiet. No one to disturb you.'

'Why?'

'Because no one is up yet.'

'Why?'

'Because they are all asleep.'

'Why?'

Kitty looked at Merritt. 'This is her new thing. Enjoy.'

Merritt laughed.

'Well, I'm heading off on a tour of the other gardens. Anyone want to come?' he asked.

'Me!' cried Poppy.

'What about Lucian?' he asked the small boy, who stared straight ahead.

'He wants to come too,' said Poppy with authority.

'Do they have some sort of secret language, like twins?' he said quietly in Kitty's ear.

She shrugged. The truth was she had no idea about Lucian and Poppy's bond, and even less idea about Lucian's reluctance to speak. His fascination with his blocks and Thomas the Tank Engine hadn't waned since she had started working for Willow, and she figured if he was happy then she shouldn't interfere.

'Well go and get dressed,' he said to Poppy and Lucian. 'Quickly. I'll meet you out the front.'

'I'll leave you here with Jinty for a moment, OK?' Kitty said as she hustled the two children upstairs.

Jinty and Merritt eyed each other, and Jinty promptly burst into tears. 'Oh dear. What a roar,' he said, undoing the straps on her highchair. He picked her up and she stopped crying, looked at him and smiled.

'Hello Jinty,' he said seriously.

She blew a raspberry at him and covered him in bits of soggy toast. He laughed and looked up to see Willow watching him.

'Morning,' he said, and held Jinty out towards her mother.

'Hi,' she said, and took Jinty in her arms. Jinty started to cry again and reached out for Merritt.

'It seems she likes you,' said Willow tiredly.

Merritt was surprised. He had little experience with children and Jinty and Poppy's enthusiasm for him was unusual, and flattering. Taking Jinty back into his arms she settled with her blonde head against his shoulder and Willow smiled.

'You have a fan.'

Merritt snorted but was secretly pleased. Jinty was warm and soft and her little wisps of breath on his neck tickled him.

'I'm about to take your other two for a tour. I hope that's OK,' he said.

'Fine,' said Willow. She didn't mind as long as she could have a coffee and time to make her phone calls.

Willow started opening random cupboards and Merritt watched her. She was dressed in leggings and a t-shirt with a long cardigan over the top. Her legs were so thin he thought they might snap.

'Have you lost something?' he asked.

'The coffee pot,' she said. 'I was sure Kitty had packed it.'

Kitty walked back into the kitchen with the children dressed for outside, although Poppy had added her purple feather boa. 'Kitty, where's the coffee pot?' snapped Willow.

Kitty thought of the coffee pot and remembered she had left it sitting on the bench back in London. 'Oh no, I knew I forgot something!' she cried.

'Christ Kitty, do I have to remember everything?' Willow glared at her and thumped out of the kitchen.

'She's lovely in the morning,' said Merritt under his breath.

Kitty looked crestfallen and took Jinty from his arms. 'Don't let them near the lake,' she said.

'Sure,' said Merritt and he took one of the children's hands in each of his. 'Alright explorers. Let's go!' he said and Kitty watched as they headed down the gravel driveway together.

As she took Jinty upstairs for her sleep she heard Willow on the phone in the drawing room.

'Of course I will. Thanks Simon. No, I haven't heard,' Kitty overheard as she walked past the room towards the stairs. 'He's a shit, I know.'

Simon was Willow's agent. Kitty had only seen him in the flesh once in three years, at a party Willow hosted at her home, which had gone well until Lucian had come downstairs and set up his Thomas the Tank Engine train set in amidst the feet of the guests.

Lucian had been so engrossed in his trains that he had refused to move, and Kitty had been called to try and shift him back upstairs. She had sat next to him in the centre of the room and talked quietly to him for over fifteen minutes until Lucian finally let her pack up the tracks and the trains and take him back to his room. Willow had laughed nervously to Simon, who she was chatting to, and Kerr had shaken his head and gone outside onto the balcony for a joint. Most of the guests had tried to ignore the scene, except for a young man who had observed from across the room. He had watched Kitty's face as she talked to the child, whose face was absent of expression, and saw how gently she spoke to him. He noticed her wet hair and long fingers and how they touched his little face to turn it towards her, and how the child's eyes never met her wide brown ones. He saw how the room full of London's glitterati didn't faze her, and how her intention was solely to help the small, lost boy.

Kitty had had no idea she was being watched. The party was just after she had started with Willow and Kerr and all she wanted was for Lucian not to make a scene. She had been in the bath when Willow had banged on the door telling her to come and get him.

She had put Lucian back to bed and made sure he was asleep. Then she snuck down the back stairs to the kitchen to see if there were any of those *crèmes brûlées* in tiny teacups left that she had seen the waiters handing around.

As she walked into the kitchen there were a few waiters and a guest. Kitty ignored them and walked over to the bench, which was filled with leftover delights from the party.

'Hello,' said the guest.

Kitty looked up and saw a handsome man, maybe a few years older than her. He was wearing a dinner suit with the tie casually undone and hanging around his neck.

'Hi,' said Kitty shyly.

'You did very well with your little friend in there,' he said, sipping from a highball glass.

'Thanks,' said Kitty and wondered if he would think her greedy if she got a tray and piled it high with tasty morsels to take back to her bedroom.

'You the nanny then?' he asked, eyeing her over and noticing her tiny waist and large breasts in her tracksuit bottoms and long-sleeved thermal top. Kitty wished she had put on a bra when she had jumped out of the bath.

'Yes,' said Kitty, trying to cover her breasts with her arms.

'I had a nanny when I was small. Never looked like you though.' He raised one dark eyebrow at her.

Kitty didn't know what to say, so she stood silently.

'You're a bit of a kiddie whisperer then?' he asked.

'That sounds terrible when you say it like that,' she said, startled.

'No, no, no tawdry intention; just commenting on your brilliance with the kiddies,' he laughed.

'Are you a friend of Willow and Kerr's?' she asked, wanting the conversation with the handsome man to continue.

'Me? No. I don't think they have any friends here. I don't think they have any friends at all actually. No, I'm sleeping with one of the guests, who's here with her husband,' he said.

'Oh,' said Kitty, shocked and disappointed. Of course a

man like this would be with the fabulous people; she had forgotten her place.

'Are you shocked?' he asked her, liking the flash of disappointment that had fleetingly crossed her face.

'Yes,' she answered honestly. 'It's not very nice for the husband.'

'I suppose not,' said the man, clearly not caring.

Kitty stood waiting for him to say something else, but the room was silent except for the sound of glasses and plates being packed up by the catering staff.

'Well I'm off to bed,' she said finally.

'Alone?'

'Yes!' she said, shocked again.

'Shame. What's your name then?'

'Kitty,' she said shyly.

'Goodnight little pussy,' he said sexily, and Kitty felt herself go weak at the knees.

'Night then.' Kitty left the kitchen without anything that she had come for.

Boys had always pursued Kitty, but this one was different, she had thought. The last boy she had slept with she had met at a pub nearby when she was exploring the nightlife in her new city. He was a funny New Zealander who had plied her with vodka and taken her back to his hostel. They'd had quick fumbling sex and she'd passed out on his bunk bed, to awake to him packing his rucksack and telling her he was off to Prague that day and to look after herself.

Kitty had done the walk of shame home to Willow's, where she had snuck upstairs before the rest of the house had awoken.

After her recent bad experience she was trying to stay away from the opposite sex. She always seemed to choose the wrong ones. She had lost her virginity to Merritt's friend Johnny Wimple-Jones, which she would never be telling Merritt about. It had been a mistake, she realised in hindsight, but Johnny had been so nice when he had turned up at Middlemist claiming he needed to speak to Merritt urgently. Merritt had already left the country and her father was in London for the night. Brandy and flattery had got Kitty into bed, and Johnny had taken her in a haze of drunkenness and a small amount of pain. Truthfully, she was happy to get rid of her virginity. It sat in the corner of her adolescence, in turn berating her and scaring her until she finally laid the ghost to rest – or Johnny did, so to speak.

After Merritt told her about Eliza cheating on him with Johnny, Kitty was shattered and had vowed to keep her tryst with Johnny secret forever.

The young man at Willow's party unnerved her. His grace and casual elegance was something she had never seen in a man. Her own father and Merritt were men of the land, all dirty fingernails and work boots. There was a feline quality about this man in his dinner suit, and his upper-crust, lazy accent reminded her of Alan Rickman and Jude Law rolled into one.

She had never seen him since, but she thought about him sometimes, never daring to ask Willow who he was. Instead, when she was lonely in her bed, she would make up her own fantasies about him. It was easier than actually having to have a real conversation with a man; small talk and secrets. Kitty preferred the world in her head to the world outside. She knew why Lucian kept to himself.

Kitty left Jinty sleeping and found Willow waiting for her in the hallway.

'I have to go back to London. You going to be alright here for a few days with the children?' Willow didn't give Kitty time to answer; she started walking towards her bedroom expecting Kitty to follow, which she dutifully did.

'I'm seeing a new PR girl. Some young gun apparently; Simon recommended her. If I need money quickly then I have to get back to work. Simon believes – and I agree with him – that my re-entry into the public eye needs to be managed carefully.'

Kitty nodded. It all seemed so hard, this celebrity life of Willow's. Nothing was ever done honestly, she thought, her mind on the hair and makeup artists who would spend hours on Willow to get her looking like she was naturally fabulous. If they could see her now, thought Kitty as she looked at Willow in her leggings and odd socks.

'I'm pleased this woman will take me on as a client actually. She set up the deal for Gwyneth to work for Estée Lauder. And Simon has a film he's putting me up for that Kate Winslet's just dropped out of because of her divorce, so that's good.'

Kitty was silent, although she wasn't sure Kate Winslet thought her divorce was good. She wondered if Willow had any empathy for the woman, who was only in the same situation she was in herself.

'I'm going to shower and head off now. I'll be staying at the Dorchester until I get things sorted.'

Kitty wondered how she was going to pay for the Dorchester if she was running low on cash. Willow, as if reading her mind, spoke up. 'Simon set it up. I'm going to be photographed coming and going – they'll give me a suite for as long as I need.'

'That's nice of them,' said Kitty.

'Nice? No it's business, Kitty,' said Willow. 'So call me, OK?'

'Are you going to wait for the children to return?' asked Kitty.

'No, no time. You can say my goodbyes. They'll be fine,' she said, taking her large Louis Vuitton toiletry bag and walking towards the bathroom, with Kitty following her out down the corridor. As she was about to go through the bathroom door she stopped and turned. 'Kitty?'

Kitty turned and looked at her employer.

'Thanks.' Willow looked uncomfortable as she spoke the word.

'It's OK,' said Kitty, and she smiled at Willow. For a brief moment the women looked at each other as equals. Then Willow shut the bathroom door on her, and Kitty was outside again.

CHAPTER SIX

Eliza slammed down the phone and screamed from her white wood and glass desk. 'Lucy! Lucy!'

A harassed girl with thick ankles and premature worry lines ran into Eliza's office. 'Yes Mrs Wimple-Jones?' Lucy felt ridiculous calling her boss by her surname. The last place she had worked at, she had known all three of the directors by their first names.

When Eliza had personally headhunted her and wooed her Lucy had felt flattered. Eliza made all the noises of a woman who wanted to share her vision with Lucy, dangling the possibility of a partnership with her in the new PR firm she was setting up, and speaking at length about her belief in a well-run business that didn't require the crazy hours Lucy was putting in as an account manager at her current firm. Lucy had taken the job with Eliza even though her old bosses had pleaded with her to stay and offered her a higher salary. Times were tight; they'd already let go of all the juniors and Lucy was scared that she might end up as one of the unemployed if she stayed there, however much they liked her. She had been heady on Eliza's dream.

It didn't take long for the dream to turn into a nightmare. Every night, Lucy dreamed of walking into the office and stabbing Eliza with her silver Asprey letter-opener. Instead she sucked up Eliza's demands and her constant bitching and dreamed of a day when she would open her own place.

Lucy imagined a PR company where people rang and had their queries answered. Where they were billed for actual work, not for Eliza's dry cleaning and lunch bills, which padded out clients' invoices as 'project disbursements'. Eliza had forced Lucy to include the costs of her most recent art installation on a client's bill, much to Lucy's horror.

Eliza had come from the most successful modern art gallery in London, and through her network she had turned herself into a PR maven. Her clients in the art industry and her marriage to Johnny Wimple-Jones meant she had in her BlackBerry some of London's best-known people, whom Eliza always referred to as friends. She always said to anyone who would listen that her agency wasn't a job, it was just catching up with friends every night of the week.

Lucy groaned internally whenever she heard this catch-phrase. True, it wasn't work for Eliza; it was left up to Lucy to ensure the guests had drinks and the photo shoot was set up and the reputation of the latest art *enfant terrible* was saved.

Eliza had the network, but Lucy had the smarts. She was sure that one day karma would assert itself and she would be at the top of the PR game.

The truth was that most of Eliza's clients only stayed at EWJ Agency because of Lucy. Her calmness and sensible advice had saved the day on many an occasion. Whether she was talking down a waiter high on coke and threatening to set fire to the hostess's hairpiece with the chef's blowtorch, or consoling a WAG whose husband's philandering had just been made public, Lucy was in control.

Eliza was looking at Lucy shrewdly. 'You've lost me the Piper Esprit Champagne account.'

Lucy looked at her boss confused. 'I don't think we ever had that account,' she said.

'Well we could have, but now I've just found out that they are launching with Karin Burchill.' Eliza spat out the name of her biggest competition, as though it left a bitter taste in her mouth just to speak it.

'I didn't know they were looking,' said Lucy.

'You should have known. That's your job,' snapped Eliza.

Lucy felt a myriad of things rise to the surface that threatened to fall out of her mouth, so she closed it firmly, thinking of her small flat in Islington that she was paying off.

'I'm sorry,' she said instead.

'You should be,' snapped Eliza.

Lucy looked down at the diary in her hands.

'You have two appointments back to back. Willow Carruthers first. She'll be here in ten minutes,' placated Lucy.

If there was one thing Eliza loved more than herself, it was celebrity. Eliza raised her eyebrows as if in disdain, but she was wondering if what she was wearing was impressive enough for the most stylish woman in the world. When she had got ready that morning, Eliza hadn't known Willow would be coming; if she had she would have pulled out all the stops. Instead she looked down at her black silk Burberry dress, worn with the double strand of Wimple-Jones family pearls and her towering black patent leather Jimmy Choos, and figured it would have to do.

Eliza had decided that she would only dress in black and white once she started the agency. 'Like the news,' she told people when they asked. Lucy was always tempted to remind her that more and more people were reading their news online and that perhaps she should wear a Google logo dress, but she knew to keep her mouth shut.

Lucy left Eliza's office and went back to her small desk, where she also acted as a receptionist and did whatever else Eliza decided to throw her way.

Sitting down, she opened JobSearch on her computer, typed in 'PR' and started to trawl through the results. She was either overqualified or underqualified for everything. No middle-entry positions, she thought. So fucking depressing.

The bell sounding Willow's arrival startled Lucy from her gloom. She pressed the buzzer to let Willow into the upstairs office.

Eliza had made the EWJ offices look like a small gallery. Modern art covered the walls, changing constantly as Eliza rotated her sizeable collection between her three houses in London, the country estate and the house in Ibiza.

Today Willow was greeted by a giant installation of latex fried eggs hanging at different heights up the stairs. She pushed open the heavy glass doors. Lucy walked forward to greet her, but Eliza had pushed past and stretched out her long thin hand towards Willow before Lucy had had time to even open her mouth.

'Hello, I'm Eliza Wimple-Jones,' she said, with her most welcoming smile plastered on her face. 'Please come in and we'll have a chat, OK?' She guided Willow to the small boardroom and tossed a look at Lucy over her shoulder. 'Coffee and mineral water please, Lucy.'

Willow smiled at Lucy almost apologetically and Lucy smiled back. Lucy was used to Eliza's rudeness and dismissive tone. She knew that eventually Eliza would tire of her new client and then all the work would fall to her. She took a tray into the boardroom, notebook and pencil under her arm, and placed it down quietly on the glass table. A giant sculpture of a woman in pieces was strung above their heads. While it was ugly, it was better than the baby *in utero* talking on a mobile phone that had hung there a few months ago.

Willow sat nervously as Eliza talked about her boutique agency. 'I don't publicise. My job is to ensure you are in the media for the right reasons, and seen with the right brands and the right people. Your comeback, if you want to call it that, needs to be carefully orchestrated; by not only me but also your agent and manager, both here in London and back in LA.'

Willow nodded.

Eliza went on, liking the sound of her own voice. She was great at the pitch and she knew it; this was where she did well. She just wasn't so great at doing the work.

'This could take several months actually, so we need to be careful about how quickly we push you out into the marketplace. Slowly, slowly is the key.'

Willow thought about her dwindling current account and felt sick. 'Actually I was hoping to move faster than that.'

Eliza nodded, 'I understand. Want to show the world you're fierce and fabulous, huh?' She smiled conspiratorially. 'I get it, I did the same after my first marriage went down the gurgler. OK, well then to launch you sooner – that's a different plan altogether.'

Willow smiled her most winning celebrity smile. 'Great. So what's the plan?'

Eliza preened under the gaze of Willow and looked at Lucy. 'This is Lucy Faulkner; she's my assistant and planner.

She has fabulous ideas, and she's already run a few past me this morning after Simon called telling us of your interest in our agency.'

Willow looked at the pale girl, who seemed about twenty-five years old. She was wearing a brown cashmere sweater that made her bust look like a single bolster pillow and a horrible black skirt that sat at an unflattering length on her thick legs.

Lucy panicked. She hadn't run any ideas past Eliza at all. This was typical Eliza form: all icing, no cake. Lucy took a breath and looked at Willow. She was going to have to wing it and hope it was enough for her to sign them on.

'I think that if you want to relaunch yourself quickly the best way is to get you a cosmetics contract. It's a great way for people to see you in a different light and for the industry to see you're ready to work again. You don't have any projects lined up yet?' asked Lucy briskly.

Willow sat back. She had underestimated the smart tweedy-looking girl. 'No. I have a meeting this afternoon for a film though,' she said.

'OK, so I suggest we start shopping for a contract. Anyone would be happy to have you, either in fashion or in cosmetics as I said. Then I think we do a big interview: a tell-all with a magazine of substance. *Vogue*, *Vanity Fair*, nothing less than that, otherwise it cheapens the whole thing. I suggest you make no comment in public about your husband or your children either. Take the high road.'

The buzzer went in the office and Eliza looked at Lucy, expecting her to stop mid pitch and answer the door. Willow looked at Eliza, and then back at Lucy. 'Perhaps you can get it. I'm interested in what Lucy is saying,' she said almost imperiously. Eliza smiled graciously but was fuming inside. How dare that washed-up bitch tell me to answer my own door, she thought.

As the door to the boardroom shut Lucy looked directly at Willow. There was a fragility about her that she found interesting, as though there existed something more behind the brittle veneer she used to mask her feelings.

'Listen, can I be straight with you?' she asked suddenly and not even believing she was saying it.

'I guess,' said Willow warily.

'There are rumours that you and Kerr are in the shit financially, big time. I don't know if that's true – and unless you're my client it's none of my business – but if it is true then Eliza's not the agent you want. She's indiscreet and a social climber. Your sorrows are her gains and she will use it against you. I suggest you look for another agency if it's true. It's not me, I could solve this for you – but don't trust Eliza.'

Willow looked at the sensible, plain girl with the golden advice and nodded.

Eliza came back into the room. 'Sorry, bloody couriers,' she said and sat down again. 'Now where were we?'

Willow stood up. 'I'm sorry to waste your time. I'm afraid this isn't really the agency for me; perhaps it's a little premature,' she said, smiling at Eliza.

Eliza glared at Lucy. What had she said to her? The stupid dumb clodhopper of a girl was useless. 'Are you sure? I think we could work well together,' pleaded Eliza.

'No, I'm afraid not; but thank you for your time, I really appreciate it,' said Willow. She backed out of the room, ignoring Lucy, ran down the stairs under the giant hanging eggs, and didn't stop to take her first breath until she was on the street outside. A few people passed her, doing double takes at the glamorous star looking as though she had seen a ghost. Willow pulled herself together and thought about her options. If word got out about her financial woes then she would never be taken seriously. No one could know about this, she thought; she needed to act as though she hadn't a care in the world except for her beloved children. The last thing she wanted was to do cheap media for money; she might as well light some hoops in Trafalgar Square and jump through them for small change.

Eliza was horrible, she thought: so instantly see-through and a definite social climber. Willow shuddered. She would never associate with someone like Eliza; why on earth had Simon recommended her? Lucy, on the other hand . . . Well, she had definitely underestimated the girl, who reminded her of Mrs Tiggy-Winkle from the story that Poppy liked so much. Round, comforting, sensible. That's what I need more of in my life: sense. And dollars, she thought as she pulled out her phone.

After Willow left EWJ, Eliza screamed at Lucy for ten minutes, demanding she tell her what she had said when she left the room, but Lucy played dumb. The truth was she had found out about Willow and Kerr's finances from her friend who worked in PR at Kerr's record label. As soon as Lucy overheard Eliza taking the call about Willow, she had rung around her mates in PR to get the lowdown.

Eliza's tirade only stopped when the phone rang and she stomped off to her office, slamming the door. Lucy picked up the phone. 'EWJ Agency, Lucy speaking,' she said efficiently, although she felt like crying after Eliza's onslaught.

'Hi Lucy, it's Willow again.'

'Hello,' said Lucy, surprised.

'I just wanted to thank you for your honesty and advice. Suffice it to say there are a few things happening in my world at the moment which are less than appealing,' said Willow wryly.

'I figured,' said Lucy.

'Listen, this may seem odd, but is there any chance you would consider working for me as my private PR person? I don't have any money yet but I think I can get back in front, and I really need people I can trust at the moment,' said Willow down the phone.

Lucy was silent, thinking.

Willow continued, 'I know it's a big risk for you but you were amazing in that room, and I honestly think you could help me. And I could help you, I hope.'

'I would need to think about it,' she said quietly, looking down at her desk.

'No private calls!' hissed Eliza and Lucy looked up to see Eliza's reptilian face peering at her.

At that moment Lucy realised she had had enough of Eliza and her bullshit and she smiled down the phone. 'Actually that sounds lovely. I'll text you from my mobile and we can meet in a minute,' she said.

Eliza looked at her as she hung up the phone. 'You've had lunch; you don't get time off to meet people. I need you here,' she barked.

'Actually Eliza, I'm leaving.'

Lucy stood up and took her handbag from the filing cabinet.

'When will you be back?' asked Eliza, unnerved by Lucy's calmness.

'On the first of never, Eliza. I can't work for you any longer and I was too well raised to tell you what I think of you, so please consider my notice immediate and final,' she said, and with that she walked out of the door.

Eliza started to follow her down the stairs, screaming her name. 'Lucy, Lucy! Come back here!' she called, and then the phone rang and Eliza turned on the stairs to go and answer it and lost her balance and reached out to grab something. The only thing her desperate arms could find was one of the hanging fried eggs. She yanked it and fell down the stairs to land on her bony bottom, a giant latex egg on top of her.

And that was Lucy's last vision of her ex-boss: at the bottom on her bottom with egg on her face. Perhaps karma did exist after all, she thought.

CHAPTER SEVEN

Merritt was back from his tour of the grounds with Lucian and Poppy. Kitty watched them as they rounded the side of the house and thought for a moment what a shame it was he'd never had any children, but she pushed the thought from her mind. That would mean Eliza would be their mother, and that was a fate she would not wish on anyone.

'We're back!' called Merritt from the foyer, and Poppy echoed him. 'We're back!' her little voice rang out.

'How was that?' asked Kitty as she took their muddy boots off.

'Awesome,' said Poppy, using her favourite word of the week.

'Depressing,' mumbled Merritt. He followed the little party into the kitchen where Kitty had set up a morning tea of pikelets and milk and a pot of strong tea for Merritt.

'Really?' asked Kitty as she sorted out the children.

'Oh Kits. It's in such bad shape. I don't even know if it's worth saving. Perhaps we should just let the National Trust have it,' he said, slumping in his chair.

Kitty sat opposite him not knowing what to say.

'The gardens are overgrown – hideously overgrown in fact. The fences are falling down, some of the trees are in bad shape, will need to be looked at as soon as possible. And that's just outside,' he said sadly.

Kitty frowned. This was not her area of expertise. In fact, she thought, she didn't even have an area of expertise.

'I am going to write a big list this week of everything, inside and out. I could use a hand when you have a moment,' he said.

Kitty thought about the children and all she had to do for them and was about to speak up when she saw Merritt's forlorn face and decided against it. 'Of course,' she said, although she wondered what help she could be.

'We have the money Dad left us but that's about it,' he said, thinking aloud.

'We could turn it into a hotel?' suggested Kitty, having seen it done on TV before.

'What the hell do we know about that, Kit? It would be worse than Fawlty Towers I think,' he said.

Kitty laughed. 'Yes well, I suppose you're right.'

'I wish there was buried treasure somewhere. Dad always said that his great-great-great-grandmother had said there was something of worth in the house, but I have no idea what he meant. He spent his life searching for it, but who knows what she was talking about?' he said.

Poppy looked at Merritt, her eyes wide. 'Treasure? I'll find it!' she said.

Kitty smiled at her indulgently. 'Well if you do then you can have some of it,' she said to the small girl, whose cheeks were flushed from the country air.

Merritt stuffed two pikelets into his mouth at once. 'I wonder what the hell she meant,' he pondered.

'I have no idea. There aren't even any paintings left of

George's,' said Kitty as she refilled her chipped mug, referring to their ancestor who had built the house. His paintings, once worthless, were now well regarded by the art community. Their father had watched with painful fascination every time a new painting went up for sale at one of the major auction houses.

'Should be our money,' he used to say to the children when he saw the rising prices of George Middlemist's works in the marketplace.

Family legend was that once George and his wife Clementina had separated, she sold all his works to keep herself and her children in the lifestyle they were accustomed to. Divorce was not an option in Victorian England, Edward's father had told Merritt and Kitty, and once George had had the affair with his life model Clementina threw him out of Middlemist, where she stayed until she died of old age.

Clementina had been an artist too, but not of the same calibre as George, and the only paintings left in the house were hers. They weren't likely to get the same price as George's art and so the family had them stacked away in the eaves, in what was once George's studio.

Merritt stood up and bowed to Kitty and Lucian. 'Well, Lady Poppy and Lord Lucian, it was my pleasure to escort you today. Please feel free to see me at any time and let me know if I can be of assistance. No matter is too small or too big; I am at your service.'

Poppy giggled and Lucian looked straight ahead. Merritt walked over to the phone on the bench and took the pen and pad that lay next to it.

'I'm off to see what work lies ahead of me,' he said, and

he walked out the door. Lucian got out of his seat and watched as Merritt walked away.

'He'll come back,' said Kitty to Lucian, who was peering through the dirty glass. He turned to Kitty and then looked back out of the window again. That's odd, she thought, he never notices anyone.

Kitty forgot about Lucian quickly as Jinty's wails came crackling through the kitchen on the baby monitor. 'Your sister's awake. How about I get her up and we see what she's up to?' said Kitty cheerfully, and she took the two other children upstairs to see their sister.

Merritt walked around the Lady's Garden, as it was known, taking notes and thinking about Willow's children. He hadn't spent much time with children at all, but Lucian reminded him of a client's child he had seen in Florida. He was the eight-year-old son of a wealthy polo player from South America. They were a lovely family, he remembered, enthusiastic about Merritt's ideas, and they included their child in everything. Merritt had stayed nearby the house for six weeks to ensure the proper placement of their large collection of rare trees, and he had spoken at length with the wife about her son. He tried to remember what she had said her child's condition was. She had asked Merritt to design a sensory garden for him and he had had much delight in working with the boy, getting him to choose plants and flowers that would stimulate him.

A few times a week a special teacher would come and work with him and mostly they worked outside on the green lawn, playing games and rolling on sports equipment, even crawling together. Merritt had watched with interest and he even saw small improvements by the time he left. Merritt reminded himself to email the woman to ask for more information so he could give it to Kitty for Willow.

Inside the house Kitty was fighting with Poppy, who was insisting on using her crayons on the wooden oak panels in the hallway. 'No,' said Kitty. 'These are not for drawing on.'

'Well I want to draw. I want my art things and you didn't bring them,' moaned Poppy accusingly.

'Well I'm sure we have some paper somewhere,' said Kitty, licking her thumb and trying to get the green crayon off the wall.

'I want real art things,' said Poppy, making a face that Kitty knew from experience would turn into a giant wail.

Kitty thought of the eaves, where all of Clementina's paintings were housed. Perhaps there were things up there. She remembered her mother and her father had dabbled in art, and they had also encouraged Merritt and Kitty to paint, hoping that their ancestor's genes would come through – but to no avail. Eventually it had all been packed away. Kitty wondered if it was all still stored up there in the eaves.

'Alright, come on then,' she said impatiently, and picking up Jinty and gently pushing Lucian ahead of her she led the way for Poppy to follow her up to the eaves. The stairs got smaller as they climbed and it became darker, the air mustier. Jinty started to cry and squirm in Kitty's arms. 'Hang on, nearly there,' she said, and they came to a small wooden door. Kitty hadn't been up here in years, and she pushed open the door wondering what she would find.

The room was dank and smelt of stale air and oil paints. Kitty held Jinty as she drew back one of the blinds and sunlight flooded the room. All of Clementina's paintings leant against the far wall and there were many easels and canvases with half-finished paintings. A red chaise longue in tattered velvet was the only piece of real furniture in the room apart from a small table with a tarnished bowl sitting on top of it. There were shelves of books and art supplies and a small sink in the corner of the room.

There were trunks stacked on top of each other and a few boxes marked 'Iris'. No doubt her mother's things that her father had hidden away after her death, thought Kitty sadly. She remembered how desolate her father had been. That's when he forgot me, she thought, trying to hold back the tears that pricked her eyes.

Kitty's father had been so enveloped in his own grief that he'd let Kitty do as she pleased. He had ignored her failing at school, her lack of confidence and her sadness. She had lost her mother, but that was not enough to pierce his veil of desolation, and so they had lived in the same house, sometimes not speaking for days. She felt like her mother had abandoned her first by dying, then Merritt had abandoned her when he and Eliza split up, and then her own father had abandoned her in her own house.

Kitty sat on the sagging chaise longue. The emotion threatened to overwhelm her and she wondered at the strange turn of events that had brought her here, back at Middlemist with Willow's children and Merritt, sitting in the eaves.

Poppy danced around the room. 'Look at all the things! Can I have them?' she asked, expecting the answer to be yes, as it usually was. 'No, but you may borrow them,' said Kitty firmly.

'OK,' said Poppy, turning up her little nose. 'This will be my playhouse,' she said decidedly, 'and you two cannot come in unless you ask,' she said to Jinty and Lucian. Lucian was standing by the window staring ahead over the grounds, watching Merritt in the garden. Jinty was sitting on Kitty's lap, playing with a long strand of torn velvet.

'Can I come up here whenever I want?' asked Poppy.

'You must ask me first, and I will have to do a scout around to see you can't get hurt on anything.'

'OK,' said Poppy happily.

Kitty placed Jinty on the floor and she promptly pulled herself up to a standing position to continue playing with the velvet strand. Kitty looked around; there was nothing major Poppy could hurt herself with. The windows were too large to lift, so she couldn't fall out the window. She pushed the easels against the walls so they wouldn't topple over and lifted one of the trunks down onto the floor to ensure that it too would not fall on Poppy. Looking through the shelves of art supplies, she found some watercolours and paper. She took out a brush and filled up a glass jar with water. 'Here you go,' she said to Poppy. She placed the paper on the table and put the bowl next to it. 'You use them like this,' and she painted a few strokes for Poppy to see what she was doing.

Poppy snatched the brush out of Kitty's hand. 'I'll do it,' she said, and Kitty looked at her. 'Don't snatch, Poppy. And say thank you.'

Poppy turned her head towards Lucian. 'Lucian needs to go to the toilet,' she said, and Kitty jumped up. 'You need to do a wee, Lucian?' she asked. She took him by the hand, lifted Jinty expertly with one arm, and started down the stairs. 'Stay there. Don't paint on anything but the paper and don't hurt yourself. I'll be back in a minute,' she called up.

Poppy smiled as they left. She had no idea if Lucian wanted to go to the toilet, but she always found this the best way to get rid of Kitty or her mother. Poppy looked around the room and sighed with delight. Although she didn't know the word for it, it felt good to be alone. To have a place where Jinty and Lucian couldn't come.

She walked over to the trunk that Kitty had moved and examined the strap that was holding it together. It was worn leather, fraying in parts. Poppy wasn't strong enough to pull it open, so she picked at the leather until it fell apart. Straining at the large lid, she struggled till it fell backwards with a thud. She waited for Kitty to yell out to her, but heard nothing from downstairs.

Peering into the trunk, she saw layers of yellow paper with fabric underneath. Pulling off the paper, Poppy lifted up a hat covered in roses, faded but still pretty. Poppy put it on her head. Digging deeper into the trunk, she found old fans, some broken but some still in good condition. Small shoes and coats. A large petticoat and huge cream dress with lots and lots of buttons and lace.

Poppy pulled everything out of the trunk into the middle of the floor and climbed into the empty space, wearing a pair of the tiny shoes. I could lie down in here, she thought, and she jumped on the box's floor until she heard a crack. Looking down she saw her foot had gone through the bottom of the trunk, but when she lifted her leg out carefully she couldn't see the floor below it. She squatted to the side of the hole and picked at the old, splintering wood, lifting up small pieces. Worried about a splinter, which she had had once before, she pulled on one of the kid gloves lying in the heap on the floor and noticed her hand nearly fitted it perfectly.

Once she had both gloves on, Poppy worked furiously until she had made a large hole in the base of the trunk. She slipped her hand in to see if there were any other items underneath. *Maybe this is the treasure that Merritt and Kitty talked about,* she thought excitedly.

Her gloved hand brushed against something and she gasped as she pulled it out. It was a bundle of letters bound by a pale blue ribbon. Poppy was disappointed; she couldn't even read yet. She threw them on the floor and continued searching the cavity in the trunk. Next she pulled out a few small leather-bound books. She threw them over with the letters – they were no good either. She put her arm back into the trunk's false base one last time and stretched her hand as far into the corner as she could. She drew out a small box. Opening it, she found a beautiful ring. It was a large square-cut emerald with small diamonds around it set in silver on a gold band. Next to it lay a gold wedding ring.

Poppy knew she had found the treasure. Not waiting a minute longer, she stood in the doorway and screamed for Kitty in her loudest, most piercing voice.

Kitty, who was still in the bathroom with Jinty and Lucian, heard the cry and panicked. Merritt, who heard from the garden, ran inside in alarm. He and Kitty met on the stairs. 'Where is she?' he cried.

'In the eaves,' she said breathlessly, trying to run up the stairs with Jinty on her hip and dragging Lucian along behind.

'The eaves? For fuck's sake Kitty, that's not safe!'

'I thought it was,' said Kitty crossly as she mounted the top step, and together they reached the door. Poppy greeted them in a Victorian bonnet, kid gloves and beaded dancing shoes.

'I've found the treasure,' she said proudly, and held out the box to Merritt and Kitty.

Merritt took the box and opened it. 'Fuck a duck, Kit. She's found Clementina's engagement ring.'

CHAPTER EIGHT

Willow was nervous. It had been too long since she had spoken to anyone about a film role, and now she had to meet with the director and have a 'chat'. After her Oscar she could have chosen anyone she wanted to work with, but that didn't last. Nothing lasts, she thought, thinking of Kerr.

Sitting in her suite at the Dorchester, she decided that if she landed this part then today would be a good day. She had bought clothes specially for the meeting, with Lucy's approval. Funny how such a dowdy girl could have such good ideas about fashion, she had thought as Lucy had assessed the choices laid out on the bed.

'Yes to the Yves Saint Laurent. No to the jeans and Chloé top,' said Lucy knowingly.

'But the top is so pretty,' said Willow, touching the delicate lace.

'I don't think Harold Gaumont has ever worn jeans in his life, nor have I ever seen any of his actors wear jeans in his films,' said Lucy, raising her eyebrows at Willow. 'The dress is perfect,' she said, holding up a finely pleated silk chiffon number with a print of autumnal flowers on it. 'Wear it with those shoes you have on now,' she said, pointing to her soft suede brown kitten heels, 'and pull your hair up in a messy bun.'

'Well, it would help if I knew what the film was about. Simon had no idea. He's very mysterious, this Harold,' said Willow.

'You have to assume that with Kate Winslet being cast before it will be a period piece of some sort. I can't see her in jeans,' laughed Lucy.

After meeting with that awful Eliza woman, the best thing Willow could have done was to ring back and convince Lucy to leave to work solely for her. They had spent the afternoon drinking tea in Willow's suite and exchanging stories.

Willow had admitted to Lucy that she was indeed broke and would need to get to work as soon as possible. Lucy hadn't been surprised; she knew so many of her clients' secrets that they filled her dreams at night.

'So you have no money, only assets?' Lucy had asked.

'Do shoes count as assets?' asked Willow, almost seriously.

Lucy's laugh had given Willow her answer. 'Don't worry too much. As long as you have a roof over your head you'll be OK. I'll have you earning in no time.'

'Jesus, you sound like a pimp.'

Taking the Yves Saint Laurent dress from Lucy, Willow's mind turned to the terrible story she had just been telling her about Eliza. It was meant to be funny but had ended up making Lucy sad she had put up with her for as long as she did. 'How did you stand working for her for so long?' Willow had asked.

'I didn't really have a choice. I have a flat with a mortgage and there isn't a lot of work out there for people in my industry. The first thing companies do is slash marketing and PR budgets when times are hard.'

Willow felt the weight of Lucy's mortgage as if it were her

own. 'Well, you better get me to work soon so I can help you pay for your flat,' she had said, half joking, half seriously.

'Oh don't worry, I will. I already have many, many ideas – but first we need to get you ready for your audition.'

'Oh it's not an audition, it's a "chat",' laughed Willow.

'It's an audition,' said Lucy firmly.

Lucy was astute, but she deliberately underplayed herself; it made the clients feel better about themselves, she thought. She took an academic approach to her work: learn, offer advice when asked, and dress to underwhelm. That way when brilliance came out of her mouth, people would always be surprised. The biggest perk of being dowdy was that people told you their secrets more readily when faced with lace-up shoes rather than stilettos.

'Now I'll head off home and get started on your re-entry into the world of bullshit. You ring me straight after, OK?' Lucy had said, as she gathered up her plain black bag and coat.

Willow laughed. There was something about Lucy that was so practical and sensible; she reminded her of someone. She thought about it. Yes – she reminded her of Kitty, only smarter. What was it about the two English girls that made them so likeable? Although Willow had been in England for years, she had yet to make close girlfriends with anyone. Most women were either jealous or in awe of Willow, and her home-schooling experience hadn't helped her socially. She didn't know how to make friends, but she decided as she gossiped with Lucy and talked about everything from fashion to interior design that this felt good. Sometimes she and Kitty talked, but Kitty seemed afraid of her and they didn't have anything in common besides the children.

Lucy was not as she seemed, Willow had learned. She knew everything about fashion, parties, and people, and how the machinations of reputation worked, yet she refused to be a personal part of it. 'I know my side of the room,' she had said to Willow. 'Besides, as my uncle used to say, you should never shit where you eat.'

Willow had laughed and laughed. 'Good point.'

'Right, now I know a bit about this director. He's a bit mad,' said Lucy.

'I had heard that. In what way, do you think?' asked Willow.

'Well, he's a visionary. Only makes a film every few years, when the creative urge strikes him. Always epic and huge. Total creative control freak,' Lucy had said.

'I must admit I've only seen one of his works; the one about the geisha. It looked amazing,' said Willow, remembering the lush art direction but not much about the story.

'Yes, I saw that too. No idea what the hell was going on, but I loved the costumes,' Lucy had agreed.

And now Willow sat waiting for the legendary director to come to her suite for their 'chat'.

She had offered to meet him but he was averse to the public in general, Simon had told her. Instead he was driven from place to place in a black Bentley with darkened windows. Reclusive, brilliant and married four times without any children, he was a fascinating and influential director whom the critics adored and the general public treated as an artist.

The doorbell to Willow's suite rang. She wiped her clammy hands on the cream sofa, flipped her hair and answered the door with a smile.

'Hello,' she said.

A small man of about sixty, maybe older, stood on the other side of the door, wearing a silk smoking jacket, velvet slippers and a large pair of dark sunglasses. 'Willow,' he said in a transatlantic accent. 'Harold Gaumont.' He gave the briefest flicker of a smile and Willow threw her most charming one back.

'Please come in.' She stepped back to let Harold through into the living room. 'I was about to order afternoon tea. Is that OK?' she asked.

'Can I ask you something before I make my decision about the tea?'

'Of course,' she said casually but racked with nerves.

Willow stood in the centre of the room waiting for the question, aware of his reputation for odd requests during auditions. She had once heard that he had put an actor through a secret audition: he had hired actors to push the man to breaking point while waiting in line at a railway station, all the while secretly filming him.

'Can you please speak in a British accent while I visit with you?' asked Harold.

'Any particular region?' asked Willow, more confidently than she felt. Please don't ask me to do a Welsh accent, she thought desperately.

'Think well bred, country house. Yes to the tea,' he said.

Willow thought for a moment and Kitty jumped into her head. Channel Kitty, she thought, and she walked over to the phone, dialled the number for room service and gave the order for tea in a perfect English accent.

Harold sat down, smiled, took off his glasses and laid them on the table between them. 'Excellent start, Willow. Now why do you want to be in my film?' he asked, and sat back in his chair, resting the tips of his fingers together and placing them in front of his face.

Willow looked at him closely. He was quite handsome without the glasses, sort of like David Niven crossed with Willy Wonka, she thought.

'Well, I would love to be in one of your films. Your work is legendary,' answered Willow honestly, in an accent that could have cut glass.

'Naturally,' he said, with no arrogance at all. 'But why do you want to be in my film *personally*? You haven't worked in what? Five or six years? You won an Oscar for a film that really wasn't worth an Oscar nomination. You must have been surprised when you won?' he said, not unkindly.

Willow paused for a moment.

'I was surprised to win,' Willow said, still speaking in a perfect accent. She looked down at the table and straightened his sunglasses. 'Honestly? I need the work. I need it more than you will ever understand. I want to work, I need to work, and I want to do something that I can actually be proud of, not like that silly film I won the Oscar for.' As she spoke her eyes filled with tears and she realised it was all true. She was unworthy of the Oscar and she did want to work. She had three children and a fuckwit of a husband. It was time to get real, even in a faux English accent.

Harold lowered his hands and rubbed them together. 'Good answer. Now where's my tea that you promised me?'

Just as he spoke the doorbell rang again and Willow let the waiter in with their afternoon tea. 'Thank you. I'll take it from here,' said Willow to the waiter, still in her accent.

The waiter recognised Willow. He tried not to roll his eyes. Those bloody Americans who spent a few years here and then ended up speaking like the Princess of Wales, he thought as he left her suite.

Willow set up the tea in front of her and Harold. 'Shall I be mother?' she asked as she turned the teapot.

'Yes please,' he said. Willow poured the tea and set the tiny sandwiches and cakes out in front of them both.

'Milk? Sugar?' she asked.

'Both please,' he answered, as he watched her carefully pour the tea into the fine china cups.

'Are you married, Willow?'

'I was,' she said. 'Now separated.'

'Ah; very modern thing, divorce. I've done it many times. You get used to it,' he said.

'I suppose I will. I have to,' she said.

'Yes, nothing to do but to get on with it, I've found.'

'I'm trying,' she said, and smiled as she handed him a small plate.

'You're from New York originally?' he asked.

'Yes,' she answered, unsure whether he wanted her to continue with her English accent.

'And how have you found England?' he asked.

'It's very much to my liking.' She decided to stay with the accent. 'I even like the weather.'

'Well then, you must have an English soul.' He laughed. 'Will you stay here in England, once you're divorced?'

Willow realised she hadn't thought about geography. Moving to Middlemist was the only plan she had made, and she knew she couldn't stay there forever.

'I don't know, to be honest with you. Perhaps. There's not

86

much in the US for me now. My parents work in New York but my children like it here; it's all they know.'

Willow was still speaking in her English accent, but she was speaking from the heart. Harold watched her closely.

'It must be hard to be the responsible one now. To have to make all the decisions.'

Willow felt her eyes filling with tears and looked down at her lap, trying to focus on the flowers on her dress as they became increasingly blurred. 'Yes,' she mumbled.

'And to have to plan ahead while their father gallivants across the world,' he said, pushing her, 'worrying about their futures and the gossip – what will happen to you, will you ever be happy again?' Harold spoke in low tones; it seemed like he was hypnotising her.

Willow saw a tear drop onto one of the flowers on her dress, and her throat felt as though it was closing over. She had refused to cry when Kerr had left her when she was pregnant with Jinty; when she had laboured with only Kitty at her side; when she had held her darling daughter for the first time. She hadn't shed a tear when she saw the photos of Kerr on the yacht with another woman's nipple in his mouth and that woman's sister with her hands down his shorts. She hadn't wept when she had learned about her precarious financial position, or when she had moved into Kitty's ramshackle family home; but now, in this suite, which she couldn't pay for and which she would be allowing herself to be photographed in front of for the next few days like a fame whore, she felt the tears come. Not now, she screamed inside as she felt them flow, not in the goddamn audition! Lucy was right: it was an audition. And she was failing miserably.

Harold sat still, watching her shaking shoulders, and she looked up at him, her carefully applied makeup running down her face. 'I'm sorry,' she said.

'Don't be sorry. It's still hard to be a woman, no matter what that Oprah woman says,' he said.

'It's so hard – and I've made so many mistakes,' she cried.

'Well that's what helps us learn. Mistakes are lovely actually. I've made so many, and from them I pushed myself to be better. You must do the same, my dear.' He picked up his cup and sipped elegantly from it.

'I want to,' she said sadly.

'You will. Now dry your eyes and I will tell you about the part, if you want it,' he said brusquely.

Willow looked at him surprised. 'Are you serious?'

'Deadly.'

Willow went to the bathroom and looked at herself in the mirror. Her eye makeup was everywhere and she had a red nose from crying. Her lipstick was coming off and she thought she looked a fright. Cleaning herself up, she walked back out to Harold.

'Was that an audition?' she asked as she stood by her chair.

'No, my dear. You had the part before I rang the doorbell. Anyone who stays at the Dorchester has my vote. I don't like those modern hotels with their glass edges and ugly sculptures. You showed class by being here.'

Willow pushed back a hysterical urge to laugh and sat down again.

Harold sat forward. 'The film is a period piece set in Victorian England about a woman who wants to speak to her dead husband. She is so overwhelmed with grief that she starts to dabble in black magic and starts an occult group at her home. She has an affair with a younger man who joins the group, whom she is convinced is her husband returned, and the audience thinks so also. But then we find out he is actually trying to marry her and send her mad so he can have her committed and take her wonderful home.'

Willow listened. 'It sounds amazing.'

'Yes, it will be,' said Harold, certain in his own genius. 'If I can find a house.'

'You don't have a location?' asked Willow, her heart sinking. Finding a location could take months, and she needed to start work as soon as possible.

'Well everything seems to be done up nowadays. They're all bloody B&Bs and awful hotels. There are very few original homes left that haven't had the National Trust attack them yet,' he said, turning his nose up in distaste.

Middlemist House popped into Willow's head, and before she knew what she was doing she spoke. 'I know a house I think would be perfect.'

'Really?' asked Harold, leaning forward. 'Tell me more.'

CHAPTER NINE

'That's nice,' said the brunette as she lay on a mattress on the floor. Her large breasts were being kneaded gently. She spread her legs for the third time in the last six hours. Ivo entered her and they started to move together in rhythm. Just as they were about to come together, there was a loud knocking at the door to the bedroom.

'Ivo, mate, I need that fifty quid you borrowed.'

'I don't have it mate,' called Ivo as he kept fucking the brunette.

She started to moan and then she came with a cry, and Ivo, so turned on by the urgency of her orgasm, felt himself reach orgasm too. 'I'll have it tomorrow!' he cried in the midst of his throes of ecstasy.

'Fuck Ivo. You said that last week,' said Henry, his host, whose spare bedroom he was staying in. Well more like squatting in. Since his lover Tatiana had moved on to a new toy boy, Ivo had been unceremoniously dumped without anything but the clothes she had bought him and his Patek Philippe watch.

He had been staying at Henry's, an old school friend, but he was wearing his welcome a bit thin and he was flat out of cash. He could have rung his mother but then he knew that the information would go back to his father, whom he despised, so instead he grinned and bore it.

Nothing really got Ivo down. He was decidedly chipper about any setback, figuring it would all work out in the end. Things usually did for him. Look at me now, he thought, in bed with the hottest pop star in London right now. She was an Australian soap star who had made it big with a shitty single and spectacular breasts that made her popular with men's magazines and websites.

Maybe she would take him in, he figured, even just for the sex. They had met at a party the previous night given by some Eliza Wimple-Jones woman for her PR clients. The news of Tatiana and Ivo's separation hadn't yet hit the gossip wires. He had figured he might as well get the free booze and finger food while he could.

The pop star was lonely and he was charming, and soon he had her drunk and on her back, which is where he liked his women.

Now in the cold light of mid-morning, Ivo sat with his back against the wall and lit one of her cigarettes. 'What shall we do now?' he asked sexily, his dark hair flopping over one eye.

'I have an audition to go to,' she said in her broad Australian drawl.

'An audition?' asked Ivo, his perfectly formed ears pricking up.

'Yep, I've been taking acting lessons. I'm gonna be an actor,' she said proudly.

Not with that fucking accent, he thought, but he smiled indulgently at her.

She smiled back at him. She was so pretty. He thought for a moment; she could take care of his cash and his cock for a while.

'Need a hand remembering your lines?' he offered.

'There were no lines to learn. I just have to meet the director and have a chat. Will you come with me? I'm so nervous.'

'Sure.' He had nothing better to do – and she might buy him breakfast, he calculated, listening to his rumbling stomach. The only thing he had eaten yesterday was a few sandwiches at the party, and he had drunk copious amounts of champagne.

She got out of bed and stretched. Her figure was amazing, he thought. Sexy and round, but without a trace of fat. He felt a stirring in his groin again.

'Come back to bed,' he said huskily.

'Nope, sorry. Don't want to be late,' she said and pulled on the clothes she had worn the night before. 'I'm gonna dash home and change first. You coming?'

Ivo stood up, his hard-on on display. 'You sure?' he asked, looking at his magnificent dick.

She paused, and then thought of her career. Despite what people thought, she was very ambitious. She knew this audition was a big chance for her. 'Save it for 'ron,' she said.

'Who's Ron?' he asked, aghast. Did she have a boyfriend called Ron who she wanted a threesome with? He only did threesomes with women, he thought, remembering Tatiana and her sister.

'Later on,' she laughed. 'It's an Aussie saying.'

'Right,' he said, and pulled on his jeans and an old white t-shirt. Padding into Henry's room, he looked around and found Henry's Paul Smith blazer. Admiring himself in the mirror, he noticed that the t-shirt had a stain on it, so he grabbed a scarf of Henry's girlfriend's, a paisley shawl thing, and slung it around his neck. Pulling on his Converse, he waited by the door. 'Come on then Ron,' he called, laughing at his own convenient joke – he couldn't remember her name in his champagne fog.

Leaving the house, they took a cab to her flat. Ivo waited while she quickly showered and changed into jeans and a tight sequined singlet. Teamed with gladiator heels and a yellow Bottega Veneta bag, she looked the very image of a Eurotrash heiress.

'You like?' she said, spinning around for him.

'Very much,' he said, thinking she looked overdressed for daytime. 'What's the role?'

'I have no idea. The director is very private and brilliant my agent says. It's not a big role but it could lead to other things, help people to see me as more than a pop star,' she said.

Lose the heels, the sequins and the feather earrings and that would be a start, he thought, but he said nothing. 'Where you meeting him then?' he asked as he held the door open for her.

'At an art gallery,' she said, pulling out her small diary. She opened it to today's date. 'The V&A? Is that a hospital?'

Ivo stifled a laugh. 'No, it's the Victoria and Albert Museum. A funny place for an audition,' he said as he hailed a taxi.

'Well, film people are very creative you know,' she said importantly.

'Apparently,' he said drolly, and they took the cab to the V&A.

Inside they waited in the foyer. A small man walked towards them. 'Jodi?' he asked politely.

93

Jodi! That was her name, Ivo reminded himself.

'Hi,' Jodi replied enthusiastically.

'I'm Harold Gaumont,' the small gentleman said.

'This is my friend Ivo,' said Jodi. 'I said he could come along.'

Ivo stretched out his hand. 'Lovely to meet you, Mr Gaumont. I can make myself scarce if you'd like.'

Harold looked at the beautiful boy in front of him in the pink paisley scarf that reeked of good breeding and sex. 'No, it's fine. I thought we would take a turn in my favourite collection and have a little chat.'

Jodi and Ivo followed Harold, who seemed to know his way about the gallery with no problems and greeted the security guards by name.

'Have you been here before, Ivo?' he asked as they walked together, Jodi's heels making a loud clacking noise on the parquet floor.

'Yes, I have spent quite a lot of time here actually,' said Ivo, thinking back to his days at university.

'I find it calming.' Harold said. 'All this artistic brilliance in one space. It is quite heartening.' Ivo smiled at the man in the velvet slippers. Harold drew in a sharp breath. Ivo was truly beautiful, almost like a painting.

'You spend much time in galleries, Jodi?' asked Ivo, trying to draw Jodi into the conversation, aware it was her audition after all and unnerved by the looks the man was giving him. Perhaps he was gay. It wasn't the first time he had been hit on by older men.

'Me? Galleries? Not really. I had to go to a few for school and that, but I prefer the movies.' She smiled at Harold, proud of her answer.

'Tell me, my dear, can you do an English accent?' he asked.

'Too right I can,' she said, launching into her best Eliza Doolittle. 'I 'ave a brill voice coach.'

Harold stood with his eyes raised in surprise. 'Wonderful. Any other type of English accent?'

'Well I can do Received Pronunciation as well,' she said. 'I am very proud to meet you 'arold,' she said, slipping between RP and Cockney and sounding like Maggie Thatcher doing a guest appearance on *EastEnders*.

'Well done,' said Ivo encouragingly. If he was going to find his next meal ticket then she needed to get this gig. She smiled at him and adjusted her breasts in the strained singlet.

The three walked in silence towards the paintings. It was early and the gallery had almost no one in it. 'Do you know this painting?' Harold asked Ivo.

'I do. It's a Baxter. *The Day Before Marriage*,' said Ivo without having to read the note next to the painting.

'Tell me about it,' said Harold.

'She's about to be married. She's wearing traditional Victorian love jewellery, common in those days, as was mourning jewellery. She's holding a letter in her hand, perhaps a billet-doux from her husband to be. She's well dressed and elegant, which shows she's perhaps from the upper class. The emotion is in the letter in this painting. It shows the power of love letters and their effect on women.'

'Have you ever received a love letter, my dear?' asked Harold to Jodi.

'Not really a letter, but I did get a nice email from a boyfriend once. That was nice,' she said, smiling at Harold.

'Ah,' he said, and turned away.

'What about this one?' Harold asked Ivo.

'It's a George Middlemist, of his wife Clementina. She's in a garden surrounded by clementine trees creating an arbour over her. The yellow roses suggest joy.' Ivo looked closely at the woman in the painting. Her black hair was pulled up into a loose bun, and her dark eyes peered back at him. 'The basket of fruit next to her suggests she's responsible for the abundance in the garden, like Ceres the Goddess of the Harvest, and her hair and dress, which was not ornate for those days, imply this is casual, that it's even a folly for her to be playing the role of a rural woman.'

Harold smiled and looked closely at the painting. 'You're right. How do you know so much about art then?'

'I read art history at university,' he said, leaving out the part where he got expelled for dealing coke and ecstasy to his fellow students, something the esteemed university had been quick to cover up.

'What do you do now?'

'Oh, a bit of this, a bit of that,' said Ivo vaguely as he watched Jodi take a call on her pink mobile on the other side of the room.

'Have you ever tried acting?' asked Harold.

'Only at school and a bit at university,' admitted Ivo.

'Not for you then?' asked Harold.

'Well let's just say my father didn't approve, and while he paid the bills I did what he asked,' said Ivo, thinking back.

'And does he still pay the bills?' asked Harold.

'No, no. We haven't spoken in two years,' said Ivo, scuffing the floor back and forth with his foot.

'Well, how about you come and do a little reading with me, and let's see if you still have it?' asked Harold.

Before Ivo could answer, Jodi came clumping over in her heels. 'I'm so sorry,' she said, smiling brightly, 'I've been offered a film in LA. A big new action movie with Michael Jackson's son Blanket. It's gonna be huge. I have to take it. You get it don'tcha?'

'Naturally,' said Harold. 'If the blanket calls then you must attend.' He smiled at the girl with the feathery earrings.

'I've gotta go to my agent's now. I'm sorry Ivo. I'll call you from LA, OK?' she said as she rushed out the door. Ivo waved at her as she left, knowing she never would. She didn't even have his number.

Harold watched her leave. 'Who's Blanket again?' he asked, savouring the name as though it had a taste.

'Michael Jackson's son,' said Ivo seriously.

'I don't need to know any more. Americans and their names! Blanket indeed,' mumbled Harold. 'Now Ivo, let's get a script and try you out, OK? I have a feeling you might be better than you think.'

Ivo hoped he was right now that his meal ticket had given him up for a blanket. He smiled at Harold. 'Alright, I guess I have nothing to lose,' he said, shrugging his shoulders.

Taking a cab to Harold's apartment, Ivo sat nervously waiting for Harold to return to the room with a script. There were pictures everywhere and books too. He stood up and looked at the many photographs of women on the mantelpiece. 'Those are my wives,' said Harold as he came into the room with a few sheaves of paper.

'All of them?' asked Ivo, breathing an internal sigh of

relief that Harold hadn't returned in lipstick and stockings, like one older gentleman had done to him a few months before.

'All of them. And now they are all happily married to other men. I'm not very good at relationships.' The petite man sat down in the huge red leather armchair, which threatened to swallow him. Ivo silently agreed with him; relationships weren't exactly his forte either. A quick fuck or being kept were more his style.

'Here, read these through and then we'll have a go. OK?' said Harold, handing him a script.

Ivo read it over quickly and looked up at Harold. 'Victorian? Occultism?' he asked.

'Good pickup,' said Harold. He had only given Ivo a few pages of the script but he had chosen ones that referred to the occult group.

Harold started to read and Ivo said his lines. His accent, his timing and his look were perfect. Harold felt himself start to relax; his intuition was right. He had only seen the Australian actress because her agent had pushed him to at least meet with her. What an enormous stroke of luck that she had brought her one-night stand with her, he thought.

'I think you'll do nicely, Ivo,' said Harold, taking off his glasses.

'Wow. Really?' Ivo was relieved. A small role would keep him off the streets for a while, and he would be able to pay Henry back.

'Well, I am pleased to be considered. Is it much of a role?' asked Ivo, hoping he wouldn't have to learn too many lines.

'Of course my dear. It's the lead,' said Harold, smiling at the boy, whose face had suddenly lost all of its colour.

Fuck me twice and call me Blanket, thought Ivo as he sank back into his chair.

CHAPTER TEN

'I won't do it,' said Merritt to Kitty firmly.

'Why not?' she pleaded with him.

'I don't want all those film wankers traipsing over our house and ruining things,' he said.

'Thanks very much!' said Willow.

'Well, it's true,' he said indignantly. Ever since Willow had come back from London yesterday with the news, he had been fighting against having the shoot at Middlemist.

'You're crazy, Merritt,' said Willow. 'Simon says this is a huge film. You could get most of the work done outside without any disruption, and the production will pay for everything. Harold Gaumont is a genius and his films are always brilliant, and the time period's always depicted perfectly. Stop being a bullheaded idiot and do it for god's sake.'

Merritt looked at her with dislike. 'How dare you tell me what to do?'

'Get over yourself,' she said to him. 'The house is half Kitty's. What do you want to do, Kitty?' She turned to her and waited.

Kitty looked between her brother and her employer and paused. What Willow was saying made sense and she knew that it would take a miracle to be able to do up the house.

Maybe this was what they needed. She wanted to see Willow back to work, for Willow's sake and for her own. She took a big breath. 'I agree with Willow. I think you're being bullheaded. You're not thinking about what Middlemist needs, just what you want,' she said carefully.

Merritt looked at her strangely. She'd never gone against his word before. When Edward died she had agreed with all of his choices for the funeral and the burial and had even agreed to leave Middlemist, pretending she had a friend to go and stay with for a while, even though he had since found out she'd had nowhere to go at the time.

Willow sat with her arms crossed in the living room looking at the strange pair of siblings, so completely different to each other. Merritt looked at Willow. 'Alright, you win. But if even a daffodil bulb is ruined I will hold you liable,' he said.

'Whatever,' said Willow, repeating Poppy's phrase, and Kitty laughed out loud.

Merritt glared at his sister as she tried to stop laughing, but tears fell down her cheeks.

'What's so funny, Kitty?' asked Willow, bemused at her nanny's hysteria.

'I don't know. Everything's funny at the moment. Us being here, the film, Poppy finding the ring and the papers, and the fact that Merritt does have a head a bit like a bull, if you look at it closely.'

Willow looked at Merritt. He didn't look like a bull to her. When he was being pleasant he was almost handsome, she thought, in an outdoorsy sort of way.

Merritt sat sulking in his chair. 'I need a drink.'

'Yes please!' called Willow as he left the room.

'He hates me now,' said Kitty, the laughter leaving her.

101

'No he doesn't, he'll get over it. He's just angry because he knows it's the right thing to do even though he doesn't want it,' said Willow.

'You think?'

'I think he has been alone for so long he's always had his own way, so considering other people isn't really something he's used to,' said Willow knowingly. Growing up with therapist parents had taught her a thing or two about people and their actions. Shame she didn't apply it to Kerr when she met him, she thought.

Merritt walked into the room with a bottle of claret and three glasses as a peace offering. Opening the bottle, he poured for the women and then sat in the chair opposite them.

'It's not that I don't think it's a good idea in theory, but I am so overwhelmed with the details, trying to fix up the house and work out where the money will come from. The garden I'm all over, but I can't afford a proper interior designer to get it back into shape inside. I don't know the difference between a chaise longue and a credenza.'

'Don't look at me,' said Kitty throwing her hands up. 'I have no idea about that stuff either.'

'I do,' said Willow slowly. 'Let me come up with a few ideas. I won't be like a real interior designer, but I can pull pages from magazines and books and give you a feel to get you started,' she offered.

It was her favourite thing to do. She would be so excited if Merritt let her. Merritt raised his hands as if surrendering.

'Whatever,' he said, and they all laughed.

On the morning that Harold Gaumont was due to arrive for the appraisal of Middlemist, Willow was in a flap.

'Kitty, keep the children away if you can. I don't think he likes children. Well he doesn't look like he would like them,' she called down the hallway from her bedroom.

Poppy screwed up her face as Kitty dressed her. 'I don't like him then either,' she said.

'Shhh,' said Kitty as she brushed Poppy's golden curls and put a red ribbon in her hair.

'Where's Lucian?' Kitty asked.

'Out with Mewwitt,' said Poppy.

Kitty lifted her off the bed and set her on the floor. 'Go and watch Jinty while I make the beds,' she said, and Poppy ran down to the playroom where Jinty sat surrounded by Merritt's old building blocks, which Kitty had found in the nursery.

Lucian had taken an immediate liking to Merritt, following him around the garden and watching him work. Merritt kept up a continuous monologue with Lucian, as he had seen the mother and father do with the child in Florida, and occasionally Merritt saw Lucian open his mouth to speak.

Willow didn't mind Lucian being out with Merritt; in fact she encouraged it. It meant he was less likely to follow her around, which got on her nerves, she had to admit.

Willow had dressed carefully for this next meeting with Harold. She wanted him to see her at her best, and considering the limited wardrobe she had brought with her to Middlemist, she had managed to pull together the appropriate look, she thought.

Black, tight Calvin Klein pants and black suede ankle boots – a neutral base – but on top she had taken her lace Chloé blouse and layered over it one of the red Victorian hunting jackets that Poppy had found in the eaves.

She and Kitty had gone through all the trunks upstairs and had found clothes from nearly every era. It was a costume party shop's dream, and Willow looked the part today with the blouse, the jacket and another discovery: a beautiful golden brooch with what looked to be a plait of hair inside it.

Willow made her cheeks a little flushed and applied eye makeup. She had washed and dried her hair, setting it in rollers so it hung in gentle rolls down her back, and sprayed herself with the violet water, which surprisingly still smelled quite fresh, that she found in the bathroom cupboard. Applying a quick sheen of nude lip gloss, she ran down the stairs two at a time.

Merritt looked up as she came bounding down towards him and he felt his stomach give way. She looked beautiful. Not like the pale, harassed woman he had seen over the few days he had come to know her.

She smiled at him and stood posing on the steps. 'Enough?' she asked.

'More than enough,' he smiled, looking at her in a way that Willow hadn't seen for a long time, and she felt her stomach flip.

'Thanks,' she said, blushing. 'Sorry about bullying you into this, but I do think it could be the miracle you need to save Middlemist.'

Merritt shrugged his shoulders. I gave up on miracles a long time ago, he thought, but he said nothing and put his hands in his pockets.

Merritt had washed his hands for the occasion, but that was it. In his old work boots, trousers and flannel shirt he looked like a roadside labourer, but Willow knew it didn't matter. Harold was here for the house, not for its owner.

104

Merritt heard a car pull up and opened the large Gothic front doors. The driver came around and opened the door to the Bentley. Harold emerged. 'Hello. I'm Merritt Middlemist. Pleased to meet you,' said Merritt, stretching out his hand.

'Indeed,' said Harold, taking the hand in his tiny paw and looking beyond Merritt at the house. 'What a grand dame.'

'Yes, she is wonderful, although a little tired I'm afraid,' said Merritt apologetically. Harold waved his apology away.

'Willow, how lovely you look.' He kissed Willow on each cheek as she emerged from the house. 'Is this your lovely boyfriend then?' asked Harold, looking at Merritt.

'No, no. No. Not at all. Of course not,' said Willow, suddenly nervous.

Merritt looked down. 'No, I'm the brother of her nanny. She's staying with us,' he said.

'Not that I meant it would be terrible. God, I sounded so rude. Of course you could be my boyfriend. Oh dammit!' she said, fumbling over her words.

'No offence taken,' said Merritt, still looking down. Harold watched them with interest.

'Show me the house then,' said Harold, and Merritt and Willow walked him through it, which took over an hour.

'I would like to sit now. The lovely drawing room at the front would be fine,' said Harold, and Willow led the way back.

'Can I get you tea, or something else?' she asked, hoping he wouldn't ask for coffee, thinking of the pot sitting on the stove back in London.

'A water would be fine,' he said to be polite, and Willow left the room. He and Merritt sat in comfortable silence.

The double doors at the other end of the room, leading into the billiard room, were flung open. An angry Poppy stood in the doorway.

'Why don't you like children?' she demanded to know of Harold.

'I do like children. Wherever you're getting your information from, I would consider getting a new source,' said Harold, not at all fazed by Poppy's arrival.

'I only like sauce on chips,' she said. She walked over to Harold and stood in front of him. 'Mummy says you don't look like the sort of person who would like children, so she told me and my brother to stay away.'

Merritt sat watching the precocious child, who reminded him so much of Willow. He tried not to laugh.

Willow walked into the room with Harold's water and glared at Poppy. 'Poppy darling, why are you in here?' she asked, her voice steely.

'I wanted to see the man. I've seen him now. He does like children, Mummy, you were wrong. And he doesn't want water, he wants sauce,' she said, smiling angelically at Harold.

Harold laughed uproariously. 'What a mind she has. A wonderful child. Tell me – what's your name?'

'Poppy.'

'That's very pretty.'

'I know. What's your name?'

'Harry,' said Harold.

'That's a good name. His name is Mewwitt. It's a silly name. I'm not being rude – even he thinks so, don't you Mewwitt?'

Merritt nodded his agreement and Poppy sat down close to Harold. Willow sat down and tried to give Poppy a look to tell her to leave but Poppy ignored her and crossed her legs, like her new friend Harry.

Harold spoke. 'Merritt, I understand this is a terrible inconvenience but we are prepared to do all the legwork in the gardens and inside where we need to get things up to scratch. While we won't be planting anything, we will need to get the fences and the retaining walls fixed and some of the gardens cleared. I imagine it would be quite costly to do.'

'Yes, the costs are high,' said Merritt with a sigh.

'We would require a month to get the house ready for production and we would be here for six weeks for the shoot. I can get my assistant to send you over all the details. We will pay you a weekly fee for use of the house and also a fee for any props we use. You can guide us on the garden work, as we would like it to be as authentic as possible, and we will also give you a credit for the work in the film,' said Harold.

Merritt sat stunned. He had no idea it would be as easy as this. He looked at Willow, who was smiling at him, and she raised her eyebrows as if to say, 'I told you so.'

'I suppose there's nothing else to say. Send me the details and I'll get back to you,' said Merritt.

As he and Willow saw Harold off back to London, he turned to Willow excitedly.

'You're a life saver,' he said, and he picked her up in his large embrace. He spun her around and then he kissed her on the mouth quickly. 'You're amazing. I'm going to find Kitty,' he yelled, and he ran back into the house.

Willow stood in shock at the kiss. Although it was chaste she had felt a stirring in her that she had forgotten existed.

Merritt's arms were so strong and he was so tall, she felt tiny next to him. She stood in the driveway, watching Harold's Bentley navigate its way around the potholes.

For the first time in a long time, she felt excited. About what, she wasn't sure, but it felt better than being depressed, and for that she was grateful.

Summer

CHAPTER ELEVEN

Over the next few weeks, Middlemist House was a hive of activity. Kitty had her work cut out for her trying to keep the children away from the diggers and cherry pickers that surrounded it. The minute she and Merritt had signed the consent papers for the filming, an army of crew arrived and set to work.

Merritt was in his element and Kitty couldn't remember when she had last seen him so cheerful. While at first he had hated the idea of the film being shot at Middlemist, now he chatted with the art director and production designer constantly, bringing out books and old photographs from the library to show them Middlemist's former glory.

When Poppy had discovered the letters and journals, Merritt had given the journals to Kitty to read. He'd said he would go through the letters, but he had been so busy with the work at the house that he hadn't even begun. Kitty, however, looked over at the journals sitting on her bedside table each night, and could only feel guilt for not even opening the small books, which were falling apart at the spine.

The ring was now housed safely in Merritt's room, but only after Kitty and Willow had tried it on. It was too small for Kitty's ring finger but it fitted Willow's hand perfectly. 'It looks lovely,' she said, holding out her hand to admire it. 'You should save it for your wife, Merritt.'

Merritt harrumphed. 'Not bloody likely that'll happen again,' he said. Willow looked at Kitty in surprise. There had been no mention of an ex-wife. 'I'll save it for Kitty when she gets married.'

Kitty laughed. 'No chance of that, Merritt. I don't see the men knocking down the gates for a date with me.'

'What a fine pair we are,' said Merritt, and he tousled Kitty's hair.

'Don't forget me,' laughed Willow. 'A single mother and nearly thirty-two years old. It doesn't get much more tragic than that. I'll be known as a cougar once word gets out I'm on the prowl again.'

'Oh you won't have any trouble meeting men,' said Merritt.

'You think?' laughed Willow.

'You're attractive and intelligent. Men like that,' he said.

Willow thought of Kerr with his Russian sisters. 'It's not enough for some men,' she said.

'Then they're idiots,' he said, in a practical tone of voice.

Willow had thought about his comment for days afterwards. Why did she always choose such immature men?

Her mother had warned her about Kerr. 'I think he has growing up to do,' she had said when Willow took him to New York to meet her parents.

'He's fun, Mom,' Willow had said.

'He's a child,' said Janis. 'He's Peter Pan.'

'Jesus, Mom, you've known him for two days and now you can analyse him?'

'I know what I know, honey. It's my job. I think you should have fun, but don't get serious. He ain't a keeper.'

Ringing her mother with the news after Kerr left her was hard, but Janis wasn't judgmental.

'Let him be, he may come back. See if he gets it out of his system,' she had advised, but Kerr hadn't come back. Now the paparazzi photos of him meant Willow couldn't lie any more – to the world or herself – about her marriage.

It was over.

Not that she and Kerr had ever discussed it. He never returned her calls or her emails. He had disappeared, and now that the news of her taking over the role in Harold's film had broken, the paparazzi would be coming down the motorway any day, breaking the relative peace at Middlemist.

Even though the house was busy with the production crew, Willow was enjoying pretending Middlemist was hers. Given carte blanche from Merritt and Kitty to redesign the interiors, she thought about nothing else. She spent hours looking at magazines and sending off for expensive interior design books, which she charged to Kerr's credit card. Actually she charged a lot of things to Kerr's credit card. She was surprised the bank hadn't stopped it yet.

As soon as her lawyer had told her she was in dire financial straits she had stopped spending immediately. Since Kerr was refusing to speak to her or send her any money, if he had any, she would live it up on Kerr's remaining credit instead.

Willow had a new laptop and printer, clothes and toys delivered to her at Middlemist, along with organic groceries, skincare products and makeup that she had ordered online. The local village was out of bounds due to Willow wanting to lay low, but Merritt said the gossip had already started once the film crew arrived. Thankfully he didn't give anything away about Willow being Middlemist's houseguest, but Willow knew the peace wouldn't last for long.

She had managed to avoid Merritt as much as she could, although it was hard in the evenings when the film crew had gone and it was just her and the children, Merritt and Kitty. Once the children had gone to bed, Willow would stay in the drawing room, her favourite room in the house, surfing the net and printing out pictures to stick into her large Hermès notebook.

Just the night before, Merritt had come and stood over her, leaning over her shoulder to see what she was working on. She could hardly breathe with his head so close to hers. 'What's that?' he had asked, looking at the screen.

'It's a company that reconditions antique bathtubs,' she had said, her voice cracking slightly.

'No, over there,' he said, putting his large hand over hers and moving the cursor further down the screen.

Willow was torn between wanting him to leave his hand there and snatching her own away. What a silly, sex-starved woman I am. The first man I meet, I get a crush on, she thought. She told herself off. Merritt isn't vaguely interested in me, she reminded herself.

Kitty was lying on the sagging sofa with her iPod in her ears and her eyes closed. Merritt left his hand slightly longer than necessary on Willow's and she felt the same butterflies she had had when he'd lifted her up after Harold left. His display of affection and joy at the film had been surprising and it seemed completely out of character for him. She had mentioned it briefly to Kitty in passing but Kitty had laughed, saying Merritt used to be fun and it was good he still had it in him.

Just as Willow was about to turn to Merritt, she heard Jinty's cries on the baby monitor. Willow looked at Kitty, but she seemed to have fallen asleep on the sofa. Willow got up wearily.

'I'll go,' offered Merritt.

'Really? She's probably just lost her dummy,' said Willow.

'No problem. I'll go upstairs and you put the kettle on. I'd love a cuppa,' he said as he left the room.

Willow walked into the kitchen and set about making the tea. It felt odd having a man offer to help with her children. It was Kitty who had always done everything. Since Willow and the children had moved to Middlemist, she had a true understanding of what Kitty's days were like and Willow felt guilty for the amount of work she made the young girl do. Not that Kitty ever complained. She was so patient and kind, especially with Lucian, who was still in deep worship of Merritt.

'You were right, it was just the dummy,' Merritt said as he walked into the kitchen. Willow felt her body tighten at the sound of his voice.

'She was so sweet when she saw me. She smiled this big sleepy smile. Gorgeous,' he said as he reached up for the biscuit tin on top of the cupboard where Kitty had hidden it from Poppy.

Willow turned and saw him stretching, his t-shirt riding up and showing his flat stomach with tiny blond hairs on it. She felt weak at the knees. Stop it, she reminded herself.

Spinning around back to the stove, she put her hand down on the hot stovetop for a second and felt a searing pain through her hand. 'Ahhh!' she cried. 'Fuck it!'

Merritt dropped the tin, grabbed her hand, put it under

the cold tap and held it while the water washed over it. 'God, I'm so stupid,' she said, tears filling her eyes.

'No you're not,' said Merritt, and he lifted her hand to inspect the burn. 'It's not too bad, but you will need some cream and dressing.' He started looking in the cupboard above the fridge, to see what first aid they had in the house.

'Here, sit down and I'll play nurse,' he said and he gently pushed Willow onto the kitchen chair.

He took out a tube of cream and some dressings that had his father's name on them, and decided they would do the job unless it got worse. He gently applied the cream, placed a dressing over it and wrapped it up in a bandage. When he had finished he looked down at Willow. 'All better?'

She nodded. The pain of her burn was nothing compared to the sickness she felt in her stomach when he touched her, and she was slightly breathless.

'You're a bit pale. Need a drink?'

Oh, I need a lot more than that, she thought, but she nodded her consent. Merritt pulled out a bottle of brandy from the cupboard along with two small glasses, and he poured them both a drink.

'Hurts, huh?' he asked.

'It's not too bad,' she said quietly.

'Are you OK?' Merritt looked at her closely.

'I'm fine, really. Just shock I think.'

'I know what you need,' he said playfully.

I'm sure you don't, she thought, but she smiled anyway. Merritt picked up her hand and kissed it. 'All better,' he said proudly.

Willow laughed and smiled at him, and Merritt smiled back. For a moment that seemed like an eternity to Willow their eyes met and she wanted to reach out and touch him. Instead she stood up.

'Actually I don't think I want a drink. I might take some painkillers and go to bed. I have this interior design job I'm trying to finish,' she said, trying to ignore the tension in the room.

'Yes – when will I get to see your work?' he asked.

'Soon, I'm nearly done,' she said, standing in front of him. There was an awkward pause and then she leant down and kissed him briefly on the cheek. 'Thanks,' she said.

'No problem.' He smiled and she went upstairs to her room.

Merritt sat for a long time in the kitchen nursing his brandy and thinking about Willow. Was he imagining it? Was she acting oddly around him?

He was attracted to her; what man wouldn't be? She was beautiful and elegant and had a sense of self-possession he found fascinating. The idea of her being a parent didn't bother him at all; he liked her children, although he worried for little Lucian. He stood up, drained the rest of his brandy and rubbed his eyes with his hands. Get over yourself Merritt, he thought.

It had been over a year since he had had sex. His last lover was a woman he met in Jodhpur, at the hotel whose magnificent gardens he had designed. It was the opening night party and he'd felt uneasy in his dinner suit surrounded by celebrities. He watched as Madonna sat at the bar waiting for people to present themselves at her feet, her new boyfriend by her side. Hers was the only face he recognised, but he'd had no doubt there were many other celebrities there judging from the stench of self-importance in the air. He had headed out to the immense stone balcony to escape the heat and bullshit, and found himself alone with a beautiful woman.

'Hello,' she had said in her soft Indian accent.

'Hello,' he said in return, and they watched the stars as they emerged one by one in the dusky pink and blue Indian sky. They stood for what seemed like hours and watched as the sun set and the sky darkened.

'You like the party?' she asked.

'Not really,' he said. 'I'm here because I have to be.'

'Me too.' She laughed and they looked at each other and smiled. 'Want to escape?' she offered.

Merritt looked back at the room, filled with flesh and ego. Nobody had bothered to turn up for the tour of the gardens he had been asked to give. He felt alone and far away from anything real.

'What did you have in mind?' he asked, turning to the woman impulsively.

Taking his hand, she pulled him towards the back stairs of the balcony, took off her shoes and ran down the steps into the dark. Merritt paused for a moment and then ran after her. They walked through the gardens he had spent so much time on and she put her arm in his. It was companionable and felt right even though they didn't know each other's names.

'The gardens are lovely. I walked through them today,' she said in her lilting accent.

'Thank you. I designed them,' he said humbly.

'Well you are very clever.'

Merritt said nothing. Her praise didn't matter to him; he was saddened that people didn't care for gardens any more.

It used to be an art, he thought, now people just wanted quick overhauls with instantly grown plants.

He and the woman walked down towards the pool, which was silent, the air thick with the scent of gardenias. She looked at him and arched an eyebrow. 'Swim?'

He looked at her confused.

She peeled off her cerise silk slip and stood opposite him in tiny cream silk pants. She was in her late twenties and her body was toned and taut. He felt a stirring in his groin and looked back up to the palace. The music echoed out and Merritt realised no one there missed him – hell, no one in the party knew him.

Pulling off his dinner suit and shoes, he stood naked opposite the woman, his cock jutting out in front of him. She didn't look at him, but instead dived into the water. He followed her in. She swam around him and threw her pants onto the side of the pool, and he swam over to her, reached down into the water and pulled her towards him. The nipples on her tiny breasts were erect and he sucked them gently. She was naked except for the rings and necklaces that glittered in the water, and he held her as she wrapped her legs around him. They rubbed together in the water and kissed gently until he felt himself slip inside her, and they fucked in the water, breathlessly. He pushed her against the tiled walls and she grabbed at his back, her long nails digging in, and then they came together. Afterwards she had lifted herself off him, swum underwater to the other end of the pool, and pulled herself out of the water.

'Thank you,' she had said as she tied her hair into a bun. He had wondered how she did it with no pins to hold it. Taking a towel from the trolley at the side of the pool, she dried herself and then pulled her dress back over her head. She took her pants and dropped them into the bin by the side of the pool, and then she bent down next to Merritt at the water's edge. 'Enjoy your stay.' She smiled and walked in the direction of the party.

Merritt had stayed in the pool, unsure of what had just happened and if it was real. The scratches on his back would sting under the shower when he finally made it back to his room, reminding him it was true. He wondered who the woman was.

Leaving the next day, he sat in his business class seat and pulled out the airline magazine while he waited for the plane to finish boarding. There was an article about the wedding of the year that was about to happen between one of India's richest men and the daughter of a Maharaja. The man was thirty-five years her senior and the woman was a rising Bollywood star. Merritt looked at the pictures and recognised the woman he had had sex with the night before. Merritt closed the magazine and sat back in his seat, wondering when his life had become so devoid of intimacy.

Now he was back at home, pining after a Hollywood star, not a Bollywood star, and this time she came with three kids and what sounded like an idiot of a husband. Merritt hadn't allowed himself to even entertain a crush since Eliza had broken her promise to him, and he had managed successfully to limit himself to no-strings, even nameless sex occasionally, and by travelling the world, to stay away from England and its memories.

Part of him, though, was excited to know he felt something again. He had wondered if Eliza had broken him for good.

He had loved her but he had let her have control, and she had made a fool of him with his best friend.

Merritt wondered now about Willow. There was no way she even spared a thought for him, he decided, and he went to bed.

Upstairs in her bed, Willow heard Merritt heading to bed and she willed him to come into her room. Outside her door he stood and paused, then he walked down the hall. He swore he heard someone call his name.

CHAPTER TWELVE

'Over here,' called a woman's voice and Ivo, panicking, looked up and saw a woman with a clipboard coming towards him, with a headset and a bumbag.

'Hi,' said Ivo. 'Ivo Casselton,' he said to the woman.

'Great. Come with me,' she said and led the way to the house, where she handed him a large package. 'Here's your script, your notes, your schedule and your accommodation details.'

'Thanks,' said Ivo, trying to juggle his duffel bag and the heavy papers.

'Table reading at twelve pm today at the house. My number's on the call sheet if you need anything. I'm Jenny,' she said officiously. 'Who's your agent again? I haven't had those details sent to me yet.'

'I haven't got one,' he said, looking round at the house, which was having lengths of fake wisteria strung from it by men in a cherry picker.

Jenny looked at him oddly. 'No agent?'

'Nope,' said Ivo. 'I'm new to this game.' He laughed.

'I suggest you get one quickly.' Jenny looked at her clipboard.

'Any idea who?' he asked.

'I'm not sure. Maybe ask the other actors?' said Jenny as

her mobile phone rang. 'Sorry, gotta take this,' she said, and Ivo smiled as she walked away to answer the call.

Ivo felt out of his depth. When Harold had told him he would play the lead in his new film, Ivo had been struck with insecurities he didn't even know existed in him. He hadn't received the script till now and felt a panic slowly rising into his throat. He read through the accommodation details and looked at the map. He was to be put up in a local hotel in a nearby village, the one he had sailed through on the bus up to Middlemist. He had borrowed another few hundred quid from Henry, confidently telling him he would be able to pay it back once he found out what he would be paid for the film. Ivo hadn't even signed the contract yet and he had no idea what and when he would be paid, but he was sure he wouldn't be working for free. Well he hoped as much.

Glancing at his watch – a vintage Rolex, the most expensive thing he owned – he saw it was ten o'clock and there was no point waiting for the bus to take him back into the village. By the time he got there he would just have to turn around and come back. So he wandered towards the house, and, seeing the front doors open, he stepped over the tracks for the cameras that were set up and walked inside.

The grand foyer was empty and he stood with his bag over his shoulder and looked up at the vaulted ceiling. It was a stunning house. He thought of his own family home. He had wondered if he should tell his mother about the film, but then thought better of it. He decided to save her from the endless lectures from his father about Ivo's lack of responsibility and direction.

Hearing footsteps behind him, he turned and saw a girl walking towards him. Small with dark hair and eyes, she reminded him of someone, but he couldn't remember who it was.

'Hello,' he said nervously.

The girl stopped and peered at him. 'Hello,' she answered shyly.

'I need to set my stuff down. Do you know where the table reading will be? I'm a bit lost,' he admitted.

'Ah, yes, sure,' the girl stammered. 'It's in the ballroom in the other wing of the house.'

'Great. Do you think you could show me?' he asked, taking in her lovely face as she blushed. Ivo knew he had a way with women, and this girl was like all the others. Maybe she could provide a bit of distraction on set. She was obviously an actress; too pretty not to be, he thought.

The girl looked upstairs and then back to Ivo as though she was torn, and then she quickly walked in the direction of the opposite hallway. 'Alright, quickly then,' she ordered, and Ivo followed her as she expertly guided him through the long hall to a set of double doors. Swinging them open, Ivo stood entranced by the large room. It had French windows on one side leading onto an overgrown terrace. Inside, there were several tables set up in a large U shape.

'Just leave your things here, I guess,' she offered, and Ivo dumped his bag and package on one of the tables.

'I better go,' she said, and started to walk out the door.

'Will I see you later at the reading?' he asked.

'Um. I'm not in the film,' she said, confused. How could he think she was an actor?

'You working on set then?' he asked.

'No,' she said, not looking at him. He didn't remember her, although she had remembered him.

124

'Oh?' It was Ivo's turn to be confused. 'It's amazing,' he said, looking at the crystal chandeliers. Some of them were missing a few crystals, but they were still breathtaking.

'Yes,' said the girl, looking at the way his dark hair touched the collar of his blue shirt.

'I hope I see you around then,' said Ivo, turning on the charm and smiling.

'Perhaps,' said the girl, and she turned and left the room.

Ivo watched her leave. Yes, she would do nicely, he thought. Small, large breasts, innocent and obviously shy around him. Ivo rubbed his hands together as he dragged the script out of the package and sat down to read. She would be a lovely distraction.

Kitty had been going downstairs to get baby Panadol for Jinty when she had seen Ivo standing in the foyer. She had nearly passed out. It was the boy from Willow's party years before. He didn't have any idea who she was, but she knew him. He had stayed with her since that night, and she had a feeling that she should stay away, or else he would be trouble. Big trouble.

Kitty dressed Lucian, put Jinty to bed and left Poppy watching the activity from the bedroom window. She and Lucian went and sat in the tiny sitting room off the kitchen, where Lucian watched Merritt in the driveway waving his hands and yelling up to the men above him.

Merritt turned and saw Kitty and Lucian and he waved at them, smiling. He proceeded to do a silly dance for Lucian, and Lucian waved back. Kitty was shocked. 'Can you say Merritt?' she asked the small boy. He never waved to anyone, ever.

125

The small boy looked out of the window at Merritt and held his hands up against the glass, but he said nothing.

Merritt had approached Kitty with the idea that things with Lucian were not quite right. She knew it was true, but unless Willow accepted it then he wouldn't be able to get the help he needed.

'You can look it up on the internet,' Merritt had said. 'Aspergers, autistic spectrum disorders. He reminds me of a child I knew in Florida. I emailed the mother and she sent me all this information and links to websites. There is a great teacher who specialises in this sort of thing. Maybe you can give some information to Willow?'

'I don't know, Merritt. She doesn't think there's anything wrong with him,' Kitty said.

'How's he going to go to school if he can't talk?' asked Merritt, concerned.

'He's not going to school. Willow believes in homeschooling,' said Kitty.

'That's rubbish. Children need school,' said Merritt firmly, remembering his days at boarding school. He had loved the culture of school and university: he had had wonderful times, made friends for life, until Johnny had fucked his wife. Merritt had pushed Johnny from his mind and continued championing Lucian.

'The child needs help, Kitty. I think it's remiss of you as one of his carers not to see it,' he admonished her.

'I'll look up the sites and I'll see what Willow says,' said Kitty to placate him, but she still hadn't got round to it. She hated the computer, and surfing the web didn't come easily to her.

Her answer had satisfied Merritt, and since the film crew had taken over the house he hadn't mentioned it again.

Kitty sat with Lucian in the sitting room and thought about the young man she had just met again. She had imagined him in her life after the night she'd met him, she wasn't sure why; she had found his energy magnetic and harboured secret fantasies about an unnamed man for the past two years. Don't be such a fool, Kitty, she told herself. There's no way he would be interested in you, he's a film star. He probably just wants you to get him coffee.

Kitty knew she was kidding herself; she would give him whatever he wanted, and he just had to ask. Looking across the trailers and vans that stretched down the side of the house, she saw Willow exiting one of them in full Victorian dress, holding a black parasol over her head.

She looks incredible, thought Kitty, and she watched as Merritt mock-bowed as she walked past. Kitty laughed and tapped on the sitting room window and Willow smiled and waved at Kitty and Lucian.

'Wave at Mummy,' said Kitty, and to her surprise Lucian waved his hand at Willow as she sailed past. She stopped at the window and her face broke into a broad smile.

'Hello handsome,' she said, and from inside, Kitty could see tears in Willow's eyes. 'Merritt, Merritt!' she called, and Merritt ran over. 'Lucian waved at me,' she said, emotion breaking in her voice.

'Oh yes? He waves at me all the time,' said Merritt, confused.

'Really?' asked Willow.

'Of course,' said Merritt. 'He stands in the windows when I'm in the garden and we have a little waving ritual,' said Merritt.

Willow reached up and kissed his cheek. 'You're a dream,' she whispered in his ear, and then she walked in the direction of the house to be photographed for Harold's approval. Merritt watched as she walked away, and he touched his face where she had kissed him.

Kitty watched from the window and saw the look in Merritt's eyes, the way he ran when she called, the way he closed his eyes when Willow kissed him. The way he drew in his breath as she whispered something in his ear.

Yep, thought Kitty, she wasn't the only one in trouble here. Merritt had it as bad as she did.

CHAPTER THIRTEEN

Kerr was positioned between Tatiana's thighs.

'See, I can hold you in my grip like this?' she said, tightening her thigh muscles. 'And then I can flip you like this. Da?' she said, and swiftly flipped Kerr off the sun lounger onto the decking of her yacht.

Kerr landed with a heavy thud on his coccyx. 'Bloody hell Tatiana, that hurt!' he yelled out in his broad Scottish accent.

'Hmm,' she said, and readjusted her diamond-encrusted Dior sunglasses.

She was bored with Kerr now. They had been sailing around the Mediterranean for five weeks and all he wanted was blowjobs and coke, which she had an endless supply of, but what was she getting out of it? She was sick of these pieces of shit that leeched off her. What she wanted was a man who had his own life; a man who could do things, make things happen.

Kerr had promised her a recording contract and that he would do a duet with her on her album, but so far nothing had come through. What Kerr hadn't told her was that he was on notice with his record company, and that he was behind on his deadline for his next album.

He was supposed to be in London, writing and recording, but he wasn't inspired. He hadn't been inspired for years, he realised. He didn't have the music inside him any more, and he wondered how he could get it back. The last time he had written great music was when he met Willow. The songs had just poured out of him, and he had had a hard time trying to keep up with them. That was the album that produced three Grammys and went platinum several times. The follow-up album did alright, mostly because it was filled with songs he had written when he was with Willow, but the album after that had failed dismally and ticket sales for his concerts were slow.

When his lawyers and banker rang to tell him he was out of cash, he was incredulous. How could it be? he wondered, until they sent over the list of chattels and houses and he saw where his money had gone.

Now Willow and the children were gone, his reputation was in tatters, his mother had been emailing him articles about what people thought of him. It wasn't flattering, he thought.

Kerr ran his finger down her muscular thigh but she moved it away.

'Don't,' she said, rolling over onto her stomach and opening her copy of *Hello!*, the only thing he ever saw her read.

As he peered over her shoulder, still sitting on the deck, he saw pictures of Willow in Victorian costume. Snatching the magazine, he read, '*Willow Carruthers has wasted no time mourning the death of her marriage and has stepped into Harold Gaumont's new picture epic, filming in Bristol. It is believed that Willow will be in Bristol for six weeks with her children filming the multi-million dollar epic.*'

Kerr looked at the pictures of Willow. She did look beautiful, he thought, and then he looked at the muscular and groomed Tatiana on the sun lounger.

So different; the Madonna and the whore, he thought. Tatiana grabbed the magazine back from him.

'That is your wife, yes?' she said with distaste.

'Yes,' said Kerr, looking into the distance. No other boats in sight.

'She is an actress, yes?' asked Tatiana, her thoughts ticking.

'Yes,' said Kerr vacantly.

'I think I would like to be an actress. I think I would be good, yes?'

'Sure, sure,' he muttered. Three words from the article played over in his mind. *Multi-million dollar.* How much would she be getting paid for this role? he wondered.

Walking over to his phone on the table on deck he picked it up and saw he had thirteen missed calls and eight new messages. He ignored them and rang his lawyer, who took his call immediately.

'You're alive,' came the voice down the phone.

'Yes, I've just been having some time out,' said Kerr. 'Rethinking my options.'

'Willow is desperate to get a hold of you, as is your manager,' said the lawyer.

'Tell me, if Willow and I are split up then does she have to share with me what she earns still?'

'Not really. The kids are with her full time aren't they?'

'Yes.'

'If you have the kids then yes, but otherwise no.'

Kerr waited for a moment and then looked at Tatiana. He knew she was tiring of him. It was time to get his life back on track: music and money, that was what he wanted, and Willow held the key to both of them.

'I think it's time I came back to London,' said Kerr.

131

'High time,' said his lawyer. 'Call me when you get here. There are a few things we have to discuss. Actually many things.'

Kerr hung up the phone and turned to Tatiana. 'I have to go home,' he said.

She didn't bother to turn around. 'OK.'

Kerr waited. 'Can I use your jet?'

Now Tatiana rolled onto her back and sat up. 'What's in it for me, darlink?' she asked slowly.

'I could fuck you,' he offered.

She shrugged. 'Boring. What else?'

'I could write you a song?' he offered again. He was tired of her games and bullshit. He just wanted to be back in England with a pint in his hand and a full bank balance.

'Maybe, but first I want to be an actor. I want to meet your wife. Maybe she can help me.'

Kerr looked at her, shocked. She couldn't be serious? There was no way Willow would ever entertain this woman, whose nipples he had been seen sucking in pictures all over the world.

'Umm, I don't think that's a very good idea,' he stammered.

'Then no jet,' she said and she rolled onto her stomach again.

Kerr picked up his phone, dialled his phone banking number and keyed in the details. He would check his bank balance and then make his own way home. He had hidden this credit card from Willow, and it was strictly only to be used in an emergency. He considered being held hostage off the coast of Sicily as an emergency, and he waited while the automated voice gave his balance over the phone.

'You have one hundred and eleven pounds available,' the automated voice stated.

That can't be right, he thought, and he pressed the button to hear it again. 'You have one hundred and eleven pounds available,' said the voice again. 'To hear the last six transactions press two.'

Kerr pressed two, his hands shaking. There had been twelve thousand pounds on this card. 'Last six transactions. Monday the twelfth of June – The Apple Store – two thousand and twenty-one pounds. Tuesday the thirteenth of June – Net-A-Porter – three thousand one hundred and two pounds. Tuesday the thirteenth of June – Ralph Lauren – one thousand and seven pounds, twelve pence. Tuesday the thirteenth of June – Whole Life Foods – five hundred and forty-two pounds, eighty-two pence. Wednesday the fourteenth of June – Harrods – two hundred and twelve pounds, eleven pence. Thursday the fifteenth of June – Harrods – eight hundred and fourteen pounds, ninety-nine pence.'

Kerr hung up, rage pouring from him. Fucking Willow had his card details. Well she could go fuck herself. She was going to teach his girlfriend how to act and he was going to claim half of her wage; maybe even more if he got the kids.

Looking over to Tatiana, he said, 'Fuel the jet babe. I'm taking you to London to visit the Queen.'

'Really?' she asked, sitting up again. Perhaps she had misjudged Kerr.

'Not the real Queen, but I'm going to make you an actress. I spoke to Willow – she can't wait to meet you,' he said, and Tatiana clapped her hands and opened her legs.

'Then come and get your ticket to ride,' she purred and Kerr smiled at her open legs.

God knows Willow wasn't much in the sack, he thought as he moved towards Tatiana.

133

As he swapped positions with Tatiana and lay on the sun lounger, she jumped on top of his cock and rocked back and forth until she felt herself beginning to come.

'And the Oscar goes to Tatiana Rusellov!' she cried as she came, and Kerr watched her with bemusement. What the hell, if Willow could win one then there was no reason Tatiana couldn't either, he thought as he felt himself beginning to finish, and he grabbed her face as he came.

'You know it baby,' he said, and the two of them smiled at each other, each absorbed with their own satisfaction and their own sets of plans.

CHAPTER FOURTEEN

Willow and Ivo glanced at each other over the table.

She thought she knew him and sat racking her brains until she remembered. Yes, he was that boy Dicky Henley Smyth and his wife Tricky had brought to her cocktail party in London a few years before. Rumour had it that Dicky and Tricky were both in love with the boy, but Willow noticed the way he was eyeing Harold's assistant's ass as she bent down to adjust the legs of one of the tables, and assumed he must have been fucking Tricky, not Dicky.

The boy was pure testosterone, and Willow raised her eyebrows at him when he caught her eye to reprimand his ogling. He shrugged his shoulders as if to say, 'What can I do when faced with a wondrous ass like that?'

Willow made a face at him across the table, similar to the one she would have given Poppy had she been sprung doing something naughty, and Ivo poked his tongue out at her playfully. Willow suddenly felt old. There was a time when this young boy would have been making a play for her; now he was checking out the crew. Never a great sign, she thought, and she wondered when she had gone from ingénue to old crone.

Willow felt her phone vibrate in her pocket, and pulling it out she saw Lucy's number come up.

'Hey,' said Willow.

'Hello! I have good news,' sang Lucy's voice down the phone.

'Great, I could do with some,' said Willow softly, getting up from the table and leaving the ballroom to step outside on the terrace.

'I've had a call from Blessings' rep, and they want you to be the face of their next campaign.'

'Really? Oh my god!' cried Willow. She had forgotten what it was like to be wanted and chased after for work. It felt good.

'Yes, they saw you in *Hello!* and Kelly was adamant that you needed this gig. Their last face was Sapphira De Mont, who did really well for them, but she's having a baby and doesn't want to work for a while. It's yours if you want it.'

Willow did a little dance on the empty terrace. 'Tell them yes, yes!' she cried and Lucy laughed down the phone.

'Alright, I will, and I'll get back to you with the details.'

'Lucy, you are a star,' said Willow gratefully down the phone.

'No, you're the star. I just hold the spotlight,' said Lucy, doing her best Eliza impression, and she and Willow howled with laughter.

Willow put down the phone. Things were looking up finally. Blessings were the fastest-moving makeup line in the marketplace, created by makeup artist to the stars, Kelly Ryder. Kelly was the coolest person in the business and Willow had worked with her once before on a shoot for *Vanity Fair*. Then she had moved to London with Kerr and lost all contact with Kelly and Hollywood.

Willow looked back at the people at the table reading. They

were still awaiting Harold's arrival; people were milling about and drinking coffee and getting to know each other. It felt good to be a part of something again, and Willow felt happy for the first time in a very long time. She felt tears run down her cheeks. Walking down the steps onto the lawn, which was thankfully empty of crew, Willow sat on a stone bench and wept openly.

'Are you alright?' she heard a voice say, and she looked up and saw a figure looming over her. She rubbed her eyes and they adjusted to the light, and she saw Merritt standing in front of her.

He sat down on the cold bench next to her. 'Anything you want to share?' he asked, concerned.

'No, I'm happy,' she said, smiling.

'I never quite get Americans and their emotions,' he said drily and Willow laughed.

They sat in companionable silence for a while and then she spoke. 'You see, I have been unhappy for a long time. Over two years, I think, and I got used to living with it. Every day blurred into another day, and I did things to try and push the feelings away, and I thought that I would never know happiness again. And now, right now, I'm happy. And it feels fucking fantastic,' she said, looking into the distance, her hands clutching either side of the bench.

Merritt looked into the middle distance with her, not focusing on anything.

'Are you happy because you're working again?' he asked.

'I'm happy because I'm working, I'm making a difference to my children, I'm happy to be a part of something again and I'm happy to be here with . . .' Willow's voice cracked a little and she stopped.

Merritt sat still, desperate for her to continue, but she said nothing.

'I'm happy you're happy, and I'm happy you're here,' he said, his voice low with a touch of nervousness. He hoped and prayed that she wouldn't brush him off; he hoped he hadn't imagined the way he thought she looked at him. He waited, as though for the executioner's axe, and Willow said nothing; but he felt her hand touch his on the bench and he held it, thin and cold, in his warm soft paw, and the thrill of the touch brought butterflies to Willow's stomach.

They sat together holding hands and looked across the lawns at the dancing butterflies and the birds that came and went, until Willow heard a voice calling her name. Looking up she saw the young boy from the table reading who ogled asses looking over the edge of the terrace.

'Oi, they're calling you. We're ready,' he said, noticing the hands being held, and catching her eye he gave her the exact same look that she had given him earlier. She poked her tongue out at him as he had done and he laughed and turned inside again.

'I have to go and work,' she whispered.

'Off you go then. I'll meet you after work, OK?' he asked, and Willow nodded and blushed.

'Bye,' she said swiftly and kissed his cheek.

They faced each other and then Merritt smiled and leant down and kissed her gently on the mouth. His soft lips met hers and she parted them slightly and felt the tiniest flicker of tongue in her mouth. Then he pulled away and she stood, her knees weak. 'If I continue I don't think I'll be able to stop,' he said huskily.

'Don't stop,' said Willow, pushing herself against him.

'I have to stop. You need to go to work and I need a cold shower,' he laughed.

Willow let herself go. She pulled his face down to hers and kissed him with the passion of a woman who hasn't had sex in a long time and is feeling desires that she didn't know existed in her, and Merritt responded the same way. As they parted breathlessly, she smiled sexily at him.

'Wait for me?' she asked as she ran up the stairs.

'Always,' he said, and after she left he sat down on the stone bench again and wondered if he had just dreamed the interlude with Willow. But his tender mouth told him otherwise, and he laughed out loud. He too had forgotten what happiness felt like. It felt good.

As Willow went in for the table reading, she sat down and accepted the water bottle that was handed to her and then looked up to see Ivo looking at her with an amused expression. 'What?' she mouthed at him.

'Nothing,' he replied, and winked at her.

Willow blushed, remembering Merritt's kiss and her passionate response. Her thoughts were interrupted by Harold's arrival in a black astrakhan cloak, even though it was midsummer.

'Good afternoon,' he announced regally as he walked towards the end of the table and waited for Jenny, his assistant, to pull out his chair for him. Ivo wondered if he should stand – it was as though the Queen had entered the room – but he looked around and saw that people seemed quite relaxed. Only he seemed anxious, he realised, recognising several famous faces from British films. They seemed chummy and Ivo felt sick with nerves. As soon as we start to read they'll know I'm an imposter, he thought as he sat down and leafed through his script, trying to look like one of them.

Harold sat down and opened his script.

'I shan't bother with the introductions. I am sure you will all meet each other at the ball tomorrow. Please be aware that I will be filming part of it for the flashback scenes, so please try to be on your best behaviour and in character for at least the first part of the evening.'

The room laughed and Ivo looked around. What ball? he wondered, and he opened up his pack and found a stiff envelope containing a piece of card inscribed with black copperplate handwriting asking him to the ball tomorrow night. All costumes provided.

'Right then. Shall we start?' asked Harold.

Ivo was pleasantly surprised that no one looked at him like he was a hack and he even got a few compliments during the break, mostly from women, but an older man whom Ivo had watched as a child on his favourite show, a stalwart of British film, television and theatre, spoke to him too.

'Well done young man,' he said to Ivo over an orange cake on the catering table.

'Thanks,' said Ivo gratefully. 'It's all a bit nerve racking.'

'Oh no my dear. Just keep on doing it and you will find it comes more and more naturally,' said the older man. 'Thornton Wills,' he said, extending his hand.

'Ivo Casselton.'

Thornton eyed Ivo. 'Is Peregrine Casselton your father?'

Ivo paused. 'He is.'

'Ah, I went to Harrow with Perry. He was quite the actor too. I was always surprised that he never trod the boards,' said Thornton as he poured tea for himself and for Ivo.

140

'Really?' asked Ivo, intrigued. His father had been so against him acting, wanting him to take over the family estate instead, but Ivo couldn't imagine living in the country away from friends, women, drugs. Ivo tucked the information away at the back of his mind, unsure what to do with it but knowing it was important.

'Thanks for the advice,' said Ivo.

'No problem. Any time you need a hand with anything let me know. It's good to have a mentor when one is new. I would have been lost without Larry when I started out,' said Thornton in his cut-glass accent.

'Larry?' asked Ivo.

'Larry Olivier!' exclaimed Thornton.

'Of course,' said Ivo, trying to remember who Larry Olivier was and wondering if he was still around to coach him when he saw Willow walking towards them.

'Hello love,' said Thornton, and kissed her on both cheeks.

'Hi darling,' she said. 'How's James?' she asked.

'Heavenly,' said Thornton. 'Now how are you?' he asked, his face serious.

'OK. It's good to be working,' said Willow.

'Well if that is the panacea you need, then do it. Idle hands are the devil's work and all that,' said Thornton.

Ivo tried to walk away without being noticed, but Thornton grabbed his arm. 'Have you met Ivo properly?' he asked Willow.

'No, not formally,' she said to Thornton, and she turned to Ivo and put out her hand.

'Willow Carruthers.'

'Ivo Casselton.'

'Thornton, they need you in costume,' said Jenny as she walked up to the group.

'Oh dear, I think I need to stay off the cake or the waistcoats won't fit me,' laughed Thornton, and he handed his plate of cake to Ivo and walked away with Jenny.

'Thank you for not mentioning what you saw on the terrace,' said Willow, formally. 'Thornton's a bit of a gossip I'm afraid. I know him through mutual acquaintances.'

'No problem. Thanks for not mentioning my lecherous behaviour earlier.' He laughed and Willow found herself smiling at the young man. His energy and intensity during the reading was exciting, and she knew they would have a good chemistry on screen.

'So we're lovers,' he said.

'Pardon?'

'In the film,' said Ivo.

'Yes, we are,' said Willow. 'It's an amazing script.'

'Seems like a good yarn,' said Ivo casually, and Willow looked at him. 'Have you been in a film before?' she asked.

'Nope,' said Ivo, flushing a little as he munched on Thornton's orange cake.

'Really?' asked Willow. She was surprised at how good he was; he had a natural understanding of the timing and the text. The language in the film wasn't easy, it was very formal, but Ivo spoke it as though he was a Victorian suitor brought forward in time.

There was an awkward pause between them, Willow thinking about his prodigious talent and Ivo mistaking her silence for disappointment in his skills.

'It's an amazing house,' he said politely to break the silence.

'Yes, it is.' How was it so easy for him? thought Willow.

His natural talent was something she had worked so hard for, and there he was, like a young Lord Byron.

'You been here long?' asked Ivo again.

'Yes, a few weeks,' said Willow.

'Wow, then you must know the girl who owns the house,' said Ivo excitedly.

'What?' asked Willow, confused.

'The girl who owns the house. I met her this morning, she mentioned a brother too. Any chance you can introduce me?' asked Ivo.

'Kitty? You mean Kitty?' asked Willow.

'Is that her name? Kitty.' Ivo rolled it over his tongue and smiled wickedly at Willow. 'She's bloody stunning.'

'She's also my nanny,' said Willow sternly.

'Well, I might have to be a naughty boy then and see if she'll tell me off,' said Ivo.

Willow shook her head at him. 'I have a new name for you,' she said.

'What?' he asked, small crumbs of orange cake at the edges of his beautiful mouth.

'Ivo the Terrible,' she said, her voice serious.

'Let's hope so,' said Ivo and he sauntered off, his jeans loose on his slim hips, with the cocky stride of a man who knew he could have everything he wanted and come back for seconds.

CHAPTER FIFTEEN

Kitty looked at herself in the mirror and frowned. She felt ridiculous. The bodice of the dress was pushing her breasts up so high she could practically rest her chin on them, and the bones of the corset were digging into her ribs.

No wonder they carried smelling salts with them everywhere, thought Kitty as she tried to slip on a shoe without bending over.

Harold's insistence that Kitty and Merritt attend the ball along with a fully costumed crew and cast had Kitty terrified, but at Willow's insistence she went to the costume department, where racks of dresses ran along the walls of the trailer, and they squeezed Kitty into a sea-green taffeta ball gown with a wide neckline and small bows at the sleeves. The colour enhanced Kitty's dark features, and while her bobbed hair wasn't really the style of the day, the hair and makeup girls had pulled it back and pinned a matching hairpiece fashioned into an elegant bun at the nape of her neck.

As she opened the door, she saw Merritt pacing the hallway. Waiting for Willow, she thought. His handsome face broke into a smile when he saw her. 'You look amazing Kits,' he said.

'Thanks, but it's bloody uncomfortable,' she said, sighing.

'It looks wonderful,' he said. 'I might just wait and see if Willow needs help.'

144

Kitty raised her eyebrows at him. 'I'm sure she's able to dress herself,' she said. 'Anyway, she's not in there, she's being dressed in costume,' said Kitty. 'I took the children down there to say goodnight and set them up with the babysitter,' said Kitty.

'Oh,' said Merritt, looking dejected.

He had hardly seen Willow since their kiss in the garden yesterday. She had been held back late by Harold, who had wanted to discuss her and Ivo's scenes, and they had worked till midnight. Exhausted, she had returned to the house to find Merritt asleep in the drawing room. She had carefully laid a rug over him and crept up to bed, disappointed and relieved. All afternoon Merritt's kiss had remained in her mind, and the longer she thought about it the less it seemed like a good idea.

Then she had been up early to start shooting and had not even had time to see the children, let alone Merritt.

Merritt pulled at his white bow tie and waistcoat. 'What do you think?' he asked, his face suddenly clouded with doubt.

'I think you look great. This look actually suits you,' said Kitty. It was true; Merritt's body shape and height gave him the distinct look of a hero. 'You should be on the front of a romance novel,' laughed Kitty.

As they walked downstairs together, Kitty's pace slowed. 'Hurry up slow coach,' said Merritt.

'Shut up. This dress does not encourage fast movements,' said Kitty. 'I have no idea how I'm supposed to dance in this. Do you think they'll have a DJ?' she asked.

Merritt laughed, 'Kits, it's a formal ball, Victorian style. Harold is filming it for flashbacks in the film or something.'

'Shit,' said Kitty, almost standing on the hem of the dress. 'It sounds boring.'

'I think it'll be fun,' said Merritt, his eyes dancing with enthusiasm. Kitty had never seen him like this before.

'You're being weird,' she said. 'Are you in love with Willow?' she burst out.

Merritt spun and looked at her on the stairs. 'No. Why do you say that?' he barked.

'Well, I've seen the way you look at her, that's all,' she answered honestly.

Merritt continued down the stairs silently.

'Sorry I brought it up,' said Kitty quietly.

'Don't worry about it,' said Merritt, but Kitty's words rang in his ears. Was he in love with Willow? He hardly knew her, and yet something had sparked in him when Kitty asked him.

As they neared the ballroom they took in the chaos, with Harold on a large crane with a camera and a man to work it. Crew who weren't in the ball scenes were rushing about with cords and tracks and lighting rigs.

Kitty and Merritt stood to the side, alone, waiting for instructions, while other costumed crew laughed and milled about. Kitty felt very isolated even with Merritt by her side.

Harold's voice boomed out over a loudspeaker.

'Thank you. I would like silence please. Tonight it's vital that we get this right. I have a few requests. Please try and be Victorian; gentlemanly men and feminine women. You may flirt and drink the champagne on offer, but please don't get drunk and ruin my picture.'

Kitty looked up at Harold, who was wearing a silk turban and headphones as he continued his instructions.

'I have four cameras set up and I also have hidden cameras around. We have dancers coming who will fill the dance floor, but if you are so moved and can do a basic waltz, then please

146

join them. Be yourselves, only be a better, more refined version. And have fun,' he ordered.

Music floated out over the speakers and Kitty saw a small group of musicians playing along in the corner of the ballroom. Waiters walked about the room in full costume handing out glasses of punch and champagne and Kitty gratefully accepted one.

'You better take small sips,' said Merritt, looking at her tiny waist in her dress.

'Good idea,' she said, and sipped from the glass delicately.

The mirrored doors of the ballroom opened and Merritt stood silent and expressionless as Willow entered the room. Her dress was a copy of an original Charles Worth, the Chanel of his day. In golden yellow silk with beaded crystals catching the light, the dress came down in a low-cut sweetheart neckline. Lace hung at her shoulders, gently beaded so as to caress her arms when she danced.

Willow's long blonde hair was swept into an elegant chignon with matching crystal hairpieces, and her earrings were original Victorian gold and diamond teardrops. Kitty felt her mouth drop open at the sight of her employer in all her splendour, and she turned to Merritt, who seemed equally stunned.

Willow stood patiently as a makeup artist powdered her face and décolletage, and then Harold yelled from his perch in the ballroom's eaves.

'Ready when you are!'

Kitty felt nervous although she had no idea why. She wondered if he would be here, and she tried to scan the room without looking desperate.

The dancers were gorgeous to watch, and she eventually

forgot to look for the boy with the hooded eyes and sexy mouth. Instead, she watched the colour and movement in the centre of the room.

Willow walked over to Kitty and Merritt and snapped her fan at them. 'What do you think?' she asked coyly, and Kitty laughed.

'You look amazing,' she answered honestly.

'It's so uncomfortable,' said Willow. 'I'm trying not to fidget.'

'I know the feeling,' said Kitty, feeling an itch on her back.

'You look lovely Kitty,' said Willow and Merritt nodded.

'She does look quite the part,' he said.

'No compliments for me, Mr Middlemist?' asked Willow, flirting gently.

Merritt felt his face redden.

'There are not enough compliments in the world that I could bestow upon you, so instead I will say, "You are beautiful".' He bowed slightly as he said this and Willow felt her knees weaken. Any resolve she might have had to tell Merritt that their clandestine kiss on the stone bench was a terrible idea disappeared.

Kitty stepped away silently towards the small group next to them.

'I wanted to see you last night,' he said in a low voice to Willow.

'I know. I got caught up,' said Willow. The space between them was electric, and she held back the desire to pull his face towards her.

They stood side by side, Merritt standing tall in his costume.

'Do you dance?' he asked, looking at the floor of spinning petticoats.

'A little, although not like that,' said Willow.

The music stopped and the sound of a waltz rang through the ballroom. Merritt bowed towards Willow again. 'Will you do me the honour of giving me this dance?' he asked, and Willow looked at him, surprised.

'I don't think Harold wants us to dance,' she said.

'We shall start, and if he wants us to stop then we will,' he said, and taking her arm he led her to the edge of the dance floor, and artfully pulled her into his arms as they turned about the floor.

The other dancers looked at them surprised, but continued dancing around them. Willow had never felt more real and alive, even in the midst of the bizarre setting.

'Imagine living in these times,' said Willow, 'so caught up in rules and reputation.'

'Yes, I couldn't do it at all,' said Merritt.

'You could have fooled me, with all your bowing and manners,' laughed Willow.

'Manners are one thing, but the truth is I am having very modern thoughts about you, Miss Carruthers, and none of them would have passed in Victorian times,' he whispered into her ear. Willow burst out laughing and tried to stop it.

'I should be shocked at you, Mr Middlemist,' she said, tapping him on the shoulder lightly with her fan.

'I hope you are; I want to shock you,' he growled, and Willow felt desire in every part of her body.

'Jesus Christ,' she whispered. 'You have to stop or I don't know what I'll do.'

Merritt held a respectable distance between them as he turned her about the floor, but he looked into her eyes and smiled a little. 'What would you do, if you could?' he asked.

'Everything,' she whispered.

'Tell me,' he demanded, tightening his grip on her back.

Willow felt herself lean against his arms. She felt lightheaded and strange.

'I think I might faint,' she said, and Merritt spun her out onto the terrace into the cool air.

There was no one else out there yet. Willow clasped the edge of the stone balustrade.

'Are you OK? Should you sit down?' asked Merritt, concerned.

Willow tried to draw breath and Merritt stood helplessly. 'I think I should get someone to help you,' he said, his voice anxious.

'I don't need help,' she said as she turned to him, her eyes flashing.

'What I need is for you to kiss me,' she burst out. 'I've been alone for so long, I forgot what it's like to be wanted, to be desired again. I want you so much I ache. I know you don't want some sad, washed-up, broke actress with three kids; I wouldn't want me. And I know you're not the marrying kind and you travel the world and are generally fabulous, and you think it's fun to flirt with me; but you have to understand – I am gone. Lost. The minute you look at me I fall apart. I haven't felt like this in a long, long time.'

Merritt tried to interrupt her but she held her fan out as though it was a sword.

'Shut up. I don't expect anything from you, but I can't play games. I don't have the time or the energy. If you want to kiss me again, which I am pretty sure you do, then take me – because I'm dying here.'

Merritt started to laugh.

'What? Do you think I'm tragic?' she almost yelled at him.

Merritt pulled her to him. 'No, I told you, I think you're beautiful,' he said. He kissed her hard and she fell into his arms, kissing him back.

'We have to go,' she said, pulling away from him.

'Where?' he asked, breathing heavily.

'Anywhere.'

'What about the film? Harold?' he asked.

'NOW,' she demanded, and she pulled Merritt to her again, kissing his mouth so hard he thought she might bite him.

Merritt pulled her towards the stairs.

'Wait,' she said, pulling at her dress, which was caught on the stone balustrade. Finally it pulled free, and Merritt took her hand and dragged her across the grass into the darkness.

As they ran they stopped every few steps to kiss and Willow thought she might die from desire, but Merritt kept pulling her along by the hand till they came around to the outside of the house. Merritt stood in front of the wall and then felt inside a gap in the stone. He pulled on a handle and a door shifted open in the side of the house.

'You've got to be kidding me!' exclaimed Willow, her desire forgotten for a moment.

'Nope. Secret passage,' said Merritt, and he pulled her into the tunnel. The door closed behind them. It was completely dark, and Willow stood scared for a moment till Merritt's calloused hand took hers again.

'This way,' he said, and in the darkness she followed him, tripping on the rough granite, but Merritt caught her arm and held her up.

He stopped and pushed on a door with all his body weight

while Willow stood there waiting, and suddenly they were in a bedroom.

'Where are we?' she asked, looking around the room. It seemed to be untouched: heavy wood furniture and a four-poster bed with a blue silk counterpane. Surprisingly, the room wasn't dusty. 'Why's it so clean?' she asked Merritt suspiciously.

'The film production crew cleaned the whole house in case Harold wanted to shoot here.'

Willow felt nervous and silly in her dress in the old-fashioned room. She stood in front of the stone fireplace, her hands clasped in front of her.

Merritt stepped forward. 'It's my turn to speak now.' He held his hand up to Willow's mouth to stop her speaking.

'I'm not famous or rich. I am the marrying kind. I was married once, but she cheated on me in a most spectacular fashion. It broke my heart. That's why I travel. I haven't ever found anyone that I wanted to stick around for. Till now.'

As Merritt spoke, he pulled at the pearl buttons that ran up her back till the dress fell open, and he slipped it off her shoulders. He kissed her collarbones and his tongue gently flickered on her throat. 'What I feel is more than desire, and you can do what you want with that statement. I knew as soon as I saw you walking down the stairs as though you owned the place that you were exactly what I needed.'

Willow stood in her petticoat and slip and Merritt moved away from her and walked to the bed, pulling at his tie and undoing his waistcoat. Sitting on the edge of the bed, he pulled off his jacket and sat in his shirtsleeves, part of his chest showing. Willow felt exposed and vulnerable.

'Undress,' commanded Merritt.

'Pardon?' asked Willow, her eyes widening.

'Take off your clothes,' said Merritt, leaning back languidly on an elbow.

Willow looked at Merritt as though he was a new man. Gone was the angry, bullying gardener. Gone was the opinionated man she had first met, and the gentle listening giant that had held her hand on the stone bench. Instead here was the sexiest man she had ever seen, in Victorian costume, in a room where time had stopped.

Willow smiled at him and pulled at the ribbons on the petticoats. They fell to the floor. Now she stood in Victorian bloomers and a camisole with a corset over the top.

Merritt's eyes flickered over her and despite all her coverings, Willow felt naked.

She walked towards him and turned her back. 'Unlace me,' she said, and Merritt did as she asked. Taking it slow he pulled at each lace, gradually releasing her. Willow felt her ribcage expanding again.

Pulling off the corset, she stepped out of the bloomers and the camisole and stood naked before him, in nothing but the beaded headdress.

'Jesus you're beautiful,' he said, and pulled her towards him onto the bed.

Pulling off his shirt while they kissed passionately, she ran her hands over his chest. He had the body of a man who knew what real work was, tanned and with chest hair and muscles that rippled under her slim hands.

They kissed again, and this time it was slower. Merritt worked his way down her body, kissing her breasts and stomach and between her thighs. Willow arched her back towards him and Merritt slipped out of his trousers and lay next to her.

'How do you want it?' he asked her.

'What do you mean?' she asked, her face worried.

'You tell me what you want and I will do it. There are no strings, no expectations, so tell me. I don't know you, you don't know me. Let go.'

Willow lay still. She had never had this offered to her before, and she was unsure what to do with the proposition.

Merritt rolled towards her and leaned above her. 'You tell me what you want. Do you want me to kiss you here?' he asked and he kissed her left breast.

'Yes,' she murmured as he sucked her left nipple gently.

'Or here?' he asked as he moved over to suck her right nipple.

Willow grabbed his face and held it in her hands. 'Enough with the small talk; just fuck me and we can fill in the blanks later,' she demanded, and reaching down she found his cock with her hand and tried to guide it in between her legs.

Merritt rolled on top of her and she parted her legs; he entered her and she arched her back moving in rhythm with him. They flipped over and she straddled him and rode him with a fervour that she didn't know was in her. 'Jesus, oh shit!' she cried as she came, and Merritt watched pleasure wash over her face.

She rolled off him. 'Your turn,' she said, trying to catch her breath. Merritt pulled her to him and, spooning her, he stroked her head. 'Better now?' he asked and she laughed.

Merritt started to fondle her breasts and she found herself moaning again. He entered her from behind and they moved slowly this time, without the intensity of before; he felt himself moving in and out of her wetness and thrust harder, pushing himself into her. She moaned with ecstasy and he whispered hoarsely, 'I'm going to come. Come with me.' Willow let herself go and went for her second orgasm with Merritt, laughing and crying at the same time.

Across the house, Harold watched the footage of Merritt and Willow dancing and then them on the balcony, filmed by the night vision hidden camera. He watched them talking. Arguing perhaps? he wondered, and then he saw them kiss and she fell into his arms.

'Delightful,' said Harold in the edit suite, and he clapped his hands together with joy. He sat back in his chair, put his velvet-slippered feet up on the desk, and took a sip of his warm, sweet tea. He raised it to the still on the screen, of Willow in Merritt's embrace.

CHAPTER SIXTEEN

Kitty stood in the ballroom and wondered where Merritt and Willow had gone. She felt alone and out of place, aware of the cameras and self-conscious. She wanted to disappear to her room and put on her tracksuit bottoms and warm cardigan and watch *Britain's Got Talent*. I wonder if I snuck out if anyone would notice, she thought, and she edged towards the ballroom doors. As she tried to move through them she tripped on a cable and went sprawling into the hallway. Lifting her head she saw a pair of shining dress shoes in front of her eyes.

'You OK?' she heard, and she knew whose voice it was before she had tried to lift herself from the ground.

She felt strong arms lift her up and she peered into Ivo's face.

'Hello,' he said, and smiled at her.

'Um, hi,' she said, and tried to pull herself together.

Ivo glanced down at her and then looked back at her face. 'Your breasts are lovely, but I don't think it's quite in keeping with current fashion.'

Kitty frowned at him. 'This is how they wore it back then,' she said huffily.

'Really?' smiled Ivo. He stood back, crossed his arms and looked down at her chest.

Kitty stared at him. 'Are you alright?' she asked.

'Fine actually. I could stare at your breast all day if you let me.'

Kitty looked down and saw that part of her breast had fallen out of her dress when she had tripped and the edge of her nipple was on display. 'Fuck,' she said and tried to tuck it back in.

'Yes please,' said Ivo.

'What?' She looked at him horrified.

'I thought you were offering, displaying your wares et cetera,' laughed Ivo.

'You're gross,' said Kitty, reprimanding herself for liking such a lascivious prick. Clearly he was just like every other guy she knew.

'Not gross, but horny, definitely,' he said, and Kitty made a face at him.

'Go away. To think, all these years,' she said, shaking her head as she walked away.

'Kitty, Kitty!' She heard a female voice call her name and turned to see the babysitter Willow had hired from an agency in London walking quickly towards her.

'Hi. Is everything alright?' Kitty asked.

'Not really. It's Lucian. He refuses to go to bed and instead he's under it and he won't come out,' she said, exasperated. 'I'm sorry to interrupt you.'

'Oh, it's OK. I was coming upstairs anyway,' she said pointedly to Ivo who was watching with interest.

'You go back to your hotel and I'll take care of it,' said Kitty.

'You sure?' asked the woman, obviously happy to be away from the child who didn't speak.

'It's fine. Get your things and I'll sort it out,' said Kitty as she followed the babysitter up the stairs to the children's rooms. The woman grabbed her bag and ran down the stairs, only too happy to get away.

Kitty went to her room, pulled off the dress, put on her tracksuit bottoms and a t-shirt and cardigan and padded into Poppy and Lucian's room. Ivo watched her from the corner of the hallway. She was unaware of his presence, and she left the bedroom door open.

Poppy was sleeping peacefully in one of the twin beds. Kitty sat on the floor.

'Hello Luce. It's Kits. How are things under the bed? Find any treasures like Poppy?' she asked gently.

Silence greeted her questions, so Kitty tried a new tactic. 'Lucian, how about you come out and we go on an adventure?'

Lucian remained under the bed. Kitty had a flash of inspiration and got up from the floor. She sprinted down to Merritt's room.

Looking around, she opened his wardrobe, and reaching up to the top shelf she found what she was searching for. She came back quickly with her prize, and sitting on the floor she started to talk.

'Poor Custard. Nobody loves him any more. What's that?' she asked.

'Ah, yes, I know you miss Merritt, but he's all grown up now. I don't know anyone who can look after you,' she said and waited. Silence greeted her. 'You want someone to look after you? Poor Custard, I'm sure there might be someone here. I would ask Lucian but he's under the bed and won't come out,' she said sadly.

Ivo stood hidden by the door watching Kitty as she spoke to a worn teddy bear.

'Perhaps if Lucian would come out then he might be your new friend. I know that Merritt would love if he would help you, Custard,' she said, and Ivo saw a small blond head pop out from under the bed. The small boy looked at the object of Kitty's conversation and waited.

Kitty continued as though Lucian was still under the bed. 'Don't cry, Custard. I'm sure I can find you someone to love and take care of you. Perhaps Poppy, although you may end up wearing jewels and covered in crayons; or Jinty, but she only likes to suck things.'

Lucian darted out from under the bed and snatched Custard from Kitty's hand.

'Hello Luce,' she said, as though him being under the bed was perfectly normal. 'This is Custard. He was Merritt's friend, but he has been so lonely. Do you think you can look after him for Merritt? I asked him and he said it was fine.'

Lucian held the bear close to his face as though he was inhaling it and he kissed it. It was the most affection he had ever shown anything, and Kitty smiled at him joyfully. 'Will you take good care of him, Luce?' she asked, and Lucian nodded slowly. Kitty felt her heart bursting.

'I love you Lucian,' she said as she scooped the small boy up and popped him into bed. 'Now Custard is very tired and needs to sleep. Will you lie here with him while he sleeps?' Lucian snuggled down under the covers and Kitty kissed his head. 'Goodnight darling,' she said, and she left the room, closing the door behind her.

'I know you,' she heard behind her and she spun around to find Ivo leaning against the wall.

'What are you doing up here?' she asked angrily. 'Were you spying on me?'

'Yes,' answered Ivo simply. 'I know you from Willow's party. You helped that child leave the party when he was in some sort of train trance,' he said.

'I don't remember you,' lied Kitty.

'Really? We spoke in the kitchen for a while.'

'Nope, don't remember,' said Kitty as she walked towards the nanny quarters, where the heating worked best, desperate for a cup of tea.

Ivo followed her down the hall and into the room.

'You shouldn't be here.' Kitty felt nervous in his presence.

'Maybe, but the ball is boring and you are much more fun,' he said as he walked in and sat on one of the armchairs. 'You did well with the kid. He's not right, yeah?' he asked.

'He's fine,' bristled Kitty as she set about making the tea.

'I'll have mine black with one sugar,' he said.

Kitty frowned, but took an extra mug down and dumped a teabag in it.

'Where's their mother?' asked Ivo.

'I have no idea,' said Kitty.

'With the gardener no doubt,' laughed Ivo. 'It's all very D H Lawrence isn't it?'

'Who's D H Lawrence?' asked Kitty in spite of herself.

'The writer? Wrote *Lady Chatterley's Lover*? The book about the lady who has an affair with her gardener. Or perhaps it was a gamekeeper,' he mused to himself.

'I haven't read it,' said Kitty.

'Then you must,' said Ivo. 'I'm Ivo, by the way,' he offered.

'Kitty,' she offered in return.

'I know,' he said.

'How do you know?'

'Lady Chatterley told me when I asked about you, and I

160

remember you told me when I met you in her kitchen in London.'

Kitty said nothing, wondering what Willow had told him about her. Then she spoke quickly. 'How do you know about Willow and Merritt?' she asked.

'Is that his name?' asked Ivo. 'I saw them snogging in the garden yesterday,' he said, his eyes glinting in the lamplight.

'Really?' asked Kitty, intrigued. Merritt had got to work fast, she thought.

'Yes, all very sexy,' said Ivo, stretching out his long legs and putting them on the worn ottoman in front of him.

'Wow,' said Kitty, breathing heavily. 'I hope this doesn't end badly,' she said aloud.

'Why does it concern you? Probably just a quick fuck while she's on location,' said Ivo, looking at her cardigan straining against her breasts.

'Well, Merritt's my brother,' said Kitty with a shrug of the shoulders.

'Ah yes, then it could be a problem.'

Kitty put the tea beside him on the table and sat opposite him. 'Do you like being an actor?' she asked politely.

'Dunno yet. This is my first real job,' said Ivo, blowing on his tea. 'Do you like being a nanny?' he asked.

'I suppose it's alright. I don't think I'd be much good at anything else,' she said. 'I like the children. I love them actually.' She smiled and Ivo thought how lovely her face was when she felt joy.

'You didn't go to university?' he asked.

'No.'

'Why not?'

'I didn't want to,' snapped Kitty.

161

Ivo put the tea down and looked at the pile of worn leather journals. Kitty had taken them out of her room and left them there.

'What are these?' he asked.

Kitty looked at him. 'Are you always so nosy and rude?' she asked.

'I'm not being rude, I just asked what these are,' he said, not looking up from the journals, which were now in his elegant hands.

'They're journals. They were found last week but I haven't had time to go through them yet,' she said.

'Look at this handwriting. It's like art,' he said, turning the pages carefully. 'Some of it's in French,' he said. 'Do you speak French?'

'No.'

'I do. I could translate it for you if you like,' he said.

Kitty paused. She had promised Merritt she would go through them, but now they were in French she had a perfect excuse.

'Really? You would do that for me?' she asked, her dark eyes narrowing.

'Absolutely, on one condition,' he said, looking at her.

'What?' she asked carefully.

'You show me your other boob,' he said, and Kitty laughed at him.

'Very funny!'

'No, I'll do this for you and you can help me with my lines. I only got the script yesterday and it's so wordy. Would you?'

Kitty felt her stomach sink, and she tried not to look at him as she felt tears pricking her eyes. She could think of nothing better than to help this gorgeous, flirtatious man, the one she had been thinking of for so long, with his lines – any excuse to spend time with him – but instead she looked away.

'I don't think so, I'm really busy with the children. Sorry.'

Ivo looked at her closely, his eyes narrowing a little. 'No drama, I can learn them on my own. But I would still like to help you with these; gives me something to do besides learn lines and chase you.'

Kitty looked up at him quickly to see if he was serious and she saw he was. He raised an eyebrow at her, as if to say, *If you'll let me.*

'If you want,' she said quietly.

'What? Read the journals or chase you?' he asked, leaning forward, and Kitty felt her face flush.

'The journals, of course.' But her face gave her away and Ivo winked at her, the tiniest of winks, and Kitty felt her stomach give way to butterflies.

'Then the journals it is,' said Ivo, and he drained his tea, picked up the books and headed to the door. 'Night Pussycat. Sleep tight.'

And then he left, and Kitty breathed a sigh of relief and disappointment.

CHAPTER SEVENTEEN

Willow and Merritt snuck back into the other wing of the house in a state of undress and bliss. They crept into the hallway and stopped outside her room. 'I'd ask you in, but the kids come into my bed in the morning,' she said, and Merritt smiled.

'I know,' he said.

They stood facing each other, clutching their costumes.

'Right then. Night,' said Willow, embarrassed.

Merritt pulled her into his arms and kissed her gently on the mouth. 'Thank you,' he whispered, and Willow felt her knees buckle. She opened the door with one hand and dragged him inside. They dropped the clothes and headed to her bed kissing, and she pulled the covers back so they could slip underneath them, the cool sheets a shock to their warm bodies.

Lying her down on the bed he kissed her all over, and Willow let him take her. This time he lay on top of her and watched her face as he entered her, and together they reached a climax that Willow thought was going to drown her.

They lay together, Willow's head on his chest, and they slept soundly.

Merritt was woken by breath on his face. He opened one eye and saw Lucian standing in his pyjamas at the edge of the bed, face to face with him. Merritt, startled, woke Willow, and she sat up and saw Lucian.

'Hi Luce,' she said casually.

He smiled at her and she felt her heart pound. He never smiled.

'What you got there?' she asked, pulling the covers up around her nakedness.

Lucian clambered onto the bed and sat in between them, pulling the covers up over his lap, and held out Custard.

'Is that Custard?' asked Merritt, surprised.

Lucian held the bear close to him. Merritt smiled at the small boy. 'I'm glad you found him, although I have no idea where.'

'Who's Custard?' asked Willow, looking at the worn bear.

'My bear from when I was a child. Maybe Kitty found it,' said Merritt, looking at his childhood friend. Willow went to get out of bed and felt Lucian's hand on her arm pulling her back in. 'I have to get up, Luce,' she said, but Lucian held her arm tightly.

'Alright, just a minute then,' said Willow, settling back into bed. The three of them lay there in silence while Lucian tucked Custard under his arm. He held his mother's arm and put his head on Merritt's pillow.

Merritt lay still, smelling the boy's clean hair. It was so bizarre to experience this feeling of contentment. He wondered if Willow felt it as well.

Willow, however, was silently freaking out, panicking that Poppy would soon come darting into the room. The door opened quietly and Kitty poked her head around. 'Sorry, is Lucian . . .?' she started, and then saw the three of them in bed. Willow felt her face turn the colour of beetroot.

'Hi Lucian,' she said, not missing a beat. 'Morning Merritt, morning Willow. When you three are ready I have eggs and bacon,' said Kitty, a small smile filling her voice. 'Or I could bring them up to you if you like.' She looked at Merritt, whose turn it was to flush red.

'No, no, we are just coming,' said Willow, not moving.

'Come on Luce, you get first pick of the bacon!' Lucian jumped over Merritt and ran towards the door and down the hallway. Kitty closed the door, held her hand over her mouth and ran down after him. Well done Merritt, she thought as she served up the bacon.

Willow sat on the edge of the bed. 'Oh god, I'm so sorry,' she said, her head in her hands.

Merritt rolled over and ran a finger up her spine. 'It's fine. Lucian's sweet,' he said honestly. 'I liked it actually.'

'You say that now. Wait till you have three of them in the bed,' she laughed, shivering at his touch.

Merritt nuzzled against her back. 'Come back to bed,' he whispered.

Willow tried to stand. 'I have to get up. God, what will Kitty be thinking?' she said.

'She'll be fine. She won't care. Kitty's pretty Zen about things, I think you'll find.' Merritt pulled her about the waist and laid her back on the bed. 'Now, there is something I like to do in the mornings. Want me to show you?' He laughed, and leant down to kiss her, his unshaven face rubbing against her cheek.

'Make it quick,' she said, half jokingly.

'Not a chance lady,' he said, and disappeared under the covers.

Kitty fed the children and waited for their mother to come downstairs. Today was Saturday and there was no filming, so Willow had promised Kitty she could have some time off. She sat waiting in the kitchen. It was now ten o'clock and there was still no sign of her brother and her employer. I knew this would get messy, she thought, and she pulled out the vacuum and started to clean the hallway, hoping to disturb them.

It worked, and Willow, wearing a robe, poked her head out of the door. 'Just going to have a shower and then you can head off, Kitty,' she said casually, as though she hadn't just been fucking her brother all morning.

'Thanks,' said Kitty. She left the vacuum where it was, went to her bedroom and looked at her reflection. She had the urge to head to the village where she knew Ivo was staying and hang around until she saw him. She had tried to think of a better plan but couldn't come up with one. It had worked in school, so why not now? she thought.

Dressing carefully, she pulled on her jeans and her black boots. She wore a white t-shirt with a blue jacket of her father's over the top, the sleeves rolled up to show the pink silk lining.

She went into the nanny quarters where she had left the piles of clothes that Poppy had found in the eaves and she pulled at them till she found what she was looking for: a silk paisley-print scarf in purples, pinks and greens, almost a shawl, that she rolled up and slung casually around her neck.

As an afterthought she pulled a thin gold chain out of the box of costume jewellery and put it around her neck. It hung long on her, and it was a little tarnished. On it hung a gold pendant: a circle of seed pearls surrounding a painting of a man's eye. Hair curled around the image.

It swung between Kitty's breasts and she liked the weight of it around her neck. Applying a small amount of lip gloss she skipped down the stairs, where she found Merritt waiting for her by the front door, dressed for gardening.

'Sorry about this morning,' he said sheepishly.

'Doesn't bother me,' she said cheerfully, as she grabbed her bag.

'Where you off to?' he asked. 'You look nice.'

'The village. Need anything?' she sang as she swung open the huge front door.

'No,' said Merritt, wondering what had put such a spring in her step.

Kitty walked down the driveway and went to the bus stop at the end of the street.

The buses ran every half hour on a Saturday, so Kitty sat down to wait. She thought about Merritt and Willow. Although it seemed odd, they kind of made sense together. Her brother was misunderstood, but he was inherently good; he just didn't always know how to deal with people, she thought. He was smart and clever and could grow anything. Why did all the talents in the family bypass her? she wondered.

Kitty saw the bus rumbling towards her and she stood up as it came to a stop. There was someone waiting at the door and she stood back to let him step off. It was Ivo.

'Hello. I was coming to pay you a visit,' he said.

'Oh,' said Kitty, flustered and pleased to see him. 'I was heading into the village,' she said, and they stood awkwardly, Kitty on the ground and Ivo on the bus steps.

'On or off?' called the impatient driver. Kitty jumped on and Ivo grabbed her as the doors closed behind her and the bus lurched forward.

Ivo led her to a seat and squashed in beside her. They were the only ones on the bus. Kitty tried to act cool as she looked out the window.

'Aren't you going to ask me why I was coming to see you?' asked Ivo, nudging her with his elbow.

'Oh yes, right. I forgot. Why?' she asked, staring out of the window at the green fields.

'I thought about you all night,' he said, and Kitty turned to look at him. 'I was reading your journals.' Kitty nodded.

'Oh,' she said for lack of anything else to say.

'Why didn't you tell me that your great-great-great-grandfather was George Middlemist?' he said.

'I didn't think it was important. Why?'

'Those journals you gave me are written by his wife, Clementina,' said Ivo.

'Really? That's amazing. What does she say?' asked Kitty excitedly.

'I've just started them and the language is very formal, but it seems to be her diary of her marriage,' said Ivo.

'Amazing,' said Kitty, her eyes widening.

'Do you know much about her?' asked Ivo, looking at the necklace between her breasts.

'Nothing really. Maybe Merritt knows something. It's all a bit sad really. We don't have one painting of George's in the house; it was the bane of my father's life,' she said.

'Not one?' asked Ivo, surprised. 'I thought he was quite prolific.'

'Do you know much about him? I would love to know

more,' said Kitty, turning in her seat, her knees pressed against his.

'I know a bit from university. I rather liked his work. Some people thought it was a bit poncy but I like how he painted women as women. Women who looked like you,' he said, his eyes searching her face.

Kitty felt herself blush.

'You can read the journals after I've translated them,' he said, and Kitty looked away.

'So, why were you heading into town? Looking for me perhaps?' he said, noticing her carefully applied eyeliner and lip gloss.

'Does every girl fall for your routine?' asked Kitty, not looking at him, feeling more stupid than usual thanks to him guessing her plan.

'Yes,' answered Ivo with a shrug. 'Usually.'

'I'm not one of those girls, so you needn't bother,' said Kitty, wondering why she had bothered to dress up. Ivo wasn't boyfriend material; he was a major player and she was fooling herself.

'Alright. Friends then?' asked Ivo and he held out his hand. Kitty took it. It was smooth and soft; the hand of a man who didn't know hard work.

'OK,' she said softly. Maybe being friends with Ivo would be OK. She knew his type; he reminded her of Johnny the lying bastard, she thought, and she looked back out of the window.

'So, what shall we do in the village? Not much to do – I had a look around; took me all of ten minutes,' laughed Ivo.

'Yes, it's not London, I'm afraid,' laughed Kitty. And they

sat easily together as the bus rounded the corner into the village centre. Kitty alighted and waited for Ivo to descend from the steps.

'So what are you going to do?' he asked.

'I have to go to the shop and buy a few things,' mumbled Kitty.

'That will take all of five minutes. Then what?' he asked, putting his hands in his pockets.

'Um, then I guess I'll go home,' she said, squinting into the light.

'No – how about a pub lunch?' he said, pointing in the direction of the pub. 'It's the least I could do for a friend.' Ivo had checked his bank account the night before and had been thrilled to find it topped up. His first instalment for the film had come through.

'OK,' said Kitty shyly.

'I'll meet you there then?' asked Ivo, his face searching hers.

'Yep,' said Kitty, and she walked in the direction of the store.

Wandering about the small store, she pulled random items out and put them in her basket. Tampons, nail polish remover, a magazine, chocolate, hairspray; she didn't need any of them.

She stood at the counter as Mrs Turner, the wife of the shop owner, rang up her goods.

'You've set the village in a tizzy,' she said.

'Pardon?' asked Kitty, wondering how the town knew of her lascivious thoughts about Ivo.

'The film,' said Mrs Turner. 'It's all anyone is talking about. All the B&Bs are full up and you can't move in the pub at night,' she said knowledgeably.

'Ah yes,' smiled Kitty politely.

171

'What's she like then?'

'Who?' Kitty feigned ignorance.

'Willow Carruthers. I read all about her in *OK!* magazine. Poor thing, with her husband being such a cad and all,' she said as she put the items into a plastic bag.

'She's very nice,' said Kitty.

'Oooo, you met her then,' said Mrs Turner.

'Just briefly,' said Kitty, knowing that if she said anything to the town gossip, Willow would never get any peace. The Middlemist family had always kept to themselves, and Kitty was happy to keep the tradition going.

'Thanks Mrs Turner,' said Kitty, and she went to leave the store, wondering if Ivo would be waiting for her. She thought of his eyes when he was sitting with her on the bus; she knew he was looking at her breasts but she found herself not minding. She had actually hunched her shoulders and pushed them closer together at one point when she saw him looking at her. This behaviour was new to Kitty. The sex she had had was pleasant but not earth shattering, but she had the distinct feeling Ivo would know his way around a girl's body. Just thinking about it made her groin throb. She felt dirty and blushed as she stood by the counter.

'Is it all sex then?' hissed Mrs Turner, as Kitty turned to leave.

'Sorry?' asked Kitty. Was the old bat reading her mind?

'On the film set, in the house – you know what you read about in the magazines.' She pointed at the rack of magazines near the counter.

Kitty opened the door to the shop and looked across the road. She could see Ivo sitting at a table outside in the sun nursing a pint, with another one waiting for her. Kitty admired the easy way he leaned back in the chair. He was pure sex, and Kitty knew that if she wanted, she could have him, no strings attached. She thought about Merritt in bed with Willow, a sight she was both comforted by and envious of, and she saw Ivo wave at her. Kitty waved back and turned to Mrs Turner.

'Yes Mrs Turner, I'm afraid it is. All sex, sex, sex and then some more sex. That's why I'm in the village – to get away from the sex,' said Kitty seriously, and she heard Mrs Turner's little cry as she danced across the road towards the waiting Ivo.

'Get everything?' asked Ivo.

'Yep,' said Kitty, and she drank from her pint.

'Want me to get a menu?' asked Ivo.

'No, I always have the same thing when I come here,' said Kitty. 'Fish and chips.'

'Alright, then I'll have the same,' he said, and he went inside to order. Kitty felt pretty good, sitting in her village with such a handsome man.

She smiled to herself and Ivo walked out.

'What you laughing at then?'

'Nothing. Just nice to be out,' she said.

'I like your necklace,' he said.

'Thanks, I found it in a pile of crap from the attic this morning.' She held it out for him to see.

'Do you know what it is?' he asked.

'Nope,' said Kitty, looking at it again.

'It's a lover's eye pendant. The Victorians made them,' he said. He reached over and brushed her breast with his fingers as he took up the pendant in his hand. Kitty felt her nipples harden.

'This is real hair. Perhaps it was Clementina's – a picture of George,' he said excitedly.

'Why do you know all of this stuff about art and jewellery? Are you sure you aren't gay?' asked Kitty.

'Nope, not gay. Not everyone who knows about this stuff is gay. I studied art and art history, and the reason I know about the necklace is because my mother has one,' said Ivo easily. He was so sure about his sexuality Kitty felt dizzy from the testosterone pouring from him. She wasn't used to men like Ivo, so sure of themselves and so unapologetic about who they were and what they wanted.

Ivo opened the satchel he had been carrying and pulled out a journal. 'Here; read this,' he said, and he pushed the book over to Kitty.

Kitty sat still. 'You read it. I find it hard to make out the letters,' she said, and she pushed the book back towards him.

Ivo took the book and read. 'I sit in the orangery and I feel the baby inside me. George is painting me and I wonder if anyone could be happier than I at this moment. *Rempli d'amour et de soleil, c'est le meilleur des jours, mais combien de temps ils durent? Rien ne dure toujours, tout meurt.*'

Ivo's voice was low and resonant, and although Kitty had no idea what he was saying when he spoke French, she leaned forward, mesmerised by his voice.

'What does that mean?' asked Kitty, watching his lips as he spoke.

'Filled with love and sun, it is the best of days, but how long will they last? Nothing lasts forever, everything dies.'

'Well that's depressing,' said Kitty as she sat back in her chair.

'Maybe, but you know Victorian times; they were used

174

to death. Perhaps Clementina was worried about childbirth; you know so many women died in childbirth back then,' Ivo said.

'Why are you so smart?' asked Kitty.

'I'm not smart, I just know a lot of things. That's different. I know silly useless things that are of no help to anyone,' said Ivo, laughing.

Kitty wasn't convinced. Ivo was above her in every way: intellect, looks, even his casual style made her feel dowdy and unimpressive.

Kitty looked across the village. There were more people around than usual, she noticed. She felt Ivo's eyes on her.

'You dress like an artist,' he said.

Kitty was unsure as to whether his comment was a compliment or not, so she said nothing.

'Your jacket, the scarf, the necklace, your hair. It's all very French,' he offered as an explanation, aware she was bewildered by him. 'I like it.'

'Thank you,' said Kitty. 'I don't really think about clothes. I wear the same things all the time for work; kids are messy.' She laughed.

'I've heard that. Do you paint?' he asked.

'No,' laughed Kitty, 'I haven't an artistic bone in my body.'

'You look like you do. Perhaps you channel it through your style.'

'Are you sure you aren't gay?' asked Kitty again.

'I'm very sure.' And the way he said it and the look he gave Kitty erased any doubts.

Kitty pulled her sunglasses from her bag. 'I'm not sure what you want from me,' she said.

'What do you mean?'

'You. Your attention? I'm not the type of girl who sleeps around. So you might as well head off now if that's what you're after,' said Kitty, her directness startling Ivo.

'That's good; I'm not that type of girl either,' he said flirtatiously.

'No really. I'm not.' Kitty was firm in her decision, although the pulling in her groin was trying to convince her otherwise.

'Listen here, Pussycat. I have no friends here, no girlfriend, and I am stuck here for six weeks. I thought it would be nice to make a friend; maybe meet some of yours.'

'I don't have any,' said Kitty.

'None here?'

'None anywhere,' said Kitty, thinking back to her horrid time at school, her loneliness in London.

'Why not?' asked Ivo, taking his turn to be direct.

'I don't know,' said Kitty. 'I'm not very good with people, just with children.'

Why was she being so honest with him? And why was she so pleased he didn't have a girlfriend if she had just told him she didn't want to be involved with him? God, she was so stupid, she thought.

Ivo changed the subject. He thought she looked as though she might cry.

'Tell me about your family. The journals of your great-great-great-grandmother are delicious to read,' he said as the waiter brought their fish and chips over to the table.

Kitty salted her meal and shrugged. 'Well, the house was built for Clementina. That's all I know. All of George's paintings have disappeared and the only art left is Clementina's, which isn't worth much. When my father died, he left the house to Merritt

and me with the instruction not to sell it till after ten years.'
Kitty popped a chip into her mouth and munched, waiting for
Ivo's response.

'So now what? How long has it been since your father
passed away?'

'Three years,' said Kitty.

'Were you sad when he died?' asked Ivo, his own father's
face flashing before his eyes.

'Not really. Didn't know him very well,' she said without
any emotion.

'Why, did you live elsewhere?' asked Ivo as he ate his lunch.

'No, I was at home with him,' said Kitty.

'Where was your mother?'

'At home too, but she died when I was twelve.'

'So, what happened then?' asked Ivo, leaning forward.

'Nothing really. My father was an angry man; about what
I don't know. I never understood him. He kind of ignored
me really; not outright, but he didn't worry about me or
wonder about me. He was all about Merritt, which I think
was hard for Merritt to live with. After Merritt's marriage fell
apart, my father was angry at him. I think he hoped Merritt
would solve all the financial issues and take over the house.'

'Right,' said Ivo, thinking of his own father and his
disappointment at Ivo's choices.

'So after he died you went to London.'

'Yes, I fell into a job with Willow and I've been there ever
since.'

'Did you like London?' asked Ivo.

'Not really; it's so busy and dark. I like the country more,'
said Kitty, realising she sounded like a hick and that she didn't
care.

'So the state of the house now? You and Merritt planning to fix it up?' asked Ivo with his mouth full.

'Maybe. It would cost a bomb which we don't have, and what would we do with it once we'd finished? I'm not married, neither is Merritt. I doubt he will marry again. It's only good for a family or the National Trust,' she said.

'Maybe Merritt will marry Willow and then you can all live there happily ever after,' said Ivo, laughing.

'I doubt it,' said Kitty. 'I think it's just a sex thing.'

'Nothing wrong with that,' said Ivo in a low voice.

'No, I guess not, but some people want more.'

'Is that what you want, Kitty?' asked Ivo, leaning further forward. There was a simplicity about Kitty that appealed to him; no designs or expectations, and even a primness that he found intoxicating.

Kitty pondered the question. She wanted so much; she wanted to love and be listened to, to be read to and caressed, to be touched and told she was clever; to be loved. And yet she said nothing.

Ivo could provide none of those things. And while it was fun to flirt around the edges, she knew not to get too close; men like Ivo burnt a girl's wings if they flew too near to him.

'I don't know what I want yet,' she said, and concentrated on her meal.

They ate in silence and then she stood up. 'I might pay and head off home.'

'My shout,' said Ivo, wondering when the conversation had halted and why the awkwardness now.

'Thank you,' said Kitty, and she was standing wondering whether to shake his hand or kiss his cheek when Ivo made the decision for her and pulled her into a warm hug.

178

'Nice to see you Kitty. If I come across any revelations in the journals, I'll let you know.' And Kitty let him hold her for longer than necessary.

Then she turned and walked away to the bus stop. And as she left, Ivo was surprised to find he was very sorry to see her go.

CHAPTER EIGHTEEN

Merritt and Willow moved into intimacy quickly and found they enjoyed it. The ease of living in the same house and the presence of the children gave Middlemist an unrealistic energy, and Kitty wondered how long it would keep before the bubble burst. Perhaps Ivo was right; maybe they would marry and they would all live happily ever after. Part of Kitty hoped it would happen; then she would never have to go into the world again. She could stay here and be the nanny forever. Except there was the problem of Willow's ideas about homeschooling, Kitty remembered, but she pushed it from her mind.

Willow filmed most days. Ivo was always on set too, and he was polite and witty and professional and he made a point of seeking out Kitty when he could. Poppy was instantly in love with him – as most girls probably were, thought Kitty. He and Willow had settled into a jokey relationship and even Merritt tolerated him, although he wasn't really Merritt's type of man.

Kitty found herself fascinated to see the new sides of her brother and her employer emerge. His tenderness; her kindness. The selfish side of Willow that she knew in London had all but gone, and she would watch as Willow carried a tray into the drawing room, with mugs of tea and some exotic organic biscuits from Harrods on a plate.

It was odd to be served by your boss, thought Kitty, but her and Willow's relationship had shifted and there was a seed of equality sprouting between them. Willow suddenly cared about what Kitty thought, and Kitty was unsure about the new dynamic.

Kitty watched Merritt and Willow walking around the garden away from the set, Willow in full costume and the children gambolling behind them, Jinty in Merritt's arms. It was so perfect that Kitty felt tears prick her eyes.

'Hello Kitten,' she heard, and she turned to see Ivo in costume, standing in the kitchen.

'Oh hi,' said Kitty flatly.

'How're things?' he asked.

'OK,' said Kitty.

'What you doing tomorrow?' asked Ivo.

'Not much, why?' she asked, crossing her arms to cover herself, although she wasn't sure why.

'I have discovered something I thought you might like,' he said.

'Oh.'

'Can I show you tomorrow?' asked Ivo, uncertainty in his voice.

'I guess so,' said Kitty, shrugging. 'What is it?'

'It's a surprise,' said Ivo. 'Be ready at nine o'clock.' He disappeared again and Kitty wondered what she had got herself into.

Merritt and Willow waved at her through the window and she waved back rather forlornly.

'Is she OK?' asked Willow to Merritt.

'I think so,' said Merritt, glancing back over his shoulder to look at her through the window, but she had gone.

181

'She seems a little lost lately,' said Willow.

'It must be odd for her; us and so forth,' said Merritt, suddenly unsure about what the 'so forth' was. Was this a relationship? he wondered.

Willow was silent. What did he mean, 'so forth'? she wondered. Her dress became caught on a lavender bush and Merritt stopped and pulled it away. 'You right now?' he asked, and Willow smiled at him.

'Thank you,' she said, and they kept walking.

'What's this garden for?'

'This is the Lady's Garden, as it was known. A garden for picking flowers. It was once filled with roses and lavenders, dahlias, anything that looked good in a vase.'

Willow looked around the garden, now stripped of any blooms. 'It must have been lovely.'

Merritt looked at her in her full skirt – a tea dress, she had called it – and smiled. 'Yes. Lovely.'

She looked at him and turned her head to one side quizzically.

'I mean it will be lovely, when it's done.' He fumbled as he spoke and his words fell out in a rush.

Willow smiled at him. 'You're lovely also, Merritt,' she said, and when they walked back to the house, she felt his hand take hers. She left it there, not caring who saw them.

As they rounded the corner onto the driveway, Lucian and Poppy following and Jinty now asleep on Merritt's shoulder, Jenny, Harold's assistant, came to them. 'Do you have a minute? Harold wants to see you both,' she said.

Willow looked at Merritt, who shrugged his ignorance as to why Harold would want an audience with him.

'I'll pop Jinty down and set the little ones up with the electronic babysitter. I'll be down in a minute.'

Jenny and Willow watched him go inside, children trailing behind him like he was the Pied Piper. 'He's good with the kids,' said Jenny.

'He is,' said Willow.

Merritt had taken to the children with the same passion he had taken to her. He was patient and selfless, entertaining and firm. He was more of a father than Kerr had ever been, and it dawned on Willow that she was not the only one in this. Her children were in deep also. Lucian, who had shown more affection to Merritt than anyone, Poppy, who stopped all her rubbish with one look from him, and Jinty, who reached for him each morning.

Willow felt clammy and scared. What if he didn't want her and the children forever? She started to panic. She thought it was sex she wanted, but now she had more she was terrified of losing it. And Merritt was not the sort to stay around – Kitty had told her he always travelled. She was sure he didn't want to be saddled with three kids and a broke woman.

Willow wiped her hands on her dress.

'You OK?' asked Jenny. Small beads of sweat appeared on Willow's brow.

'Fine; it's just the corset,' lied Willow.

'Right, well if the Great Oz commands us, we must see what he desires,' said Merritt, emerging from the house. 'The bigger two are watching some show with a talking vacuum cleaner and Jinty is asleep. Shall we go?' he asked, and he took Willow's arm as they walked to Harold's trailer.

Jenny knocked and poked her head around the door. 'Willow and Merritt are here, Harold,' she said.

'Send them in,' said Harold, and Willow was nervous about the meeting. Why had he invited Merritt?

'Hello luvvies,' said Harold.

'Hello,' the two of them said, trying to see him in the darkness of the trailer.

'I have something to show you,' said Harold, and he turned on a TV screen. An image of the ball came up.

Harold pressed play on a remote somewhere and the screen sprang to life. Willow saw the ball in full swing, then she saw her and Merritt talking and him taking her onto the dance floor. She saw her face as he seduced her as they danced and her rushing to the balcony. Then she saw them kiss. She stood still, aware of Merritt next to her, and she felt ashamed and aroused and shocked.

'What do you think of that then?' asked Harold.

Willow spoke up. 'I'm sorry Harold; I think we got carried away. If we ruined any scenes for you then I apologise. I promise it won't interfere with the shoot.'

'Absolutely,' said Merritt. 'If we can reshoot or something, whatever you need to do, then I will stay away of course.' He felt like a chided schoolboy being caught with his hand up a girl's jumper.

'What do you mean?' asked Harold in the darkness. 'I called you here because I want to use this footage in the film. I think this will be a lovely flashback to your character, Willow, remembering her husband. I think, Merritt, you will be Willow's husband. Is that alright with you? Do you think you could be Willow's husband?'

Merritt turned to Willow, who looked back at him, equally surprised.

'I do,' he said.

'And you Willow? Do you think you will be OK with this?'

'I do,' said Willow, staring into Merritt's eyes.

'Lovely then; all settled. Merritt, Jenny will get you to sign a release form.' Merritt nodded, still looking at Willow.

'That's love there on the screen,' said Harold. 'Nobody can act that well. Not even you, Willow.'

Merritt and Willow turned to look at where he had paused the shot. Merritt was holding her and she was looking up at him, the moment before they kissed.

They left Harold's trailer in silence, Harold's observations hanging heavily between them. It's too soon to be in love, thought Willow.

Harold's crazy, thought Merritt as they walked beside each other. 'I have to go now,' said Willow as they arrived at the set in the garden for the afternoon shoot.

'OK,' said Merritt, his hands in his pockets.

'Are you OK with that about Harold? He's a bit crazy I think,' said Willow, putting her hand up over her eyes to shield them from the sun.

'I gathered that,' said Merritt. 'I'm fine. My one and only chance to be a movie star.' He laughed and Willow joined in, although she felt absurdly sad and she didn't know why.

'OK, bye then,' she said, and she walked away.

Merritt watched her leave, and it felt like one of them had just told a lie. The only thing was he wasn't sure who had told it.

Willow worked late, and when she returned to the house she was tired, grumpy and happy to see that Kitty had put the children to bed, and then filled with guilt that she felt that way.

There was no sign of Merritt. He was probably scared

shitless after Harold's proclamations of their love today, she thought as she climbed the stairs wanting a bath. She was just deciding she was too tired to be bothered to run one when she saw a note taped to her door.

Evening,
I have run you a hot bath. I am available for a back rub and other entertainment either before or after should you require it. Please send me a note under my door if you need anything.
Love Merritt

Willow smiled. He must have written this hours ago, she thought, not realising she would be held back for so long. She took the note off the door and went to drain the cold water from the bath, in case Poppy went to use the bathroom in the night.

Opening the door, she was met with candlelight and the scent of mimosa. The water in the old claw-foot tub was steaming and a soft fluffy towel that Willow hadn't seen before was folded on the chair at the end of the bath.

Undressing, she slipped into the warm water and felt her muscles relaxing almost immediately. As she sank under the water, she tried to think about the last time someone had done something for her where she didn't have to ask and pay for the duty. It was the single kindest thing that anyone had done for her in so long that she felt like crying, but she was too tired. Staying in the silky water till her fingers were pruned, eventually Willow got out, dried herself and put on the soft cashmere robe that she had brought with her from London.

When she walked into her room, still clutching the note, she saw that Merritt had closed the curtains, turned on her nightlight and turned down the bed. The room was warm and cosy, with a small vase of pale yellow tea roses by the bed, clumsily arranged. Willow felt a lump in her throat. What a tragic figure she was that a mere bunch of roses could reduce her to a puddle of tears.

She sat on the bed holding his note, thinking of Merritt writing it, fussing around the house, picking the flowers and choosing a vase. She quickly stood up, turned the note over and wrote a reply in her quick writing. She paused, then she signed her name, crept out into the dark hallway and slipped it under Merritt's door.

Merritt had heard Willow come upstairs but stayed away. He knew he would have liked to be left alone when he was tired and so he didn't want to harangue her, even though he would have loved to see her again. When he heard her enter her room and shut her bedroom door, he was disappointed not to have her company but hopeful she was feeling better. She looked tired and seemed to be losing more weight as filming went on.

Merritt stood and started to undress for bed when he saw the note slip into his room under the door on the floorboards. He almost ran over to it and scanned it quickly.

Bath was perfect. Bedroom cosy but lonely. Take some time to smell the roses with me. I am incapable of anything except a goodnight handshake and will be wearing some sort of passion killer nightgown, as you English say, but if you are interested knock twice.
Love
Willow

Merritt pulled on a pair of his father's pyjama trousers, even though he usually slept naked. He figured that he should make the effort since Willow had told him sex was off the menu.

He knocked twice softly at her door. Willow opened it and stood there wearing a knee-length flannel nightgown, a pair of aqua bedsocks and her hair pulled up in a messy bun on her head. Merritt thought she had never looked more real or lovelier.

'This is me,' she said, gesturing to her bed wear.

'Hello me,' said Merritt, and held his hand out for her to shake it.

Willow smiled at him and pointed to his pyjama trousers. 'No top?'

'Yes, well, I've had to pull these from the dark and a top might be asking too much. I didn't want you to think I was after anything more than a handshake. And maybe a little spooning.' His eyes were dancing. Willow laughed and then pulled him inside and shut the door.

Merritt went and stood by the bed. 'Right or left side?' he asked.

'Left.'

'Good. Can I look at this book?'

'Yes, if you want to learn about Victorian occult practices.'

'I do actually. Do they have a money spell?'

'Probably. They seem to have a spell for everything,' Willow said as she got into bed and applied hand cream, her evening ritual every night.

Merritt flicked through the book and Willow checked her phone for messages.

It was easy and domestic and something neither of them

had experienced before. They both found they rather liked it, but they didn't say anything to each other.

Merritt settled into the bed, thumping his pillow. 'Night night.'

Willow reached out to turn off the bedside lamp. 'Night Merritt.'

And they slept solidly for eight hours, and when they woke they made love, slowly, the type that is best for the morning. When you know you have all day ahead of you and you're lazy in your movements and you don't quite want to wake up.

Then the children came into the room and Kitty tried to usher them out but somehow they all ended up in bed – Poppy with a book, Lucian with Custard and Jinty with a packet of sultanas – and Merritt had never felt happier. He looked across the bed at Willow, who was being force fed sultanas by Jinty while trying to read to Poppy, and Lucian was dancing Custard on Merritt's feet, and he was overwhelmed.

'He's a fool you know,' he said.

'Who?' asked Willow, as she shifted Jinty off her hip bone.

'The man who chose not to be in this bed at this moment with all of this,' he said, as Custard danced on his head.

Willow looked at the mess of feet and blankets and toys. 'Perhaps it's not for everyone,' she said diplomatically.

'Well, it's for me,' muttered Merritt under his breath.

'Sorry? I didn't hear you,' said Willow, pulling a sultana from her ear.

'Nothing,' said Merritt.

Poppy leaned over and said loudly in Willow's ear, 'He said, "It's for me".'

Merritt felt himself colouring and Willow said nothing, afraid to show her hand, and Poppy watched them both, wondering why they didn't say what they wanted. Like the time she told Tilly at the park she liked her doll better than hers and Tilly agreed and they swapped and neither nanny noticed. It was easy and all they did was tell each other the truth.

Poppy folded her arms. 'Mewwitt?'

'Yes Poppy?'

'Do you love my Mummy?' she asked, in her queer transatlantic accent.

Merritt paused. He could feel Willow stiffen in the bed, waiting for his reply.

'Well Poppy, that's a big question for a little girl,' he said, stalling for time.

'Poppy, don't ask Merritt such personal things. I am sure he is quite fond of all of us,' she said, her heart sinking a little.

Merritt listened to the quaver in Willow's voice when he heard her answer Poppy, and he decided to lay his cards on the table.

'Actually Poppy, I'm more than fond of you all,' he said.

'What's morethanfond?' asked Poppy, pronouncing it as one word.

'I love you all,' he said, and Willow stared ahead, wondering what he meant and in what way, and she wanted to scream at the children to leave the room so she could question Merritt with a flashlight in his eyes, but she said nothing.

'I love you Mewwitt,' said Poppy solemnly.

'I love you too, Poppy.'

Jinty threw herself at Merritt, knowing there was a

190

conversation of importance in the room, and shoved a sultana into his mouth. Lucian cuddled Custard with great sincerity and Poppy moved away from the centre of the bed.

'You better kiss Mummy now,' she said and Merritt leaned over to Willow and looked into her eyes.

'I love you Willow,' he said and he kissed her on the lips, briefly but warmly.

Willow felt her heart soar and she kissed him back. 'I love you too Mewwitt,' she said, mimicking Poppy; but her eyes were serious and Merritt was happy.

'Right, Saturday! What shall we do?' he asked and jumped out of bed in his pyjama trousers. 'Picnic? Day trip? What?' he asked.

'Picnic!' cried Poppy, and Merritt clapped his hands together.

Merritt took the children downstairs with an old t-shirt over the top of his pyjama trousers and started breakfast, talking loudly. Willow dressed in her old sweats and walked into the hallway.

Kitty rushed past her looking stressed.

'Hey, you OK?' Willow asked.

'I'm going out today and I have nothing to wear. I have one good outfit and I wore that last time he saw me,' she said, her eyes filling with tears.

'I'll help you find something. Borrow something of mine,' offered Willow as she pulled her hair up into a high ponytail.

'That would be so weird. You're my boss,' said Kitty, frowning.

'Boss schmoss,' said Willow, taking Kitty by the hand and leading her towards Kitty's bedroom. 'If you hadn't noticed, I am sleeping with your brother, so I think that allows certain boss–employee lines to be crossed.'

'I'm fat,' said Kitty, not listening. 'Nothing would fit me.'

'Shut up. You're not fat and I can dress you for anything. Where're you going?' she asked.

'I don't know. He just said he would pick me up at nine this morning and he'll be here soon,' cried Kitty.

'OK. Who're you going out with?' asked Willow, as she flipped through the hangers in her wardrobe.

'Ivo,' said Kitty quietly.

Willow spun around and put her hands on her hips. 'Really? He's a devil that one,' she said archly. For some reason she felt protective over Kitty all of a sudden.

'I know, but he hasn't tried anything; we just talk. He's quite funny and he's really smart,' said Kitty, dreamily.

'Don't expect too much,' said Willow sagely. 'I married a man like Ivo. They're fun, but not the marrying kind.'

'Oh I don't plan on marrying him, but when I'm with him, I feel smarter and prettier and it's nice,' said Kitty, and her face lit up.

Willow smiled, thinking of Merritt. When she was with him, she felt sexy and interesting. She knew what Kitty felt like.

'OK, so you have jeans?'

'Yes, but I wore them last time,' said Kitty mournfully.

'Jeans again are fine. What shoes do you have with you?' asked Willow, digging through Kitty's messy wardrobe floor. 'These are fine,' she said, pulling out a pair of black suede flats. 'Now come with me.' And she led Kitty into her room and pulled open the drawers of the large oak dresser.

'This, I think,' she said, holding up a blue and white striped singlet, with draping on one side and a white strap on the other shoulder.

'I don't know,' said Kitty doubtfully. 'Stripes? With my boobs?' She looked down at herself in her t-shirt.

'These are large stripes. And the draping will actually enhance your breasts, not draw attention to them,' said Willow.

Kitty took the top and looked at the label as Willow kept moving through the wardrobe and opening the drawers with abandon. 'Do you like her stuff?' she said, moving her head in the direction of the top Kitty was holding.

'Who?' asked Kitty, confused.

'Hers,' said Willow again, and Kitty looked again at the label.

'I haven't heard of her,' said Kitty.

'You haven't heard of Vivienne Westwood?' asked Willow. 'Really?'

'Um no,' lied Kitty, her face flushing.

Willow took a black jacket down from the rail in her wardrobe. 'This Chloé will work with that,' she said, holding up a military-style jacket. 'Tell me you've heard of Chloé.'

'I have,' lied Kitty again, and she took the jacket from Willow.

'Alright, pop them on, let's have a look at you,' demanded Willow, and Kitty fled back to her room to get changed in peace. Changing in front of Willow would be too weird, she thought, and she pulled on her jeans and the top. It did work, she thought as she looked in the mirror.

Slipping the jacket on, Kitty felt unlike herself, but instead like a fashionable French girl with an eye for style and handsome men.

She slipped the lover's eye necklace on over her head and put her feet into her shoes. Opening the door, she found

Willow waiting impatiently in the hall. 'Let me look,' she said, and she turned Kitty around.

'Excellent. Now to gild the lily.' She pushed Kitty into the bathroom and flipped down the lid of the toilet.

'Sit,' she commanded, and Kitty did as she was told.

Kitty threw the hand towel over the front of Kitty's clothes and started to apply foundation and eye makeup. Skilfully she used the brushes and powders and then finally brushed on a slick of lipstick and gloss that she mixed together on the back of her hand. She stood back and looked at Kitty. 'Perfect,' she said.

Kitty looked at herself in the mirror. Her eyes seemed wider and deeper set. Her skin was flawless and her lips were slicked in a red lipstick that seemed to work wonderfully with the striped top.

'It's a bluey-red,' said Willow as she saw Kitty's eyes darting from her mouth to her top. 'It has navy in it, so it works well with blues,' said Willow importantly.

Merritt's voice came up the stairs. 'Kitty? Ivo's here.' Kitty starting panicking but Willow stopped her.

'Bag, keys, phone, lipstick, condoms,' she said.

'Oh my god. No way,' said Kitty as she rushed to her bedroom.

'What, no phone? No keys? No lipstick?' teased Willow.

'No condoms,' said Kitty primly.

'Well, you know best,' said Willow, pursing her mouth.

Kitty ran down the stairs leaving Willow in the bathroom and saw Ivo in the foyer, with his back towards her. He turned and raised his face up to hers and smiled, his dark hair flopping over one eye. The way he looked at her and took in her whole appearance, and the way she knew he

194

approved, made her turn on the stairs and rush back to the bathroom.

Willow was leaning against the bathroom door holding out a strip of condoms in her hand. Kitty snatched it from her and tucked it into her bag.

'Not a word,' hissed Kitty.

'Never,' whispered Willow, and Kitty stopped at the top of the stairs.

'Thanks,' she said, and Willow met her eyes.

'My pleasure,' said Willow. And for a moment, she felt like a real older sister.

CHAPTER NINETEEN

Ivo leaned over Kitty in the car and pulled open the glove box.

'You can be navigator,' he said, and threw a map onto her lap.

'I don't do maps,' said Kitty. 'Absolutely hopeless,' she said apologetically.

Ivo pulled over. 'Really?'

'No idea, I'm sorry,' she said, and she smiled at him so sweetly that Ivo thought for a moment he could forgive her anything.

'OK, give it here,' he said, and he traced a line over the map. Kitty shuddered slightly imagining that finger running over her body.

'You cold?' he asked.

'No, I'm fine,' she said, embarrassed. 'Where're we going?' she asked quickly to change the subject.

'A surprise,' said Ivo and he started up the engine.

'Alright. Off we go,' he said and he drove the little hire car fast through the country lanes until they were on the motorway.

'Are we going to London?' asked Kitty, looking at the motorway that she and Willow had travelled on weeks before.

'Yes. Now stop prying – I want to know all about you,' said Ivo.

'There's nothing to know,' she said, but with Ivo's clever questioning and his continual interest in her answers Kitty found herself sounding quite fascinating, as she aired her opinions on education and child raising and celebrity and the perfect bacon sandwich.

In turn Ivo found himself telling her about his schooling, his lack of direction and falling into the film by mistake. His father's disapproval of his choices and his discouragement of acting when in fact he himself had acted as a younger man.

'At least he gives a shit,' said Kitty moodily as they sat in London traffic.

'True,' said Ivo, remembering her mentioning her father's lack of interest in her.

Ivo pulled into a car park and put a disabled sticker on the windscreen. 'Where did you get that?' she asked, shocked.

'It's a friend of mine's mother's. She doesn't need it – hasn't driven for years – so I bought it off him for emergencies,' said Ivo, and he took Kitty's arm in his and walked them down the street. Kitty saw a few heads turn as they sauntered down the street chatting.

'Do you get used to it?' she asked as they walked.

'To what?' he asked.

'To people looking at you because you are so handsome,' she said, without a trace of flirtation.

Ivo stopped in the street and looked at her. 'No, silly. It's not me they're looking at, it's you.' He laughed.

Kitty made a face at him and he dragged her to a shop window. 'Look at you,' he said, and Kitty looked at them both, so casually cool and sexy. She smiled.

'Maybe they are looking at us,' she admitted.

Ivo was intoxicating. No man this gorgeous had ever been

interested in her, and she wondered what he saw in the shop reflection that she couldn't see.

They walked and talked until they arrived. 'We're here,' he announced proudly, and Kitty looked up.

'Wow,' she said. 'What are we going to do here?'

'Look at art, silly,' chided Ivo gently, and he pulled her into the Victoria and Albert Museum.

Kitty breathed a sigh of relief. I'm glad it's not a library, she thought.

Taking her to the second floor, he walked through the imposing doors and took her to a large painting.

'Look,' he said proudly, and Kitty looked up at a painting of a woman standing inside a conservatory, surrounded by fruit. She was wearing a white dress with a yellow ribbon around her waist, and Kitty thought she looked happy.

'She's pretty,' said Kitty.

'She's you,' said Ivo, looking at her.

'What do you mean?' asked Kitty, confused. She looked again at the woman in the painting; she did bear some resemblance to Kitty. Dark hair, dark eyes; but that was all she could see.

'Read the label,' said Ivo, his voice filled with excitement. 'I knew you reminded me of someone, and I couldn't think who. Read,' he said, and he pushed her towards it.

Kitty looked at the words and started to feel the tears prick at her eyes. She blinked several times, aware that Ivo was watching for her reaction.

She looked at him. 'That's amazing,' she said, her voice hollow, and Ivo looked at her, sudden understanding clouding his face.

It all made sense.

198

'You can't read, can you Kit?' he asked softly, and Kitty felt the tears fall. She ran from the gallery, tripping down the stairs into the light outside.

Ivo rushed to follow her small figure crossing the street.

'Kitty, Kit!' he called, but she kept running away from him, away from the words.

You stupid idiot, she thought, of course he was going to find out – he's so clever and I'm so dumb. She kept pushing through the crowds of people. When she stopped and looked up she realised she had no idea where she was.

She felt herself being spun around. 'Kitty! Kitty.' Ivo was breathing heavily.

'Go away!' she cried, and she pushed him; but he remained in front of her.

'Kitty, it's fine, really,' he said, and he took her to the side of the busy street, ignoring the faces peering at the attractive couple having a lovers' tiff.

'It's not fine. No, I can't read, and now you know,' she spat at him.

'It's all OK, really it is Kitty,' said Ivo helplessly. He had no idea what to say. He had thought something was up when he asked her to read the map, and now it all came together. Her refusing to help him with the script; asking him to read the journals; not wanting a menu at the village pub.

Kitty started to cry openly now, and snot and tears poured over her face, ruining Willow's makeover.

'You have no idea how hard it is to be me. To be so stupid. I can't do anything, ever. I want to, but I don't know how. The letters and words don't make any sense,' she cried, and Ivo thought she looked about four years old.

'So now you can go and be smart somewhere else and I will leave you alone because I'm so stupid,' she said angrily.

'Kitty, that makes no sense. Why would I want to go somewhere else because you can't read? For fuck's sake,' said Ivo, angry now. 'I don't give a shit about you reading. Trust me, there are plenty of genuinely stupid people who know how to read,' he said.

'Who?' asked Kitty forlornly.

'Me,' answered Ivo.

'Don't be daft. You're so smart and I wish I were like you. That's why I've been hanging around you even though I said I wasn't interested. It's not that you aren't attractive – you are – but when I'm with you I feel smarter,' cried Kitty.

Ivo felt his heart melt. He took Kitty into his arms and hugged her tight. 'Don't worry Kits, we can work this out,' he said, and he held her till her sobs subsided.

She pulled away from him and looked in her bag for a tissue, but all she found was an old packet of dried-out baby wipes. She wiped her nose. Ivo took one from her, wiped her eye makeup away and stood back to look at her.

'Better,' he said, and he took her hand.

'Come on, I'm not letting a silly thing like you not being able to read twenty-six letters get in the way. I can think of twenty-six things that I don't know, so let's call it even,' he said, and he took Kitty by the hand and led her back to the museum.

As they walked back to the painting, Ivo spoke. 'The reason I wanted you to see this is because this is your great-great-great-grandmother, the woman whose journals you let me read. This is her, and I think she bears a striking resemblance to you. Now you look while I read to you what this label says.'

200

Kitty stood back, trying to compose herself.

'*This painting is called* In the Orangery *by George Middlemist – 1851. George Middlemist used his wife, Clementina, as his model for many of his paintings. Clementina was born in France to wealthy parents who disapproved of the marriage. She and George resided at their home Middlemist House. The orangery was built for Clementina and filled with exotic fruits, including clementines, which symbolise joy. Soon after this painting was finished Clementina had their first child, Albert.* Who was your great-great-grandfather,' pointed out Ivo proudly.

Kitty forgot about her problem for a moment and stood gazing in wonder at the painting. 'Didn't you know about this?' asked Ivo.

'No idea,' said Kitty. 'Actually I don't know anything about George at all,' Kitty said, embarrassed.

'We have to sort that out,' said Ivo. 'I know so much about him, and about art. How about I tell you?' he said, liking the feeling of usefulness that washed over him.

Kitty looked up at him shyly. 'I would like that,' she said, and Ivo felt proud of himself and proud of her for telling him.

'Now, we need a drink,' he said. Kitty nodded, desperate for something to calm her nerves.

Ivo took her hand and they walked towards the nearest pub and sat down. It was cosy and not crowded and Kitty felt herself relax slightly.

'Gin and tonic?' asked Ivo, and she nodded. He gave the order to the waiter and they sat quietly till the drinks were served.

'So I have to ask you about it,' said Ivo, and Kitty grimaced. 'Just so I understand,' he added gently. 'How did you get through school?'

'I didn't. I fudged my way through for as long as I could and then I left once a few teachers began to get clued in,' she said, twisting the drink in her nervous hands.

'How do you get through life?' he asked. 'Forms, banking, driving, reading to the children?'

'I don't drive. I look at the pictures in the story books and I just make it up.' Kitty paused. 'You actually get to be quite clever. I got someone at the bank to show me how to use the ATM a few times and then I just remembered the process, and when I have really hard forms to fill in . . .' she took a deep breath, 'I wear a sling.'

'A sling?' asked Ivo, confused.

'Yes. I pretend I've hurt my arm and get someone at the place to fill it in for me,' she said, taking a sip of her gin and tonic.

'Jesus,' said Ivo, trying to imagine his life without reading. 'Does your brother know?'

'No, he just thinks I'm a bit thick,' she said sadly.

'I'm sure he doesn't,' said Ivo, frowning.

'He does. Everyone does,' she said, feeling tears springing into her eyes again. 'I think that's the hardest part,' she said quietly.

'What?' asked Ivo.

'Being underestimated. Nobody having any expectations of you. When you talked about your father and how he was disappointed with your choices because he thought you could be so much more, I wondered what that was like. My father had no expectations of me. My mother got sick when I was five years old, when I should have been learning to read, and it kind of took over the house. Merritt was so much older than me – he wasn't about to sit and explain the letters to me.

202

Then Mummy died and I was forgotten. I guess that's why I'm with children; they don't know any better, and they don't realise that I'm the same intellectual age as them,' she said sadly.

'Oh bullshit. You're not retarded, you just don't know how to read,' said Ivo, impatiently.

'You don't understand,' said Kitty crossly. 'It seems so big now, the whole reading thing. It's like a giant mountain of letters jeering at me.'

Ivo sat thinking about his father and the last time he had seen him, when he had gone to borrow money from his mother. His father's words rang in his ears.

'Ivo, you are wasting your future and your talents. You are making a complete cock-up of your life. Do something with it, boy, or stay away. You hear me?'

He held Kitty's hand over the table.

'Kits,' he said, and she looked up at him sadly. 'How about I help you? I'm not a teacher but I can help you read the letters. I could look it up on the internet,' he said, wondering if he could do it.

Kitty looked up, her eyes red ringed – but still so beautiful, he thought. 'Could you?' she asked.

'I could try,' said Ivo, feeling more confident as he looked at her. She gave him a watery smile.

'Well, I guess I could try too. Can you promise me one thing?' she asked.

'Anything,' he answered, looking at her pinched face.

'Can you promise to not tell anyone? Ever?' she implored him.

'Of course,' he said.

'No, I mean it. No one must ever know. Do you promise?' she asked him again urgently.

'I promise, Kitty. Cross my heart and hope to die,' he said gravely.

She smiled wanly. They finished their drinks and walked side by side back to the car in silence, each absorbed in the thought of the task ahead of them.

As Ivo unlocked the car Kitty got into the passenger seat, held up the disabled sign and looked at it.

'At least you have a real reason to use this now, at least whenever I'm in the car,' she said sadly, a single tear falling down her cheek, and Ivo couldn't help himself. He burst into laughter.

Kitty looked at him, shocked, and then she started to see the funny side of it and laughed with him.

And Kitty felt like she had just made it to first base camp on the mountain that loomed before her.

CHAPTER TWENTY

Merritt and Willow lay under a tree in the field near the house on a blanket. Jinty slept in the pushchair next to them and Lucian was being bossed about by Poppy, who was holding a large stick, in the distance.

'Happy?' asked Willow, who already knew the answer.

'Perfect,' answered Merritt, and Willow rolled over onto her elbows and looked at him.

'This morning, in bed . . .' she started, and Merritt opened one eye and looked at her. 'What did you mean?' she asked.

'I meant what I said,' he replied, not looking at her.

'You love me?' pushed Willow.

'Does that scare you?' he asked, carefully looking at Poppy still.

'I don't know,' she said. 'It's been a long time. My life is complicated and big.'

'My life was small and easy,' he said. 'Until you came into it.'

'I'm sorry.'

'Don't be. I like it much more now,' he said, and he turned to her and smiled.

They slipped into easy harmony together over the next few weeks and Willow all but forgot her financial woes back in

London. Kerr still hadn't returned her calls and she had stopped ringing him. He seemed so far away now, and Willow didn't want his memory spoiling her daydreams.

When Willow watched Merritt sitting with Poppy on his knee, Lucian next to him on the sofa in the drawing room, all shiny and clean after their baths; and when Merritt read them story after story and listened when Poppy constantly interrupted; and when she saw Jinty asleep on his shoulder, dribbling on his shirt and him not noticing, she found it hard not to wish he was their father.

Willow found herself doing more for the children when she wasn't working. Partly because Kitty was asking for more time off to spend with Ivo, and also because she liked to pretend that she and Merritt were married and that they lived a perfect, easy, uncomplicated life.

They didn't push for answers about each other's intentions. Instead Willow worked on the film and Merritt worked on the house.

Their nights were spent in the drawing room, her putting together the final touches to the scrapbook for the interior design inspiration for Middlemist House, Merritt poring over garden books and plans from the library.

Ivo visited Kitty every night at the house after filming and stayed till late, but Merritt and Willow stayed out of their way. Merritt figured he had no right to ask about Ivo's intentions for Kitty when he didn't know his own towards a woman not yet divorced, with three children.

Merritt tried to not think about the three weeks left on the film and what would happen after that. He found himself becoming more attached to the children, and there were times when he looked at Willow and his heart swelled with something unfamiliar. He was sure he loved her, but enough to take on three children and a complicated career? And what could he offer her anyway? he wondered while she worked away at the computer. Her phone rang and she left to go and answer it.

Her plans, although he hadn't seen them, would cost money he didn't have. Even with the money from the film, and discounting the cost of the clearing work the crew had done in the garden, he wasn't even close to having what he needed for the repairs to Middlemist.

He put his thoughts away when Willow came beaming into the drawing room.

'That was Lucy,' she said. 'She's organised the shoot for the makeup line I told you about.'

'Right,' said Merritt. It rang a bell somewhere in the recesses of his mind.

'They want to shoot it here, with the children in it,' she said. 'Is that OK? I said I would ask you first, in case you went nuts at me again.' She sat on his lap.

Merritt put his face into her shoulder. 'Don't remind me what a shit I was,' he said.

'Yes, you were a prick,' laughed Willow. 'Although in a kind of sexy, Mr Darcy way.'

'Yes, it's fine for you to shoot here; I'm sure Kits will agree,' he said, and she wiggled in his lap to get comfortable.

'Great.' And she kissed him softly on the forehead and he breathed in her scent of roast chicken and mimosa and felt her hair fall onto his face. He cupped her face in his hands and kissed her on the mouth. They melded into each other in the chair, and he slipped his hand up her t-shirt and felt her braless breast.

Their kissing became more urgent and Willow felt his hard-on underneath her. She reached down and rubbed her hand against it gently and Merritt moaned.

Standing up, still holding Willow, he took her over to the worn, sagging couch and laid her on it. They made out on the couch, seeing how long they could last before they needed to tear each other's clothes off. They lasted for half an hour, grinding against each other, Merritt allowing himself to taste her breasts as he shoved her t-shirt up under her arms, and then finally she stood up and wriggled out of her t-shirt and leggings and stood naked in front of him.

'No underwear?' he asked, his voice low with desire.

'I've wanted you all day,' she said. 'So I came prepared.'

'Well I hope you do come – prepared or unprepared,' he said, and he watched as she lowered herself, unzipping his pants and pulling them down as she went, releasing his cock from his boxer shorts.

Lowering her face, she peeked up at him and winked as she took him in her mouth. She sucked and licked and tantalised until Merritt groaned.

Willow stood up and straddled him, lowering herself onto his cock, and sat waiting for him to get his breath.

Merritt looked up at her and saw how truly beautiful she was, without makeup or accessories and with pure ecstasy on her face. They moved together and she pulled Merritt's t-shirt up over his head. He pulled her down onto him and as their skins touched, she felt her body shudder at the electricity between them. They kissed, their tongues meeting in each other's mouths.

As she felt herself about to reach orgasm, she stopped moving and Merritt looked at her, feeling her internal pulse against him. He held her. 'You OK?' he asked.

'I'm great. I'm about to come and I want to be prepared,' she said.

Merritt laughed. 'I love you Willow,' he said, and she felt her body lose control. She came to a body-shaking orgasm, and then she looked down at him and smiled.

'Lucky I was prepared,' she said, and then she rode him with abandon. As she felt his legs come together and sensed that he was about to shudder to his own orgasm she took his face in her hands. She peered into his eyes as his pupils dilated and she whispered.

'I love you too Merritt.'

And then they lay in each other's arms and dreamed it would always be like this.

Upstairs an angry Kitty was telling Ivo he was a dick.

'Spell it out,' he told her, pencil in hand.

'Fuck off,' she said.

'Can you spell it?' he asked again.

For two weeks, whenever Ivo wasn't filming, they had worked on her letters. She had to learn them and the sound they made and she was bored of it. Ivo had come with flashcards and tapes for her to listen to that he had bought online, and he worked her hard.

Kitty was practising on Poppy and Lucian, and Willow was pleased to see her work.

'Excellent Kitty! I'm so pleased you're starting their education already.' Kitty had smiled and kept on going with a bored Poppy and an unresponsive Lucian.

Twenty-six letters, Ivo reminded her, but it seemed endless to Kitty. And she kept mixing up her 'd's and her 'b's.

Ivo realised that Kitty wasn't another bit of skirt he could bed and leave behind. He felt strangely responsible for her, although he didn't know why. He had taken his own education and intelligence for granted for so long; was this why his father was angry with him?

Mostly he and Kitty had settled into a nice routine. They would work on the letters, and then have a cup of tea, a chocolate biscuit and a chat. Sometimes Ivo would read from Clementina's journal. Then they would walk the house exploring, to find the rooms that Clementina had described.

Kitty showed him the hidden tunnels that led to each wing of the house, and the art studio and the boxes of old clothes and jewellery that Poppy had found.

'It's like a museum,' said Ivo as he stood in the old orangery, now without most of the glass, that had once housed the beautiful fruit. 'I love doing this stuff with you,' he said. 'I feel like one of the Famous Five,' he whispered.

'Are you Julian or Dick?' she asked.

'How do you know about that? I thought you couldn't read,' he said, as he needled her side with his elbow.

'Yes, well I watched the TV show sometimes,' admitted Kitty.

Ivo found Kitty's company soothing. He hadn't really touched a drink since he had started on the film, he was sleeping properly, and the rest of the time he was either working, reading or helping Kitty. He looked forward to their time spent together and began to see her as more than just a potential shag. Kitty was the first female friend he had ever had that he hadn't fucked first, and he found that he liked it.

Kitty was the opposite though. She hated the reading

210

lessons, dreading the time spent over the flashcards with her trying to make the sounds and remember the letters. The only thing that got her through was the idea that she and Ivo would be alone. Sometimes, when they walked through the unlit parts of the house with only their torches guiding the way, Kitty would pretend to trip so Ivo would grab her arm to steady her, and Kitty would lean against him for a moment longer than necessary.

Then Ivo would leave and she would have to start the charade all over again. Learning to read and falling in love were the hardest things Kitty had ever done.

Kitty's routine was to sneak into the Lady's Garden each afternoon, far away from the hive of activity near the house where no one could hear her, to practise her sounds aloud before she practised on the children.

It was a surprise when Harold, the film's eccentric director, appeared as if by magic in the garden. Kitty had mostly stayed away from the film crew and the actors, except of course for Willow and Ivo. The others intimidated her, with their jokes and witty puns.

Sometimes Kitty saw Harold wandering around the shoot dressed bizarrely; one day hunting clothes, complete with top hat and whip, and other days all in black, with a fabulous cloak made of peacock feathers.

Today he was wearing what looked to be a yellow silk waistcoat embroidered with pansies, and a linen morning coat so long that it dragged on the ground.

'Hello there,' he said, wandering up to Kitty.

'Hi,' she said shyly.

'Practising our vowels and consonants are we?' he asked with his hands behind his back as though surveying the garden.

'Um . . .' Kitty was at a loss what to say. He had clearly heard her, and now she couldn't lie. She tried to make up an excuse but was left sitting silent as her mind raced.

Harold smiled benevolently at her, reached into the pocket of his waistcoat and pulled out a card. 'I hear you most days, I just never want to interrupt; you seem so hard working,' he said.

Kitty nodded at him, somewhat pleased that someone had noticed how much she was trying.

'If you're ever in London, I know a wonderful voice coach who specialises in working with dyslexic actors. I can set up an appointment with her if you like.'

Kitty blushed. Dyslexic. 'No, I'm not dyslexic.' I'm just stupid, she thought.

'Oh right then,' said Harold, sitting down beside her. 'You don't mind do you?' he said, gesturing to the bench. Kitty shook her head, afraid of being rude.

'So, the problem is what then? You can read but you need help with the sounds? Or you can't make out the symbols?' he asked.

Kitty sighed. 'Please don't tell anyone,' she said to the kindly man in his odd getup.

'It will be kept in confidence absolutely,' said Harold gravely.

'I can learn most of the letters; it's putting them together. My eyes get fuzzy, almost.'

'Yes, that's dyslexia my dear,' said Harold. 'You know, there are many famous people who have it.'

Kitty looked at him. 'Who?'

'Da Vinci, Picasso,' Harold said.

Kitty looked unimpressed, so Harold thought back to

212

the actors he knew of and had worked with. 'Keanu Reeves, Keira Knightley, Orlando Bloom. Those names ring any bells?'

'Really?' asked Kitty, incredulous.

'Really. They just need help with their scripts; doesn't affect their ability to act at all.'

'I love Keira Knightley,' said Kitty dreamily.

'She's a doll isn't she? And so clever. So, so clever,' said Harold as he stood up. 'Let me know if you get to London, yes?' he asked.

Kitty stood up and impulsively kissed Harold on the cheek. 'Thank you,' she said, and Harold laughed. If I were ten years younger, he thought, but he had seen how Ivo chased her. She was meant for another, he thought as he walked away.

The conversation with Harold was soon forgotten by Kitty though. Her obsession was with Ivo and his lack of advances. It was made worse by watching Merritt and Willow playing happy families. Kitty was jealous and happy for them at the same time, and she tried to give them time together when she wasn't working with Ivo on her reading. So desperate was she to learn to read so she and Ivo could concentrate on other things, that she practised whenever she could, with Poppy and Lucian as her unwilling students.

Kitty was walking outside in the driveway practising her sounds under her breath when a young woman pulled up in a battered Golf.

'Excuse me – I'm looking for Willow,' said the girl.

'Um, she's in the house,' said Kitty, and she kept on walking, saying her sounds aloud.

Actor wankers and their vocal warmups, thought Lucy as she kept driving towards the house.

'Jesus Christ,' she said as she pulled up and parked in front of Middlemist.

A man rounded the corner pushing a wheelbarrow with a small blonde girl on top of a pile of dirt. 'Hello,' said the little girl brightly.

'Hello,' responded Lucy.

'Can I help you?' asked Merritt warily. Willow had said she had seen a few 'papanazis' around, as she and Kitty called them, and he was careful with the children around strangers.

'Yes please. I'm Lucy, I work for Willow. Is she around?'

'Oh hi, Lucy. I'm Merritt,' he said. 'And this is Poppy.'

'Hello Poppy,' she said again, and Poppy smiled at her. Lately her behaviour was improving and gone was the rude, brattish child that had once inhabited Poppy; instead a happy, smiling, funny little girl replaced her.

'I'll get her for you,' said Merritt. He went to the front door and poked his head through. 'Willow?' he yelled, and he looked at Lucy. 'Come in then; she's upstairs changing the beds,' he said, and Lucy looked at him shocked.

She stood in the foyer and waited till Willow appeared at the top of the stairs, in jeans and an old t-shirt of Merritt's with the name of a local plant nursery on the back.

'Hey,' called Willow, and she jumped down the stairs. She looked amazing, thought Lucy; calm and natural and happy.

'Hey yourself,' said Lucy. 'I have to come and organise you for tomorrow,' she said. 'Sign the papers and all that.'

'Cuppa tea?' asked Merritt as he padded into the foyer in his socks, having left his work boots by the front door.

'Lovely,' said Willow. She and Merritt drank endless cups

of tea, and she still hadn't replaced the coffee pot that Kitty had left in London.

Lucy followed Willow into the drawing room and sat down on the chair that Willow gestured to as though she had grown up there.

Lucy knew not to ask questions of her clients until they offered information, and then she would do what she was best at: running through the good and bad, the facts to be embellished and the ones that needed to be buried. Now she sat and waited for the right time to tell Willow the bad news.

Willow spoke first. 'So I think you should know. Merritt and I have kind of got together while I've been here,' she said.

'Oh right,' said Lucy. 'I kind of picked something up.'

Willow smiled. 'Yes, so I have no idea what's going to happen, but I'm happy, which is a lovely change.'

Lucy looked at her and saw the happiness that emanated from her. She felt a little sick. Maybe she would wait to tell her till after the shoot, she thought.

Lucy opened her iPad and pulled up the schedule. 'So hair and makeup and wardrobe will be down tomorrow at nine o'clock. I'll be there. They're going to video it for the website too – I have all the papers to sign. Sorry I didn't get here earlier, but I've been flat out in London.'

'It's fine, I've been crazy here also,' said Willow, as she went to the desk to find a pen. She saw a missed call and a message on her phone but guessed it was either Simon or Janis, so she left it to return tomorrow.

Merritt arrived with cups of tea and a plate of biscuits, Poppy trailing behind him like a shadow.

215

'Here you go ladies,' he said, and set down the tray.

Willow looked up at him and smiled. 'Thanks sweetie.'

Merritt sat down with his cup and Poppy settled in beside him. 'Should I stay or go?' he asked Lucy and Willow.

'Stay,' they both cried, for different reasons. They spent the morning chatting, and Merritt gave Lucy a tour of the house.

'It's amazing. You must let me know when this is done up so I can get some press about it. You might be able to hire out the ballroom for weddings and parties, or do tours of the gardens, recipe books; it's endless,' enthused Lucy.

'Oh we will,' said Willow confidently, and then she looked at Merritt and covered her mouth. 'I mean he will.'

Merritt put his arms around her and pulled her to him. 'She's very bossy this American girl,' he said playfully, but inside he was happy she had used the word 'we'.

Lucy left to stay at the local B&B and promised to be back in the morning to field any issues and make sure all was going according to plan. She knew she would have to face the matter of what was about to arise in Willow's world sooner or later, but she and Willow needed this job for Blessings to go perfectly and she didn't want anything to ruin it for them.

The next morning, Willow woke up to a perfect day and a perfect orgasm courtesy of Merritt, who took it upon himself to wake her while he was under the bed sheets. A light breakfast as Kitty wrangled the children, and soon she was made up as the perfect American girl in the English countryside.

The children were dressed in Ralph Lauren from head to toe and Willow had multiple costume changes. Ball gowns, tweed skirts and wellingtons, silk cocktail dresses and parasols. Merritt and Kitty watched from the sidelines, Merritt in his gardening clothes: his torn jeans, his faded blue flannel shirt with the sleeves rolled up and his work boots. After the photographer and art director had got all the close-ups of Willow in the Lady's Garden, they asked the children to come into the picture and play on the lawn with Willow on a bright pink tartan rug.

'Why won't the little boy smile?' asked the photographer, who had been flown over from New York. 'Come on kiddo, smile!' he called from behind the lens.

But Lucian remained lifeless, standing in the middle of the rug as Jinty crawled and toddled and Poppy twirled in her pink cotton dress.

Willow tried not to look stressed but she felt her face tightening.

'Hang on,' called out the producer, and he spoke to his art director. 'Take a break for half an hour and then we'll do it again,' he called, and Willow stood holding Lucian's hand, feeling silly in a turquoise cocktail dress with a tight skirt and high heels that sunk into the grass. Her right arm was covered in jewelled bracelets and her fingers were bare of her wedding rings. She played with the bracelets for Lucian, who seemed to be entranced with the colours and the sounds they made.

Merritt wandered over. 'You look beautiful,' he said.

'Do I? Do I?' asked Poppy.

'You do, you do!' laughed Merritt.

'What's up old boy? You not feeling it today?' he asked Lucian.

Willow interrupted. 'People don't understand Luce, that's

217

all. He's just shy and takes his own time to warm up to things,' she said quickly.

Merritt looked at Lucian and said nothing. This was the one topic that he and Willow had not touched upon. Instead, he ruffled the boy's hair.

The photographer came back after half an hour. 'OK, so I got an idea. I just want you to stand there and watch as I do something and go with it. It will either work or it won't. I'm just gonna take shots and you act natural, OK?' he said to Lucian, who stared past him.

Willow felt nervous. She liked to be in control and this was out of the ordinary.

She stood with the children in front of her as the photographer's assistant walked back with something in her arms. She whispered to the photographer and then put down her bundle. A small chocolate-brown Labrador ran towards them and Poppy squealed with joy.

Lucian fell to the ground and the puppy started to jump all over him and lick him and Lucian started to make a noise that Willow, Kitty and Merritt had never heard before. The photographer ran around them clicking and Willow and Merritt ran to Lucian, only to realise he wasn't crying; he was laughing.

Loud guttural sounds came from him that rang out to become delightful peals of laughter, and Willow and Merritt laughed too and she hugged him.

'He's laughing, he's laughing!' she cried, and her eyes brightened with tears and Merritt joined in.

'I know, listen! It's wonderful,' he said in her ear; and the photographer kept taking shots, and the children all sat on the rug with the small brown puppy and played, and Merritt and Willow held each other for a long time.

Kitty wiped tears from her eyes and looked at Lucy, who was wondering what the hell was happening.

'He doesn't talk,' she cried to Lucy. 'This is a big moment.'

Lucy nodded, trying to understand, happy that the shoot was going well.

When the photographer had got the last shot, Merritt walked over to the assistant and started to speak quietly. They went away while Kitty took the reluctant children off to get changed.

Willow stood with Lucy. 'Wow, that was amazing,' she said. 'I hope they got the shots they needed.'

'I think so, it looked incredible,' said Lucy honestly. 'Actually, I need to have a chat, if you have some time.'

'Sure, let me get all this off and meet me inside,' said Willow, and she went in.

Lucy waited in the living room for her client's return, nervous and anxious.

Willow returned in jeans and a shirt, her hair pulled off her face, and sat down. 'So, what's up?' she asked.

As Lucy was about to answer, Lucian and Poppy ran into the room. 'Where's the doggy?' Poppy cried.

'He's gone home,' said Willow. 'I'm sorry.'

Poppy's bottom lip came out and Lucian looked at his mother and frowned. Willow watched his face.

'But it was nice of the puppy to visit us, wasn't it Luce?' she coaxed. Lucian said nothing, and Willow felt her heart sink again.

'Look who's come to stay.' Willow heard Merritt's voice and she looked up to see him holding the small pup.

'Puppy!' cried Poppy, and she and Lucian ran to him as he put the dog down.

Willow looked up at him. 'What do you mean?' she asked, incredulous.

'I bought him from the owner. The assistant helped me work it out. A family needs a dog I think,' he said, and Willow felt tears fall down her face. She ran to Merritt, narrowly missing stepping on Poppy, who had the dog sitting on her head.

She hugged Merritt tight. 'I love you,' she said, and he held her tight.

'I love you too,' he said in return, trying to push back his own tears.

Lucy sat on the couch watching the family moment. Shit, bugger, fuck, she thought.

'Come on kids,' said Merritt, 'let's go and get him sorted. Has anyone got any ideas for names?' he asked.

'Poppy!' Willow heard her daughter cry as she followed Merritt and Lucian and the new dog out of the room.

'Poppy the puppy? Not sure that works,' Merritt answered in the distance, and Willow laughed and came back into the room.

'Wow. Sorry about that,' she said, shaking her head and laughing still. 'Now, what did you want to tell me?' she asked as she sat down.

Shit, fuck, shit, thought Lucy again, and she drew a breath for confidence.

'I hate to tell you this at this time, but you have to know from me. Kerr's back in town and he's hired Eliza as his PR rep and publicist. He's also hired a big gun divorce lawyer and they're coming down tomorrow to see you. Kerr's bringing his new girlfriend; she wants to be an actress. He's hoping you will introduce her to Harold,' said Lucy.

'Shit. Fuck. Shit,' said Willow, her perfect world slipping away from her reach.

'My thoughts exactly,' said Lucy.

CHAPTER TWENTY-ONE

'I know this house,' said Eliza, as she peered through the window of the rented car that Tatiana and Kerr had hired for the drive. She looked at Johnny, who had accompanied them on the trip once he had seen photos of Tatiana online with no top on and Kerr sucking her nipple.

'It is very beautiful,' said Tatiana as she peered over the top of her Polaroid sunglasses.

'Yes, but it's falling down,' said Eliza, as though she could taste the mildew.

Johnny looked nervous. He hadn't seen Merritt since he had caught him in bed with Eliza, who was now his wife, and he wasn't up for any confrontations.

The car stopped and the driver alighted, opening the doors for his passengers.

Tatiana got out first and then Eliza, next Johnny, and finally Kerr.

Willow watched from upstairs. She had told Merritt and Kitty that Kerr was coming to see the children but she hadn't elaborated any more. Merritt had been good about it, actually enthusiastic for him to see the children. 'They need a father,' he had said.

They have you, thought Willow, but she didn't say anything. The evening had been pleasant, with the dog finally being

222

named George at Poppy's insistence, and it was given the seal of approval by Lucian, who smiled a little when it was floated as an option.

Kitty was nervous for Willow, knowing what a prick Kerr was, and anxious for Merritt too.

On the morning of the meeting, the children had played up – it was only natural, with all the tension in the air – and Kitty had had her hands full.

Finally the guests were there, and Poppy was bursting to see Kerr.

Kitty went down with them to see him. Lucian remained behind Kitty, holding Custard. Jinty was asleep upstairs. Poppy threw herself at her father.

'Pops!' he yelled, and Willow felt sick hearing his voice. 'Hey Luce. You're a bit old for a teddy mate.' Lucian ran upstairs and hid under the bed. It took Kitty all morning to try and coax him out.

Kitty's surprise at seeing Eliza was nothing compared with her horror at seeing Johnny. Remembering him taking away her virginity and never calling, even though she had followed him around for weeks until he threatened to call the police on her and called her a stupid dumb whore in the street, made her want to get under the bed with Lucian.

Willow was all charm, as she welcomed them into Merritt's home.

Merritt stayed away, not aware of the party that had come with Kerr. He figured that Willow and Kerr had things to discuss, so he spent his day in the garden, being busy, worrying.

When he finally came to the house, he kicked off his work boots and walked into the drawing room to find Eliza, Johnny and a strange European-looking woman in shorts, a fur coat and Ugg boots drinking his scotch. He felt his perfect world slip away.

'Hello Merritt,' said Eliza coolly.

'Hello old man,' said Johnny, as though nothing had ever occurred between the three of them.

'What the fuck are you doing in my house?' asked Merritt, his eyes flashing.

'Oh, we're here as guests of Willow,' said Eliza, her eyes daring him to make a scene. 'I'm representing her husband. Johnny's just here for the ride.'

Merritt turned and walked out. He slammed into Willow in the foyer. 'What the fuck are they doing in my house?' he hissed.

'They came with Kerr,' she said. 'Why? Do you know them?'

'Know them?' he spat. 'That bitch is my ex-wife and that other bastard is my ex-best friend, now her husband.'

'Oh fuck,' said Willow, in shock.

'Yes,' said Merritt as he walked up the stairs.

'I want them out! Do you hear me?' he yelled, as he stalked up the stairs.

As he came to the first floor he heard crying from Poppy's room. 'But I like it here!' she was sobbing. He thought at first she'd overheard his shouting and misunderstood, but then he heard a man's voice.

'You'll like it in America too, Pops,' said the voice. It sounded Scottish. 'Just you and me; and we'll leave Lucian and Jinty here for Mummy so she doesn't get sad.'

Merritt stopped outside the room and saw Lucian standing in the hallway listening to his father.

'Can we take George the dog?' sobbed Poppy.

Merritt held his breath as Kerr answered. 'Of course we can. He's your dog now. Lucian doesn't want him,' he said, and Merritt wanted to kick him. Instead he picked up Lucian and swept into the bedroom.

'That's not true, Luce. George and Poppy will stay here, with me and your mum and Jinty,' he said firmly, not quite believing himself.

When Kerr finally left with his guests, Kitty put the children to bed and Merritt went to bed himself, closing his door firmly. Willow wondered whether to knock as she stood outside his room, but she decided against it and went for a restless night's sleep.

The next morning she was filming again, and since it was near to the end of the shoot they were in for long days.

Kerr arrived by himself at the set to see Willow and he waited for her inside the house, talking to Poppy and ignoring the other children. Kitty sat with them and tried to include them in the conversation, but Kerr ignored her as well.

Finally Willow arrived. 'I think we better go for a walk,' she said to Kerr, and she took him in the direction of the Lady's Garden.

'What do you want, Kerr?' she asked, as they sat down on the bench where she and Merritt had first kissed.

'I don't know,' he said as he looked out over the field.

'You fucked us up so badly, Kerr,' she said hatefully.

'I know.'

'We have no money,' she said.

'Well you do now, with the film; and Eliza says you're doing some big makeup brand promotion,' said Kerr. 'We're still married, so I get half of that.'

'Are you kidding me?' She stood up. 'I will fight you all the way to court,' she said.

'No you won't,' he said calmly.

'I fucking will.'

'No you won't, and you know why. Because I will get Eliza to release your secret and then you will be a complete laughing stock, you fucking idiot,' he said. 'I want half of the money for the film, I want half of the money for the makeup gig and ongoing royalties.' He paused. 'And I want Poppy and the dog.'

'What?' she cried, feeling as though she was in a horror movie.

'You heard me. Do it or I'll slander you all over town. And I know about you and the dumb hired help you've been fucking here. Poppy told me. You are so sad. Fucking your landlord so you don't have to pay rent, huh?'

Willow went to slap him but he grabbed her wrist and spun her around onto his lap.

'He's brought out the tiger in you has he?' he asked menacingly. 'Shame I never saw it; might have stopped me having to find it elsewhere.' He shoved his hand up her top, grabbed her breast and kissed her hard on the mouth.

Merritt was coming out of the side garden when he saw her on Kerr's lap, being kissed and fondled. He stood watching and then turned and walked away. Of course it would end like this, he thought; as it started, with Eliza and Johnny orchestrating the whole finale from afar.

Willow stood up and punched Kerr in the face. Where the force came from she didn't know, but she felt satisfied with the punch as she saw him fall backwards off the bench.

'Do it. Tell everyone. I don't give a shit. You will not have anything else of mine; not my money, not my children and not any more of my time. Now fuck off or I'm calling the police.' And she ran into the house.

That night, after he left Middlemist, Kerr took Eliza out for dinner and left Tatiana to her own devices. He needed a strategy, and Eliza was a real-life Lady Macbeth.

Tatiana threw a tantrum in her room and wrote CUNT FUCKER ARSEHOLE all over the walls in makeup, along with some unpleasant Russian and a giant penis playing a guitar. Johnny heard her throwing things in the room next door and went to investigate.

'You right darling?' he asked smoothly as he heard the shattering of glass. Tatiana opened the door wearing knickers, a bikini top and sunglasses. She looked at him.

'I hate him,' she said, and she pointed to the wall.

Johnny looked at it, and then looked at her and smiled. 'That's really something,' he said. 'Ever thought about a career as an artist?'

Meanwhile Eliza and Kerr were getting pissed in the pub and she was planning his career in America. 'They love accents over there. You should leave the band and go solo. Launch in America,' she was coaxing him. She was sick of London and she was sick of Johnny. What she needed was a rich rock star and LA, where she could hang out with Posh Spice and maybe join Scientology with Katie and Tom.

Kerr listened to her. 'You're fucking right,' he said. 'I'm better than England. Fuck it, let's do it.'

'Excellent,' said Eliza, draining her vodka.

'What about Johnny?' he slurred.

'Who's Johnny?' She laughed and Kerr joined in, although he didn't understand.

Later when they fucked in his bed underneath Tatiana's mural, Eliza looked up at it as she rode him. 'You're such a rock star, trashing your hotel room like this,' she said, her head spinning.

Kerr had no idea what she was talking about again, but he pumped harder. They fell asleep together.

In the room next door, Tatiana was holding a mug of hot chocolate as Johnny cut up the cocaine she had produced earlier.

'You think I could be an artist?'

'Absolutely,' he said. 'I can make you a star of the art world.' He leant down and snorted.

To be a star was all Tatiana had ever wanted, and she nodded. 'I am vey passionate. I just need an outlet.'

'Well how about you start on me then,' said Johnny, undoing the robe he had slipped into and showing her his hard dick, completely devoid of pubic hair.

Tatiana smiled. Johnny was much more her type, she thought as she peeled off her shorts.

PART TWO

To George Middlemist
27 Rue du Moulin Vert, 14ème
Montparnasse
1865

George,

*   You have broken my heart. You have broken it and
I will never forgive you. I have been left alone with this
house and our children and nothing else. What can I do?
What shall I do?*

*   I am now faced with a future that is uncertain, except I
know you are no longer in my heart.*

*   You promised me the world and delivered me nothing
but your lies. I hate you. I loathe you.*

*   When you were with her and not with your wife, you
destroyed everything wonderful we had.*

*   I gave up everything for you. I have no family; no
country; no art. I have destroyed all your paintings so I
will never see your name again.*

*   I have poisoned the orange and clementine trees; dug up
your garden; salted the earth. It will be years before
anything grows here again.*

Things only grow when there is love, and there is no love in the earth at Middlemist any more.

Do not write to me, do not visit me. You will never see your children again. Ever.

If not for them then I would die, but they give me reason to go on.

Fin.

Clementina.

Autumn

CHAPTER TWENTY-TWO

Lucian picked up Custard the bear and walked downstairs. He could hear his mother and Merritt talking heatedly in the kitchen. Kitty wasn't around, nor was Poppy. His father had left the house a while back. He found George asleep in the drawing room and he picked up the small puppy. Tying a long red hair ribbon of Poppy's around the dog's neck, he dragged him out through the French doors, out onto the terrace, and found himself on the lawn.

He looked each way. Where to go? he wondered. He reached down and patted the dog, and then set off in his red jumper and blue jeans.

He walked through the trees and came to a fence. Clambering under it, he was in a large field, and he looked around again. He let go of George's ribbon and George ran ahead. Lucian chased him and they ran to the other side of the field, and soon they were both exhausted.

Coming to a road, Lucian put out his foot and stepped on the trail of ribbon to pull George back to him. He must be careful on roads, he always remembered Kitty saying that.

He walked up the road further. He had no idea where he was going, he just wanted to be away when his father tried to take Poppy and George away from him. He didn't mind Poppy going so much, she was annoying, always talking when he was trying to find the words, but George was another story. George and Custard were his only friends. And Merritt, but he was a grownup after all, and you can't trust grownups.

Taking a small path off the road, he walked along a bit further; but he felt tired. So tired. And hungry.

He sat down under a large tree and George settled in next to him. Lucian sat and closed his eyes for a moment. The sun on his face was nice. He liked the country, he thought. He liked lots of things, but no one understood him. No one tried. Maybe Merritt, a little, and Kitty; but not his mother or father. At the thought of his father, Lucian started to cry. Big fat tears rolled down his little face and he cried with sheer abandonment. He knew more than people thought; he had things he'd say one day. He knew stuff, plenty of stuff, if someone would listen.

George looked up at him and jumped up and licked the salty tears from his face and Lucian laughed. 'George,' he said in a faltering voice, and the small dog wagged his tail.

'George,' he said again. George would listen, he thought, and then he fell asleep.

CHAPTER TWENTY-THREE

Merritt and Willow were having an almighty row. Filming was halted until they had sorted out their differences, but it seemed they were at a stalemate.

'You were kissing him,' said Merritt accusingly.

'You didn't see me clock him in the face!' she screamed at him.

Merritt chose to ignore this. The jealousy he was experiencing far outweighed what he had felt when he caught Eliza and Johnny together. He was furious with Willow and with Kerr for spoiling his idyllic life.

'Stop being such a jealous pig, Merritt. You have no right,' she said wearily.

'No right? I fucking love you! That's what right I have!' he screamed.

Jenny the production assistant popped her head around the doorway. 'I know this is a terrible time, but we have to push on; it's the last day,' she said, embarrassed.

Merritt glared at her and Willow walked towards the door. 'If you are going to act like this then I'm going back to London,' she said and she walked into the hallway.

'Have you got a pen and paper?' she asked Jenny, who handed her the clipboard.

Scribbling quickly, she ripped off the piece of paper and

handed it to Jenny. 'Get this to Kitty, my nanny, will you please?' she asked, and Jenny nodded.

Willow walked out and went to costume to prepare for the next scene, ignoring the stares from the crew and extras and holding her head up high. Fuck you Merritt, she thought; you're no better than Kerr. How dare he be so rude and accusatory? she thought. Well fuck him. She would head back to London for a while and see how he liked that.

Shooting through the afternoon, Harold worked her hard and she barely had time to think about Merritt. When she finished shooting she changed and walked back inside the warzone. She could hear Jinty crying, and Poppy was sitting in the dark watching television, her nose pressed up to the screen.

'Where's Kitty?' she asked, looking around.

'Dunno,' said Poppy.

'I don't know,' corrected Willow.

'Yeah, I dunno,' said Poppy again, and Willow shook her head. Merritt was nowhere to be seen, and walking upstairs she found Jinty in her cot, screaming and purple in the dark. She was sweaty when Willow picked her up, and her nappy was dirty and wet through. She must have been alone for hours, thought Willow angrily.

She changed Jinty and, soothing her, carried her downstairs. She started to make scrambled eggs and toast with one hand while holding Jinty in her other arm.

'Poppy, Lucian, eggs!' she cried.

Settling Jinty into her highchair, she set the plate in front of her with a sippy cup of juice. Poppy wandered in. 'Can I eat it in front of the TV?' she asked.

'No,' said Willow firmly.

'Lucian!' she called again.

'He's not here,' said Poppy sitting down.

'What do you mean? Has he gone somewhere with Merritt?' she asked, remembering the sound of Merritt's car speeding off from the house and interrupting a scene.

'No, he went with George. He's gone to America I think,' she said, licking the butter off the toast.

Willow felt panic welling up inside her.

'America? What do you mean, Poppy?' she shouted at the child.

Poppy looked at her mother. Gone was the happy version she had come to know, and back was the angry Mummy she remembered from London.

Poppy said nothing, afraid of what might happen if she spoke.

Willow felt sick. 'Where has he gone, Poppy? Where?' She started to shake the child. 'Where?' she screamed again, and Jinty and Poppy started to cry.

'What's going on?' she heard, and she looked up to see Merritt standing in the doorway.

'Lucian's gone! Poppy said something about America,' Willow screamed at Merritt. 'Where were you?'

'America? He's not going to America. Kerr wants to take Poppy,' said Merritt, trying to soothe the girls. 'I just went out for a while to clear my head.'

'It's OK, it's OK,' he said, lifting Jinty from the chair. Poppy ran to his side, sobbing desperately into his leg.

Willow ran to her mobile phone and dialled Kerr's number. He didn't answer.

'I swear if you have taken Lucian as some sort of

punishment for me hitting you I will fucking kill you, you hear me?' she spat down the phone. 'Bring him back at once!'

She hung up and wrung her hands together. 'Where is he? Why weren't you here? Where's Kitty? Fuck, she's stupid,' said Willow.

'That's enough, Willow,' said Merritt, with a warning in his voice.

'I sent her a note.' Willow picked up her phone again, and tipping a sheaf of papers out onto the table, she leafed through them till she found what she was looking for: the numbers of everyone in the production from the call sheet.

She started to dial with shaking hands and tried three times to get the order of the numbers right.

'Jenny, hi. It's Willow. Did you give that note to Kitty? You did? When? OK, thanks. No, fine, all fine,' she said and hung up.

'I gave Jenny a note for Kitty to get the children ready and to help me and she has left them here, alone. What sort of a person does that?' she screamed at Merritt as she ran into the hallway calling Lucian's name.

She ran back and dialled Kitty's number. 'Kitty, where are you? Have you got Lucian? Please call me back.'

She ran around the house, calling Lucian's name and then calling Kitty in between, her messages becoming more desperate.

'God dammit Kitty! Call me back.'

'Kitty, where the fuck are you?'

'Kitty, for god's sake, you better have a good excuse.'

Finally she sat on the stairs and cried. Merritt walked

out with the girls. 'I think we'd better call the police,' he said.

'No police, no – they'll make it all too hard with the press and everything,' she wailed.

'Who gives a fuck about the press? Your child is missing,' he said to her.

'You think I don't know that, you fucking idiot?' she screamed at him, and she dialled another number.

'Lucy, Willow. Can you come down? We have a situation. Yes. Lucian's missing,' she said. 'OK, see you soon.'

'A situation? You call your autistic son missing a *situation*?' asked Merritt, incredulous.

'He's not autistic! How dare you?' she said, standing up. Poppy watched them from behind the banister.

'He fucking is and you know it,' said Merritt back to her. 'You have to hear it at some point. You are living in a made-up world, Willow.'

'Fuck you,' she said, crying. 'You don't know anything! Stop trying to be their father, they have one already. You are so fucking needy with your love bullshit and waving at Lucian and all that crap. It's so transparent, you make me sick.'

Merritt put Jinty down on the floor, pulled Poppy out from behind the banister and pushed her towards her mother.

'They're your kids, you deal with them!' he yelled. 'Now get the fuck out of my house!'

Willow fell to the floor with Jinty and wept while Merritt stepped over her and walked upstairs. It was Poppy who knelt over her mother as she slumped there, stroking her hair like Kitty did to her when she was sad.

241

'It will be OK Mummy, you can come to America with Daddy and me and see Lucian. We might need to leave Jinty here though. Daddy said she was a mistake.'

And Willow wept harder than ever before.

CHAPTER TWENTY-FOUR

Kitty had heard Willow and Merritt fighting. Listening outside in the hallway, she pieced together that Willow had been kissed by Kerr. Merritt was angry and now they were screaming at each other. Lovers' tiff, she thought, and she wandered upstairs and checked on Jinty, who was fast asleep.

Walking down again, she saw Willow out of the window walking towards costume and she was stopped by Jenny. 'Willow wanted you to have this,' she said, handing her a note. She hurried away before Kitty could pretend to have forgotten her reading glasses and get her to read the note out loud, so she stuffed it into the pocket of her skirt. Probably more organic items she wanted Kitty to order from London.

Her mobile phone rang and Ivo's face popped up on the screen – this was the best way to know who was calling – and she answered it excitedly. He still hadn't made a move on her, although she was desperate for him to do so.

'Hello,' she purred into the phone, as she had seen Willow do to Merritt on occasion.

'Hello yourself,' said Ivo, surprised at her tone. She had been a reluctant student and perhaps, he admitted to himself, he had been a little overzealous in his Professor Higgins role. 'What are you doing now?' he asked.

'Nothing. Wandering around looking for something to do,'

she said, thinking – more like some*one* to do. Wanting Ivo between her thighs had become her newfound obsession, and she was surprised at how attractive she felt around him. Sometimes when they read together, it was all she could do to not reach out and touch his face; pull off his shirt; but she didn't. She told herself it was just a crush on the teacher, but that was a new feeling too. She had hated all her teachers through school, and now here she was fantasising about school uniforms and rulers.

Kitty made a decision. She had had enough of waiting; of learning; she needed to start practising.

'Fancy a visitor?' she asked. She heard her phone beeping. Low battery. Shit. Hurry up, she willed. She needed Ivo to make a decision before they were cut off.

'Sure,' said Ivo easily, wondering what Kitty was up to. She was impossible to read, excuse the pun, he thought to himself as he hung up the phone. At times he thought she looked at him with pure lust, but then other times it was just hate. Usually when he was trying to teach her the letters of the alphabet.

It wasn't as though he wasn't attracted to Kitty. He was; she was divine – and those breasts, he thought to himself, but he felt differently about her. More protective of her somehow.

He would be heading back to London soon, and he wondered if she would visit him there. Probably not, he thought, thinking of how she had said she disliked it when they visited there together.

Ivo stretched and sniffed his armpits. Wrinkling up his nose, he decided he should have a shower before Kitty's arrival. As he washed himself, he thought about her breasts again and he felt his cock becoming stiff under the streams of warm water. He hadn't had sex in five weeks. He could have with any of the extras, but somehow his friendship with Kitty stopped him. Commitment was new to Ivo, as was celibacy, and he soaped up his cock and thought what the hell.

Kitty stood outside his door knocking. She had managed to hitch a ride in with one of the crew and was in town in ten minutes. Ivo's door was unlocked, she found when she tried the handle. She heard the shower going and smiled to herself. Taking a deep breath, she pulled off her short denim skirt and white tank top. Kicking them across the room, she pulled down her underwear, undid her bra and stood with her hand on the bathroom door handle.

Now, she told herself, and she walked into the bathroom and pulled back the shower curtain. There was Ivo, naked with his hand on his large cock.

'Oh!' They both said startled, and Kitty was frozen with embarrassment. She tried to cover up her nakedness.

'I was just thinking about you,' said Ivo, with a small smile on his face, 'but I must say the reality is far better than what I had going on in my mind.'

Kitty started to laugh and Ivo pulled her into the shower and kissed her on the mouth. She felt herself swimming in desire.

'Just so you know, I have never done anything like this before,' she said.

'Really? I have, plenty of times. Let me teach you,' he said, rubbing the soap over her breasts. As he washed her body, Kitty felt herself getting weaker and weaker.

'I don't think we can do it in the shower. I'm such a klutz I might fall over,' she said in his ear.

Ivo slipped the soap between her legs and felt her wetness. 'No, no, I'll hold you up,' he said, and he bent his knees a little and guided his cock inside her. She gasped and looked at him. Lifting her up he pushed against the wall and with one hand directed the warm water onto her. She began to move with his rhythm and soon they were fucking so loudly she was sure the whole B&B would be able to hear them.

They fucked until the hot water ran out, and then Ivo carried her to the bed and they started all over again. Now Kitty knew what it was to have great sex. The time with Johnny had been awkward and painful, and then the New Zealander had left her high and dry in every way, but with Ivo, she wanted him so much she wondered if he could live inside her forever.

They spent the afternoon in bed, and soon it was evening. Kitty was still in raptures in Ivo's bed. Three orgasms, positions she had never even entertained before, and some moves she had only seen Samantha do in episodes of *Sex and the City*.

'You are incredible,' she said.

'You're not too shabby either,' he said, nuzzling into her breasts.

'Can I visit you in London?' she asked quickly. 'Or is this just a one-time thing?'

Ivo raised his head and looked at her.

'I would like that very much,' he said seriously, and it was true: he would like to see her. She was the first person he thought of when he awoke and the last person he thought of at night.

Kitty hid a shy smile in his shoulder. 'I have to go. I'm sure Merritt will be sick of the children by now,' she said, getting out of bed. She checked her phone. Dead.

Ivo lay in bed. 'How about I come back with you?' he said.

Kitty looked down at his beautiful form and felt wet again. How could it be possible? How can the body make that much liquid? she thought crossly to herself.

'I think you better had,' she said sexily, and he laughed as they pulled on their clothes.

Walking across the square to the bus, he wrapped his arms about her. 'I like you very much, Pussycat,' he said into her hair.

'I like you too, Ivo the Terrible,' she said back to him.

He laughed and pulled away. 'Did Willow tell you about that?' he asked.

'Yes. Your reputation precedes you.'

'That's a big word,' said Ivo mockingly. What did she know about all the other girls? Even a few men were in love with him.

'I remember you, you know,' she said.

He looked at her oddly. 'When?'

'From the party at Willow's. I said I didn't but I did,' she said, and she looked down at her feet, her nails painted silver and pink by Poppy.

Ivo pulled her to him again, and they held each other all the way back on the bus to Middlemist.

CHAPTER TWENTY-FIVE

Kerr walked into Middlemist with Eliza in tow. 'Just in case you need to release a statement,' she said on the way over after Kerr received the message about Lucian.

'So, you've lost the little idiot have you?' asked Kerr as he saw Willow sitting on the sofa, pale and drawn.

'Take it back,' said Merritt, stepping out from the double doors that led into the library.

'What? Fuck off mate,' said Kerr, and Merritt took one step and put his hands around his throat.

'Take it back or I will hurt you. You're the fucking idiot,' he said in a low voice.

Kerr started to shake in his biker boots. 'I'm sorry Willow,' he said.

Merritt released his grip and Eliza stepped out from behind Kerr.

'I see you are still rough trade, Merritt,' she said.

'I see you are still a pretentious whore, Eliza,' he said.

Willow stood up. 'Enough!' she yelled. 'We need to find Lucian.'

'Then call the fucking police,' said Merritt.

'No, no police,' said Eliza, Kerr and Willow in unison.

Merritt shook his head and walked out to try Kitty's phone again. Still nothing.

He heard the front door open and rushed to greet her hoping she had Lucian, but instead he found Johnny and Tatiana on his doorstep.

'What the fuck do you want?' he asked Johnny.

'We come to say our goodbyes,' said Tatiana in her thick accent, cutoff denim shorts and thigh-high Robert Clergerie boots.

Now that was rough trade, thought Merritt, looking at the skull and crossbones scarf tied around her head like a female Jack Sparrow.

'Well fuck off then. No goodbyes needed,' said Merritt, pushing the door and walking back into the drawing room, not realising Johnny had blocked the door open with his foot. Johnny and Tatiana invited themselves in and followed him into the room where Eliza and Kerr looked up with surprise.

'What are you doing here?' asked Eliza guiltily.

'We come to say goodbye,' said Tatiana.

'OK, bye then! See you in London,' said Eliza, distracted by her phone.

'No darling, here's the thing,' said Johnny charmingly. 'Hello there,' he said to Willow who looked at him as though he was insane.

Eliza looked up at him. There was something in his voice that told her she ought to pay attention.

'What, Johnny? We have a crisis here,' she said. 'The autistic child has gone missing.'

Willow stood up. 'Don't fucking call him that, OK?' she cried, wanting Merritt to take her in his arms but knowing she had burnt her bridges with him too.

'Hey, I say it as I see it,' said Eliza. 'Kerr said he was an idiot or something. Imbecile?' She tried to find the word.

'He's just a little slow,' said Willow loyally, her heart breaking.

'That's a bit harsh isn't it, old fella?' asked Johnny to Kerr.

Kerr looked at him as though he didn't matter, which to Kerr at this point he didn't really.

'What?' asked Kerr.

'Well you don't call your own child a fool, do you?' asked Johnny. However reprobate he was in life, he had certain values when it came to animals, children and most art. He had wanted to have children with Eliza but so far she was holding out, claiming she could be like a Scientologist wife or the Time Traveller's Wife or something and give birth when she was fifty.

Lucy walked into the room and into the middle of the drama. Everyone was watching Kerr yell at Eliza's husband, and the moment Eliza set eyes on her, she started to scream too. 'You fucking whore, you ruined my business! You stole Willow from me!' she accused, and she tried to jump over the coffee table towards her former employee. Lucy stepped sideways and Eliza went sprawling across the floorboards.

Lucy walked straight to Willow and took her in her arms, ignoring Eliza.

'What's happened?' she asked.

'Lucian's missing with the dog. Poppy says he's gone to America.'

'OK, well he can't have gone far. What did the police say?' she asked Merritt, who hunched his shoulders and snorted at her.

'We didn't ring them,' said Willow. 'Too many questions and all the media hanging around.'

Lucy shook her head. 'No, they need to know. How long has he been gone for?'

'Two hours,' said Willow, feeling sick again.

'Two hours? Jesus. I'll call them. You get me a recent photo of him, OK?'

Willow nodded and, desperate to have a task, she ran to the bedroom to get the digital camera.

Johnny seemed unflustered by the chaos around him, while Tatiana looked bored. 'Come on Johnny, let's go,' she said in her little girl voice.

'Yes, well, we are heading back to London,' Johnny announced to the room, but only Eliza listened.

'Together?' she asked.

'Yes, Johnny will make me star. I'm an artist,' she said proudly.

Eliza snorted. 'Well, good luck with that,' she said, laughing.

'I don't need luck, she has talent,' said Johnny easily.

Tatiana preened in front of Kerr. He was useless as far as she was concerned. Useless and a boring fuck.

'So, you're leaving me for that?' asked Eliza.

'Yes. I think we've run our course, don't you?' said Johnny simply.

Eliza stood shocked. 'You are leaving me for some fucking Eurotart with no class?' she bellowed.

'Now, now Eliza, don't be such a snob,' said Johnny, pulling Tatiana back as she lunged at Eliza. 'Don't forget that you are just a grocer's daughter after all,' he said, referencing the shopping centres that her father owned in Manchester.

Merritt tried not to laugh at the shock on Eliza's face. She tried to cover up her background but when she was angry, as she was right now, her Manchester accent came out. She screamed at Johnny. 'You fucking prick. You'll never get any decent PR without me!'

Johnny shrugged. 'Get over yourself Eliza. It was me that brought in the PR and the contacts. Without me you're nothing,' he said.

Willow rushed back into the room with a photo she had printed off from the camera.

'Where's Lucy?' she asked, but no one answered her. She ran into the hallway and bumped into Ivo and Kitty in each other's arms, kissing. 'Where the fuck have you been?' she screamed at Kitty.

'What?' asked Kitty, looking around.

The others came out of the drawing room into the foyer at the sound of Willow's voice. 'I have called and called you. Where the fuck were you?'

'I was with Ivo,' stuttered Kitty.

'While you were fucking him, my child and *your charge* has gone missing!'

'Which one?' asked Kitty, panicking.

'The stupid one,' said Kerr under his breath. Johnny heard it and frowned at him.

'Lucian, with the dog! I wrote you a note to tell you to look after them! Jenny said she gave it to you, why didn't you read it?'

Kitty reached into her pocket and pulled out the note. She could make out a few of the words.

Willow was hysterical. 'Why, Kitty? I entrusted you with my children and you left them here alone? Jinty was soaked and screaming, she was crying and crying!' Willow was gulping for breath. 'And Poppy alone in the dark, the TV as the only light? You know she hates the dark Kitty, you know that!'

252

Kitty was crying now, sobbing as Willow's face loomed close to hers. 'I know, I know,' she spluttered.

'No you don't know. You don't fucking know! You have no idea. You left them here alone. Fuck you Kitty, fuck you. Why didn't you read the fucking note? Why?' She was leaning over Kitty, who was a head shorter than her, now. Kitty fell to the ground.

Willow leaned over her, screaming. 'Why didn't you read the fucking note, tell me?' Poppy watched from the top of the stairs, while Jinty cried in her room at the sound of her mother's voice.

Merritt stepped in and pulled Willow away. 'Stop it,' he said. 'Stop it.'

'Why, Kitty?' screamed Willow again, and Ivo stepped forward.

'She didn't read the fucking note because she can't fucking read, you bitch!' he yelled at Willow and the room went silent.

'Ahhh, of course, she can't read,' said Johnny out loud. 'When we shagged I sent you that letter asking for you to come and visit, but you never did. Even after I took your virginity and everything,' he said with realisation dawning on his face.

Ivo stepped up as though to hit Johnny, but Merritt got in first and punched him squarely in the nose.

'She is my sister after all,' he said to Ivo.

Ivo nodded with respect as Lucy came into the foyer, her mobile pressed up to her ear. 'They found him; at the police station; were about to send out a report when I rang, been there about an hour. A farmer brought him in. Found him under a tree asleep.'

Willow started to cry again. She instinctively ran to Merritt's arms, but he pushed her away.

'No one speaks to my sister like that, ever. Pack your things, get your children and get the fuck out of my life,' he said to her in a quiet voice. And striding past the group, their mouths agape, Merritt walked away from what he had once believed was his future.

CHAPTER TWENTY-SIX

Willow fled with Lucy to pick up Lucian from the police station and Kerr stood helplessly looking at the sobbing girl on the ground. Johnny sat next to her, rubbing his jaw where Merritt had hit him.

Tatiana watched with a vested interest. 'You OK, darlink?' she asked Johnny, concerned whether he would still be able to make her a star of the art world.

'Fine; I probably deserved that.' He laughed and got to his feet. 'You care to have a go now that I'm running away with your lover?' he asked Kerr.

'No, I'm fine thanks,' said Kerr, rubbing his own face in the same place Merritt had hit Johnny and thankful it hadn't been him on the end of those enormous hands.

Tatiana tottered over to Kerr. 'Darlink, we're over, you know. I just wanted to come and meet the director but instead I meet Johnny, so it all works out, da?' she said, in that cloying voice that annoyed Kerr more than he could explain.

Kerr shrugged. 'Fine, fine, whatever,' he said, and he meant it. He had new plans now, and they certainly didn't involve Tatiana and her need for public adoration. He had his own public to adore him and he was planning on getting a new fanbase, in the US.

Tatiana touched his face. 'You're a good man,' she said insincerely.

Johnny looked at Kerr. As far as he could see there was nothing about Kerr that was decent, and certainly not the way he spoke about his own flesh and blood. So the child was simple; what was the harm in that?

Probably took after his old man, thought Johnny, as he left Middlemist with Tatiana.

Johnny had a younger brother who wasn't the sharpest knife in the drawer, but he did OK. Didn't get through Eton of course, but his parents had made sure he learned the basics and now he had a good life on the farm, working with the animals. Johnny liked his brother's company; he kept it simple in an otherwise complex world of art and reputation.

Kerr had watched as Willow and Lucy left to pick up Lucian. Eliza stood beside him.

'Where's the weeping retard?' she asked.

'Her gay friend has taken her up to bed,' said Kerr of the boy in the pink scarf.

Eliza raised a perfectly groomed eyebrow. That boy wasn't gay, she was sure of it, but she knew it was best to keep her mouth shut.

'So what now?' she asked. 'America?' She looked at his doughy profile.

The last few years hadn't been kind to Kerr and his looks were puffy. Too many carbs, too much cocaine, thought Eliza.

Kerr nodded. 'But first I have to sort a few things out with my children.'

Eliza tried not to roll her eyes. Hopefully he would give up on his dream of taking the girl with them to LA. She seemed vile and looked just like her mother, the hysterical tyrant. Even Eliza was shocked at Willow's outburst. Americans, she thought; too many emotions.

Kerr pulled out his phone, walked into the drawing room and dialled a number.

'Gerry; Kerr. Listen, we've had a situation up here with Willow. Yep, she lost one of the kids, fucking her boyfriend at the time I think, and then she had a complete meltdown. I'm going for complete custody,' he said down the phone.

'Yeah and one more thing mate, I need you to look into a school that takes retarded children. Yep, full-time boarding,' he said, and he hung up the phone.

Eliza stood in the doorway, watching and listening.

'You cannot be serious?' she said. 'There is no way I am looking after three children, Kerr; not even for a minute. You have completely the wrong idea about me.'

Kerr laughed, 'So the evil stepmother does exist.'

'Yes, I'm afraid she does,' said Eliza in her primmest voice.

'Don't worry darlin',' he said. 'It's just for the money. She has a cosmetics contract and this film. There's more to come, and she can fucking look after me in my old age,' he said, and pulled Eliza into his arms.

She wrapped one leg around him, her black Jil Sander trousers pulling across his thin thigh, and she shoved her tongue into his mouth.

'I like the way you think,' she said as she pulled away from him.

Merritt stood outside the French doors watching them. He realised Willow had been telling the truth about Kerr. He was disgusting, and a pig of a father.

It still didn't redeem her for her treatment of Kitty though, he thought, and he wanted to weep thinking of Kitty struggling for all those years, trying to learn to read on her own. The way her father used to yell at her, calling her stupid and telling her to try harder at school.

He couldn't hear what Kerr and Eliza were saying, but he knew it was something Machiavellian. Eliza was awful and it hadn't taken him long into the marriage to realise it. Actually he was grateful that Johnny had taken Eliza off his hands, otherwise he would have had to have given her half of Middlemist.

He had wondered over the years what Johnny had seen in her, and now he understood. Eliza was the sort of woman a man needed when they didn't know themselves. Before they matured.

Merritt was socially inept when they met. She had brought him into the world with her vivacity. Johnny was living with the pressure of a younger brother who would never amount to anything, so his ambitious parents had put the heavy mantle of success onto Johnny's shoulders. Eliza gave him direction and pushed him the way he needed to go. She was a muse with standards, he thought, and Willow came to his mind.

She wasn't back yet. Kitty had left with Ivo. He didn't know where she had gone; she still wasn't answering her phone.

He heard the sound of tyres on the gravel driveway and he walked around to the side of the house. He saw Lucian and George tumbling out of Willow's Range Rover.

'Hello there! Go off on an adventure did we?' he said to Lucian, who ran to Merritt holding Custard and a piece of paper.

Willow walked straight past him with her head held high.

Ignoring Kerr waiting in the hallway, she walked into her room, picked up her jewellery case and a file filled with documents. Taking a sleeping Jinty from the cot, she dragged Poppy out of bed by the hand and walked downstairs again.

Putting Jinty into the car seat, Merritt watched her. 'What are you doing?' he asked her.

'You told me to go and we're going,' she said.

Poppy climbed into the car and Willow took Lucian by the hand and put him in the car beside her. Kerr walked out. 'Just a minute Willow, we need to talk,' he said, looking serious and folding his hands across his chest.

Willow looked at him. 'We've nothing to say to each other. You want to talk to me, then go through my lawyer,' she said, and she got into the car.

'You remember, we talk or I spill the secret, Willow,' said Kerr, his head turned to the side as though giving her a warning.

'Oh fuck off, I don't care any more,' said Willow wearily.

She looked at Merritt and Lucy. 'You want to know my big secret?' she asked. They stood silent, unsure what to answer.

Willow started to laugh. 'You know my Oscar? You know how it was presented by Roger Wood? The oldest man in show business – he died soon after, you know? Well guess what? I didn't fucking win. It was a mistake. He read out my name as a nominee, not the actual winner.'

Willow started to laugh and laugh, as though relieved to finally have the monkey off her back.

Lucy's jaw dropped open. Merritt stood in shock.

'So there, Kerr, I have done it. I have told the big secret. I was contracted to secrecy by the Academy and only Kerr, me and Roger know – but he's dead now so no worries there,' she said to Merritt and Lucy.

'I am a terrible actress, a terrible mother, a terrible wife, and now, it seems, a terrible lover. Lucy, you would do best to be rid of me. I'm a hoax,' she said, laughing and crying at the same time.

'Do you want to take George?' Merritt asked, holding out the puppy.

'What, and fuck him up as well?' she asked, and she looked at Merritt and stopped laughing. 'And I fucked it up with you, and I really love you. I was horrible to Kitty. And you want to know something?'

Merritt nodded, his own eyes welling with tears.

'Lucian knew he belonged here, because he knew how to write down some letters at the police station,' she cried.

'He wrote Middlemist?' asked Kerr, astounded.

'No,' said Willow as she got into the car. 'He wrote Merritt's name. He missed one "r" and one "t" and they thought he wanted a certificate of merit. So they printed him one out.'

And she wound up the window and sped off down the driveway with a spray of gravel flying into Merritt and Kerr's faces.

CHAPTER TWENTY-SEVEN

Kitty sat despairingly on the bed where she and Ivo had spent the afternoon in bliss.

'Why did you tell them?' she asked for the thirteenth time.

'Because I had to stand up for you,' he explained patiently.

'I didn't want anyone to know,' she cried again, shaking off his arm when he tried to comfort her. 'Now everyone knows that I'm stupid.'

'Nobody thinks you're stupid; just that you can't read yet.'

'I won't ever be able to read,' she said, and she stood up defiantly. 'And you know what?'

'What?' he asked, her swollen eyes and pale face breaking his heart.

'It doesn't matter. I'll be a cleaner or something,' she said.

'How will you read the instructions on the bottles?' he asked gently.

'Then I'll be a chef.'

'How will you read the recipes?' He looked at her little face and wanted to kiss her, but he knew she would push him away.

'I'll find something to do, something that doesn't require fucking reading,' she said, and she walked to the door.

'Where are you going?' he asked.

'Back to Middlemist,' she said, nervous at facing Willow

– that was, if she was still there. She had heard the way Merritt had told her to leave, and it broke her heart.

'What's there? I'm here,' he said, suddenly fearful.

Kitty looked him in the eye and set her small shoulders. 'I know you thought you were doing the right thing, but I can't forgive you for telling everyone, including that awful Eliza, the most gossipy person in the world.'

'Kitty please,' implored Ivo. 'Don't do this.'

'You did this Ivo,' she said, and she walked out of the room and down to the bus stop to wait for her ride. If she could read then she would be able to pass her driving test, she thought to herself, and then she wouldn't have to sit at the bus stop like some sort of sad backpacker.

Ivo chased her across the street. 'Why are you punishing me when all I did was try to help you?' he demanded, his face angry.

Kitty saw the bus coming in the distance and felt in her pocket for some loose change.

'Just leave me be Ivo, it's not like we were ever going to be forever anyway.' She turned to him.

'Why not?' he asked. 'Why do you even assume that?'

'Because I know about you and your life, and there's no room in it for an illiterate girl, I'm guessing,' she spat at him.

'Well I guess you'll never find out, will you?' he yelled at her.

The bus pulled up and Kitty got on. She paid her fare and sat down at the back, away from the side Ivo was on.

Ivo jumped onto the steps.

'Fare please,' said the driver.

'Um, I don't have it. Can I pay you back tomorrow?' asked Ivo.

262

'No fare no ride,' said the driver, looking ahead.

Ivo swore under his breath and stepped off the bus. 'You're making a huge mistake Kitty!' he yelled, and she looked away as the bus pulled onto the road.

I already made it, she thought, when I let you into my life. And she steeled herself for her reunion with Willow.

CHAPTER TWENTY-EIGHT

Merritt walked through the house, happy to have it to himself again. Kerr and Eliza had skulked away; hatching evil plans for another day, he thought. Kitty walked through the front door. She took one look at him and burst into tears again.

Taking her in his arms, he held her for a long time. 'Why didn't you tell me, Kitty Kat?' he asked quietly.

'I couldn't tell anyone,' she mumbled.

'You told Ivo though.'

'I didn't, he guessed.'

Merritt held her close and felt pain for the years he'd spent away from her when she needed him most. Why did Ivo realise so swiftly about Kitty's reading problems and not him or Dad? Deep down he knew the answer was because he and his father were completely self-absorbed. Forgetting Kitty had just lost her mother and worrying about money and reputations instead. All those years she had suffered and she hadn't said a thing. Merritt wondered if he could ever forgive himself.

'I should have been there for you,' he said, his voice cracking.

'You had your own life, Merritt . . . and Eliza,' she said, and Merritt started to laugh.

'You never liked her did you?' he asked his younger sister.

'Never,' she admitted, and they laughed and cried at the same time.

'Is Willow here?' she asked, listening for the children.

Merritt looked down and Kitty realised she had gone.

'Oh Merritt, it's all my fault,' she cried, and he led her by the hand to the kitchen.

'None of that now please. We had to sort things out once Kerr got here and things just went a bit silly, that's all,' he said, sounding calmer than he felt.

'Do you think you will talk to her soon? Can you tell her I'm sorry?' said Kitty. 'I feel so terrible.'

Merritt put the kettle on and sat down opposite her.

'Listen. I want you to know something; it's really important,' said Merritt, reaching across the table.

Kitty looked up at him mournfully. 'What?'

'When they found Lucian, they took him to the police station. They asked him to write his name down so they could try and find out where he came from. Do you know what he did?' asked Merritt.

Kitty shook her head. 'He can't read or write. Poor thing, it must have been awful.'

'That's the thing, Kits. He did know. He wrote down Merritt, minus the extra r and t. Your teaching him helped, Kitty – it helped him. And when all the drama dies down then Willow will see what you taught him. He can learn; he just needs to find the right teacher.'

Kitty cried again, and Merritt watched her.

'It's a bit like you, Kits,' he said.

'What's like me?' she asked, accepting the box of tissues that Merritt handed her.

'You just need the right teacher,' he said, 'to help you learn how to read.'

She nodded.

Merritt continued, buoyed by acceptance. 'I know Ivo tried, and he did an OK job, it seems; but you need professional help from people who do this all the time.'

At the mention of Ivo's name Kitty felt the tears come back.

'What? What's happened?' asked Merritt, confused.

'I can't believe he told everyone,' she said, her cheeks turning red with shame.

Merritt shrugged. 'Willow was being awful, even you could see that. He tried to stand up for you.'

'But I left and I didn't check my messages. I assumed you would take care of the children when it was my job; she was right,' said Kitty in a small voice.

Merritt didn't say anything. She was right, she had neglected her care, but then so had Willow and so had he and Kerr. They were all wrapped up in their own dramas, and it was the children who had suffered the most.

'So what do you want to do?' he asked as he poured her a cup of tea. Kitty stirred some sugar in.

She sat and sipped the sweet liquid, and then she looked at Merritt. 'I want my inheritance, and I want to go to London to learn how to read,' she said.

Merritt raised his chipped willow-patterned mug to her. 'Then off to London it is,' he said.

'What about you and Willow?' asked Kitty, emerging from her own personal crisis.

'Willow? Oh she's long gone,' said Merritt, almost cheerfully.

'Aren't you sad?' asked Kitty, her face clouded with worry.

'Oh no. I don't think we were meant to be long term; just a bit of fun, that's how those actors like to play it,' said Merritt as he crossed his long legs. 'I'm sure she's had lots of lovers since her dickhead husband left her.'

Kitty shook her head violently. 'No Merritt, she hasn't. I've lived with her since before Jinty was born. You have no idea how lonely she is. Did you know Kerr told her to get an abortion with Jinty? I was her birth coach – he didn't even come to the hospital.'

Merritt looked at his cup as she spoke, thinking about Willow. There was no doubt she had had a tough time, but that didn't entitle her to be abusive to the girl who had raised her children for the last two years.

'Merritt, don't be too hard on her,' said Kitty softly. 'I would have fired me today too; she just did it badly, that's all.'

Merritt smiled at her. 'Of course you're right, Kits; but what do I want with three kids and a mad-as-a-snake actress in a country home?' he scoffed.

Kitty looked at him closely and took his hand. 'I'm not blind, Merritt. I know how you feel about her.'

Merritt took his hand away. 'And now she's gone. She was telling the truth about Kerr, and I punished her, and then she punished you because of me. It's all a massive cock-up, eh Kits?'

Kitty put her head on the table and groaned.

'Is Ivo coming back here?' he asked her as he cleared the cups from the table.

'No, we're over too,' said Kitty.

'Because he stood up for you to Willow?' asked Merritt.

'Because he promised he would never tell and he did.

267

He made people feel sorry for me, and that's the last thing I wanted.'

'Don't you think you're being a bit harsh?' asked Merritt.

'No harsher than you,' answered Kitty, and she stood up. 'I'm going to head back to London tomorrow.'

'I'll drive you,' said Merritt.

'No, I'll take the train,' she said. 'Gives me time to read.' She slapped her hand on her leg as though she'd just made the funniest joke in the world.

Merritt laughed in spite of her terrible joke. 'At least you can laugh,' he said as he switched off the light in the kitchen.

'God knows I'm sick of crying,' she said in the darkness.

CHAPTER TWENTY-NINE

Willow stood in the modest London townhouse and looked at the freshly painted walls. The parquet floors were clean, it had a small garden and four bedrooms. It would do, and it was all she could afford.

Her money from the film and from the Blessings cosmetics contract was just enough for the down payment. The bank had been kind enough to oversee her precarious financial position as long as she committed to working more. She had a budget for the first time in her life, drawn up with the lovely young bank manager whom she had flirted with, just a little. Her accountant had overseen the transactions and now she had a home. Living with the children at the Dorchester had been hard, and she was sure they had worn their welcome a little thinly.

The new nanny, Sally from Australia, was fine. Not as gentle as Kitty, but the children seemed to like her. Poppy asked continually where Kitty was and Willow found it hard not to get cross with her asking, but mostly she felt sick about her treatment of the poor girl. How did she get through life without reading? She had left the odd note for her before; maybe she got the cleaners to read them, she thought.

The doorbell rang and she went to answer it, knowing it

would be the first of her scant possessions arriving. She had sent for her things to be delivered from Middlemist, but there had been no word from Merritt. He had made himself clear, she thought sadly.

'In here,' she said to the moving men who carried the boxes, carefully marked by the packers, and they placed them down, one after another. And then she was alone again. The beds were set up.

The new couch from The Conran Shop was in the sitting room but she had no kitchen items, no linen, nothing. She sat on the couch, still covered in thin plastic, and cried. How did she get here? she was wondering, when the doorbell rang again.

Wiping her eyes, she went to answer it and saw it was Lucy holding a box, with another at her feet.

'Hello,' said Lucy, smiling.

'Hi,' said Willow dejectedly.

'Moving is awful,' commiserated Lucy.

'I know. Come in,' said Willow.

Willow picked up the box from the ground and led Lucy into the kitchen.

'What's this?' she asked, nodding her head towards the box as she placed it on the countertop.

'A little housewarming gift,' said Lucy.

Willow opened the box and saw six small terracotta pots with herbs in them and pretty tin plant tags with the names of the herbs stamped on them.

'Oh how lovely,' said Willow, taking them out and putting them on the window sill.

'I have a list of potential magazine interviews for you to go through with me,' said Lucy.

'Do any of them pay?' Willow asked, only half joking as she rubbed a mint leaf between her fingers, the pungent smell filling the kitchen.

'Well, no. I stayed away from those ones. We need publicity, not charity. I want to spread the word that you are back and as fabulous as ever,' said Lucy, as she opened her bag and pulled out her notebook. '*Harper's Bazaar* and *Tatler* are both interested; I think I can get you the cover of one of them,' she said, looking at her neat handwriting. 'Also good news. I wanted to tell you this in person. Devon and Squires, the jewellery house, are looking for a new spokesperson. Are you interested?'

'What would I have to do?' asked Willow nervously. It had been a long time since she was the spokesperson for anyone – even herself.

'Print interviews and wear their jewels exclusively for red carpet events; be alluring and fascinating,' said Lucy checking her notes again. 'It's worth two hundred thousand pounds over two years. I can get you the first year upfront.' She raised an eyebrow at Willow.

'You are amazing,' she said, and she hugged Lucy. 'Do it, say yes.' Willow smiled at Lucy, who was fast proving to be her guardian angel.

'You have to meet with the CEO, Richard Devon, first. He's the grandson; just taken over the business,' said Lucy. 'He's a bit of a player from what I hear. Dated lots of gorgeous women; tried to lure Liz Hurley from Shane, but no luck.'

Willow nodded. 'I can be fascinating,' she said, looking down at her jeans and her worn American Vintage t-shirt. 'Not sure about alluring.'

'I know you can. Just lose the flip-flops, I suggest,' said Lucy, pointing to Willow's feet.

'These? These are the height of fashion,' laughed Willow.

'So, I'll set up a meeting?' asked Lucy, opening her diary.

'Yep,' said Willow firmly. She had to earn money, and wearing jewellery wasn't that hard a task, she thought.

'Where are the kids?' asked Lucy, noticing the silence.

'Out with the nanny,' said Willow tiredly.

'What's happening with Kerr? If you don't mind me asking,' said Lucy. 'I'm being hassled by the press, so what's the unofficial status so I can work out the official status?'

'We have to meet with an independent psychologist and have an assessment to see that Kerr and Eliza are fit parents. Then pending that report, we have mediation next week with a judge. If we can't work it out then we have to go to court and I really don't want that to happen.' Willow looked dejected and Lucy nodded understandingly and then paused.

'I have to ask, and I'm sorry to bring it up, but was what you said about the Oscar true?'

Willow folded and refolded the tea towel. 'I'm afraid it is. I'm sorry; I'm a bit of a fake really,' she said quietly.

Lucy shrugged, 'I don't care, but the Oscar does give you currency in the celebrity world. You don't think Kerr will release it to the media? To Eliza?'

Willow sighed. The confession at Middlemist was all she could think about. She wondered what Merritt thought of her now.

'I don't really care about it, to be honest with you. The

Academy won't be happy and they will, of course, deny everything. It's not in their interest to let this out.'

Lucy nodded again. 'Then let sleeping dogs lie,' she said and as if by magic, George the puppy tottered into the room from his basket near the back steps.

'Hello George,' said Lucy, reaching down and patting the wiggling puppy.

Willow looked at the little dog fondly.

'Kids still love him?' asked Lucy, although she knew the answer.

'They adore him; he's just what we all needed,' said Willow, trying to push Merritt out of her mind.

'No word from Kitty or Merritt?' asked Lucy, standing up.

Merritt had sent George down with the last of Willow's possessions, along with a charming note written to the children as George.

Willow had read it over and over, trying to find a clue or a message, but she couldn't see anything other than kindness towards her children, which in many ways made everything feel worse.

Willow shook her head. 'I've fucked that one up royally,' she said sadly.

'Things have a way of working out,' Lucy said kindly.

Willow nodded, hoping she was right.

'So I'll leave you to unpack, unless you need a hand?' asked Lucy.

'No, I'll be fine, we haven't got much,' said Willow, looking around.

'Let me know how you go with things and I'll set up some interviews and that meeting with Richard Devon, OK?'

'Thanks Lucy, I am so grateful for your help,' said Willow as she waved goodbye from her new front step, determined to treat Lucy the way she deserved. If she had learned anything from life at Middlemist, it was to never take those you love for granted.

CHAPTER THIRTY

Ivo headed up the driveway towards Middlemist and felt sick with nerves. No girl had ever made him feel like this. He was unsure what to say to Kitty.

He had promised her he wouldn't tell her secret but he had; he had announced it in front of the worst possible people. He hoped – no, he had actually prayed – she would forgive him.

The house was silent when he arrived. No doubt Willow had run off with the children after the dressing-down that Merritt had given her, he thought.

The film crew had left and there was no sign of Merritt. He rang the bell by the front door and waited. No one answered. He walked around to the back of the house and saw a lone figure in the distance; Merritt, he thought; and he walked towards the man with the spade and wheelbarrow, his usual accoutrements.

'Hey there,' he said.

'Hey yourself,' said Merritt, and he continued to dig the soil over. He had worked so hard in the last week since Willow had left. Every time he plunged the spade into the earth, he felt as though it was digging into his heart.

'Kitty around?' asked Ivo casually, as though nothing was riding on her being there.

'Nope,' said Merritt.

'Will she be back?' asked Ivo again, trying unsuccessfully to keep the disappointment from his voice.

'Nope,' said Merritt again.

Ivo sat on the stone seat dejectedly. 'Shit,' he said.

'Yes, it's all a bit shit,' said Merritt, stopping his work to look at Ivo. He was clearly devastated that Kitty had gone.

'I was made to promise I wouldn't tell you where she was,' said Merritt with a shrug. 'Sorry.'

Ivo nodded. At least one of the men in Kitty's life could keep promises, he thought.

'You heading back to London?' asked Merritt.

'I guess, although I don't have much to go back to,' said Ivo, thinking aloud.

He had no solid work lined up. He had managed to get an agent from the film but the offers weren't exactly pouring in; no one knew he existed yet. He wasn't even sure he wanted to act; it all seemed a bit silly, he had decided.

Henry had told him in no uncertain terms that his tenure as houseguest was up, and there was no rich girl on the horizon for him to shack up with. The only girl he wanted to be with was Kitty, and she had disappeared.

Merritt looked at Ivo. He felt sorry for him. 'You can stay here for a while I guess. I could use the company.'

He was surprised at himself for being so honest. It was lonely in the house without everyone around him. He had become used to the sound of the children and talking to Willow at night and chatting with Kitty over a pot of tea in the morning.

Ivo looked up. 'Really?'

'Why not?' said Merritt, going back to his task of digging the same area of soil, over and over again.

Ivo reached into his jacket pocket. 'I have Clementina's journals. Kitty lent them to me,' he said, holding them in his hand.

Merritt looked over. 'Ah yes. There are letters too, but I haven't gone through them yet,' he said.

Ivo looked up. 'She mentioned that there were also some letters. Would you mind if I had a look at them? The journals are fascinating, and I would love to piece them together with the letters.'

'Go for it,' said Merritt. 'They are in the drawing room, I think, near the computer.'

Ivo jumped up. 'I'll head back to town and get my things then. Do you think Kitty would mind me being here after everything that happened?' he asked carefully.

Merritt looked over at him. 'I understand why you did it. I would have done the same thing. Willow's behaviour was appalling. Kitty will understand one day,' he said, a frown on his face.

Ivo nodded. 'Thanks.' He started to walk away.

'I don't think she meant it,' he said as he turned back to his new housemate.

'Who? Kitty?' asked Merritt.

'No, Willow. I think she was under enormous stress and while it doesn't give her the right to say or do what she did to Kitty, she just lost it. I think it was actually about everything,' said Ivo slowly, thinking. 'She's not a bad person, she's just a bit out of touch with the real world,' he said.

Merritt said nothing. He went back to the earth, and Ivo walked away.

He had run through his time with Willow over and over again in his mind. It was as though there were two sides to her: a lovely, warm person and then a spoilt brat with a huge sense of entitlement. Her treatment of Kitty was unforgivable, thought Merritt, but when she had revealed her secret to him and to Lucy, he had been shocked. No wonder she was so insecure, he thought as he packed up his tools and headed back to the house. Kerr cheating on her, denying her child was clearly not right, no money, accolades for an Oscar that didn't really exist.

As he walked towards the house, he saw a flash of blue in the grass. He picked up Lucian's Thomas the Tank Engine. He would miss that, thought Merritt, and he wiped away the dirt from its little face and put it in his pocket.

Ivo was back within the hour and had set up in one of the draughty bedrooms of the manor.

He found the letters where Merritt had said they would be, next to the new computer that Willow had installed.

'Did Willow leave this here?' asked Ivo as he sat down at the screen.

Merritt looked over from where he was sorting through the accounts on the sofa.

'Yes, she sent for most things, gave a list to the packers, but she left that and a few other items here,' he said. 'I think she forgot about it. I'll return it to her,' he said distractedly.

Ivo nodded and opened up the internet browser. 'I might use it for a bit then, if that's alright?'

'Go for it,' said Merritt.

Ivo sorted through the pile of papers on the desk and found a black linen-covered sketchbook. He opened it and saw individual pictures of every room in Middlemist. On the other side of the page, fabric swatches were pasted onto the paper, with images cut from magazines and printed off the internet with recommendations for the interiors of the rooms.

Paint swatches were also included, as were images of light fittings, even taps and door handles, and notes in an uneven scrawl.

'Here you go, you left your book here,' said Ivo. He stood up and passed the book to Merritt and went back to his desk.

Merritt looked at the front and was about to say it wasn't his until he opened it. His heart skipped a beat. Every page was a work of art and inspiration. Her choices were perfect and considered, he thought. As he leafed through the book, he saw how much care she had taken, writing little notes about the way the sun came through the windows in certain rooms, their draughts and their sounds.

He turned to the last page and gasped. There was a picture of the front of the house, dressed in wisteria for the film, the light shining on it. Willow had cut some figures out of a photograph from the Blessings shoot and pasted them on top of the photograph of the house. Willow in all her glory, the kids smiling and Merritt standing behind her proudly. George the dog was actually sitting down for a brief moment. The photographer had taken it for the light reading, but Willow must have got him to print it out for her.

She had written underneath. '*Merritt and Willow Middlemist and their children at their newly renovated family home, Middlemist House.*'

And then she had drawn a big smiley face beneath it.

'*Don't worry Merritt, I'm only teasing.*'

And Merritt felt his stomach tighten, as it always did when he thought about what he had lost. His eyes ran over the collage of faces again and he looked at the old house in the background of the image.

Please let her come back to me, he wished silently.

Somewhere he heard a door slam and he jumped a little and then closed the book of everything that could have been.

CHAPTER THIRTY-ONE

Kitty rang the bell of the elegant Georgian townhouse, and it was opened almost immediately by Harold.

'Hello Katinka,' he said regally, with a little bow.

'Hi Harry,' she said, and she kissed his cheek shyly.

'Come in, come in; I have the Assam tea steeping,' he said, and he led Kitty into the hallway. The walls were painted vermilion and every part was covered in art. Most of the pictures were in gilt frames: Russian and Greek icons, mirrors concave and flat, a huge portrait of a nude woman bathing over a seashell. Kitty looked up, her eyes feasting on the lavishness of Harold's taste.

Harold watched her taking it all in. 'Come into the sitting room,' he said, and Kitty followed him to the small but cosy room.

The same vermilion colour covered the walls and even more art surrounded them. The deep purple velvet sofa was piled high with cushions of every colour and candles of different sizes filled in the fireplace.

A small Moroccan table sat to the side of the sofa and a large wooden coffee table was in the centre of the room. Snuffboxes and books covered it, along with a huge crystal ball. Kitty wondered whether it would foretell her future if she peered into it.

'I call this interior style "Jackie Collins meets opium den",' said Harold cheerfully.

'It's amazing,' said Kitty truthfully.

She had called Harold from her small hotel when she first arrived in London. He had been insistent she stay with him.

'My secretary has headed abroad for a time and I'm lost without her,' he had said. 'Perhaps you can fill in for her.'

'But I can't do any typing or reading or anything,' she had protested.

'Yet,' Harold had said firmly, 'you will. Meanwhile I need someone to answer the phones, take messages – you can tell me them using a small Dictaphone perhaps – make the tea, do a tidy-up,' said Harold.

Kitty had paused, wondering about his intentions, and Harold had sensed it.

'Don't worry my dear Kitty, you're far too young for me. I like them around thirty,' he had said and Kitty had laughed.

Staying in a hotel for the time in London while she found a teacher to help her with reading would eat away at her meagre inheritance, which Merritt had released to her when she left Middlemist.

Also, she thought being with someone else would be nice company, especially someone as witty and clever as Harold.

Now she was in Harold's house with her small bag of belongings and hope in her heart, where once there was none, that she might be able to conquer reading.

Harold insisted she join him for tea and then she could head up to her room and do as she pleased. He was out for the evening; the opera, to which Kitty declined the invitation.

After tea and divine shortbread, which Harold had had

flown down from Scotland, Kitty learned, he took her up to her room.

She almost cried when she saw its beauty. A wooden four-poster bed in the middle of the room against a delightful wallpaper of sprigs of daphne that looked as old as the house but perfect.

The bed had a canopy of dove-grey silk and the linen was white, with a blue silk patchwork counterpane over the foot. The rug was large and dark brown with a woven pattern of a basket of flowers in each corner, and a chintz armchair that looked as though it had taken the weight of a thousand behinds sat peacefully in the corner, with a small footstool in front of it.

Bookshelves lined with books and decorative plates high-lighted the room, as did a gorgeous window that overlooked the street below. The mantelpiece was bare except for a silver box, and a small fire was laid ready to be lit in the grate.

'Oh it's lovely,' cried Kitty.

Harold beamed. 'It *is* lovely. Many a famous body has lain in that bed after too many clarets downstairs,' he mused. 'I'll leave you to it then,' said Harold. 'Make yourself at home, bathroom next door. I'm on the next floor. I like to be in the ivory tower, overseeing everything.' He laughed and Kitty kissed his cheek.

'You are so kind to me. Why, I have no idea – I hardly know you,' she said, her eyes brimming with tears.

'I know enough about you to have you stay with me,' he said and he smiled as he walked to the door. 'Will Ivo be visiting you here?' he asked innocently.

Kitty's face darkened. 'No,' she said, and went to look out of the window.

Harold nodded. 'Right then,' he said and he left Kitty in peace.

Kitty set about exploring her room. The thoughtfulness of Harold towards his guests was delightful. The silver box on top of the mantelpiece housed chocolate coins by Debauve & Gallais. If Kitty had been able to read the label, it would have told her that they were the chocolates which were originally made for Marie Antoinette, but she just popped one in her mouth, the delicious flavour melting over her tongue. The cabinet at the end of the bed disguised a state-of-the-art television and DVD player.

A small brass carriage clock sat on the bedside table along with a bowl of grapes, a notepad and pen and a phone.

The desk in the corner of the room was bare except for a crystal vase of purple roses, whose scent filled the room. Kitty opened the centre drawer and a set of stiff blue stationery with Harold's address on it sat neatly inside with a pen and a box of stamps.

The wardrobe had scented paper lining the drawers, padded satin hangers and garment bags for travel. It was the most supremely elegant room Kitty had ever seen and she wondered how on earth she would be able to leave.

Downstairs, as he made more tea, Harold was thinking.

There was no doubt that Ivo was in love with the girl. He had seen them in between takes on set, sometimes with Willow's children in tow.

Willow had told him that Ivo visited her most evenings at the house. A shame, thought Harold as he pottered about his white and blue kitchen. The boy seemed better when he was with Kitty; less anxious and cocksure.

Harold knew enough about love after his four marriages

to understand heartbreak. The women he chose were works of art; beautiful. He was a collector of beautiful things, but they didn't last, he thought as he rinsed a delicate white cup carefully.

No more marriages, he decided; no more beautiful women. He felt fatherly towards Kitty, although he wasn't sure why. She was lovely, but not his type – too French, he thought; he preferred cold, distant and fragile. Kitty's warmth leapt out at you and her gentleness, her childlike enthusiasm, was intoxicating. No wonder Ivo fell for her. She was the realest person he had met in a long time.

Yes, he decided, as he put away the china in the ancient Japanese tea cabinet, it was a shame to let love linger with no reward; and he decided that he would be Cupid. He had a bow and arrow and a set of wings in storage. Now he just had to retrieve them and get to work, he thought as he climbed the stairs to his ivory tower.

CHAPTER THIRTY-TWO

Willow sat outside the room waiting for the psychologist and the speech therapist to finish testing Lucian.

Poppy and Jinty had already been assessed, but the psychologist had insisted she come back with Lucian to 'look at a few things'.

Willow, in a panic, had rung her mother in New York.

'What do you mean he's not talking yet?' Janis had screamed down the phone.

'Mom, you knew this,' she said, in an equally high-pitched tone.

'I didn't, I mean I did, but still,' said Janis.

'Janis, you never see them, you never come over; I offer all the time but you say you don't want to leave your practice,' said Willow tearfully. 'I have had the worst time in my life and you haven't bothered to help me. Didn't you think I might need some help? I know you're all about this being my journey and my independence but I need some help here,' said Willow, her voice breaking.

Janis was quiet on the end of the phone.

'Mom?' cried Willow.

'We're on our way,' said Janis and she hung up the phone.

Willow wasn't quite expecting that to be the outcome. It was true that Janis and Alan were avoiders when it came to their daughter and her problems. They were so proud of her successes and her glory, but they refused to see she might not be coping, for that would mean they had failed in their alternative style of parenting that they had written books about.

Willow had no idea where she was going to put them if they decided to stay with her. She was half hoping they wouldn't come, although she could do with the help.

She could only afford the nanny when she was actually working, not full time. Just last night she had been up twice to Jinty, who was restless with the new sounds from the street outside. Poppy had refused to dress that morning and was now at the park with the nanny and Jinty, wearing her pyjama bottoms, a ballet skirt and a bikini top.

The women walked back into the room with another younger girl and Lucian.

'Can we have a chat with Mummy while Penny stays with you?' asked the speech therapist. Willow felt the knot of fear tighten in her stomach. It had been there for almost two years, since Kerr had left. It had disappeared at Middlemist but it had found her again in London, she thought as she followed the women into an office and sat down facing them.

'How is he?' asked Willow anxiously.

'We think Lucian has a disorder known as dyspraxia,' said the speech therapist slowly.

'Is it terminal?' asked Willow, tears filling her eyes.

'It's not a disease,' said the woman gently. 'It's a neurological speech development issue.'

Willow took the tissues that one of them set out before her and she wiped her eyes. 'I'm sorry, I'm having a tough time at the moment,' she said.

'It's a very stressful time when a child is diagnosed with something like this, but please take heart that this is treatable,' said the speech therapist.

'Really?' asked Willow doubtfully.

'Really. I think the main issue with Lucian is anxiety, as well as a significant development delay,' said the psychologist.

'Anxiety?' asked Willow, her mind racing.

'Yes, it's obviously become an issue for him between the ages of two and five; that's really when he should have had intervention. Children teasing him often makes it worse. How has he coped at school?' asked the speech therapist.

'He's not at school,' said Willow, looking down. 'I was going to have him homeschooled.'

'By you?' asked the psychologist with interest. How on earth was a celebrity mother planning on homeschooling her child? she wondered.

Willow was silent and then told the truth. 'By my nanny,' she said, leaving out the part that her nanny, now ex-, was illiterate. There was no way she wanted to bring that up.

'If homeschooling is something you want to do still, then I suggest you work with a therapist to ensure he is getting everything he needs. But I think he would do well in school with intensive work,' said the psychologist, looking to the speech therapist for agreement. The speech therapist nodded.

'I agree. Children are the best way to get other children talking. He's only five, so you can hold him back this year. I suggest kindergarten, where he can have a carer. Start him as soon as you can. We can give you a list of names.'

Willow nodded.

The psychologist looked at her and leaned forward. 'How is Lucian's relationship with his father?' she asked.

Willow put her head back, hoping the tears would go back into her tear ducts. She looked at the white ceiling. 'He doesn't have one,' she said. 'Kerr thinks he's retarded. I have tried to tell him he's just special and he'll find his own way, but Kerr insists that he is stupid.'

'Has he said this to Lucian?' asked the psychologist.

'Yes, many times,' said Willow, her face reddening. 'But I knew he wasn't correct. Lucian definitely understands me. There is intelligence in his eyes, I know it,' she said passionately.

The psychologist nodded. 'He's not stupid, you're right; he's a little delayed, but hopefully we can get him working and talking in a much better way for himself and for those around him.'

'Why did you ask about his father?' asked Willow suddenly. 'Did he say something?'

The psychologist looked at the speech therapist and spoke quietly. 'He seems to freeze when we mention his father. It was a noticeable reaction; enough to worry us. You said he spoke in Bristol, when you were there?'

'Yes,' said Willow. 'I didn't hear him but he said the name Merritt to a policeman when he was lost. That's how they managed to get him back to us.'

'And Merritt is the name of your nanny's brother?' asked the speech therapist, looking at her notes.

'Yes, Merritt. He also waved at him, which I did see; he never seemed to react before to anyone, except maybe Poppy a little.'

'These are very good signs. Is there any chance that he could spend some more time with Merritt? Maybe we could teach Merritt a few of the exercises to help him in his therapy?'

Willow shook her head. 'No, I'm afraid that's impossible,' she said.

'That's a shame,' said the psychologist, pulling out a picture from the folder. 'I asked him to draw a picture, and this is what he did,' she said, putting it in front of Willow on the table.

Willow was shocked; she didn't even know he could draw.

She looked at the drawing. It was quite good for a five-year-old, she thought proudly as she assessed the picture, and then she saw what he had drawn. Middlemist, albeit crude, was still recognisable.

There was she, with Poppy in her red shoes, Jinty and Lucian with a small dog at his feet with only three stick legs. At the back was a stick drawing of a man, holding a spade.

'When I asked if that was his father, he shook his head,' said the speech therapist. 'And then when I asked if it was Merritt, he smiled. He loves that man very much, it seems.' And Willow picked up the drawing and held it to her chest, trying to breathe through the pain. So do I, Lucian; so do I, she thought.

Winter

CHAPTER THIRTY-THREE

Ivo settled into Middlemist House nicely. He was used to big houses with their draughts and peculiarities. While Merritt stayed outside in the gardens, Ivo explored and read the journals and the letters of Clementina and George.

'She was quite a fiery one,' said Ivo one rainy day to Merritt, who was absorbed in his seed catalogue.

'Who?' asked Merritt, looking up.

'Your great-great-great-grandmother, Clementina,' said Ivo. 'When George left, she says she destroyed all his paintings in this letter.'

'That must be why there are none around,' said Merritt, returning to his catalogue. 'It was the bane of my father's existence, especially when the prices for George's work went up,' he said. 'All that's left is Clementina's work, which I wouldn't get more than a few hundred pounds for. It's awful stuff,' said Merritt, shaking his head.

'I'd love to see it,' said Ivo excitedly.

'You're welcome to it. Top of the stairs, open the small door and then keep going. Wonderful view though. The studio looks out over the entire county, almost.'

Ivo jumped up and took the stairs to the attic. Upwards he climbed, thankful he had stopped smoking since he met Kitty, as the ascent was hard work.

At the top of the stairs, he found the studio.

As predicted by Merritt, the paintings were hideous. Angry works of men being castrated, crucified and stoned by Roman women, being burnt at the stake and lost at sea; the themes of revenge went on, and Ivo reminded himself never to cross a Middlemist woman again. Holding one of the smaller pieces, he walked to the window and held it to the light.

Putting it down, he picked up another larger canvas and held this one up too. He went through each piece, and then taking a few he walked downstairs again, his face puzzled.

'Don't tell me you want to put them up on the walls, I couldn't bear it,' said Merritt when he saw the works in Ivo's hands.

'No, I think I've found something. Would you mind if I take these to a mate of mine in London who works at Christie's? I promise I'll return them,' said Ivo.

'Sure,' said Merritt easily. 'Take as many as you like. I hate to disappoint you but they're not worth anything,' he said, laughing at Ivo's enthusiasm.

Ivo said nothing. Instead he asked to borrow Merritt's car, which he agreed to. Merritt liked Ivo the more he spent time with him. He was funny, self-deprecating, wicked and clearly in love with Kitty. He knew little about him as he spoke in circles when he mentioned his family, except to mention he was a huge disappointment to his father. Merritt understood that, remembering his own father's anger at his divorce from Eliza.

Ivo was well read and well bred, thought Merritt, but he didn't wear it like a badge of honour. He genuinely liked learning new things and he was clever, Merritt noticed. He had a gift for languages; he spoke three apart from English: French, Italian and a smattering of Russian.

'It's how I used to order my hookers,' he explained to Merritt when he asked why he learned Russian.

'What about Italian?' asked Merritt, shocked.

'I use it for the ladies only; and I like to order in French just to piss the waiters off in Paris,' he said, and Merritt laughed. There was so much about Ivo he didn't know, but he figured it was none of his business. At least not while he was the dumped boyfriend of his sister.

Ivo piled up the car with as many paintings as he could fit into the back seat and the boot, and he drove off towards London with a toot of Merritt's car's horn.

Dialling his phone, he pressed it up to his ear as he drove.

'Henry? Ivo. No I don't want to stay, relax mate. Listen, you sitting down? I think I've found a ghost. I've found the ghost of George Middlemist.'

CHAPTER THIRTY-FOUR

Willow sat with her lawyer in the mediation rooms. Kerr's lawyer sat opposite.

'I'm not prepared to wait any longer,' the mediator said. 'Since Kerr Bannerman has missed this second appointment, I will give temporary custody to the children's mother, Willow Carruthers. If your client deems it fit to grace us with his presence and argue for his existence in the children's lives, then please do keep us informed,' said the mediator, standing up. A formidable woman. Willow felt afraid for Kerr's sake, if he did ever front up.

Kerr's lawyer sat down wearily in the chair after the mediator had left. 'Do you know where he is?' she asked Willow.

'No idea,' she said honestly. Kerr's disappearance was not unusual, and she knew he was fine. He was too arrogant not to be. Even though the banks were pursuing him and his record label kept calling Willow for his whereabouts, he refused to show his face. She wondered where he was. He clearly didn't need the money from her now, she thought, as her lawyer turned to speak to her.

'So you're a single mother in the eyes of the law now.' She smiled at her client.

'I always have been, in my own eyes,' she said, and this time it was really true. She was up early every morning now, caring for her children, tending to the scrapes and the struggles; but mostly she was getting to know them.

She knew now that Poppy liked boiled eggs but not scrambled and that she wanted to be a puppy doctor when she was grown up; she knew her favourite story was *Madeline and the Bad Hat*, because she read it to her every night before bed.

She knew Jinty rubbed her dummies on her face when she was tired, and liked both her teddies in her cot before she would sleep. She liked the sound of the birds in the courtyard, and she ate the dog's dried food at least twice before Willow realised.

But the most special pleasure she had was in watching Lucian emerge from his silent, anxious world.

Willow was diligent with the exercises, and kindergarten had helped. His sounds were coming and his confidence was growing. She didn't know whether to scold him or praise him when he snatched the crayons off Poppy one morning, causing Poppy to burst into tears with shock at her brother standing up for himself.

Willow had known that Kerr wouldn't show up to mediation. Another month had passed since the first scheduled visit and Kerr had obviously found a source of wealth more valuable than Willow's paltry stream.

At least, it was paltry compared to what she had once spent; but now she saved. She had a savings account, and it made her laugh to see the statement on screen when she logged in on her phone. She listened when her accountant rang her about her deal for Devon and Squires, and she made decisions that gave her peace of mind.

'I have to go,' she said to the lawyer. 'I have a party to go to.'

The lawyer raised her eyebrows. 'It's work,' protested Willow, and the woman laughed.

It is work, she thought as she walked into Richard's office that evening. Work, and perhaps a little play. No woman is an island, after all.

'You look lovely,' said Richard, as Willow walked into the room. She smiled; she knew he was right. She did look wonderful, in her new Oscar de la Renta coral silk cocktail dress. Strapless with a trail of gold embroidery over the skirt, it showed off her flawless skin and tiny waist. Her hair was straight and long and her makeup, courtesy of the makeup artist that Kelly from Blessings had recommended, was exquisite. It was the best she had felt in a long time, and she reminded herself to write Oscar a note to thank him for lending her the dress for the evening.

Richard stood up from the sofa and placed a string of diamonds around her neck, to match the diamond and coral drop earrings she was wearing.

The first meeting with Richard from Devon and Squires had gone well; very well, in fact, and Willow wondered if she would sleep with him. Not yet. She reminded herself of the danger of falling into bed with a man too quickly, and then she pushed Merritt from her mind.

Richard's wealth was comfortable, not excessive. It was well rooted in tradition, and the crests of three European Royals on his jewellery boxes gave him class. His family had an apartment in Paris, an apartment in New York and a villa in Anguilla, which Willow liked saying in her head as she ran around St James's Park.

In some ways, it was nice to be back in the city and in the social circuit. Richard had wined her and dined her in London. She had been careful to keep him away from the house and from the children. She met him at his office mostly; that way it still felt like business and not romance. Richard, though, had other ideas, and she didn't mind being wooed. Kerr had been hopeless at wooing, she remembered. She had been bewitched by his rock star lifestyle and his coolness. Now he seemed a bit tryhard and desperate.

Merritt? Well, he was the salt of the earth. The only wooing he did was to coax his flowers into bloom.

Richard was the opposite: flowers, candy, gifts, notes, phone calls. If she wasn't such a bitter bitch she might have even enjoyed it, she thought.

What she did enjoy was the flights to Paris on his private plane. The suite all to herself at the Crillon for the launch of the campaign starring her. The photo shoot with yards of Dior lace and perfect hair. Yes, it was good to be back, she thought, and the work offers were rolling in.

An independent film with superstar Jack Reynolds was on the table, as was an action franchise playing the love interest. It wasn't an interesting role, but it offered a percentage of the backend, which would give Willow the financial security she desired.

And so would Richard, she thought, as she felt the diamonds cold against her skin. It was time to be practical after all. Could she really have lived in a ramshackle Gothic house in the middle of nowhere?

In the back of Richard's Mercedes, as they were driven to the British Fashion Council's party for Fashion Week, she tried to imagine how Merritt would fare at an event like this. Why did he keep popping back into her mind? she wondered.

She had enough going on with Janis and Alan staying at the house; it was chaotic.

Lucy's schedule kept Willow in the public eye but not hankering for attention. Lucrative deals negotiated with photo agencies meant that Willow's carefully constructed image was back in the magazines and on the internet. Photos of her doing the kindergarten run with Lucian and Poppy. Pushing Jinty in the baby swing, walking with her parents through the streets or St James's Park.

Janis and Alan had stepped up as parents and Willow was beginning to see another side to them. Less self-involved and more present, the relationship had changed, with Willow allowing Janis to see her vulnerable side and Janis and Alan allowing themselves to be grandparents for the first time.

Janis liked to look over the pictures of herself in the magazines. 'I look fat in this one,' she would say, and Willow would try not to laugh at this woman who worried about what her weight looked like in a photo but refused to see that multicoloured rave pants with fluorescent yellow stripes, bought at a street market in London, were unflattering.

Arriving at the party, Willow and Richard stood on the red carpet outside and allowed themselves to be photographed together for the first time.

Willow smiled. Fuck you, Merritt, fuck you, Kerr, she thought, and she put her hand into Richard's. He looked at her in surprise. He had tried to make a move on Willow last week and she had begged off with a headache; this was the furthest he had got with her yet. Proud of himself he smiled broadly for the camera, his slightly receding hairline showing off his forehead, shining in the spotlights.

Richard was more attractive because of his connections

and his name and he knew it, so he went after women who wanted what he had to offer. Women who wanted to be not necessarily happy but wealthy for the rest of their lives. He knew of Willow's financial woes – Kerr's lawyer talked in the spa at the health club and Richard's lawyer repeated everything to Richard over lunch at The Wolseley.

Willow was just what he wanted. Elegant, glamorous, not talented enough to be a threat but beautiful enough to wear the Devon and Squires products with the chicness they required. The lack of sex between them didn't worry him; he had his whores for that. He liked sex with prostitutes: they were easier, less complicated and always ready to do what he asked. He saw no shame in it, just as his father and grandfather before hadn't.

He watched Willow as she was interviewed by a blonde with huge breasts wearing a fur hat. Willow was all charm and generosity. Yes, she would do nicely, he thought. The children weren't too much of a problem; he had been raised by nannies and he was fine, he thought to himself. Willow had mentioned a nanny and her mother – clearly she understood child raising was a job to be outsourced at all possible times.

Richard knew the pressure was on him to bring a new heir into the company. He was thirty-six years old and single. His mother, Magdalena, had told him in no uncertain terms that his responsibility was to manage the company affairs, keep Devon and Squires's name clean and shiny, and procreate.

Hopefully Willow would like more children, he thought, as he watched her sip her champagne and listen to a dinner guest drone on. She caught his eye and he smiled at her and made a face as though he was bored. She laughed a little.

Later when they danced to Michael Bublé, whom Willow despised but Richard loved, he asked her if she thought she had more children in her future. Willow, a little drunk, told him that she would sooner stab herself in the eye with a pencil than have more children.

Richard made sure she got home safely under the care of his driver. He had his secretary return her calls over the next two weeks and finally she got the message. He had his hookers for sex, but he needed a wife and an heir. Willow wasn't right, he decided.

Eight weeks later he announced his engagement to Ingrid, a model and the ex-girlfriend of a Swedish tennis champion. Beautiful and malleable, she was perfect for Richard and guaranteed to be knocked up within the year.

Willow wasn't devastated. Actually she was partly relieved.

'Did you see the papers?' asked Lucy when the announcement came out.

'Yes, I saw it,' answered Willow.

'You OK?'

'Fine. I don't really care; nothing happened between us,' said Willow truthfully.

'Well, I think your contract is safe for at least this year,' said Lucy, 'but I will start looking for something else just in case.'

Willow put down the phone and sighed. Working was such a chore, she thought. For the first time she wanted to be at home with the children, pottering in the small garden that she had set up with them. She tried not to think of Merritt but it was impossible. Poppy chattered on about him endlessly and now Lucian's voice had been located he too piped up with his name occasionally. Jinty was walking everywhere and Willow was waiting for the magical 'Merritt' word to spring forth from her any day.

The ghosts of Middlemist were everywhere, she thought, as she looked out over the pots of parsley and basil, just beginning to seed.

CHAPTER THIRTY-FIVE

'It's a ghost,' confirmed Henry to Ivo and Merritt. 'They all have them,' he said excitedly. 'I've run these ones through the infrared reflectography machines. There are definitely works underneath them. To be conservative I would say that they look to be a different style of work from the top layers, but I cannot say they are George Middlemists just yet. We'll need to send them off for further tests.'

Merritt stood stunned in the back rooms of the auction house.

'How many more did you say there were at the house?' asked Henry.

'At least another fifty of different sizes,' said Ivo, his voice raised to a fever pitch.

'Let's get these done first and restore at least one, and then I'll come back to you,' said Henry.

'How long will it take?' asked Ivo.

'It depends on how long it takes to take the existing layers off, could be weeks or months,' said Henry.

Ivo looked at the painting in front of him. It was his favourite so far. He called it *The Proposal*. A young man knelt in front of his love, a woman in a white dress with dark hair and dark eyes. The garden surrounded them and the man had such an expression of hope and pain on his face that Ivo related to him completely. He knew he could never afford it, not even with his wage.

Ivo nodded. 'Come on mate, we need to get you a drink,' he said to Merritt, and saying their goodbyes to Henry they headed for the nearest pub.

'You could have a fortune on your hands,' said Ivo as he settled two pints in front of them.

Merritt shook his head. 'You mean to tell me they've been in the house all these years and we dismissed them? I can't believe it.'

Ivo nodded. 'I know. It's crazy but it makes sense. Where else would they have gone? The paintings that are out in public now must have been sold directly by George himself.'

Merritt sipped his beer. 'If they are what you think then I could sell them and do up the house finally,' he said.

'Absolutely,' said Ivo excitedly. He had taken great pride in his sleuthing work, and the rush of the find was more intoxicating than any drug he had ever used.

'I have a proposal,' said Ivo carefully.

'Yes?' said Merritt, waiting. What did Ivo want? Money for his trouble? A painting? He sat still in anticipation.

'I want . . . I want . . .' Ivo swallowed. He had been thinking about this for the last two weeks since the paintings had been with Henry.

'Out with it,' said Merritt impatiently.

'I want to write a book,' said Ivo finally.

'A book? On what?' asked Merritt, puzzled.

'On George and Clementina. I know these are the paintings, I feel it; and I think it's the most amazing story. The story of the house and love and revenge and art. It's perfect,' he said.

'Go for it,' said Merritt, laughing with relief.

'But I would need to write in peace. In the place where it all began,' said Ivo, looking at Merritt for a reaction.

'You want to write it at Middlemist?' asked Merritt.

'Yes. If you don't mind,' said Ivo, looking down into his pint.

'Mind? I would love you to stay,' said Merritt. He enjoyed Ivo's company, and if the paintings were George's then he would be indebted to him forever.

'Really? Wow. Great. I mean fuck, bloody marvellous,' said Ivo, beaming from ear to ear.

'Knock yourself out, although I'm not sure anyone would buy it. I don't know how interesting it is,' said Merritt.

'I think you'd be surprised,' said Ivo with authority. 'There's a market for this type of book. Part academic, part intrigue. Look at *The Da Vinci Code*,' he said.

Merritt laughed. 'Good luck then,' he said.

'I can pay rent,' said Ivo proudly.

'No rent,' said Merritt firmly. 'I owe you, I think.'

'You owe me nothing. It's everything I wanted to do, I've finally realised,' said Ivo.

'Really?' asked Merritt with interest. 'You don't want to be an actor?'

'No, too much waiting around. I like to make things happen.'

'There's a lot of sitting around in writing a book. I should know, I've written a few gardening books in my day,' said Merritt.

'I know, but it's different – I would be learning things, writing things down, telling a story,' said Ivo, his face flushed from the warmth of the pub and his passion.

'I could put you in touch with my literary agent,' said Merritt. 'They might be able to help you get a book deal.'

'Really? That would be great,' said Ivo. 'Things have a way of working out, huh?' he said, and then he thought of Kitty. 'Well, almost everything.'

Merritt sat thinking about Kitty and Willow. He hadn't heard from Willow. Lucy had rung him about the packers. She was formal and polite on the phone, and he hadn't dared ask her how Willow and the children were. He missed them all more than he thought possible, spending nights poring over the workbook she had put together on the house.

Kitty was settled with Harold, the film's director. She insisted that nothing was going on, he was merely being a gentleman and helping her. Merritt had no choice but to believe her. He would have liked to talk to Willow about it, but she had clearly moved on, he thought. He had seen photos of her everywhere, in the street, with the children. Jinty was walking, he noticed with pride when he saw images of them in the park together.

Lucian looked happy and Poppy – well, she was still Poppy. Ridiculous clothing and a defiant attitude like her father, he thought, as he saw her wearing wellies with a fairy dress in a magazine he had bought because it had Willow on the front. She was dating too, he read with a heavy heart. First a jewellery designer or something, and then rumours of her and the actor Jack Reynolds, whom she had met with for lunch before they started their next film.

The next few weeks were excruciating while he and Ivo waited for the results of the tests on the paintings, but when the call came through from Henry confirming their authenticity, he and Ivo were exultant.

'Now I have a book!' cried Ivo.

'And I will have the money for the house,' said Merritt in shock.

And they sat in silence, both thinking for a moment of what they didn't have. It lingered longer than the short-lived joy they had just felt.

The rest of the paintings were packed and shipped off to London for restoration, but not before Ivo and a photographer had documented each canvas of Clementina's work.

Ivo worked hard on the proposal for his book and sent it off to Merritt's literary agent. They were interested; could he write three chapters?

'Three chapters?' said Ivo, reading the email to Merritt. 'I suppose I'd better get started.'

'You'll be right,' said Merritt encouragingly. 'I'll be your editor, so to speak. You write and I'll check,' he said.

'Really? Thanks Mezza.'

'Mezza?'

'I'm trying to find a nickname for you,' said Ivo.

'Not Mezza, please,' said Merritt with a frown.

'What about Tits?' asked Ivo cheekily.

'No thanks,' said Merritt, snorting. Ivo made him laugh and he was such good company; he could see what Kitty liked about him. He was fun. A few times he had nearly told Ivo where she was, but he couldn't break his promise to her.

Ivo had stopped asking now; he knew Merritt was good to his word, and he let it go. Instead he buckled down and started to write. Within two weeks he had his three chapters and an outline of the rest. It was the most productive two weeks he had spent in years, and he was mentally exhausted at the end of each day when he tucked himself into Kitty's little bed.

Merritt didn't tell Kitty about Ivo staying, but he did tell her about the paintings. He told her a white lie, that an art historian had discovered the paintings underneath Clementina's by happenstance. Kitty didn't care as long as Merritt was happy, and he seemed to be, even though she knew he was mourning the loss of Willow and the children.

Ivo and Merritt settled into a routine of writing and gardening. Ivo sometimes stretched his body and helped Merritt in the garden, and Merritt read what he had written most evenings.

'It's a shame we aren't gay,' said Ivo. 'We cohabit very well.'

'Yes, shame; but if we were, you'd be too young for me,' said Merritt laughing. 'I'm an old man now, nearly forty-two,' he said.

'Forty is the new thirty,' said Ivo.

'Said the twenty-eight-year-old,' said Merritt as he watched the fire. The weather was turning and winter would soon be here, he thought. He had done as much as he could in the garden and he was nearly out of money. He was considering a new book or a television special, but he had lost his creative urge for anything else besides Middlemist.

He needed the paintings sold as soon as possible.

'You heard from Henry?' he asked Ivo each night to the usual answer from his housemate.

'When I do, you will be the first to know.'

Word came through when Merritt was down the bottom of the garden. Ivo had to run the length of the estate to find him. 'It's Henry,' he said, holding out the phone.

Merritt wiped his hands on the side of his work trousers.

'Hello? Yes, great. OK, sure, see you then,' was all Ivo heard.

'What? What?' he asked jumping up and down on the spot.

'Auction in a month, just in time for Christmas,' said Merritt.

'Fucking hell, that's quick,' said Ivo.

'Yes it is, but it's better for me,' said Merritt, looking back at the house.

He and Merritt walked back to the house together and as they strolled through the orangery, he spotted something pink in the corner. Walking over to it, he pulled out Poppy's favourite dancing skirt, with tiny bells sewn onto the tulle.

'Yours?' asked Ivo, raising an eyebrow.

'No, Poppy's,' said Merritt quietly.

Ivo said nothing, and Merritt clung to the tiny costume until they reached the house, where he hung it on the hook of the back door in the kitchen. The bells tinkled every time the door was opened afterwards.

CHAPTER THIRTY-SIX

Kitty arrived for her first lesson with the specialist reading teacher early, as instructed by Harold.

'Always be early, it shows respect,' he had insisted, and Kitty did as he said. Harold's elegance and refinement permeated everything he touched. Staying with him, Kitty felt like Eliza Doolittle or Miss Congeniality or both. He was gentle with her but he insisted she use the right knife and fork at the formal dinner they sat down to most nights; the right heel with her jeans; the most luxurious cashmere she could afford when she said she needed a jumper. He took her to Liberty's for a knit and she left with an evening dress by Lanvin, a day dress by Cacharel, new shoes, a Givenchy leather bag, a Chloé evening bag and a Marc Jacobs winter coat.

Harold had insisted he buy the items and she could pay him back later. Kitty felt odd about it until he explained that nothing was expected, but that she had a responsibility to look as good as she could; she was merely performing a public service.

'No one wants to see someone dressed badly. If you can't help it, then fine; but if you have a choice then try to make an effort. It's an act of civic duty to be as well presented as you can be,' he said, wearing a cashmere beret and a striped sailor top.

Kitty had laughed at his peculiar opinions, but she did feel good about herself as she sat in her jeans, her pretty Kurt Geiger flats and her new Liberty of London cashmere jumper.

Harold had taken it upon himself to give Kitty an education. Not just in reading, but also in life. Manners, art, history, people; even housekeeping.

'The water for the tea must be almost boiled, but not completely. Put the milk in first. It's all about the release of the proteins. Milk first, Katinka,' she would hear him say from the kitchen. As an experiment she put the milk in later, and he knew.

'Don't try to trick me, child. Now go and pour me another cup please.' He *tsk tsk*ed at her as she left the room, giggling to herself.

The first reading lesson was always going to be horrifying – like the first time you drive a car, said Harold – but Kitty still didn't have her licence so she had no benchmark to compare against the sheer terror she felt as she waited.

The door opened and a woman smiled at her. 'Kitty?'

'Yes,' said Kitty shyly.

'Lavender Macquire,' she said, holding out her hand. Kitty shook it and followed her into her lovely home.

Books were piled up everywhere, as were CDs, and there was a microphone on a stand.

'What's that for?' asked Kitty, nervously looking at the microphone.

'I record dialect tapes for actors,' said Lavender.

'Wow, so you can do accents?' asked Kitty.

'Yes, I can,' smiled Lavender.

'Cool,' Kitty said, and walked to the chair that Lavender gestured to.

Lavender sat opposite her. 'So tell me about yourself and why you're here,' she said, picking up her notebook and pen.

Kitty paused. 'I thought Harold told you,' she said, her brow furrowed.

'He told me a little, but I want to hear what you think.' She smiled again.

'Well, I can't read and I need to learn,' said Kitty, her face reddening.

'Need or want?' asked Lavender.

'Both.'

'Good.' Lavender looked up at her new pupil. 'What words can you read already?'

'None,' answered Kitty.

'None? Right then.' Lavender took a black felt-tipped liner from the table in front of her and wrote something on a piece of card from a stack next to it.

'What does this say?' she asked, holding the card up.

'Kitty.'

'So you can read,' said Lavender.

'That doesn't really count does it?' asked Kitty.

'Why not?' asked Lavender. Then, after a pause, 'Pick up your coat. We're going for a walk.'

Kitty stood up reluctantly. She wanted reading lessons, not a personal trainer.

Lavender slipped on her coat and walked to the front door. 'Come on then,' she said, and she and Kitty stepped into the busy street.

'What does that say?' asked Lavender as she pointed to the sign at the corner of the road.

'Stop,' said Kitty.

'Yes.'

'But I knew because of the colour,' said Kitty. Lavender ignored her.

'What does this say?'

'No parking?'

'Yes.'

'But I saw the letter P with a line through it,' admitted Kitty.

'So you know your letters?' asked Lavender.

'Some,' said Kitty.

'Who taught you that?' Lavender asked as they continued along the street.

'Just someone,' said Kitty. Lavender didn't push her.

As they walked along, Lavender pointed out signs and Kitty did better than she thought she would. When Lavender used reading in an everyday way it made sense. It was the books that caused her anxiety, Kitty explained.

'Books are a while away yet; we need to work slowly and without stress. You'll enjoy books as soon as you can enjoy the story,' Lavender said as they walked back to her house. Kitty felt relaxed about the work ahead of her for the first time. Walking had been a good idea – it made the focus about something other than Kitty and the words, she thought.

Back at the house she worked through the letters, and again she did better than she expected.

'Well done! Your friend who taught you did it well,' Lavender said.

'Why?' asked Kitty.

'The sounds to go with the names. Some people get stuck by just learning the names of the letters, but not the sounds they make to go with them. You should take your friend out for a drink,' laughed Lavender.

314

Kitty softened towards Ivo for a moment, and then she remembered the horrified look on Merritt's face and the scorn on Eliza's when Ivo had blurted out her secret. She shut him out of her heart again.

After agreeing to meet with Lavender three times a week, and to practise with Harold if she could, Kitty literally floated home. She felt as though a ton of books had been lifted from her.

'How did your first lesson go?' asked Harold, waiting at the front door like a patient father.

'It was wonderful,' said Kitty. 'I know more than I realised!'

'We all do darling,' said Harold. 'We just don't understand until it's all too late,' he said sagely.

'You sound very low; you OK?' she asked, as she hung her coat by the front door. 'Cup of tea?'

'Yes please darling,' said Harold, and they wandered into the kitchen.

'What's the problem?' she asked as she set about making the tea.

'I'm not sure I like my film.' He sighed and sat heavily in the oak chair.

'Why?' asked Kitty. Harold had been in post production for days on end with the film, and Kitty didn't dare disturb him.

'I don't know. I think it's generic,' he said, waving his hands about.

'I don't know what that means,' said Kitty.

'It means common, everywhere, usual. Not exclusive,' said Harold.

'Like McDonalds?' asked Kitty as she put the cups and saucers down.

'Yes, precisely. I am the Ronald McDonald of filmmaking,' he said sadly.

Kitty laughed. 'I'm sure you're not. Is there someone you can ask to look at it for you?'

'No,' said Harold. 'I don't show anyone what I do before release. It has been chosen to open Cannes, and the final print isn't even close to being ready. It could take months.'

Kitty sat thinking. She was at a loss as to who could help Harold.

'Perhaps you might take a look?' Harold asked, looking for her reaction.

'Me? I don't know anything about films,' she said.

'I know, that's why. Just watch it and tell me when things don't make sense or if you think you have seen them in other movies. You watch movies I assume?'

Kitty nodded; she watched movies all the time. She had seen every film in the local DVD shop and then some more. When you don't read you have to find something to do with your time, she reasoned.

'I could try but I don't think I would be much help,' she said.

'Let's go,' said Harold, and he stood up.

'Now?'

'Cannes is in May, m'dear. We must get a wriggle on.'

'Harry, it's November,' she said.

'I know! No time at all.'

Kitty followed him up the stairs to his ivory tower.

Surprisingly, it was an open-plan space. The walls were knocked out to reveal a bed opulently covered in cushions and throws, but the soft furnishings were the only decoration in the room.

There was a huge screen and a number of computers and smaller screens. Soundproof walls were covered in linen and a small bathroom, discreetly screened, finished everything off.

'It's quite bare compared to downstairs,' said Kitty.

'I like my work to be the art,' said Harold pompously, and Kitty hid her smile from him. He was her benevolent landlord, after all.

She felt nervous to watch Ivo on the screen; it had been weeks since she had seen or heard from him. She scoured the social pages for pictures of him, but there was nothing anywhere. She didn't ask Merritt about him; there would be no way Merritt would know anything about him. He was stuck with his head in the soil, too busy worrying about some fancy art auction.

Kitty had no expectations of the auction's outcome, but Merritt clearly did, she thought.

Harold pressed a few buttons and a countdown came onto the screen.

Harold turned to her. 'Do you know much about the story?' he asked.

'Sort of. Willow's character is sad about her husband dying and tries to bring back his ghost, and then Ivo turns up and she thinks he's her husband reincarnated. But Ivo just wants to marry her and send her off to the mental ward?'

'Pretty good,' said Harold smiling.

He pressed play and Kitty sat back. 'Oh, Middlemist looks wonderful,' she said, smiling at her beautiful home on the screen.

She jolted when she first saw Ivo, but as it continued she became more involved with the story and less with his presence. Occasionally she would ask Harold to stop and ask questions or make comments, but mostly she just watched. When the ball scene came on, Kitty hid behind her hands when she saw herself on screen. Harold stopped the film. 'Does this scene make sense? I've had to play with this edit a bit.'

Kitty shook her head. 'Fine, why? Did I do something wrong?' she asked.

'No, no – not at all. It's just that young Ivo couldn't keep his eyes off you,' he laughed.

'What? Really?' asked Kitty, trying to remember that night.

Harold flicked to another screen. 'These are the outtakes,' he said, and he pressed play. Kitty watched as the extras and the actors milled about. She saw herself talking to Willow and Merritt; taking a drink; the whole time Ivo was across the room, his eyes following her at every turn. Kitty felt her stomach flip as she saw herself so oblivious to his lust and admiration.

'He is madly in love with you, you know,' said Harold, matter-of-factly.

Kitty looked down. 'He betrayed me,' she said quietly.

'Did he sleep with someone else?' asked Harold, leaning back on his Herman Miller chair.

'No,' answered Kitty, 'not that I know of.'

'Did he treat you badly? Hurt you?'

'Not really,' said Kitty, and then she burst into tears and told Harold the whole story of her secret coming to light, Willow's treatment of her, and the end of Merritt and Willow's union.

'He's to blame for everything,' said Kitty.

'Really?' asked Harold gently.

'Sort of. Some of it,' admitted Kitty, letting the emotional noose on Ivo's neck relax, just a little.

'So, would you be here now with me if you hadn't had the run-in with Willow?'

'Probably not,' said Kitty, looking down.

'Things have a way of working out, Kitty. Be here now and learn from me and Lavender, and then see what comes. I have a feeling you and Ivo will work it all out.'

Kitty said nothing. She disagreed. Ivo had all but disappeared anyway, she thought.

She watched the rough cut of the film and was transported into Harold's world. At times she forgot she was watching her former boss and lover in her childhood home.

'The film's really good,' she said when it came to an end.

'Do you really think so?' asked Harold eagerly. 'Not generic?'

'Not at all, I think,' said Kitty truthfully.

'Are there any bits you didn't like or didn't understand?' he asked.

Kitty sat thinking for a long time.

'Tell me please,' begged Harold.

Kitty frowned. 'Well a few times I got a bit confused,' she said, and slowly she began to tell Harold the bits she liked, the bits she didn't like, and what she would move. 'I think that scene after the séance should go in a bit later. It kind of spoils the waiting, you know.'

Harold nodded. 'I wondered about that.'

They spent the rest of the evening watching the film again, Kitty looking at the extra scenes and eating scrambled eggs and smoked salmon. By one in the morning, she was exhausted but happy, as was Harold.

'I think you're a genius,' he said, clapping his hands together.

'Not really; I've just seen a lot of movies,' she said, smiling from his praise.

'You should be a film editor.'

'Ha. That's funny,' laughed Kitty.

'I'm serious my dear. You have a natural gift for seeing the arc of the story.'

'I didn't see an ark anywhere in the film,' said Kitty, her brow furrowed.

Harold laughed. 'It's the natural rise in the story; the way things evolve.'

'Oh,' said Kitty feeling silly.

'I'm going to keep working on this. I'll show you again soon,' Harold said, elated.

Kitty sat downstairs, proud of herself. Today was a good day, she thought; even though she had seen Ivo on screen, it hadn't hurt as much as she'd thought. A film editor, she thought to herself. I wonder how much reading I would have to do to become one of those.

CHAPTER THIRTY-SEVEN

'Morning,' said Jack Reynolds, Willow's co-star on her new film. She clutched her coffee cup, just like Jinty did her dummies.

'Yes; morning,' she said shyly.

Jack Reynolds was the biggest star in Hollywood, a definite ladies' man and a philanthropist. He lived in Italy most of the year and only worked when the film intrigued or challenged him. The film he and Willow were starting was a small independent project with a first-time director and a small budget. She had done it on the advice of her agent and Lucy, who was fast becoming the most valuable person in Willow's life.

Now Janis and Alan had headed back to New York, leaving Willow on her own. And with no sign or word from Kerr, Lucy became like a partner and a parent to her in so many ways.

She read scripts, gave fashion advice – which Willow still thought was amusing from a woman who only seemed to own one handbag – and even worked as an emergency babysitter when Willow's nanny fell down and sprained her ankle. More than that, she and Lucy were friends and almost equals. Willow trusted Lucy completely and liked sitting and nattering about the day or their lives over cups of tea in

Willow's comfortable home. Her taste had become somewhat restrained as a result of her tight budget, but it was nothing that wonderful use of paint and carefully chosen furniture couldn't disguise.

'Pink!' exclaimed Lucy when she walked into Willow's newly painted kitchen.

'Yes! I always wanted a pink kitchen,' said Willow, smiling at the work around her. 'Kerr wanted a black one at the other house. So dreary,' she said.

'It works,' said Lucy, laughing.

'I know, it really does. I love it; it makes me happy,' said Willow.

'Then that's what's important,' said Lucy wisely.

Willow had made her own coffee in her pink kitchen. Part of her budgeting was not to give in to the 'latte lifestyle', as her accountant called it, and so she had taken hers in a flask to the film studio to start work with Jack. It was a relatively short shoot for her, just two weeks in the studio, but she was looking forward to it. A wordy and witty script in her natural accent. She had fun learning the lines.

Jack was supposed to be a dream to work with, she had heard, and she smiled at him warmly. They had had dinner when he first arrived in London at a Dean Street eatery. It was supposed to be quiet and private but the paparazzi had found out somehow and they were besieged when they left.

Jack had been attentive and interested in her when they ate, but she had the feeling it was purely professional and she was grateful. After Richard she had steered away from dating.

She had even said in an interview with *Harper's Bazaar* that she was over men and would remain single for the rest of her days; instead she would focus on being a doting mother and hopefully, one day, a grandmother.

Jack sat in the makeup chair while Willow sat next to him.

'What gives?' he asked as he folded his paper away.

'Nothing. I'm so tired. I was up all night with my baby – she has a case of the night terrors,' she said as she closed her eyes while the makeup was applied.

'Ah yes, one of the many reasons why procreating is not for me,' he laughed. 'I like my sleep too much. Don't you have a nanny?'

'When I work, yes, but not at night,' said Willow.

Jack made a surprised face, which Willow didn't see.

'Hey, what are you doing tonight?' he asked quickly.

'Nothing; sleeping, looking after kids. Why?' asked Willow with interest.

'I'm having a dinner, thought you might like to join. Just me and a few friends. One of them is in a play in the West End and I thought we could meet them for a late supper,' he said casually.

Willow thought about her options. What else did she have to do besides feed, bathe and get three children to bed? She hadn't been out for anything other than work and public appearances in a long time – she longed for a fun night.

'If I can get a babysitter,' she said, wondering if she could get the nanny to work a few hours late. The new nanny was nowhere near as accommodating as Kitty, she thought. Kitty was always available; always saying yes. She had taken her for granted and then treated her like shit. Just thinking of it brought a flush of shame to her cheeks.

She had wanted to write her a letter, but Kitty wouldn't be able to read it. She couldn't call her because she didn't know where she was, and there was no way she would ring Merritt to find out. Not that he would tell her anyway.

The rehearsal started and then they were straight into filming; there was no budget to discuss options. Willow worked hard but it was fun with Jack. He was hilarious and clever, and she knew her acting improved as the day went on.

Thankfully the nanny had agreed to stay the night, and Willow left the set with instructions to meet Jack at ten o'clock at J Sheekey.

Willow dressed carefully, so as not to look too overdressed for the London theatre crowd. She found an old Stella McCartney dress in pale olive green silk chiffon, pleated, full skirted and tied under the bust. It was elegant and diaphanous, with a touch of the goddess about it when Willow let her hair down. With her favourite Yves Saint Laurent heels and a delicate diamond bracelet from Richard, she was ready to go.

Slipping on her warm Prada coat and picking up her Marni handbag, she jumped into the cab she had ordered, ignoring the surprise of the taxi driver at having someone so famous sitting on the back seat.

'I picked up Michael Caine a little while back,' he said once they'd started to drive.

'Oh right,' said Willow. 'How was that?'

'He was very pleasant, very nice fella,' said the cabby. 'You off to see a play then?'

'No, meeting friends,' said Willow, wondering who Jack's guests would be.

'Got a boyfriend yet?' asked the man.

'No,' laughed Willow. 'You single?'

'Nope, not me. I got a wife and three kids,' he said. 'I hope you don't mind me saying but I think you're well rid of him.'

'Who?' said Willow. Did he mean Merritt? she wondered.

'Your husband,' said the man as he turned into busy traffic.

'Ah yes,' she said, careful to not be drawn into anything she might regret seeing in the papers later.

'I saw him a while back, maybe three weeks ago. Drove him to Heathrow,' he said. 'He was rude. Not at all up for conversation.'

Willow's ears pricked up with interest. 'Where was he flying to?' she asked.

'International. Let me think . . . America,' said the man.

'Was he alone?' asked Willow.

The man paused. He didn't want to say too much, but she was such a nice young lass, he thought. 'I'm afraid not. He had a woman with him; she was in black and white I remember. She was rude too.' He shook his head in disgust at the disappearance of manners in cabs and Willow sat back, thinking about Kerr and Eliza. So they had gone to America, she thought. No wonder she hadn't heard from him. No doubt he had had an offer he couldn't refuse, and Willow's money was not enough of an enticement for him to stay.

'I'm sorry, love, if I upset you,' said the man, looking at her in the rear-view mirror.

'Not at all,' smiled Willow genuinely. 'You have done me a huge favour actually,' she said as the cab stopped in front of the restaurant.

She paid him and tipped him generously although he insisted it wasn't necessary, and she took his card. 'I will be sure to call you when I need a lift anywhere,' she said; and an update on my shit of an ex-husband, she thought.

Walking into the restaurant, she saw Jack at the table with a woman with her back towards her. She walked over. All eyes were on their table. 'Willow,' said Jack, and he kissed her cheek in greeting. 'Rose Nightingale, this is Willow Carruthers,' said Jack proudly.

Willow smiled hello and sat down next to Jack. She knew Rose Nightingale – she was England's Meryl Streep. She had married a Hollywood movie star, divorced him and spent ten years working on her career. Then she had met Max on the set of a film with Jack, and the rest, as they say, was history. Max had brought three little boys to the marriage after his first wife had died, and Rose and Max had since had twin daughters, who were about Jinty's age.

'Willow. I am such a fan of your work,' said Rose warmly, and soon they were talking like old friends. Max was in a play and would be meeting them soon. Willow and Jack and Rose screamed with laughter at everything; they gossiped and chatted. Rose was exactly what Willow needed.

'How long are you here for?' asked Willow to Rose.

'About two months,' said Rose. 'The children are in school here and I'm playing house with the twins and doing a bit of snooping around to see what films are coming up that I might be interested in.'

'Twins! I don't know how you do it,' said Willow, imagining two of Jinty, who that morning had poured chocolate syrup into the kitchen of Poppy's dollhouse.

'I don't do it by myself,' laughed Rose. 'I have nannies and I have a husband.'

'Yes, well I have a nanny but no husband,' said Willow, with a roll of her eyes.

'No one on the horizon yet?' asked Rose.

'No; I did see someone but it didn't work out,' said Willow, wondering why she was telling Rose.

'Richard Devon wasn't it?' asked Jack.

'How do you know that?' asked Willow.

'I read the gossip columns,' said Jack with a shrug of his shoulders.

Willow tried not to laugh at Jack's admission of gossip guilt.

'No, it wasn't Richard; that was just work.'

'Then who was it?' asked Rose, leaning forward. Since her marriage to Max, her goal was to have everyone paired off; she was like Noah's wife on the ark.

'He's nobody, he's not famous,' said Willow laughing.

'What does he do?' asked Rose.

'He's a gardener. He designs gardens,' said Willow.

Rose frowned. 'Not Merritt Middlemist?' she said. Willow nearly dropped her wine.

'How did you know? How do you know him?' she asked.

'Merritt designed my garden in LA. Amazing work,' she said to Jack. 'Wow, he is sexy,' said Rose knowingly.

Willow took a deep breath inwards as she allowed herself to be reminded about Merritt while Rose rhapsodised to Jack about him.

'He is super handsome, tall, strong, cool. Knows bloody everything about plants and wears the hell out of a pair of jeans. And those hands . . . Jesus, I was pregnant when he did the house and I was so goddamned horny all the time, I made Max get out in the garden and trim the roses, so to speak, and then come and take me like Lady Chatterley,' she said, sitting back against the banquette.

Willow laughed, despite her heartache over Merritt. Jack

sat back too. 'Jesus. You make him sound so good I might ask for his number.'

Rose laughed and waved her napkin at him. 'Silly man,' she said as a tall man came to sit beside her.

'Darling, guess what?' she said.

Max looked at Willow. 'Hello! Max Craydon,' he said.

'Willow,' she answered.

Rose interrupted. 'Willow was seeing Merritt Middlemist,' she whispered.

Max made a face at Willow. 'Lucky you! He was all she talked about when he did our garden with his team. I ended up having to wave a chainsaw around with no top on to outdo him,' he said, and they all laughed.

'So, what happened?' asked Rose.

'Nothing; it just didn't work out, that's all,' said Willow vaguely.

'What a shame,' said Rose. 'I hear his paintings are about to go to auction.'

'His paintings?' Did Merritt paint? she wondered.

'Yes – the art world is abuzz. Apparently they found over seventy paintings of his great-great-grandfather or something. His wife had painted over them.'

'Eliza?' asked Willow.

'Eliza? Who's Eliza? No, his great-grandfather's wife painted over them. And anyway they found them underneath and they've had them restored. He's selling them soon; two weeks I think,' said Rose. 'He's going to be rich after they sell. There's a big interest in Victorian Romanticism. I might have a look actually,' she said.

Willow listened with interest. 'How did they find them? How did they know?' she asked.

'I don't know any more than that. There was an article in the *Independent* about it – you could probably find it if you looked it up online.'

Willow thought about the computer she had left at Middlemist. She would buy a new one tomorrow, she thought as they ordered.

The dinner was wonderful and Willow found the company stimulating and hilarious. When they left, the paps were there as they said goodbye to Rose and Max at the door. Willow kept her head down low as Jack hopped into a cab with her.

'Hello again.' She looked up and saw the cabby from earlier in the evening.

'Oh hi,' said Willow.

Jack looked at her. 'Where you headed?' he asked.

'Home,' said Willow, nervous. There had been no frisson between them at the restaurant, and she wondered now if he would try something and whether she would knock him back. It had been a while since sex with Merritt and she missed it – the sex, she thought, but not Merritt. Ah fuck, who the hell was she kidding; she missed Merritt also.

'I'm at Blakes. Mind if you drop me off?' he asked.

Willow sighed with relief. 'Of course not,' she said, and they chatted companionably with the cabby as they headed towards his hotel.

He kissed Willow's cheek as he left the car. 'See you tomorrow,' he said, and she waved him goodbye.

The cabby pulled out again into traffic and headed in the direction of Willow's home.

'I picked him up the other day,' said the cabby.

'Really? What a coincidence,' she said, looking out of the window.

'He was with his boyfriend though.'

She looked at him. 'I don't think Jack Reynolds is gay. I'm pretty sure of it,' she said.

'Oh right,' said the cab driver. 'He had a nice young Italian man with him; an actor. Dante or something. Oh well, I must have been mistaken,' he said as he drove. But he knew he wasn't. Twenty years of driving cabs taught you a thing or two about people, and he knew a gay man when he drove one. And he knew a heartbroken woman when he drove one, he thought as he glanced at her in the mirror.

Shame, he thought as he dropped her off; young, beautiful and all alone. The world wasn't fair. And all the while Willow was thinking that she must remember never to drive with that cab driver when she had a secret; it would be all over town by the end of his shift.

CHAPTER THIRTY-EIGHT

Merritt sat in the private viewing gallery that overlooked the auction room. The crowd was swelling and he could hear the hum from below. Kitty had joined him for the auction, as had Ivo, which shocked her when she walked into the room.

'Why is he here?' she hissed to Merritt, but before he could explain Henry walked in.

'So you're the Kitty I've heard about,' said Henry, shaking her hand.

Kitty smiled. 'What has Merritt told you?' she asked shyly.

'Not Merritt, Ivo,' said Henry smiling. 'I understand you have tamed the beast.'

Kitty looked at Ivo in surprise; he was looking back at her, his face flushed. She ignored his gaze.

'Well, I'm afraid the beast is back in the wild,' she said, and turned her back on them both.

Henry looked at her in surprise and Ivo mouthed the word 'sorry' to him. He had hoped that the excitement of the auction and the anticipation of a potential sale would soften her resolve, but he was mistaken, it seemed.

Kitty held the catalogue. She had had a private viewing with Merritt before the catalogue was released, and together they had chosen a painting each that they loved.

Kitty had chosen a painting of a small child reading a book

on a chair in a garden. An auspicious omen, she thought, and Merritt had hugged her when he saw her choice.

'How's the reading going?' he had asked.

'It's good actually. My teacher is so nice, and I'm not as bad as I thought I was. Some of it got through apparently. I have dyslexia, so she has this whole method that's not what they teach kids – it's designed for adults. It works, but it's slow,' she had said.

'And how's Harold?' Merritt had asked, still concerned about her landlord.

'He's lovely. I'm really enjoying staying there actually. It will be hard to leave,' said Kitty.

'When will that be?' asked Merritt.

'I don't know yet,' Kitty had said vaguely.

'You know you can always come back to Middlemist,' Merritt had said, his arm still around her.

'I know, but I don't really feel like it's my home now,' said Kitty. 'For the first time I'm enjoying London. There's so much to do and see. I hope you're not too lonely by yourself.'

Merritt had said nothing, promising Ivo he wouldn't tell her where he was living until after the auction.

Merritt had chosen a spectacular piece. It was of Clementina in the orangery with three of her five children surrounding her and a white peacock in the background. It was romantic and beautiful, filled with lace and satin ribbons and love.

Kitty looked at it and then turned to Merritt. 'Have you heard from her?' she asked.

'Who?' asked Merritt.

'You know who,' said Kitty, making a face. 'I may not be able to read, but I'm not stupid.'

Merritt shook his head. 'I'm afraid that ship has sailed,' he said. 'Anyway, I saw she's dating some Hollywood actor now. She had dinner with him and Rose Nightingale the other night. I saw it in the papers.'

'Didn't you do Rose Nightingale's garden in LA?' asked Kitty.

'Yeah,' said Merritt with his arms crossed.

'Do you think they talked about you?' asked Kitty.

'I doubt it,' said Merritt. 'I'm sure they have better things to talk about than a gardener.'

Now they sat in a row, Merritt between Kitty and Ivo, as the auction began. The auctioneer went through the history of George Middlemist and the discovery of the paintings, but Kitty didn't listen. She flipped through the catalogue distractedly, wondering what the hell Ivo was doing spoiling her and Merritt's special moment.

Ivo kept glancing at her throughout the auctioneer's spiel, but she didn't acknowledge him, although she kept glancing back whenever he wasn't looking. He looked good, she admitted to herself. Healthy, a bit of colour in his cheeks, and he had put on a little weight, which he needed. He looked handsome, and she hated him for it.

The auction started and so did the bidding. The first piece sold for sixty-five thousand pounds, and Merritt jumped up.

'That's the new wiring!' he cried.

And they were off and running. Every painting sold, and each time Merritt called out a new part of the house that would be able to be fixed.

'Twenty-five thousand pounds, that's the glass in the orangery.'

Merritt's excitement was infectious, and she danced with him when one of the larger pieces sold for over one hundred thousand pounds. Ivo stood up, and she stopped in front of him as Merritt put her down from his bear hug. She sat down, ignoring him but catching the pained look on his face.

Ivo bent over and whispered in Merritt's ear, then looked over at Kitty who kept her eye on the auction. Merritt turned and nodded to him and made a sorrowed face.

Kitty watched Ivo leave in the reflection of the mirrored glass. She saw him pause at the door and then walk away, but she kept her head held high as the auction drew to a close.

Henry watched the board and turned to them. 'That's it!' he cried. 'Over a million pounds.'

Merritt sat with his head in his hands and Kitty sat stunned. 'Oh Merritt, it's amazing. Well done!' she cried.

'I have to go and sort out the details and paperwork,' said Henry. 'I'll have champagne sent up to you.'

Merritt turned to Kitty. 'I can't spend it all on the house. I'll split it with you,' he said suddenly.

'Don't be stupid,' said Kitty sternly. 'You want to do the house up and you should. I don't care about money, I never have. You know that,' she said.

'But it's so much money, and you don't even want to live there,' he said, his eyes glassy.

'I know, but things will work out, won't they?' said Kitty. 'I don't know what the future will bring to either of us but I'm happy to not know for a while. Middlemist deserves to be brought back from its malaise,' she said.

'*Malaise*?' asked Merritt, laughing a little.

'Harold uses it,' said Kitty, blushing. 'Did I use it in the right way?'

'Yes, I think you did,' said Merritt.

'I can do it up and sell it, perhaps,' he said.

'Perhaps,' said Kitty. 'Who knows?'

Merritt opened the champagne that a staff member had brought in to them and poured her a glass.

'To Middlemist.' She smiled.

They drank and then Merritt raised his glass again. 'One more toast,' he said.

Kitty looked at him expectantly.

'To Ivo,' he said finally.

'Ivo? Why? Why was he even here? He ruined everything,' she said angrily.

'Oh Kits. You're wrong,' said Merritt, tired of keeping secrets. If Ivo wouldn't tell her then he would have to.

'Ivo is the reason we are here now. He found the paintings, Kits. He did. We owe him everything.'

CHAPTER THIRTY-NINE

Merritt was knee deep in the renovation of Middlemist. Having realised early on that he couldn't do it all, he had hired an interior designer whose number he found in the Yellow Pages.

'I have so many ideas,' said Harriet the interior designer, wearing too much lipstick in a shade of red that clashed with her red curls. So far in her burgeoning career, since leaving Laura Ashley to start her own company she had done a few country sitting rooms and three kitchens.

'No ideas,' said Merritt gruffly. 'Everything you need is in here,' he said, and he shoved Willow's lined notebook at her.

'What's this?' she asked, opening it up.

'Your ideas,' said Merritt. 'I want everything done as specified in this book, and if you come across any areas that aren't in the book, then do what you think the person in this book would do. OK?'

He was so forceful she didn't dare argue with him. She leafed through the pictures. 'Can I add my own little accents?' she asked.

'No,' he said. 'Do you want the job or not?' he asked impatiently, watching the digger move towards the pond.

Harriet paused. A house like this could make her career; she could be the next Nina Campbell or Tricia Guild or even

Laura Ashley. She nearly crossed herself at the thought of her inspiration's name.

'I'll take it,' she said quickly, just to make him get away from her.

Merritt stomped off to review the clearing of the pond. As he watched them drain it and clear away a hundred years' worth of debris from the bottom, he saw a glint of yellow in the mud. He reached down and picked it up. 'Sophie,' he said to himself.

It was Sophie, Jinty's yellow rubber giraffe that she had lost. She must have dropped it in the pond when she was out in the stroller with Kitty or Willow. They had spent hours looking for it when she cried for her 'Ophie'.

He walked to the tap, rinsed it off and put it in the inside pocket of his jacket, and then he went back to the pond.

The weeks passed. Ivo had moved out after the auction. Merritt had returned from London to find him gone, leaving only a note.

> *Thanks for everything Merritt. Sorry I can't come up with a nickname for you. I appreciate your hospitality and friendship. I'll let you know about the books.*
> *Ivo*
> *P.S. Tell Kitty I'm sorry.*

Merritt was sad to see Ivo leave, but he was too busy with the house to be lonely. His days started early and finished late. It was a full-time job overseeing the renovations and the restoration. Artisans were brought in to paint the decorative iron gates, replace some of the walls in the gardens and match the Minton tiles in the orangery.

It was arduous and endless, and every day Merritt thought about Willow and the children. They were with him when he approved the paint in the bedroom and when he planted one hundred orange, lemon and clementine trees.

Kitty came down with Harold to visit.

'I have to see how this old dame is coping with her facelift,' said Harold as he alighted from his car.

'She seems to be doing OK,' said Merritt, looking up at the elaborate scaffolding around the house.

'Wow,' said Kitty as she walked inside. 'It looks so different already. It looks cleaner.' She laughed.

'Two hundred years of dust,' laughed Merritt. 'Who knew there were actually ornate carvings under there?'

Merritt took Kitty and Harold on a tour of the house and garden and took pride in their exclamations. 'You have done her proud,' said Harold.

'Yes, she will look beautiful,' agreed Kitty.

Merritt thought for a moment how beautiful Kitty looked. More than her clothes, which looked new, he thought, looking at her soft leather bag, but she seemed more confident than he had ever seen her.

They ate lunch in the orangery, the glass replaced and the new trees surrounding them. It was lovely in the autumn sun. Harold entertained Kitty and Merritt with his stories about his films and his hopes for the one he was yet to make. Merritt found him inspiring, and Kitty was clearly as entranced as he was. Merritt understood why Kitty was spending time in Harold's world. It was a place of beauty and wit, where troubles could be put to rest over a fine cup of Assam tea and Scottish shortbread.

Finally it was time to leave as the sun dipped in the distance.

Kitty held on to Merritt for a long time. 'Come to London soon,' she ordered in his ear.

'Maybe,' he said.

Harold shook his hand enthusiastically. 'You have done and are doing a wonderful thing, Merritt,' he said. 'Houses like these deserve to be lived in with families, generations pounding the stairs. I know Kitty said that Willow is no longer in your life – a shame by the way – but keep looking. Fill the house with children and noise, Merritt; she wants it.'

'Who?' asked Merritt, confused. Did he mean Willow? he wondered.

'The house, darling; the house wants it,' said Harold.

Merritt smiled at Harold. 'I will definitely try,' he said as he waved them back to London. He walked inside Middlemist. The house did deserve a family using it. He was loath to put all this work in, only for the National Trust to have people wandering through it pointing and stealing treasures.

He put his hands in his pockets and looked up at the ceiling, at the lions in the corners of the roof with their newly fitted lights. Yes, he thought, Middlemist needed people to live in it. And he made his decision.

CHAPTER FORTY

The plane touched down at LAX and Willow stood up and opened the cabin above her.

The stewardess walked down the aisle. 'Excuse me, Ms Carruthers, but you must stay seated until the seatbelt sign goes off and we have taxied to a stop.'

Willow glared at her. 'I have three children, including a toddler, and I am flying alone. I need all the time I can get. And you and your staff have been noticeable only by your absence on this flight,' she accused the snooty girl.

'I'm sorry Ms Carruthers, but we have other people in the business class section and we cannot give all our time to you,' answered the woman, her face reddening.

'Any time would have been great,' said Willow under her breath as she sat down again, ignoring the stares from her fellow travellers. She had flown to LA after Kerr had announced he was setting up home there and summoned her over for a visit with the children.

Willow was reticent. 'He hasn't even rung them to see how they are,' she had said to her lawyer over the phone. 'He missed Lucian's birthday,' she said, remembering the cake and present festivities she had organised. A few of Lucian's friends from kindergarten had been invited, including Rose's son Milo. She had become close to Rose in London, and Rose

340

had arrived at Willow's home with presents and champagne and Rose and a few other mothers had stayed while a magician entertained the children and the nanny organised party games.

It had been a lovely afternoon, sullied somewhat by Kerr ignoring his eldest child's special day.

'I know it's frustrating,' said Willow's lawyer, 'but I suggest you head over and see what he's up to. Who knows? He may have changed.'

Willow doubted it very much. Kerr had shown his true colours, she had decided; but he was their father after all.

So she had packed up everything and, mindful as ever of her budget, had decided to fly to LA and to go business class, not first as she was used to. She had meetings set up in LA with the director and production company for the action franchise, and had rented a house in Beverly Hills for two months. She would have Christmas with the children and her parents would fly over to spend the holidays with them.

The house she had rented was modest, but it had a pool and a playroom for the children. Fully furnished, it belonged to a Hollywood actress, a friend of Rose's who had gone to Gstaad for the time Willow was there.

Willow sat with a wriggling Jinty, who insisted on throwing the headphones at Poppy, who started to cry. She was tired – they were all tired, thought Willow as the plane stopped moving and the seatbelt light went off.

Willow jumped up. 'Lucian, get your backpack and Custard,' she said, gesturing to Custard who was tucked between two seats. Lucian did as she asked and Willow sent a silent thanks to the people who were helping him in his learning. He had grown more confident and even had a few words, mostly consisting of 'Hi', 'No', 'Mummy', 'Pops' and 'Jint', but it was a start, she thought. He was far more receptive to the world; he accepted her hugs and kisses, returned them even, and laughed with George the dog, who had reluctantly been put into kennels for the time they were away.

Poppy insisted that George had to go to Merritt's to stay, but Willow said that Merritt was away on holiday. It was easier than trying to explain to Poppy that she, her mother, had ruined everything.

After an arduous time at the airport wrestling bags and children and with no help, Willow faced the American paparazzi. 'Are you reuniting with your husband, Willow?' they asked as she walked through the airport, Jinty sitting precariously on top of the Samsonite cases and waving the headphones at them that she had stolen from the plane.

Poppy walked behind her mother, in tulle, pink Doc Martens and the bonnet that she had taken from Middlemist. Lucian was next to her.

'Mummy has a new boyfriend,' said Poppy as she looked down the barrel of a camera.

'Is that true Willow? Do you have a new boyfriend?' screamed the photographers.

Willow stopped and dragged Poppy to her side by the elbow. 'Be quiet,' she hissed. 'You know I don't have a new boyfriend.'

'Yes you do Mummy,' said Poppy, her face puzzled.

'What's his name? Who is he?' shouted one photographer at Poppy.

'He's a Merritt,' said Poppy. Willow wanted to throttle

her daughter but didn't want to be arrested in a public space.

The photographers looked at each other. He's a merit? they wondered.

'He has merit?' they asked.

'Yes, she has Merritt,' said Poppy, confused.

'Jesus,' said one as Willow pulled away in the waiting car. 'I didn't even know what that word meant until I was thirty.'

'I still don't know what it means,' said one of the more aggressive photographers. 'She must be a freaking genius,' he said.

The next day gossip hit the wires that Willow had a new lover who had great merit, according to her genius, gifted child.

Merritt read it online at Middlemist and wondered what on earth it was all about. Willow has moved on, eh? he thought sadly; and so, it seems, have the children.

The house in Beverly Hills was modest by LA standards, but comfortable all the same. It was nice to be in the relative warmth, and the children insisted on swimming as soon as they arrived. Willow sat watching them, enjoying their screams of delight. Jinty floated in a giant plastic iced donut and Poppy and Lucian wore armbands and jumped in and out of the water until Willow dragged them out with the promise of ice cream. Kerr would be arriving any minute and she wanted the children to be clean and shiny and happy to see him.

The doorbell rang and she answered it. There stood Kerr. He looked good, she thought; LA obviously agreed with him.

He had lost the puffiness that he had had the last time she saw him; too much wine and cocaine probably. Now he stood fit and well, tanned and wearing relaxed jeans, a white t-shirt and flip-flops.

'Hey Willy,' he said easily, using the name he had given her from when they first got together.

'Hey Kerr,' she said, a little icily. 'Come in.'

Kerr walked inside. 'This is nice,' he said, looking around the Spanish villa.

'It's fine; it's just for the holidays,' she said. Kerr sat on a chair in the living room.

'I thought you might stay now.'

'Where? In America?' asked Willow, confused.

'Yes, well I'm going to live here, and I thought with you being American and all that . . .' His voice trailed off.

Willow thought for a moment. In theory she should live in the States – she was American, her parents were here – but she had begun to think of England as home.

She liked England, with its funny ways and manners. She felt more English than American, while clearly Kerr had become a flag-waving Yank.

'I don't know, Kerr,' she said. 'I like England.'

'Man, you don't know what you're missing,' he said. 'America is fucking amazing. The lifestyle, the people, the opportunities. They want you to succeed. I've told a few people about my financial mess and they don't care. In England I would be hung, drawn and quartered; in fact I think I was in the papers,' he laughed ruefully.

And deservedly so, thought Willow. The press had only reported what he had done; it was up to the public to make their own decision. Kerr had obviously not told his new fanbase that he was a cheating, spendaholic, absent father.

A tearful appearance on *The View*, dancing with Ellen and a few dates with a star from *Twilight* and he was soon back in the game and loving it.

Poppy danced into the living room. 'Daddy!' she cried, and jumped into his arms.

'Poppet!' he yelled, and then Jinty toddled in. He picked her up too and Willow was surprised. He mostly ignored Jinty. Lucian stood in the doorway.

'Hey Luce,' said Kerr easily.

Lucian stood uncertainly in front of his father.

'Say hi to Dad,' said Willow, her heart breaking at her son's scared face.

'Hi,' said Lucian quietly.

Kerr's face filled with joy. 'Hey! You can say hi! That's great.'

Willow watched as Lucian walked up to his father and Kerr put down Poppy and picked up Lucian in a warm embrace. She turned to wipe away the tears that fell. Kerr held Lucian for a long time.

'You want to come to my place and see Daddy's new pad?' he said.

'We have an iPad here,' said Poppy. 'I play games on it.'

Kerr laughed, as did Willow. 'I mean my new house.'

'You should say what you mean,' said Poppy sternly. 'That's what Mummy says to Lucian.'

'I will promise to always say what I mean,' said Kerr, looking at Poppy with a serious face.

'I'm not sure Kerr,' said Willow carefully.

Kerr nodded sadly. 'I understand I'm a shit father but

345

please let me try again. I can't fix it with you but I can try with the kids.'

'Daddy said shit,' whispered Poppy to Lucian, who giggled a little.

Willow looked at the smiling faces of her two eldest children and knew she must let them have a relationship with Kerr, even if their marriage was over.

Willow watched them leave in her car, Jinty tucked up in her car seat and the other two in their booster seats. Of course he hadn't remembered to have his own fitted, so now she was left with his Porsche and nothing to do until her meeting at the film studio.

She wandered about the house, and checked her emails from Lucy. Lucy was more than her publicist now; she was her assistant and manager. Willow trusted her implicitly and was grateful to have a person like her on her side.

Lucy had organised a meeting for two o'clock that afternoon with the production company and the director. Willow decided to wash her hair and change for the meeting. She wanted to look fabulous and fresh and decided today was a day for the best English style that she could muster from the clothes she had brought over. As she walked to the wardrobe where the packers had put the clothes that she had sent over before her arrival, she saw some of the other clothes left by the Hollywood actress who owned the house. They were all hanging in plastic dry cleaning wrapping. Willow flipped through them. All Chanel. Then she remembered the actress was the face of the newest Chanel perfume. She pulled out the bags of clothes and laid them on the bed carefully. All of the pieces were amazing, and she almost salivated at the fabrics and styles. It had been a while since she had bought any new things. Lucy said she could get her lots of free clothes, but Willow felt uneasy about being beholden to anyone. She had borrowed dresses but hadn't accepted anything free. Nothing was free, her father used to tell her, and she knew that was true now. Besides, one day she would have the money again to buy her own clothes, and she looked forward to that day. Meanwhile, she wondered if the actress would mind if she borrowed a few things.

Slipping on a pair of tight leather pants, almost like leggings, she put on a white silk singlet over the top. A Chanel jacket with bracelet-length sleeves covered in dull, matte sequins fitted perfectly, and Willow put on her black leather high-heeled boots with dull gold leather toes. She felt sexy and powerful. Flipping her long hair over her shoulders, she applied another slick of her Blessings lipstick in nude and sprayed herself with her Kai perfume.

The Porsche was surprisingly comfortable and Willow wondered where Kerr had got the money for such a lovely and expensive car as she drove towards the studio, Kerr's satellite navigation telling her the way in a polite American accent.

As she pulled up to the studio gates and gave her name, she was directed to a bungalow and she parked out the front. Getting out of the car, she dropped her bag and swore.

'Fuck a duck,' she said, using Merritt's favourite expression. Seeing her lipstick had rolled out under the car, she got back in, angrily started it and drove quickly backwards, feeling the power of the engine underneath her. She spun the car around, opened the door with the engine still running, reached out

347

and grabbed her lipstick and then parked again, zipping her bag up to be safe.

She got out and slammed the car door and, flipping her hair, she walked towards the bungalow. She could see faces at the window watching her and she cursed her errant driving under her breath. Americans were fastidious about car safety, and she had just been driving like she was in a PlayStation game.

'Hello; Willow Carruthers,' she said to the man at the door.

'Tim Galvin – call me TG,' he said, smiling. 'Come in.'

Willow walked into the room and saw three men and a woman sitting down.

'Thanks for seeing me,' said Willow.

'No problem,' said the producer, who introduced himself as Tom. 'Actually, things have changed a little since we spoke to your agent in the UK. We don't need a female love interest any more,' he said, and Willow felt her heart sink as she pictured her big paycheque fly out the window.

'OK,' she said slowly, 'well thanks for seeing me anyway. If you have anything else slated I would be interested.'

TG interrupted, 'No, actually I think it's a good thing. Research shows that women want to see stronger women in film roles. The films with Sapphira De Mont, Angelina Jolie, Uma Thurman made big money. So the studio has decided that they want the film to have a female star with a male love interest.'

Willow sat stunned. 'OK, like Sigourney Weaver or Linda Hamilton, but with sex?'

'Exactly!' shouted TG. He turned to the group. 'I told you she would get it.

'I want to make a sexy, fun and dangerous film. I haven't made one of these in a long time, and I can't wait to get my teeth back into it again. And Willow, the only person whose name kept coming up to play this role is you.'

Willow shook her head. 'Really? Wow. I'm flattered. Tell me about the film,' she said.

TG stood up. He always worked the pitches well. 'It's about a woman who was a secret agent who's become a stay-at-home mom. When her much-loved husband turns out to be a secret agent and then goes missing, she takes it upon herself to find him and take on the bad guys. It's a parody on the working mom theme, struggling to be good at everything but her dramas are actually life threatening.'

'So she's trying to get childcare while in the middle of a shootout type of thing,' laughed Willow.

'Oh my god, have you read the script?' shouted TG. 'That scene is in there!'

The room laughed with relief; TG was right. Willow was the perfect person to play this role. It had been confirmed when they saw her rock the Porsche in the parking lot like it was a golf cart, and her appearance in leather and sequins was astonishing.

'No, I haven't read it but I live it,' said Willow to the room. 'I'm a single mother to three.'

'Well if you take the role, we would love your feedback on the script,' said Tom. 'We would give you a writing credit of course.'

Willow sat on her hands to stop herself from clapping them together.

'I'm interested,' she said. 'Where would it shoot?' she asked.

Tom looked down at the slated locations. 'Monaco, London and Ibiza,' he said. 'Pickups and post production in London.'

Willow nodded. Back to Europe, she thought, relieved. She didn't realise how much she wanted to be there until it was offered again.

'And when would it shoot, if it gets the green light?' she asked, thinking ahead to the children's school year.

'Starts in May next year, after Cannes,' said TG. 'Are you going?'

'Maybe; I have a film that's in consideration but I haven't heard any more about it,' she said, thinking she must get Lucy to speak to Harold's assistant.

'Well the role is yours if you want it,' said TG. 'Speak to your agent, and if you are interested then we can get started.'

Willow smiled. 'Sure, I'll get Simon to get back to you with my answer.'

She stood up and shook everyone's hands. Tom and TG walked her to the door.

'Nice car,' said TG, looking at Kerr's Porsche.

'It's OK,' said Willow.

'Yours?' asked Tom.

'No, I'm borrowing it. It's not really kid friendly, huh? I'd have to put their booster seats on the roof racks,' she laughed.

Tom and TG laughed. 'We have to put that in the movie,' said Tom.

Willow laughed, got in, and drove away with a wave. Her life was a fucking movie, she thought, remembering the past six months. Now the film of her life was being made, and she was starring in it, this time with guns. Yes, she would do the film. Why? Because it was in London, and she knew that London was her home now.

CHAPTER FORTY-ONE

Kitty sat with Lavender. 'My god, she's got it,' said Lavender in her best Henry Higgins voice as Kitty read out the sentence in front of her. She placed down another card and Kitty paused to look at it.

'Is the train on time?' she said in a confident voice.

'Oh yes, she's got it,' said Lavender again, smiling. Kitty jumped up. 'I do have it, I do! I know what it feels like to read. It's amazing!' she cried. 'You are amazing.'

'No, *you* are amazing,' said Lavender firmly.

'No, it's all you,' argued Kitty, her eyes filled with tears.

'You have practised hard, and you've worked at it with Harold, and you had a good foundation to start with. Things were there but you had forgotten and lost your confidence,' said Lavender. 'You need to thank your friend for the initial work they did with you, because it made all the difference.'

Kitty sat down, thinking of Ivo. She wanted to say things to him but she didn't know where to start. She was beginning to understand, now, what he had done when he told the room at Middlemist about her not being able to read.

Lavender looked at her star pupil. 'Homework for this week.'

'Yes,' said Kitty, waiting for the instructions from her teacher. She was a diligent student, committed to ensuring she excelled for her own sake as well as because she didn't want to waste Lavender's time.

'I want you to write a letter,' said Lavender. 'Doesn't have to be long, but it has to be heartfelt; and to someone who has been there for you through this journey.'

Kitty nodded.

'And post it to them. OK?' ordered Lavender.

Kitty agreed and walked back to Harold's house. She thought about who to write to. Merritt, she decided, and she started writing the letter in her head as she made her way home.

By the time she had arrived at Harold's front door, she had chosen her words. She rushed upstairs, opened the desk and pulled out the stationery. This would have to do, she thought, and she sucked on the pen and started to write.

To Ivo,

I am verry sory I was horid to you. I have bean doing reading and writing lesons and I think I am doing quiet well. I have to write to some one who helpd me and I was going to write to Merritt but then you poped into my head. I was awful to you. I know and I hop you will forgiv me one day.

I think about you all day. You mad me feel smart and you were patiant with me.

I am greatful and think you are so clevr. Merritt told me abut the paintings and he has used the mony to fix the house.

What you tught me helped and my teacher said it made all the diffrnce. I knew more than I thoght. I know more now abut many things.

I wuld like to be frinds maybe, if you can forgiv me, I hope so.

Yors,

Katinka Iris Clementina Ceres Middlemist

(Kitty)

She wrote Ivo's name on the front of the envelope, but realised she had no idea where he lived before she had got round to sealing it. She walked upstairs and saw Harold in his usual place in front of the television screens. The screen was paused on Willow and Ivo in an embrace.

'Hello,' she said, trying not to look at the screen.

'Hello Katinka,' said Harold, not looking at her. 'How was your lesson?'

'Good actually. I had to write a letter,' she said.

'Oh wonderful! The art of letter writing is becoming lost,' said Harold, turning around to face her.

'To whom did you write?' he asked.

Kitty looked embarrassed. 'I wrote to Ivo but I don't know his address,' she said, holding out the envelope. 'Can you check the spelling? Lavender said it had to be heartfelt.'

Harold took the envelope and opened the letter. He read it quietly and then looked up at her. 'It's perfect and heartfelt.'

'And the spelling? Is it OK?'

'You have spelt the words as they sound, and that is good enough. It's a wonderful letter Kitty; send it,' he said, leaning back in his chair.

'But send to where? I don't know where he lives,' she said sadly.

'His last name is Casselton and his father went to Harrow.

354

There are some Casseltons who live up in Middlesex – I think you might find it is them,' said Harold. 'Wait a minute, I'll find the address.' He turned to his computer and typed into Google. Picking up the cordless phone he dialled the number on the screen from the directory. 'Hello, is Ivo there?'

There was a long pause, and then, 'No?' Kitty's heart sank. She had hoped Harold would be right about Ivo's address.

'Oh lovely, I have some post of his. I will send it on then. Thank you,' said Harold, and he hung up the phone.

'That was his mother; sounds dreadfully posh. She said to send it over and she will ensure Ivo receives it,' said Harold, proud of his detective work.

'Can you write the address please? I don't want it getting lost,' she asked shyly, and Harold scribbled down the address on the envelope and handed it to her with the letter.

'Seal it with a kiss,' he instructed, and Kitty rolled her eyes.

'Don't roll your eyes, it's an awful habit,' said Harold tartly and Kitty laughed at him as she ran down the stairs to her desk.

Having stuck a stamp to the envelope, she put on her coat and headed outside into the cold air to post her precious missive. She stood at the postbox and waited till the person in front had posted their enormous bag of Christmas cards. Finally they left. Kitty's hands were getting cold. She held the letter to her mouth, kissed the back and then slipped it into the box.

'You can't take it back now,' she thought as she walked away.

Christmas was coming, and she had plans to spend it with Harold and Merritt at Harold's house. Middlemist still wasn't finished and Merritt said there was no way they could have Christmas there with the water off – the new plumbing was being installed.

The house would be done by the end of January, he told her, and Kitty wondered what he would do then. Would he live there? Let it? She didn't know. He seemed preoccupied more than usual lately when she rang him.

Kitty returned to hear the phone ringing, and she knew Harold wouldn't answer it. 'Harold Gaumont's residence,' she said as she slipped off her coat in the warm sitting room.

'Hello, it's Lucy, Willow Carruthers's assistant,' said the voice down the line.

Kitty sat down on the chair next to her. 'Hi Lucy, it's Kitty.'

'Oh Kitty, how wonderful to hear your voice. How are you?' gushed Lucy warmly. She had liked Kitty the few times she had met her and Willow had spoken so well of her. She was sorry things had ended so badly between the two of them.

'Fine,' said Kitty anxiously.

'Are you working for Harold?' asked Lucy.

'Sort of,' she said vaguely.

'Tell me, is *The Romantics* going to Cannes?'

'I think so. I can get more details from Harold later and phone you back,' said Kitty. 'He said something about some stairs and opening night.'

'Wonderful. Willow has another project lined up and I am just working out schedules,' said Lucy.

'Oh,' said Kitty at the sound of Willow's name. 'How are the children?' she asked finally after a pause.

'They are wonderful. Lucian's getting great help and has a few words,' said Lucy.

'That's great; really great,' said Kitty, her eyes filling up with tears. 'I have to go. I'll call you later,' said Kitty, and she hung up quickly.

Lucy sat in her home office looking at the phone. She picked it up again.

'Willow? Hi. I've found her. She's at Harold's. Yes. You want the number? OK, got a pen?'

Willow picked up the phone and although it was the middle of the night in LA, she felt wide awake. She knew what she had to do to make it right. She dialled the number and heard Kitty's voice on the other end of the line.

'Kitty, it's Willow. Don't hang up, I have to say something.' Willow took a deep breath.

'I'm sorry. I am so incredibly sorry for everything. I was selfish and awful and ugly and vile. You don't have to forgive me, but I hope you can one day. You treated my children better than I ever did and what you taught Lucian really helped him. I wish I had known about your reading problems, and I wish I could have helped. I'm a different person now – you helped me become that, but I hope not at your detriment. You are a wonderful person, Kitty, and you deserve more than working for me and I truly hope you move forward and find something that you can put all your wonderful skills into.' Willow waited, she could hear Kitty breathing on the other end of the phone.

'How is Jinty? Walking yet?' she asked, and Willow felt a flood of relief at the question.

'Yes, and into everything.'

'And Poppy?' asked Kitty.

'Hilarious! She loves nursery,' said Willow. 'She likes the dress-up box.'

'I can imagine,' Kitty laughed.

'And Lucian's talking a little now; each day he gets more confident.'

'That's great Willow,' said Kitty truthfully. She was thrilled the children were happy, and it was good that Willow apologised.

'How's Merritt?' asked Willow casually.

'Busy,' said Kitty, thoughtfully.

'I'm sure. Please send him my love,' said Willow. 'I would like to say sorry to him also but I don't think he would take my call,' she said. Kitty wasn't sure if the phone line was breaking up or Willow's voice was cracking. She frowned.

'Write a letter,' Kitty said suddenly.

'What?' asked Willow.

'Write a letter to him. Make it heartfelt and don't worry about the spelling. Just say it as it's meant to be said,' she instructed firmly.

Willow sat thinking. 'I will. Thanks Kitty.'

'No problem,' said Kitty smiling.

'I'm back in London soon. Will you come and see the children? Have a cup of tea with me? I've stopped drinking coffee; I am a true Englishwoman now.' She laughed.

'I will. I would like to,' said Kitty, and just before she hung up she spoke again quickly. 'Willow?'

'Yes?' came the careful reply.

'I forgive you,' she said, and she meant it. Christmas was

about forgiveness after all, she thought as she looked at Harold's immaculately decorated pine tree, covered in cupids. Christmas cupids, she thought as she went upstairs. Only Harold would have such a thing.

CHAPTER FORTY-TWO

Ivo drove his new Volvo down the driveway of his parents' home.

Evelyn Casselton was waiting for him by the front door. As an only child, his appearance on Christmas Day was important to his parents. He felt the heavy weight of expectations as he stopped the car.

'A new car, Ivo!' exclaimed his mother.

'Yes,' said Ivo, but he offered no other information. He would wait until the three of them had run out of things to talk about. He calculated that the car talk could take up at least half an hour, even an hour if he got his father banging on about foreign cars and ownership.

Picking up his overnight bag – he had promised to stay the night – he walked towards his mother.

'Hello Mum,' he said as he bent down to kiss her powdered cheek.

'Dad's inside; he's looking forward to seeing you,' she said.

Ivo doubted that very much. His relationship with his father wasn't exactly warm. Ivo felt like a disappointment to his high-achieving father – and he was, he thought, in many ways. His father was Earl of Casselton; he ran the large Casselton estate and was a committed member of the local

Conservative Party. He was educated and careful. The phrase 'the glass is half empty' summed him up perfectly.

Ivo dumped his bag in the large foyer, the paintings of his ancestors frowning down on him, and walked into the drawing room.

'Hi Dad,' he said. 'Merry Christmas.'

His father stood up from the leather wingback chair and extended his hand. 'Ivo. Merry Christmas,' he said.

His mother walked into the room. 'Perry, Ivo has a new Volvo,' she said proudly.

Ivo winced. It seemed the car conversation would be sooner than he had thought.

'Do you?' asked his father, surprised. Ivo was forever cadging money from them – well, mostly from his mother, although Perry knew but didn't say anything.

'Where did you get that?' he asked his son.

Ivo stiffened. 'From my wages,' he said.

'As what?' asked Perry, folding away his reading glasses and putting them next to his cup of tea.

'I made a film,' said Ivo.

His mother gasped. 'Not pornography Ivo?'

Ivo looked at her in horror. What did they think of him? he wondered.

'No Mother, not porn. Jesus,' he said crossly.

'What sort of film?' asked his father, gesturing Ivo to be seated in front of him.

'A period romance. Directed by Harold Gaumont,' said Ivo, waiting for their reaction.

'Oh how lovely,' said his mother, relieved; and sitting down next to him, she patted his leg. 'So, you're an actor now?'

'No,' said Ivo slowly.

His father rolled his eyes. 'What now, Ivo? If you want to be an actor, I suppose it's OK with us if it buys you Volvos,' he said.

Ivo licked his lips. 'Actually I'm a writer now. I wrote a book, and it was the best thing I think I have ever done.'

'What sort of a book?' asked his mother, worry returning to her face.

'A book about art,' said Ivo, trying not to laugh. She probably thought it was erotic fiction to go with his porn film, he thought.

'An art book? I'm intrigued,' said Perry. 'Do tell.'

So Ivo launched into the story of Middlemist and the film and Merritt and the paintings and the auction and his parents sat gobsmacked. And then his mother stood up.

'Oh it's all too perfect!' she screamed, and practically ran from the room.

'Jesus, is she alright?' asked Ivo as he watched her leave.

His father jumped up – he, too, was beside himself with excitement.

'You wait my boy, you wait! Stay there,' he ordered, and hurried after his wife. Ivo sat perplexed as Evelyn walked back into the room.

'We have your Christmas present,' she announced, and Perry walked into the room holding the same painting that Ivo had admired so much from the Middlemist collection.

'It doesn't have a name,' said his mother.

'*The Proposal*,' said Ivo, stunned.

'Oh, is that what it's called? Well, makes sense. Your father and I bought it at the auction.'

'I was there. I didn't see you,' said Ivo, thinking back.

'We didn't go. We did it over the phone; all very private

362

that way,' said his father, searching his son's face for an expression.

'Do you like it?' asked his mother, dancing around him. 'I know you don't have a permanent address yet but it can hang here until you do.'

'I love it,' said Ivo, and he reached out and gave his ecstatic mother a hug and a kiss. And then he walked over to his father and pulled him into a hug too, which delighted his father more than Ivo realised.

'We went to London to see this new Russian artist's exhibition at the Wimple-Jones Gallery, but it was awful. And so *rude*,' said Evelyn. Ivo tried not to laugh. He had heard Tatiana's show was a sell-out, but it certainly wasn't to his parents' taste.

Ivo knew through his newfound friends in the art world that Tatiana had made a sculpture of Kerr, naked, gilded, with a vagina instead of a penis. The piece was entitled 'Rock Out With Your Cock Out'. Apparently Mick Jagger had bought it and housed it in his chestnut grove in France, where his guests, out of it on expensive wine and enormous joints, would dry hump Kerr all night.

'Come on then! Time for lunch,' said Evelyn. 'Champagne is in order, I believe.'

'I would have liked to have written a book,' said Ivo's father as they settled down at the large oak table.

'You still can Dad,' said Ivo, laughing.

'Did you know I trod the boards at Harrow?' Perry said, thinking back.

'No Dad, I didn't. Tell me about it,' lied Ivo, remembering the actor from the set talking about him from his school-days. He listened as Peregrine talked about his brief but successful appearance in a production of *The Merry Wives of Windsor*.

It was a lovely lunch, filled with conversation and laughter. Ivo kept glancing at the painting, which he had taken with him into the dining room.

'I do love it,' he kept saying, over and over. 'It was my favourite.'

'One day that might be you,' said Evelyn, a little tipsy from the vintage Krug.

'I don't know Mum. There's no one special in my life right now,' he said, thinking of Kitty. 'My mail box isn't exactly filled with billets-doux.'

'Oh, that reminds me,' said Evelyn, and she got up from the table and left the room.

'Not another painting, I hope,' laughed Ivo.

Evelyn came back holding a blue envelope. 'This came for you here,' she said, and she handed him the letter. 'It looks like the name was written by a child. Perhaps it's fan mail,' she said hopefully.

'I doubt it, no one's seen the film yet,' he said as he studied the front of the envelope. His name was scrawled across it but the address was written in perfectly formed letters in an almost copperplate script.

He used his bread knife to open it and started to read. His eyes welled up with tears of pride and happiness.

'Who's it from?' Evelyn pried, watching his face.

'It's from a woman I love,' said Ivo, looking up at his parents.

'I thought you said there was no one special,' said Evelyn excitedly.

'There wasn't, I thought, but it seems in fact there could

be,' said Ivo thoughtfully. He stood up. 'Would you mind terribly if I nipped back to London? You see I lost her once and I don't want to lose her again,' he said honestly.

Evelyn clapped her hands. 'Of course! Go, go,' she said.

Perry stood and shook his son's hand.

'Good luck,' he said. 'Women are a mercurial lot.'

Ivo laughed and ran out the door towards his new car. Evelyn stood watching him tear off down the driveway, and decided that buying the other Middlemist, of the woman holding the baby in the orangery, hadn't been such a mistake after all. It would make a lovely wedding present, she thought.

CHAPTER FORTY-THREE

Kitty and Merritt were walking off their Christmas lunch through the streets of London.

'My trousers are too tight,' complained Kitty. They had left Harold asleep on the sofa, propped up on cushions with a silk quilt over his knees. He had spent the entire Christmas lunch in angel wings, much to Merritt's amusement. Kitty was used to his eccentric costumes. Sometimes he was a gladiator, other times Napoleon Bonaparte. 'Christmas is about angels,' said Harold after he'd answered the door and Merritt had looked questioningly at the white-feathered wings with gold tips.

'You can undo them,' said Merritt.

'I can't! I'm in the street,' said Kitty, horrified. 'I ate too much pudding.'

'Me too,' said Merritt, burping just a little.

They turned the corner and were walking towards the house when Kitty stopped.

'What's wrong?' asked Merritt, and then he looked and saw Ivo in the distance standing outside Harold's house. Merritt looked at Kitty, then waved at his friend. They walked closer and Ivo met them halfway. 'Hello mate,' said Merritt and shook his hand. 'Merry Christmas.'

Ivo shook Merritt's hand warmly. 'Merry Christmas to you, my friend.'

Kitty stood looking at the ground.

'I might take a bit more of a walk, try and get rid of the third helping of pudding,' Merritt said, and he walked away, hunched over in his large coat.

Kitty stood in front of Ivo. 'Hello,' she said shyly.

'Hello. I got your letter.' Ivo's eyes searched her face, hoping for something more than just small talk.

'Oh,' said Kitty, looking down at her feet.

'I loved it.' Ivo leaned down so his eyes met hers.

'Oh.' Kitty felt a blush travelling up her neck to her cheeks.

'I forgive you if you forgive me?' he said, looking at her delicate face which he loved so much.

'I forgive you.'

'I love you, Katinka Iris Clementina Ceres Middlemist.'

'I love you too, Ivo . . .' She paused.

'Peregrine James Casselton.'

'I love you, Ivo Peregrine James Casselton. Just don't ask me to spell it,' she laughed. Ivo pulled her to him and kissed her in the cold air and she felt herself melting into his arms.

'Come in and see Harold,' she said, and she held his cold hand in her gloved one as they walked up the front steps. She fished the key out of her pocket and they kissed on the doorstep.

'Harold?' asked Ivo. He had read the address on the letter, but there was no name on the stationery.

'Yes, I'm Harold's protégée, houseguest and assistant,' said Kitty proudly to a surprised Ivo.

'Harold, Harold! Look at my Christmas present!' she yelled, even though he abhorred yelling. There was no sound.

'He was asleep when we left,' she said, and she rushed into the sitting room with Ivo following, laughing at her elation.

She stopped as she entered the room and looked at Harold, peaceful on the sofa, his wings still on and spread out behind him like an ethereal cloak.

'Harold?' she said, and then she moved closer. 'Harold,' she said again. Her voice rose.

Ivo stepped forward.

'Harold?' He asked for the man's attention and then held his hand.

'Call an ambulance,' he said quickly. He took the cushions away from behind Harold, laid him back and started chest compressions.

'Ambulance! Now!' he yelled at Kitty, who ran crying to the phone. Ivo could hear her stuttering hysterically as he concentrated on his task. Once she'd finished she called Merritt on his mobile phone to tell him to come back to the house.

'Come on,' he said between breaths, but Harold's body was lifeless. Merritt came running back and took over from Ivo, who was exhausted, and then the paramedics came inside and did their job.

Kitty was inconsolable. 'Harry, Harry!' she cried into Ivo and Merritt's arms as Harold's chest was punched and shocked by machines.

Although it felt like minutes, it was almost an hour before the men stopped. 'He's gone,' said one of them kindly.

'No!' cried Kitty, and she rushed to his side. 'Harold! Harry, come back! I'm no good without you.'

Ivo watched helplessly. Kitty lay across Harold's body and wept painfully, and Merritt felt his own tears on his cheeks. Harold's kindness to Kitty and him was beyond anything he had ever experienced. He knew the world had just lost a great man.

Ivo helped Kitty away from the sitting room while they waited for Harold's body to be collected. He led her into the kitchen and sat her down while he made tea.

'They think it was a heart attack,' said Merritt, coming into the kitchen.

Kitty said nothing. She was in shock. Merritt sat next to her and held her hand. 'He didn't feel anything Kits; he was exactly as we left him.'

She nodded. 'I know. It's just that I love him,' she cried.

'I know,' said Merritt.

'And I feel terrible,' she said.

'I know,' said Merritt. 'It's an enormous loss.'

'I feel terrible because I'm sadder than when our own dad died.' She wept and Merritt held her in his arms.

'Oh darling Kits. Just because he wasn't your actual father doesn't mean he wasn't one to you. He was. He was more of a father to you than Dad ever was. Just because you're not blood doesn't mean you're not family,' he said softly.

Kitty nodded into his chest and her breathing slowed down. 'I will miss him so much,' she said.

'We all will,' said Merritt. Ivo was sitting on her other side.

'Kitty? Lovely Katinka. I will look after you.' Ivo held her hand up to his mouth and kissed it. Kitty looked at him with wide eyes.

'What?' asked Ivo.

'You called me Katinka,' she said.

'Yes, sorry about that,' said Ivo, blushing. 'It just popped into my head. I don't know why.'

Kitty smiled. 'It's OK, I like it. Harry used to call me that,' she said, and she kissed his face all over. 'He would be so happy we're together.'

And above all the chaos, Harold looked down on them and was happy. He had known it was coming; he had felt it for a while. He straightened his wings and greeted his old pals. 'Wait a minute,' he said as they started to walk away, and he watched Kitty and Ivo hold each other as his body was carried out of the house.

'Fin.'

He was the last of the romantics, he thought, and he turned and walked towards his destiny.

CHAPTER FORTY-FOUR

Willow flipped the pages of the magazine as she sat by the pool. LA was boring, she had decided. Everything was done for her, and she was actually surprised to find herself missing her kitchen and her little garden back in London. I hope the snow hasn't ruined my bulbs, she thought, and she laughed to herself at her changed priorities. She had asked Lucy to FedEx some English magazines because she was homesick, and now she sat with the children reading *House & Garden*.

'Poppy no!' yelled Lucian from the side of the pool as Poppy swam underneath him pretending to be a shark. 'No shark!'

Willow looked up from the magazine.

'Good talking Luce! Poppy, no sharks OK?' she said, and went back to her reading. Kerr had dropped the children off again after a successful overnight visit. He had changed also, which would never cease to amaze her.

Eliza was long gone. Once she had found out he was almost penniless, she had headed to New York. Kerr was now dating his yoga teacher, something Willow found hilarious. He had only joined because he heard this was the place that people in LA did business, but he soon found himself in a downward dog lusting after the teacher. She was a vegan Kabbalist with her own cable TV show. She called Kerr on

371

his shit, and Willow was grateful to her for enlightening her ex-husband.

Kerr's new job as a celebrity judge on a talent show was going well. It wasn't quite the stardom he had hoped for, but he was happy, and Willow was free. But free to do what?

She had signed onto the action film and could do anything she pleased. She was wealthy again, and yet all she wanted was to tend to her bulbs and make pikelets for the children.

She turned the page absently and then looked down. She gasped. There was Merritt in front of her, looking rugged and indecently handsome, she noticed, and behind him was Middlemist looking divinely beautiful. She looked closely at him, and then turned the page over. She gasped again.

There was the drawing room, exactly as she had pictured it. Light and airy and welcoming in blues and greens; silk walls and books everywhere. She felt tears in her eyes as she looked at the next room. The dining room in red, Chinese art around the mahogany table, and chairs for eighteen. The kitchen was her dream room, filled with cupboards, with the Aga, reconditioned, within a warm, cream-toned hearth.

Her eyes travelled across the page and she saw one of the bedrooms decked out in blue, with patchwork quilts and new carpet. Books from the nursery lined the shelves, and on top of the chest of drawers she saw Lucian's Thomas the Tank Engine.

The next room was in pink and cream, with Cath Kidston wallpaper and linen. It was deliciously girly, and Willow laughed at the idea of Merritt stepping into it. On the door handle of the French armoire was a tulle skirt, which Willow recognised as Poppy's. She must have left it there, she thought.

A smaller picture of a baby's room enthralled Willow. It

was decorated in cream, with a perfect cot that turned into a bed. A beautifully stuffed armchair in red toile sat in the corner and Willow felt the tears fall as she saw Sophie the Giraffe on top of the tiny, cream bedside table.

She turned to the bathroom. It was the bathroom she had designed in her book, with the done-up clawfoot bath and a chaise longue. It was decadent and sexy and Willow felt proud of her work. She turned to the last page. A double spread of the most perfect bedroom she had ever seen. She hadn't finished the bedroom design, and Merritt must have done what he thought she would do.

He had knocked down the wall into the next room. The bedroom was enormous, with a reading area and a king-sized bed covered in white linen and pale yellow silk cushions. Merritt hated cushions, always took them off any chair when he sat down, she remembered, but he knew she loved them and that buttery yellow was her favourite colour. Above the bed was the George Middlemist of Clementina and three of her children. The pale yellow lampshades set off the citrus trees in the painting and Willow clutched the magazine to her chest. She scanned the article, speed reading for comments from Merritt, and she felt her heart beat faster as she reached the last paragraph.

'I believe this is a house for a family. I had hoped that would be mine one day, but it was not to be. So I will be putting it up for rent, sadly; that's how it must be, I'm afraid, unless some woman with three children waltzes into my life and wants to take me and my house on and can put up with my terrible temper and funny ways.'

Willow picked up the cell phone next to her and dialled. 'Lucy, I'm coming back,' she said, and she closed the magazine.

'Out of the pool,' she ordered.

'Why?' complained Lucian.

'Because I said so. Good talking by the way,' she said as she lifted Jinty out of the iced donut ring.

'Where are we going?' asked Poppy, shivering, as Willow wrapped a towel around her.

'Home,' said Willow. 'We're going home.'

CHAPTER FORTY-FIVE

The funeral was by invitation only, as expressly stated by Harold in his last will and testament. No one was surprised; Harold had rules and he expected them to be obeyed, even after he had passed.

He left his entire estate to Katinka Iris Clementina Ceres Middlemist, having no other family. A few ex-wives considered contesting the will but no one came forward.

Cremated in his angel wings, his Derek Rose tailored pyjamas and his Dunhill velvet slippers, he had instructed Kitty to release his ashes in Jermyn Street. Harold had updated his papers the week before Christmas, which made Kitty wonder if he knew the heart attack was coming.

She sat with the letter that Harold had left her, Ivo helping her through the words and through the emotion that overwhelmed her.

Dearest Katinka,
    What fun we have had together.
    As I write this I think about society and its obsession with science and proof. People are always trying to prove things, but some things don't require proof. One just has a knowing about what is.
    What I mean to say is that you are my daughter,

Kitty. Your kindness and loveliness is something I would have been proud to own, so wherever I am now, I claim you as my daughter. There is no need to prove anything more; the proof is in your dedication to learning, your service to me and your newfound ability to make a perfect cup of tea.

I am so proud of you.

Enjoy the world, Kitty. Don't run away from it. You have a gift for understanding people's emotions and their stories. Perhaps you will express yourself in film, or perhaps you will write a book one day. Tell your story any way you can, and when you have told yours, tell those of others. There are so many stories – and they don't all come from books, Kitty – so don't be afraid to tell yours.

Now down to some housekeeping. You have the details for my voyage with the ferryman; please don't forget the slippers. If I am sent below to Hades, which I am sure many of my ex-wives have wished for, then I would like something to protect my delicate feet.

If by some chance I have redeemed myself enough to head upstairs, I shall be needing my wings.

I know many think I am a silly old man, and I suppose I am, but I am grateful that I have found great love at the end. It is a perfect ending to an imperfect life.

Goodbye, lovely Katinka, and please give my love to Ivo. I know he is reading this with you. Don't roll your eyes, it's an awful habit.

Forever yours,

Harold,

AKA – Harry

Kitty was left the house in London, its contents, Harold's sizeable bank account and the royalties from his work. His last request was that Kitty oversee the final edit of the film, much to the studio's horror. Kitty wondered if she was up to the task.

'If Harold said you can then you can,' said Merritt as he and Kitty sat with Ivo in the new drawing room at Middlemist in the afternoon sun.

'It takes me twice as long to do anything,' said Kitty, imagining reading through the script.

'You'll be fine,' said Merritt.

'Thanks,' said Kitty sarcastically as she sipped her gin and tonic.

The phone rang and Merritt got up to answer it.

'The place looks amazing,' said Ivo, looking around at the shiny and glamorous Middlemist.

'I know, but it's too big for him. I get why he wants to move out.'

Merritt walked back into the room. 'That was the estate agent. He has some big celebrity coming to see the house. They're in the area, so I'll have to show them around,' he said tiredly.

All he had done since the *House & Garden* article was show the house, but there was no one he thought he wanted to let the house to. He was particular about who should live in it, much to his estate agent's frustration. The Russian oligarch would pay cash, he told Merritt, but Merritt refused.

'They have to have a family,' he insisted.

Kitty looked at Ivo. 'I wonder who it is. How exciting! Maybe it's Posh and Becks; they have kids,' she said to Merritt, who rolled his eyes. 'Don't roll your eyes at me, you snob,' she accused her brother as they got ready to greet the potential new inhabitants.

The snow was melting and the garden was beginning to show signs of life, and Merritt knew the house looked lovely. They heard a car on the newly gravelled driveway and Kitty stood up.

'I want to meet Posh and Becks,' she said.

'You don't even know it's them,' said Ivo, laughing, and he followed them out to the driveway.

A large Porsche Cayenne with tinted windows stood in the drive, silent and still. Then the back doors opened.

'Mewwiiit Oswald!' they heard, and Poppy ran screaming towards Merritt and he picked her up.

'Pops!' he cried, and then Lucian leapt out with Custard under his arm and ran to Merritt. Lucian smiled at Kitty.

'Hi,' he said, and Kitty felt tears run down her cheeks.

And finally Willow alighted from the car. She walked around the side, and Jinty appeared. Jinty toddled to Kitty and held out her arms, and Kitty hugged her for a long time.

Willow stood shyly in front of them all.

'I wanted to apologise. I tried to write a letter,' she said, feeling terrified, much worse than when she had won her mistaken Oscar. She had tried many times to write to Merritt, but the words wouldn't come and she would just end up crying and watching reruns of *Everybody Loves Raymond* on cable and realising that she actually hated Raymond with a passion. 'Not everyone loves you Raymond, you massive cock!' she would scream at the TV.

Wearing jeans and a casual jumper – cashmere with pink and yellow stripes – and black Converse, she looked like any normal young mother. Kitty noticed a smear of food on Willow's shoulder; from Jinty, no doubt.

'Are you the celebrity?' asked Kitty, smiling at Merritt.

'Sorry?' asked Willow, confused.

'To look at the house?' said Kitty.

'No, I have no idea what you are talking about,' said Willow, confusion clouding her face. 'I just drove here direct from London. We came back from LA last night.'

Merritt started to laugh and so did Ivo and Kitty as another car drove up. Rose Nightingale and her husband Max got out of a black Mercedes.

'Oh my god. You cannot be serious!' she exclaimed, laughing, and Kitty clutched Ivo's arm.

'I love her. Like seriously *love* her!' she whispered. Ivo nodded, also starstruck at the sight of Rose.

'Merritt, how are you?' asked Rose, and kissed his cheek. Merritt shook Max's hand and introduced Kitty and Ivo, and Willow stood watching helplessly as her moment in the spotlight was taken over by Rose.

Rose looked at Max. 'I don't think this is the right house for us,' she said, laughing, and walked back to her car. 'I think this house has found its family.' She waved as they drove up the driveway.

'Where was I?' said Willow, trying to recall the speech she had yet to give.

'You are here,' said Merritt, smiling at her.

'Where's here?' she asked, confused. Why was this so hard? It had gone very differently in her head when she had planned out her big moment.

'Home,' said Merritt, holding Jinty, Lucian's hand tucked firmly in his.

Kitty and Ivo snuck back inside the house just as Willow put her hand over her mouth, rushed to the back of the car and opened the boot. George jumped out. Willow walked towards Merritt and he put Jinty down on the gravel, which she proceeded to lick; and he pulled Willow into his arms.

'Are you serious?' she asked.

'I'm serious if you are,' he said and then he kissed her.

'I love you, Merritt Edward Oswald Middlemist,' she said when they finally pulled apart.

'I love you too, Willow no-middle-name Carruthers.'

They were home, and from somewhere inside, Kitty could have sworn she heard the house give a huge sigh of relief.

No more anger or revenge.

It was the time of the romantics once again.

The stairs were steep, and Willow held on to Ivo's arm as she took the first one. She felt her thin heel catch in her white lace Dior dress and she paused. Ivo bent down and unhooked it.

'Ready?' he asked.

'If terrified means ready, then yes,' she said, and she and Ivo took three more steps and turned to wave at the crowd.

The roar for Willow was enormous.

The Romantics, Harold Gaumont's last film, was opening Cannes, and Willow wished he was here. He was the reason everything had turned out so wonderfully in her life.

Ivo had done the red carpet as a favour to Willow, even though he had sworn he was done with acting. She was about to be his sister-in-law, Kitty reminded him as she held out her left hand to admire Clementina's engagement ring.

Ivo had fulfilled the prophecy in the painting his parents had given him and proposed in the garden at Middlemist on bended knee one Sunday when they arrived for lunch with Willow and Merritt.

Kitty met Ivo's parents in London several times, and finally he had taken her to meet them at the Casselton estate. She had driven Ivo's Volvo, having received her provisional driver's licence, and was stunned when she drove carefully up to the house.

'Shit, it's a frigging castle,' she had said, taking in the enormous stately home in front of her. It was so large it made Middlemist look like the gatehouse.

Evelyn and Perry were at the front door waiting. Kitty was nervous to meet them on their home turf, but they were just grateful that Kitty had managed to tame Ivo.

'This is a wonderful house,' Kitty had said, wondering if she should call it a castle.

'Yes, Casselton Hall has been in the family since forever,' said Evelyn easily, gesturing to the stunning Palladian architecture.

'Now, the wedding will be here of course,' said Evelyn. She had already planned the day in her mind, and she flung open the doors in front of them.

Kitty had gasped at the ornate room, three times the size of the ballroom at Middlemist.

'The Great Hall,' said Evelyn. 'We haven't had a wedding here for one hundred years, and now is the time I think. Don't you think Perry?'

Ivo's father had rocked back and forth on his feet. 'Now Evelyn, it is their life. They must choose where they will be married.' Ivo shot his father a look of appreciation, and Perry and he had shared a moment of mutual understanding.

Kitty turned to Ivo. 'I don't care where we marry, as long as we do,' she had said, and Evelyn wiped away a little tear.

'The future Marquess and Marchioness of Casselton deserve a proper wedding, Peregrine.'

'What?' asked Kitty, not believing her ears.

Ivo looked down. 'I was going to get to that.'

'Why yes dear, when Perry pops his clogs then Ivo inherits. Once you are married, Kitty, you will be Lady Kitty Casselton.

Ivo is already titled,' she said, looking at her son and wondering why on earth he hadn't mentioned this earlier. Part of Perry's appeal had been his title when she had met him thirty years before at Annabel's.

Kitty had held Ivo's hand as she wandered through the stunning gardens after lunch.

'Why didn't you tell me you had a fancypants name and title?' she had asked.

Ivo looked ahead. 'Because it's a pain in the arse and I hated it growing up. It's a hell of a house to have on your shoulders,' he said.

'It's very beautiful,' said Kitty, looking back at the view.

'But it's not a home,' said Ivo.

'It could be,' Kitty had said. 'A home is about love, Ivo, and we have loads of that. Anyway your parents aren't – what did your mother say? – "popping their clogs" anytime soon, so we can stay in our lovely home courtesy of darling Harold.'

Ivo and Kitty would be married in September, and besides Kitty finding a dress – Temperley London, if you must know; white silk, goddess-style with Clementina's lover's eye necklace and an armful of white irises – the rest Evelyn had organised, perfectly and tastefully with a hint of tradition. Willow was to be a bridesmaid and Merritt best man.

Two weeks after Willow arrived at Middlemist unannounced, Merritt had proposed. He had asked Poppy and Lucian for their mother's hand in marriage that morning.

Poppy, to her credit, had managed to keep Merritt's intentions secret. It was Lucian who had insisted on asking Willow if she still had her hand on, and he had kept checking regularly.

Willow realised something was up when she went downstairs from her bath – in her perfect bathroom – and found Merritt nervously trying to light a fire, even though it was spring. The house was quiet. Too quiet. 'Where are the children?' she had asked.

'Kitty and Ivo have taken them out for the evening,' said Merritt.

Willow, in her fluffy towelling robe and socks, looked at him. 'Are you OK?' she asked, and he took her hand and led her to the orangery. It was dark but the full moon lit up the sky, throwing shadows into the glass room.

'Look,' said Merritt, pointing.

The humidity felt lovely against her face. Willow looked at Merritt. 'What am I looking at? The moon?' She looked up at the glass ceiling. 'What is that smell?' she asked, looking around. 'It's incredible.'

Merritt led her over to a plant with a huge white bloom. Willow put her face into it and inhaled. 'My god, that's incredible.'

'It's the Queen of the Night flower,' said Merritt. 'I got a sample from Venezuela. I didn't know whether it would bloom here because it's so cold, but it has. It usually comes out a bit later in May, but it must know you are going to Cannes soon and wanted to be open for you.'

Willow looked at the large flower in amazement.

'I read in Clementina's diaries that they used to have one of these in the house, and they would throw lawn parties and everyone would get drunk and wait for it to open, and they would be up till dawn. Almost like a ritual of some sort. They called it the Queen of the Night Party, and someone would sing the aria from *The Magic Flute* and they would recite poetry and dance. I understand it was quite decadent,' he said to her softly.

'All for a flower?' asked Willow.

'The bloom only lasts one night,' said Merritt.

Willow held the bloom in her hand. 'One night?'

'Yes, so make the most of it,' he laughed, his voice cracking a little. 'Not out again until next year.'

'I hope I'll be here to see it,' said Willow, not looking at him. She had moved back in within two weeks of arriving on Merritt's doorstop and they had picked up where they had left off – before the fight, of course. Easy domesticity, minus the layers of dust and tension.

The children had never been happier, and Lucian had so many words that sometimes Willow wanted to tell him to be quiet – and then she remembered how long she had waited for him to speak, and she said nothing.

Janis and Alan had arrived soon after Willow had moved in, and Janis declared Merritt a keeper in front of Merritt himself, much to Willow's embarrassment. He didn't seem to mind. English people understood eccentricities. Merritt claimed they had to be earned; the more successful you were, the more eccentric you could be. Willow didn't know how successful her father was in terms of English eccentricity standards, but at least Alan kept his clothes on at Middlemist, even if it was just a sarong at times.

Now they stood in the orangery and Merritt looked at Willow, his love.

'You will be here next year, and the year after, and every night that it blooms will be the night we remember to make the most of our lives, for nothing lasts – we know that – except love.'

Willow started to cry softly, and Merritt guided her hand into the flower. She felt the cold of metal and pulled out a beautiful lotus-shaped diamond ring. It was exactly the ring Willow would have chosen for herself. Merritt slipped it onto her finger and she looked down at it. 'It's so beautiful,' she said.

'But there's a catch,' he said seriously.

'What?' She looked at him, fear flashing across her face.

'You have to marry me,' he said. 'I know I'm a bit dull and you might get bored and I tend to get stuck on things, you know, fixated; and I can be grumpy and . . .' Willow put her hands up to his face and kissed his mouth.

'Yes, you are all those things, and so many, many more, Merritt. And I can think of nothing I would like more than to be Mrs Middlemist.'

And so she was. They were married at Middlemist at Easter in the drawing room, with a party in the orangery. Everyone danced till dawn, and the world-famous opera singer Diana Damru performed the Queen of the Night Aria as a gift to Merritt from Willow.

Willow wore yellow Alexander McQueen, as a tribute to her friend who had passed away, and a smile. Kitty and Lucy were her bridesmaids, in clothes of their own choice. Lucy had allowed Willow to recommend a few designers, and she settled on a navy silk Donna Karan wrap dress, which looked lovely.

Kitty had chosen a Vivienne Westwood polka-dot strapless silk dress in a faded red and white. It made her look like a sexy fifties movie star, Ivo exclaimed, and proceeded to talk like Elvis for the whole wedding, which both annoyed and amused Kitty.

Merritt claimed in his speech that Willow was married and he was happy, but Willow protested that she was happy too, and the guests only had to look at her face to see the joy she felt.

Kerr had sent his congratulations, and he and Tori, his vegan Kabbalah yoga girlfriend, offered to take the children while they honeymooned in Italy. But Willow had said no, they were a family, and Merritt insisted they honeymoon together. The children could go over another time, or Kerr and Tori could even come there and stay in the guesthouse, Merritt had offered.

Marriage suited Merritt, and Willow enjoyed the stability. She was a good wife, but now she had money, she afforded herself a few new things. A nanny and a housekeeper-slash-cook were the first choices, and a new wardrobe from Chanel was the next.

The she had given Merritt his gift. She told him she was pregnant. A wedding night baby, she said, and he cried while she tried not to laugh at the unplugging of his English emotion.

'I want you to know,' he said, sitting up and composing himself, 'I love the children like they are my own – I feel like they are my own – it's just that I miss having a baby. Jinty told me I was ugly this morning when I asked her to finish her toast.'

Now Willow had allowed herself to laugh. 'I will have to pull out of the action film,' she had said, but TG was insistent they hold for her to shoot after the pregnancy.

All she had to do was fulfil her appearance at Cannes, and then she could have the rest of the year off till the baby was born.

And now they were in Cannes. She had arrived with Merritt, Kitty and Ivo. The children were safely in Janis and Alan's hands at Middlemist, and Willow had no doubt her father would have lost his sarong and Poppy would have stories for days.

She and Merritt had a suite at Hôtel Du Cap with a view over the ocean, and they weren't planning to leave unless they absolutely had to.

Kitty and Ivo were more excited to be there; they went to most of the parties, where Kitty met directors and producers.

'They know me from *The Romantics*,' she said. She had done as Harold had asked and had overseen the final edit of the film. She hadn't changed much, just a tweak here and there, but the response was overwhelmingly positive and those who had seen Harold's last cut knew Kitty had made important and significant changes that worked in the film's favour.

'Someone just asked me if I was free to do a documentary on champagne,' said Kitty. 'I haven't even finished my course yet.' The London Film Academy had taken her onto their editing course and she loved it. Using Harold's equipment, she spent hours in the ivory tower, as she still called it, and played with the film and the edits.

Ivo had moved quickly into Harold's house, now Kitty's, and they were so in love it was sickening, as Kitty said to Willow.

Ivo was happy at Harold's, writing and musing. He was born to be an academic, he decided, and he had been commissioned to write another art book, this time on J M Turner.

So Kitty was dragged from gallery to private house to gallery searching for paintings, and Ivo, with his incredible nose for a mystery, actually unearthed two supposedly lost Turners.

His new moniker in the art industry was Ivo the Discoverer, and soon he was loaded with requests for books and art projects. He didn't miss acting – he hadn't done it enough to miss it, he told Kitty – but he still liked to dress up, mostly at home with Harold's hilarious costumes. He and Kitty would play like children until Ivo, inevitably, turned it into something more lewd.

Not that Kitty minded. Life with Ivo was fun in and out of bed, and she was practising reading and writing with someone who loved her even when she couldn't quite manage. What else could she ask for? she thought, as she watched him on the steps with Willow.

Her friend, her sister-in-law, and once upon a time, her boss. Kitty didn't like to think back to those days; they were all different people back then, she thought.

Ivo waved to her from the steps and she smiled and blew him a kiss. Willow looked for Merritt, and Ivo pointed him out to her. She made a face and then smiled at him and he laughed. He laughed a lot these days; at the children, with Willow, at Willow and her attempts to become the next Nigella Lawson in the kitchen, and mostly at himself.

At the top of the steps Willow and Ivo paused and they both looked for a moment to the sky.

'Harold would have loved this,' said Willow with a little tear.

'He would have indeed,' said Ivo next to her.

And somewhere up there, Harold, sitting between Alfred Hitchcock and Stanley Kubrick, was loving the red carpet at Cannes.

'I do love a happy ending,' Harold said to Alfred, who nodded his agreement.

'Wouldn't it be nice if it were all as simple as in the movies?' said Alfred.

'Oh, but it is,' said Stanley mysteriously. 'It is.'

And the three directors in the big sky laughed together. Perhaps they were directing all along, they thought.

'And now we have *Fini*,' said Harold.

'Not yet,' said Alfred. 'What will they call Willow's baby?'

'Harold,' he said proudly.

And so it was.

THE RETREAT AT HOME

Not everyone can head off to a super expensive weekend retreat to restore the mind, body and soul.

With this in mind, I recommend you plan the weekend retreat at home.

It is possible to do this, even for a day if you're organised and committed.

Step one – Let those closest to you know this is what you will be doing. Ask them to respect what you need to do for yourself. If you share your home with kids and partners, ask them to honour your space and rely on each other for the day or weekend.

Step two – Clean your house or the space you will be retreating into. The last things you want is to be trying to 'Zen out' and worrying about the dust on the side table. Change your bed sheets.

Step three – Stock your fridge with healthy food and snacks. Nourish the body and the mind.

Step four – Buy yourself some treats. Nice magazine, a scented candle or bubble bath or all three if you can afford it.

Step five – Organise an 'at home massage' if you can or give yourself some lovely indulgent facial treatments like a mask or a body scrub.

Step six – Unplug your online world. Don't check emails or voicemails. If a true emergency occurs someone will come and inform you.

Step seven – Take a walk and take out the headphones of your iPod. Be present in the walk, look at the world around you and open your perspective.

Step eight – Do something creative or if you don't feel confident, read a real book.

Step nine – Watch gentle movies or try a yoga DVD. Try meditating or at least relaxing for a period of time.

Step ten – Go to bed early and turn off the alarm for the morning. Let your body find its natural sleep rhythm.

Reading this back, I have to say, this all sounds really quite nice! I know what I'll be doing soon . . .

Taking care of your self is so important, especially when times are tough. When you give yourself the time to 'just be' in the world, you will be surprised at what comes up. Write down your thoughts and see what needs to be given attention.

It's okay to retreat every once in a while. There are so many demands on our lives and we put such heavy expectations on ourselves that a little time out is helpful to recharge.

Stay present and know you are worth investing in.

Kate

x